Sarah's Quilt

Also by Nancy E. Turner

These Is My Words

The Water and the Blood

Sarah's Quilt

A Novel of Sarah Agnes Prine and the Arizona Territories, 1906

Nancy E. Turner

Thomas Dunne Books ♏ St. Martin's Griffin
New York

THOMAS DUNNE BOOKS.
An imprint of St. Martin's Press.

www.thomasdunnebooks.com
www.stmartins.com

Book design by Irene Vallye

Library of Congress Cataloging-in-Publication Data

Turner, Nancy E., 1953–
    Sarah's quilt : a novel of Sarah Agnes Prine and the Arizona territories, 1906 / Nancy E. Turner.
        p. cm.
    Sequel to: These is my words.
    ISBN-13: 978-0-312-33263-1
    ISBN-10: 0-312-33263-7
    1. Prine, Sarah Agnes—Fiction. 2. Women pioneers—Fiction. 3. Arizona—Fiction. I. Title.

PS3570.U725S37 2005
813'.54—dc22

                                                                              2004065661

D 30 29 28

For Collin,
Megan, and
Allison

Acknowledgments

Many people offered useful information that went into this book, but no one helped the story stay true to life more than Janet Dailey of Vail, Arizona. A good friend, a good writer, and a singular personality cut of the same independent, hardworking fabric as I imagine my great-grandmother Sarah Agnes must have been, Janet provided a wealth of ranching and historic lore generously laced with encouragement.

My deep gratitude goes as always to my family for cheering me on, especially my husband, John, who knows more about writing than he pretends. Many, many heartfelt thanks to John Ware, a wonderfully dedicated agent who believes in both my work and me, and without whom I would never have written this novel. Ultimately, no better ally exists for an author than a like-minded editor, and I dearly appreciate Marcia Markland for her expedient advice and personal approach. She has been a real friend all along the way. My final thanks go to the real Sarah Agnes Prine, who lent her spirit to the telling of this fictional tale and whose photo I keep on my desk just to remember.

Sarah's Quilt

Chapter One

I used the rifle to part branches as I ran. All I heard for a time was the rhythm of my boots scuffing gravel. My horse was standing where I'd left him, his reins held by my niece Mary Pearl, who'd been out checking stock with me since dawn. I knew not to ride a horse into that commotion. I thought I heard her hollering "Aunt Sarah?" but I didn't quit running toward the sound that had stopped us. As I tore through brush, an ironwood tree clutched at my clothes; thorns ripped my skirt. The troubled bellow of a cow was accompanied by a pitiful, higher-pitched bawling. Along with that, a pack of coyotes yipped.

I cleared the rise. The mother cow whirled around at that second, hooked a coyote on one horn, and threw it high over her back. They were half-hidden by a thicket of greasewood and cholla—in a clear place just wide enough for the pack of killers to trap the mother and baby. The calf had blood running down its legs and it whimpered. The mother cow dashed and whirled, fending off another and another coyote, as others circled behind her and nipped at her baby.

I tried to yell, but I had no wind left. My throat was parched as old rope. I slung the rifle to my shoulder and picked off two coyotes. The crippled one had made it back into the path of the cow. As she tried to fight the coyote, it bit into her ankle, and she dragged it, its body clinging to her foot like a rag, before she got it loose. Fierce as she was, the coyotes knew their game was to outlast her, and while the mother cow thrashed, three more closed in on the calf. I ran again, this time finding my voice, shouting the whole way. Mary Pearl told me later that what I was hollering would not be fit talk for her mother's parlor, but I don't remember it.

I pulled up the rifle again, chambering a shell as I did. With a shot, I dropped another coyote in his tracks, and he squirmed when he fell, but he didn't get up. The little calf dropped to its knees and then lay on its side. I could see then that the mother cow was torn in the milk bag. Streaky red liquid oozed from her wound. She stomped and shook that animal off her ankle as I shot another. When one coyote remained, he turned tail and lit out into the brush, gone like a drop of water in this hot desert. Well, I started to move toward the calf; then the panicked cow decided to come after me. She put her head low and scuffed at the dust. I took up part of my skirt and flapped it at her, waving my hat in the other hand, and she backed up, mooing, looking for danger from all around. The poor old girl was bleeding from the nose, too. I whistled and Mary Pearl came riding in my direction, leading my horse. Two baldhead buzzards looped in the sky overhead.

The calf made a human-sounding wail. I knelt at its side. Poor baby was not two months into this hard world. I picked his little head up and laid it in my lap, coddling him as if he were a child. He'd been bitten all around the gut and his sack was torn clear off. By the time the cow started back my way, I saw the calf's eyes sink and knew he was dead. The cow bandied her head and groaned. Mary Pearl tossed a rope around her neck and tied it off to the horse's saddle, then backed the horse, pulling that mother cow around. The coyotes had been at her worse than I'd been able to see before. I'd figured I could doctor up the milk bag—I'd done as much before. Not this one, though—flesh hung from her leg and long blue veins dangled from her neck on the left side. Mary Pearl went to my horse, and from the saddle, she slung another rope over the cow's horns. She picketed the two horses so the cow was held between them.

The cow thrashed, limping on her mangled hoof and ankle, and shook the second lariat from its loose hold on her horns. Mary Pearl backed her horse more to keep the line taut while the animal jerked against it. In midstride, the cow collapsed, breathing hard through a spew of blood and sand and slobber. Mary Pearl rode closer, easing the tension on the rope. She said, "Aunt Sarah? Has she given in?"

I wiped my face with my sleeve and hung my head. Shock and fear had done what the coyotes couldn't. I've known cattle to outlast amazing things. Some don't. Maybe their hearts burst. Lord knows I've felt that way, watching my own child die. The old girl pitched in the dirt and bellowed, but she didn't get up. I said, "Ride on back to the house. Take my horse. I want to walk. I'll bring your rope by and by."

I reckon Mary Pearl knew better than to fuss with me right then, for she did as I said without her usual commotion. I walked around the cow, talking to her, my voice soft and low. "You fought 'em off, didn't you, old girl? Don't you go giving up now. You'll have another baby round the bend." Suddenly struggling to her feet, the cow made another threatening stance, lunged toward me, but then fell into the dirt, banging her great head against a rock outcrop. She moaned: a pitiful, suffering noise. It is a hard step for me—always somewhat of a surprise—to stop hoping and accept that there is no hope for an animal but a slow, agonizing death. My foreman shrugs and says it's part of ranching, but I hurt for my animals. I lifted the rifle and in my mind drew an *X* on her skull, midpoint between both eyes and the base of both horns. It isn't kind to do it poorly.

The shot was loud in my ears, echoing as the cow slumped and went quiet. Then I sat between my dead cow and her dead calf, right there in the scrabble and brush, pulled up my knees, and cried. These last three years have seemed like an eternity of drought and poor harvest and dying animals. My boys are off at school, and to tell the truth, it's cheaper to send them to town, where they can pick up work, than to feed them here. I need money and I need rain. Both of them in good order and flowing over.

After a while, I coiled Mary Pearl's rope and hung it over my shoulder. The rifle was heavy. My feet hurt. I beat the dust off my old hat, put it on my head, and started walking. I shook my head and didn't look back. The buzzards and the coyotes would have their day after all.

April 25, 1906

I knew soon as I spotted the riders and put names to them they were up to no good. I laid into the rug draped across my front porch rail with an iron beater, watching two men amble toward the house. Both were carrying good-size packs tied behind their saddles. It was early afternoon, and I had plenty of chores tallied to this day already. No sense waiting on a couple of slowpokes. I kept on whipping that rug, and let them get as close as the gate before I looked up and showed I'd seen them coming. "Charlie? Gilbert?" I called. "You two know what day it is?"

"Yes, ma'am, Mama," they said together. Charlie is twenty-one. Gilbert is but nineteen. My sons weren't due back from school for three weeks.

"Don't you let me hear you've failed out. I'll turn you out, to boot." I feared I knew the truth before they said it.

Charlie spoke first. "No, Mama. We haven't failed, either one of us. We just—well, we changed our minds."

I hit that rug two more licks. I said, "Oh, you did?" Charlie had been taking studies in engineering and mining. Gilbert was going to be a doctor.

He said, "Yes, ma'am."

"Both of you—together—changed your minds like they were one? What did you change them to?" Felt like my eyeteeth had just come loose. There is a perfectly fine university right there in Tucson for them to use. A library full of books, some of which I put there myself, is just waiting for them to discover and love and enjoy it. And here they come like roosting pigeons. I shook all over, so mad I couldn't speak.

Charlie stepped off his horse, holding his reins as if he was fixing to get back on.

Gilbert was still on his horse. He, too, was debating whether just to keep riding. He finally said, "Well, Mama, you don't know what it's like."

"I know what hard work is like. You have a privilege not many get—to use your minds instead of your backs—and you turn away from it, like . . . like it was tedious."

Charlie scratched the animal's head between the ears and said, "We want to be ranchers. Like you and Grampa. We aren't cut out for that place."

I found myself fussing at his back. "How will you know what you are cut out for if you don't try? Charlie, you were only a year and this term from finishing. This ranch will be here when you are done. Mount up and get back there. Tell your teachers you're sorry for being knotheads, and make up your work."

"It isn't that easy," Charlie said, finally turning around to face me. He held the saddle in both hands. "I missed the final examination in geology today. I'd have to do the whole term again anyway. They just make it so hard on you, you can't get above water. Besides, all the science professor talks about is diamond mines in Africa. I've turned enough rocks here to make a mountain, and there sure aren't diamonds under 'em. School's a waste of time when there's plenty of work to do here."

I said, "You two seemed to have time enough for plenty of other shenanigans. I heard about the armless saguaro some hooligans planted right in front of the main stairs. Looks like a blessed giant finger stuck in the ground—in front of a *university*. It doesn't take a scholar to figure who might have been part of that."

Gilbert finally dismounted, turned his face toward his saddle. He was barely hiding a grin, but still scared to look me in the eye. I said, "I reckon there's some reason you're tagging along."

"I—well, I reckoned I'd think it over awhile. Doctors hardly make enough money to keep a pot of beans on the stove. I'd rather do something that puts some jingle in my pockets. Why, a vanilla drummer makes as much as a doctor, and he doesn't have to study chemistry or cut open cadavers." He eyed that rug beater in my hands as he smiled.

All my life, I've ached for the chance to sit in a real schoolroom, but I never got the privilege. I set myself to lay into them, but I'd as soon argue with the daylight. They'd already done what they meant to do. Maybe I never went to school, but I reckon I'm smart enough to know when I'm licked. Licked for now maybe, but not finished with this fight. So I said, "How are your cousins?" Savannah and Albert's twin girls and second son—Rachel, Rebeccah, and Joshua—the ones these two were supposed to be sharing my house in town with. The ones who'd stayed in school. "You say hello to your aunt and uncle as you rode in?" My brother and his wife and family lived just a scant mile up the road from me.

I could see the boys let their shoulders down. They knew they'd won this go-round. Gilbert took the pack off his horse and began loosening the saddle's cinch strap. At the same time, both of them said, "Fine. They're all just fine," mumbling something or other about Rachel's cooking.

"And what's cadavers?" I said.

Gilbert said, "Dead folks. *Pickled* dead folks. After the second one, well—"

I headed toward the house, saying over my shoulder, "Well, if you hadn't got the stomach for that, you hadn't. Come on in, and I'll feed you. Put those animals in the west corral. Pillbox just foaled, and I don't want you in the barn, upsetting her."

Even from the porch, I could see in their eyes that they were smiling, although they knew better than to look smart in front of me. One thing I know is that you can't let up on boys. Just because they're big as a man, you give them any slack, and they'll run sidelong into trouble. I'm about fed up with these two, I thought. Reckon I'll make them some lunches, and then figure what to do with them. Might as well invite Albert and Savannah and the rest for supper tonight, let them know the two renegades are back. Sorry rascals.

There's a single cloud in the sky. It looks pretty sickly, and I doubt it will prove its mettle. We as much as missed the spring rains. Maybe the summer's wet weather will come early, and get some grass growing before we go broke buying feed for cattle that already look like walking beef jerky.

My sons were still tending their horses when Ezra and Zachary, Albert's youngest boys, came along. They had a cord of some sort stretched tight between them and they trotted in circles around each other. They were each toting a slate and a book under one arm. Their bare feet stirred up dust as they came.

"Aunt Sarah," Ezra called, "watch us. Watch! Planetary motion." They whirled up the road, and Ezra howled as if he were the wind; then he jerked the string hard and tugged his little brother forward.

I laughed. Ezra and Zachary are my last two students, and I don't aim to short them on their readiness for the university.

As they got to the house, Zack was running with all his might. They both stopped at my front steps. Zack put his hands on his knees to catch his breath. He gasped, "You sorry old buzzard, Ezra. I told you to slow down. I'm played clear out."

I called through the kitchen window, "Both of you come on in. Ezra, you'll have to do your recitation first, so Zack can have enough wind to say his piece." Ezra moaned and followed Zack to the parlor, where they dropped to the floor and fanned themselves with their slates. I said, "Your cousins are home from town. We're all going to eat first, and then you can do your lessons."

Ezra said, "Can we go see 'em? May we? I mean."

I said, "Nope. Just cool off in here. They'll be in directly."

Almost the minute I'd said it, Charlie and Gilbert came at a near run to the house and flung wide the door.

Charlie said, "Mama, are you sick?"

My sons' faces bore childlike expressions of fear. Ezra and Zack cheered and howled at the sight of them, mindless of their cousins' worried looks. I had to raise my voice to be heard over the commotion. "Nothing of the kind," I said.

Charlie said, "When we put the saddles away, we saw old Mr. Sparky had been moved. Went to see what he was sitting on."

Mr. Sparky was what I reckon you'd call a toy. A scarecrow, topped off with a skull the boys had been given when the army shut down Fort Lowell and folks turned it into a marketplace. The telegrapher used to keep an old human skull in the office with glass eyeballs plugged into the eye holes and the snaggle-toothed chinbone spring-wired to the ticker line. When a message came in, that jaw would ratchet up and down and the eyes would roll in their sockets. Indians would come for miles around just to set and wait for a message, then hoot and roll with laughter at the thing. After Jack died, some of the men at the fort sort of kept an eye on my boys when we were in town, and one of them rode clear out here to see if Charlie wanted Sparky when they left. I'd laughed and told him it wasn't like a puppy, but Charlie was happy, and later he and Gilbert took some clothes they'd both outgrown and stuffed Mr. Sparky a body.

Halloweens, Sparky keeps guard duty at the outhouse for us, which saves it being turned over like most of the other privies around. Other times, he appears now and then, just for the fun of it. Once, I got up on a Christmas morning to find what looked like a saddle tramp snoozing under a sombrero in a rocking chair on the front porch, his boots sticking from under an old blanket. About the time I guessed the old cuss was dead and started to use a stick to lift the sombrero, one of Sparky's glass eyeballs fell out and rolled across the porch. Gilbert and Charlie were laughing so hard at the corner of the house, they fell clear into the dirt. That was three years ago. Now he just collects spiders in the barn.

I said, "Grampa Chess put that hat on his head. I got tired of seeing those eyeballs glaring at me in the dark."

Charlie said, "Mama, Sparky's a-sitting on a headstone with your name on it. What does it mean?"

I stood in the doorway and folded my arms. "Not a blessed thing," I said. "I just had a hankering one day and bought it. Had my name carved, says just what I want."

Gil slapped his gloves against his leg. "What in blazes do you want it to say?"

I said, "Don't swear; the little boys are here. Come take a look, and I'll show you." I headed for the barn.

Gilbert took my arm, hurrying beside me. "Mama, if there's something we ought to know, if there's something wrong, you've got to tell us." Ezra and Zack followed us, and Charlie held the door aside, frowning. I do see his father's face when he does that.

In the barn, I moved Sparky, then went to pulling down some bales of fence wire where he'd been resting his feet. I passed them to each of the boys until I got down to the tarpaulin on the stone. "There's nothing wrong except my hardheadedness," I said. Although I'll be forty-three on my next birthday, I feel eighteen and spry, and I work sun to sun without a stop. "Don't know how you managed to find it. I hid it back here so you two won't have to mind it when the time comes."

"Mama," Charlie said, shaking his head, "that's the blamed awfulest thing I ever have heard of." That boy loses all track of his grammar when he's excited.

Gil said, "It's bad luck or something. If you're not old or sick, could bring on some kind of early passing."

I smiled at the earnestness of his expression. "Not likely, boys. The only thing I've come down with was a scalded hand last Christmas. I pondered a long time about what I wanted it to say." I was holding the tarp so they couldn't see the whole thing. The stone matched the color and shape of their papa's on the hill. It will look fine next to his. My stone says "Here lies Sarah Agnes Prine Elliot, mother, rancher, and a pretty good shot." Suits me.

Charlie made a face at Gilbert. "You sure you're not sick?"

Gilbert was starting to grin. He said, "Dang, Mama. You'll probably be dead three days before you quit working long enough to notice. Let's see 'er."

Charlie smiled. He said, "I know just what it needs: 'Shake the dust off your boots and look busy, Lord, there she comes.' "

"Rascals," I said, and pulled back the tarp. "See there? All you have to do is put on the date and prop it next to your pa's."

Gilbert poked Charlie in the arm. Charlie said, "This is vexation, Mama. Why, that had to cost a pretty penny, all those letters, and should have gone against the grain of a woman who's got a five-dollar gold piece with marks from her milk teeth bit into it."

I could tell him a thing or two, since every gold eagle he's ever seen has been one *I've* earned with my two hands. I said, "I've got lessons to teach. You boys stack those spools of wire back up before you wash and come in the house."

"We'll set your sentry back on duty, too," Charlie said.

I left my sons and started for the house, with Ezra and Zachary following behind me like ducklings, heading for the only schooling they're going to get, living this far from town. My father-in-law, their grandpa Chess, came to the house for lunch, and when Gil and Charlie got in from brushing down their horses, we had a fine reunion around the kitchen table. It always has done my heart good to watch folks eat, especially my kin.

I set our noon meal in front of the boys and their cousins, enjoying the familiar sounds that filled my kitchen. They made a ring of men, plus me. Chess, Charlie, being nearly a head taller than Gilbert, who sat next to him, and Ezra, who's just starting to get stringy, followed by little old Zack, just eight years old. Chess was as happy to see the boys as if they'd only been on some long errand. He kept pushing food at them, telling them to stock up and get the town dust out of their veins so they could breathe better and work harder.

Gilbert said to Chess, although I figured it was for me to hear, "Well, Grampa, that's the whole idea. Charlie and me need to be——"

I said, "Charlie and *I*." And while I'm hearing them argue the reasons for letting out of school, I keep remembering their father went through military college when he was their age, all on his own. That was gumption.

Gilbert kept talking without missing a word: "——and *I* need to be here to help out with the ranch when Mama gets too old. It isn't going to run itself."

Charlie grins and says, "We only have until Mama's next birthday. She'll be middle-aged and put out to pasture. She knows it herself, spending cash on that stone there, like it was just around the corner of being needed. Must be getting older by the minute."

"Middle-aged, my hind foot," I said. "Wasn't I flanking every fourth calf last year? By the time I'm too old to run this place, you two will be doddering around on canes, and riding nothing but a rocking chair. Why, I haven't even got a gray hair! I'm not old. Not by a long shot. I'll see you two graduated from that university yet."

Charlie smiled. Ornery cuss. I can hire hands to do their work, but I'm not paying hands to take their grades for them. Even before they went, they'd look down at me and we'd square off until one or the other of them cuts a grin, and pretty soon we'd all be laughing at the three of us. It never let up the mad I felt at them, but it put it on a back shelf, as if it was out of my reach for a while.

Gilbert had the gall to say if I was so set on more learning in this family, I should go myself and see what they were up against. I told him to go cut a switch and I'd wear out his britches, and then he'd see what they were up against, but he just grinned. Charlie and Gil and their grandpa took off to get a better look at Pillbox's new foal, which I'd saddled with the name Elliot's Hunter.

While my boys were in the barn, I corralled Ezra and Zack, and summertime school commenced. Savannah and I don't let up on the children the way town schools do. We have school every day of the year except Sunday, unless it's roundup or harvest or Christmas. Of course, like today, sometimes our school lasts only two hours.

We went around the side where shade hits in the afternoon, and I sat on the rope swing while they used firewood blocks for a perch. I heard their recitations and Ezra did some long division. Zack said his times tables. I listened, but I wished a breath of wind would stir. We were sweating, just sitting in the shade. Both of them had some Latin verbs, which I think no boy is too young to do, and then I read to them another page from *Modern Celestial Theories: A Study of the Planetary System.* It took a while to decipher it, but we got it boiled down to a few ideas they could understand. I do fancy a well-rounded education.

Then I sent them to play, after explaining that the planets don't swirl around each other, that one of them had to be the sun, and the other one had to do all the circling. Zachary always makes me think of a child born old, for I saw him cogitating just a moment before he said, straight-faced as a judge, "I'll be the sun, Ezra. That's the boringest part." So he'd fixed Ezra after all, and his older brother would have to run rings around him for the game of rotating planets to continue.

I shooed them like critters and headed for the house. "Scoot," I said. "School's out, and I've got work to do." I pulled my flour crock from its corner on the kitchen worktable and then tried to figure how many pies I should make for supper. I could see the four boys in the yard. Gilbert had a lariat and tossed it, lassoing Zachary, cutting short Zack's game of being the sun. Ezra leaned over, hands on his knees, catching his breath.

Watching them through the window glass, Chess said to me, "Sarah, you know I don't like to interfere with your raising the boys."

I nodded slowly. Don't know how a man can be part of a family and not interfere somehow. At least he was usually spare with his advice unless asked. I said, "What's on your mind?"

"It's time you cut 'em loose. That's all."

"You saying my apron strings are too tight?"

"That. I'm saying you could talk to them until you was choked. They're men. They got to make up their own minds, or it'll go bad on you. I recommend you to let 'em have their own reins. Make less work for yourself in the bargain."

"They aren't done growing yet."

Chess picked at a thread on his shirt. He does that when he's thinking. His head has a slight tremor, though his eyes are clear and keen. "B'lieve I disagree."

"I want them to get educated." I scooped a lump of dough onto the table and went to rolling it out.

"They will. In time. No sense wearing yourself out on it."

"How did you get Jack to go to school?"

"Didn't. He just up and went."

"So you're telling me to let them be?"

He smiled. "I'm telling you that you work like two men. I suggest you get two men to lighten your load a mite. It's soon enough they'll be 'up and went,' on their own. Some girl'll come along and wink her eye, and that'll be the end of it."

"April and Morris are living in Tucson. Maybe I'll move to town, too, and go to tea parties and concerts and let you *men* run this ranch."

Chess said, "We'd take the job for you."

I said, "What in the world will make them appreciate what I'm trying to do for them?"

"Time."

"I don't have time," I said. "I'm too old."

After they were satisfied with seeing the colt, Zack and Ezra were sent home with the invitation for supper in their minds, cookies in one hand, McGuffey's Readers in the other. My boys unpacked their duds and the books they brought home while I made up beds for them on the sleeping porch. Then they went with their grandpa to ride south and see how the land had fared with the drought.

We've been three years of the sparsest rainfall in anyone's recollection. Last year was better, but still dry. We used to run over five hundred head on sixty sections of open range, and now the land's so beat-up, it won't keep four hundred on the same acreage. When Chess decided to live here permanently, he bought up some leases on another forty sections and I opened my stock to the grasslands, but then you've got rustlers and loss from natural devices, and it still doesn't pay. Only one around still making good is Rudolfo Maldonado. His land is lower and has more natural water tanks. He can keep fifteen to twenty head on a section down there. Sometimes I envy him his land. It's some of the best around, and while my place is drying out, his is just beginning to show the drought's effect.

When I went to the bedrooms to open windows to get a breeze blowing through the house, I saw the stack of newly unpacked books on Charlie's shelf, next to others with dust on the tops. I picked up the closest one to me and held it for a minute, feeling the narrow pressed lines on the front edge, the ponderous weight of it, staring at the ominous title, *Geophysical Nomenclature of the Earth's Surface.* I opened the book. A little stub of paper made the pages fall open at the place where Charlie had been reading.

Faint pencil lines underscored some words in the first paragraph—Mount Etna, Mount Kilimanjaro, Mount Kilauea. In the side margin was a note in Charlie's hand, "Xm tomorrow, remember Boltzmann Con., $PV = Nk(B)T$," some note beyond my knowing. In the bottom margin he had written in pencil a note I understood at a glance—a single word with a whole story in it. "Esperanza." After the girl's name was a little question mark.

I slapped the book shut. It felt like I'd been prying in his private letters or something. I never meant to do that. It was just a schoolbook. With a really good notion there, in writing, of why he was having a hard time studying. Well, I suppose all that remains now is to wait until he decides to tell us about this girl. Thinking about who she might be gave way to wondering who Boltzmann is, and what those other little letters were about. Real schooling. How anybody could walk away from finding out what all that means is just beyond me. I could eat it like sweet pudding.

I put the book amongst the others stacked there on the shelf, and went to the kitchen to get started with supper. While I cooked, I drifted to town in my mind, picturing myself sitting in class with other girls. Picturing someone named Esperanza across the room, now and then glancing up to see if Charlie was looking her way. Then I pictured the teacher talking about rocks and soils and streams and such, and how to know what was under the earth, whether it was coal or quicksilver you were standing over. I forgot all about my boy and just smiled, thinking I was listening to some mighty fine talk about things I'll likely never get to learn.

My sons and their grandpa came back in a couple of hours. They talked about how scorched the land seemed. If it doesn't come rain soon, there won't be any need of hired hands at all, including the ones I've already got.

I said, "You boys get any work done?" and set a plate of fried pies on the seat of an empty chair and motioned to them. They were made from scraps left from the baked ones I'd made for supper. I put out cups for drinking water.

Charlie took one and said, "Sent Flores with five bales of hay up to the fence lines near each tank."

"Spotted a herd of antelope up at Majo Vistoso. They were drinking the springwater," Gilbert said.

Chess said, "Didn't think anything could live on that water."

We all stayed quiet for a bit, thinking about how desperate a wild animal would be to drink hot water so loaded with minerals it wouldn't boil. The pie plate was empty. A fly buzzed over the crumbs, and I waved my hand over it.

Chess said to me, "Sarah, you've said nary a word. What's on your mind?"

"Where's Kilimanjaro?" is all I said. Charlie turned about six shades of red, but he didn't say a word. "I come across that word recently," I said. "Is that Japón?"

"Africa," Charlie said. "And it's not Mexican. You say the *J* in Japan."

I said, "I see you learned at least a thing or two."

"Mama, don't start in on me."

Gilbert was looking first at one of us, then the other. He said, "Want us to ride up and get mail today? We can be back by suppertime."

"Albert and Savannah will be here for supper," I said.

Chess said, "Pass me that water jug there, Charlie, and one of those cups. Sarah has a right to lay into you if she wants to. You two have disappointed her mightily." Well, at that, we all three stared at Chess like he'd grown a horseshoe out his forehead. Never once in all the years since Jack died has he stood up for my wanting the boys to go to college. Usually, he won't speak a word on the subject. Charlie and Gilbert both winced. It appears their grandpa's disapproval hit a lot closer to the bone than their mother's.

I took up the empty plate and said, "Bring the mail, and don't dawdle. Your aunt and uncle are wanting to see you boys again. They reckoned you'd need cheering up, being so sad about missing out on college and all. Buck up. I'm not fussing at you anymore. I'd been thinking of hiring. I figure I've paid your tuition, and you owe me each a good six months, working that money off."

Gilbert made a face and popped the last half of the fried pie in his mouth. Those boys know I don't really ever stay mad at them. He gulped and said, "Charlie, old man, we are now indentured servants. Maybe when the six months are up, *la doña de estancia* will hire us on regular." He went for his hat, hanging by the door, and thumped his brother on the shoulder as he passed.

Well, before too long, I had a houseful of folks: my mother, who goes by Granny, my oldest brother, Albert, Savannah, his wife, and their children living at home. There's Clover, done with his school and come to mind the farm, Esther, Mary Pearl, Ezra, and Zachary.

Almost all my folks that I know of are here. The only ones not close by being my younger brother, Harland, and Melissa and their children and, of course, my brother Ernest, who hasn't been heard from since the war in Cuba. We all talk about him like he's just been misplaced like a hat or something, but inside I know he's gone to his reward. After that slatternly gal Felicity left him, he wrote me regular, at least once a month, even during the campaign in Cuba. He sent me a picture of himself putting shoes on the horse ridden by General Theodore Roosevelt. Don't know if we'll ever know what happened to him. I know if Ernest was still living, he'd write. For Mama's sake, I say he's going to write any day now. She has me read his old letters to her now and then.

Mama has her own little house, the first one we homesteaded in, just two rooms, but it suits her, she says. She's never quite been the same since my papa died years ago, and sometimes her mind slips a little and she seems to be someplace else in her head. It comes and goes, though, and just when I think she is clear crazy, she up and surprises me with something fine she sews or some clever thing she says.

My brother Albert and his sweet wife, Savannah, have nearly finished raising their eight children in their rambling rock-and-siding place a mile up from mine. They have a pecan farm, in which I have a small interest. They expect a meager crop this year, as there has been too little rain, barely a few drops since Thanksgiving last.

Chess lives with me and my two boys, and has since my husband, Jack, died. Chess was Jack's papa, and he's tried to take the place of a papa in the lives of my boys and me. Seems he's tried to take the place of both a ranch hand and my personal tormentor, too, since his son died. My Jack was about the orneriest man to fork himself over a horse, and I miss him every second of my life.

Jack is in the graveyard there on the hill, under the jacaranda tree, next to our little Suzy, who took scarlet fever before she was three. My other two boys are buried in town, too little to have even a marker over their heads. Here in the graveyard are some soldiers who fought the Chiricahua chief Ulzana and his men right here where the round corral is now. Yonder is Mr. Raalle, our neighbor homesteader when we first came here years ago, put there by those same Indians. Harland's wife, Melissa, was Mr. Raalle's daughter. Next to Mr. Raalle is my first husband, Jimmy, who died—after being thrown from a horse—with another woman's name on his lips. And lastly, many pet dogs and cats, baby birds, and lizards that my sons felt needed a funeral.

My mama teases me about the crowded conditions under that jacaranda tree, and where she will lie when her time comes, saying she'd rather be next to the lizards than a strange man, particularly a soldier, as you know what kind of stuff they are. "Well," I tell her, "Jack was a soldier, and you always set a store by him, so I'll save a place for myself next to Jack, and you can have a spot next to me." She seems satisfied with this, and asks me every few days if I'm still saving a place for her. Lordy, you'd think it was the supper table. If I take after my mama, it'll be forty or fifty years before I need a spot for my eternal rest, and the place could get downright crowded by then. Reckon that's why I'm planning ahead, too.

Everyone stayed late as "society ne'er-do-wells," as Savannah put it—near nine o'clock. Then Albert and Savannah's family walked home, toting kerosene lanterns. Between us, we have enough lanterns to start a business, what with the rut we've worn over the years between their house and mine. When we finally put out our last lamp, it was good to hear Gil and Charlie talking past the rhythm of Grampa Chess's snoring. I drifted to sleep listening to them chatter about people they knew from town.

Out on the porch, every three feet or so along the wall, a nail is tied with a piece of cord long enough to reach to the far side of the porch. The cords are for hanging wash when it rains—if it ever does again—and putting up a sheet for privacy if you have company overnight. That night, I awoke just pure-D hot. I got up and found one of the cords, searching blind in the dark for the eyebolt at the other side turned into the wood. I draped the sheet from my bed across the cord so I could sleep without cover. Sackcloth hung by the screens between the posts, and a pitcher of water stood on a little bench. I drizzled water on the burlap, then took a handful and cooled my face and neck, pushing it into my hair, too. I lay back on the bed behind my wall of sheeting and fanned myself with my nightgown. The porch would get cool as the sackcloth started to dry.

Nights like this, I used to make Jack get up and douse the curtains with water. If we were lucky, the boys would be sound asleep, just like tonight. I think about that now and again. I reckon it's sinful, but I do. Once a person has been married, it isn't likely they'll forget the touch of a man's hands.

With the boys home, I feel happier and busier than I have in many a day. Chess said I'd been missing someone to peck at. I told him to stop his pecking at me, and I'd mind my own. I've got two hired hands, Flores and Shorty, so we have four men working, including Charlie and Gil. Funny how when I think of them working, Charlie and Gilbert are men who will tote a man's load any day of the week. When I think of them off on their own in school, or making eyes at some sweetheart, they barely seem like overlarge boys. Not a lick of sense about it all.

Chess spends a lot of time doing fancy leatherwork. He makes the finest carved work saddles I've ever seen, and he has taken to shaping silver tabs and buttons on, too. He sold one last year for $450 to some traveling dude. He uses our best hides and has gone to lengths to get them tanned at Ronstadt's Livery so they'll be just right for a nice saddle. It's a good thing for Chess to do, now that he's not able to see far enough away to help with the ranch very much.

My foreman, Mason Sherrill, is an old man, too. He was past fifty when he came here to help me before the boys were born. Trouble is, he's over eighty now, all but blind, and he forgets so much, things are showing their rust. Still, an old person isn't the same as a worn-out shoe. They don't just get tossed on the heap. What with the retired hands, horses, and old dogs, then new puppies, chicks, kittens, and colts, well, it's a long day's work for the middle-aged ones of us—Savannah, Albert, and myself—who do the most of it. I have to admit with all the work needs doing, it's a pure relief to have Charlie and Gil here. It takes up some of the work without much more than adding two plates to the supper table.

About a week after my boys came home, I saw a skunk nearly the size of a dog headed for the barn. Nip and Shiner started barking, but they were whining, too, smart enough not to go toward it. I hurried back to the house and fetched my rifle. I took a good aim and let fire, and the polecat dropped in its tracks. Everyone came running to see what the ruckus was, but no one had to get too close to figure it out. Chess hollered to Charlie to get an old board to scoop the thing on and carry it off away from the place. Reckon it wasn't as bad as taking a test in school.

Naturally, after all that, Pillbox wouldn't let me near her baby. I named her Pillbox because she seems all fair and gentle outside, but she has got some kind of bitter stuff inside. Won't be ridden unless she takes the notion, and every time someone drops a saddle on her, she goes off on a dead run for glory. I leaned on the gate to the stall, hoping she'd settle enough so I could see the colt again. Pillbox isn't as fair a ride as her mama was. Her dam was my favorite horse, name of Rose. Rose is taking her ease in the east pasture. She gave me seven beautiful foals, and six of them we still have. I have expectations for this new generation. There he was, at last. It made me smile, watching his bright eyes take in his world. He sure is a pretty thing, like the best of every horse I've ever seen rolled into one, and all trimmed and neat, with little hooves lighting on the dust like he could almost dance. To get Hunter, I had put Pillbox with Maldonado's El Rey. I just hope Hunter has his good looks, and Pillbox's sturdy qualities, too.

Rudolfo Maldonado bought himself two Arabian stallions two years ago. One of them died suddenly, and we don't know why. That one was about the prettiest thing I've seen on hooves. The surviving one, he named El Rey, which means "the King," or "God," depending on how it's used. El Rey is tougher than a mule, but he's not got much cow sense, so I'm hoping Pillbox's good quarter horse blood will make a fine colt with some of both traits. Most things that survive here are heavy and rugged, growing thorns, or wearing hopsack-and-barbwire longhandles.

Rudolfo and I swap studs when one or the other of us has some new horse we'd like to try in the line. That man has been my friend since we came to this place, more than twenty years ago. His brother wanted to marry me after Jimmy died. If he hadn't been so much younger than I was—two years—I probably would have taken him up on it. Rudolfo himself makes mentions of the same nature, now that his wife, Celia, has passed away. Mostly, I pretend that he's just teasing and will come to his senses at length.

Gilbert says he wants to try hand-raising Hunter and training him. Reckon that'd be a worthwhile thing for a boy to do. I told him I'd think on it until Hunter was a few months old, if he'd promise to think about school, and I'd not nag him if he'd do the same, and we'll see what we come to at the end of that time. He agreed to it.

Later that morning, I worked the pump handle in my kitchen, and nothing happened. That pump was old, and more times than not needed priming. I found half a cup of water I'd been meaning to drink. With that in the top of the pump, I worked it again. After a bit, water gurgled in the pipe and ran into a tin pan I meant to carry to the dogs. I didn't like the smell of it, though, and looked closely at the pan. It happens now and then. Something will stir the well water in some way I can neither imagine nor discover. It will taste off for a day or two, and then it will come back fine. I've read that there is a whole system of underground rivers and oceans just like on top, but that is a stretch for my mind. All I can picture is the stream here close by, lined with cottonwoods, and I cannot imagine one underground, without trees and blue sky overhead. It makes me wonder about old folk stories of lands under this one with people and everything. I set the pan on the porch and whistled for Nip and Shiner.

Well, I had eggs to gather, and I had just finished that when Mary Pearl, who is seventeen and Savannah's youngest girl, came with some of their morning's milking. I knew I'd have to hurry and get it turned to butter and worked into a cake before it ruined in this heat. I'm glad not to have a milk cow myself, as they are a lot of trouble, and we are happy with just a bit of buttermilk now and then for a cake. I'll be making some sweets to take to Savannah's for supper tonight. We are having supper with them.

That afternoon, soon as I could, I hurried over to Savannah's kitchen. She said she was feeling a little better since being down the day before. I took her some liver for supper, along with steaks. The girls hate the liver, but it is a sure cure for the tiredness that seems to tax us all at times. They made up about four kinds of vegetables and a peach cobbler. I made some bread pudding, too, with nice rich cream sauce to give Savannah some strength in her blood.

We girls were all gathered in the kitchen and I was just telling Savannah she ought to put up her feet and let me set the table, when Mary Pearl said in a really loud voice, "Mama, didn't Mr. Maldonado come by here this morning looking for Aunt Sarah?"

Savannah said, "Mary Pearl, just let it be and don't meddle."

"What'd he want?" I asked. "Rudolfo knows where I live."

Mary Pearl cut her eyes at the ceiling, hummed, and then said, "Oh, *I* don't know."

"Mary Pearl, hush that," Savannah said. "You are gossiping."

"Don't you ever want to marry again, Aunt Sarah?" Mary Pearl asked.

"Mary Pearl!" her mother scolded. "That is far too personal a thing to ask your elders. Sarah, he just brought us a newspaper and asked after you. Simple manners."

Waving her mother's worries away with my hand, I said, to Mary Pearl, "That's why I've got all that dust collected under my bed. Planning to ask the Lord to fix me up a new man."

Savannah and Albert have a boy, Clover, who is older than my Charlie. He finished his studies and came back to work the farm with them. Clove has put together a steam motor that will run a belt through part of the pecan house; it'll make harvest time much less work. He's a quiet man, and reminds me a lot of my brother, his papa, Albert.

My boys and Chess were there before the coffee was made. Those three would cross many a hill for a peach cobbler. They and Clove built a toy for Ezra and Zack, just a board on a log that they could balance and play on, and while we made supper, they had contests to see who could stay on longer. Then Clove said he was going to teach Ezra to walk a barrel. They went and fetched an empty one from the barn, and Clove held Ezra's hands. He walked back and forth on the barrel while Zachary cheered and clapped.

They were all having a bushel of fun, and Savannah rested on the porch and watched them. Their daughter Esther, two years older than Mary Pearl, sat near Savannah with some sewing. Mary Pearl was in the house with me, and she had just handed me a large bowl full of potatoes when we heard Savannah calling, "Look there!"

The girls and I rushed to the door in time to see a whirlwind bigger than our house lumbering up the road. It moved as if a great hand pushed it toward us, weaving back and forth like a drunk man, slowing, carrying dust and bushes and snips of leaves and bits of paper. Well, the boys reckoned it was great fun, and raced off toward it. All five of them, Clove, Ez, and Zack, then Charlie and Gilbert, ran headlong into the whirlwind.

Albert said, "It's coming toward the house."

Esther asked, "Is it a tornado, Papa? Will it sweep us away?"

"No," he said. "Hold your hats, though."

I'd seen many a duster lifting sand off the desert here, sometimes counting five or six at a time when the heat was bad like this. Still, I'd never seen one this size. A terrible premonition filled me that my boys would be swept away in it, along with Savannah's boys, too. There they went, running straight into the whirlwind. I said, "Come on out of there, you fellows. I just washed all those clothes you're wearing," but I said it softly, and no one seemed to hear me, not even Mary Pearl, who was standing next to me.

Savannah asked, "Is the wash in off the line?" No one answered.

The boys disappeared into the dust devil. Here it came, slowly gaining on the house and swallowing whole all our boys. It seemed to stop, and for just a moment, I could see all five of them. Then, like a mammoth creature interrupted on its path by something it found to eat, it started again, coming for the rest of us.

Albert and Savannah and the girls and I all took cover in the house. Now and then, we saw one of the boys come through the wall of dust or linger behind it as it turned toward the pecan barn. I declare it seemed as if it was thinking which way it wanted to go next. Then it came directly toward us again, leaving the boys standing in the yard. It swept over the house, rattling the windows, and spraying dirt against them. For a few seconds, the sky outside the windows was brown and cottony, then blue again. Quick as that, it was gone, as if it had only come to break itself apart on their house.

We stepped onto the front porch, and saw the biggest mess I've ever seen in my life. The entire porch, chairs, plants, and rug, every square inch, was peppered with rabbit dung. It wedged into every little crevice around the windowsills and the floorboards. Little brown balls of dark hail had come out of the cloud of dirt, descending on us thicker than nuts on a cake. Savannah rushed to her chair, where she'd dropped her apron while hurrying to the house. "Look at this," she said, tipping it up. The pockets overflowed and poured out piles of rabbit drops. They hit the floor, bouncing like marbles dropped from a bag.

Zachary's voice came to us, shouting, "I rode the wind! I rode the plum-busted wind!" He spun, arms outstretched, then ran toward the porch in sweeping circles, his face skyward, eyes closed. "Mama, Mama! Clove and Charlie held my hands, and it pulled me up like a sure-nuff paper kite. It held me up like a bird. Like a eagle! I rode the wind like a sure-nuff eagle. Damnation!"

Until his last word, we'd all been smiling, sharing his fun. Savannah and Albert turned and stared at him as if he'd been a wolf come for the chickens. Very softly, Savannah said, "Albert. The strap is in the pantry."

"Zachary Taylor Prine," Albert said with such sadness in his voice that I knew Zack would never guess how it pained his father, "go to the barn and wait." He slipped into the house, gone after the old piece of a saddle cinch that served as the binding to the seat of education in their home.

Zack's face bore his confusion. He clapped his hands over his mouth, stunned at what he'd let fly in the midst of his joy. Tears spurted from his eyes, clear of his hands and face, and hit the rabbit pellet–coated ground. "It was a accident, Papa. I didn't mean it, Mama."

"Still," Savannah said, "we had that talk just two days ago, and you knew the next foul word from your mouth would bring this. A boy who cannot bridle his own tongue will have nothing but the poorest life imaginable. Take thyself to the barn, Zachary."

"Thyself?" he said.

"Go," she said, and turned away from him.

Poor little old Zack started bawling out loud, suffering his mother's so gentle rebuff more than he would ever feel Albert's strapping. For Savannah to have addressed one of her sons in this way, saying "thyself" instead of "yourself," was the ultimate in rejection. It removed him from the family circle, made him a stranger. Only family members were "you" and "yours." It dampened all our spirits to see him trod off to his punishment, shoulders heaving, feet scuffing the dust around him so that he left a cloud behind him. Anyone who knew their family knew Zack had already gotten the worst of it, and that if they laid even one switch, it would be drawn back, its purpose more for effect than for a welting.

"Savannah," I said, "I'll sweep this porch for you."

She already had the broom in her hands, but she held it toward me. Tears were in her eyes. She whispered, "He's got to learn."

I took the broom and began pushing the brown hail from the doorway and off the porch. "He does," I said. It wasn't like Savannah to buckle up over disciplining one of her children. Still, she'd been poorly lately, and he was the baby.

We heard a faint snap and a loud wail. Savannah put a hand to her face and went into the house. I heard Esther calling out, "Mama, Mama? What's the matter?"

By the time I got the porch clear of the cottontail manure, Albert came from the barn, Zack at his side. The two were talking. Zack's face, now subdued, was red and streaked with clean lines through the grime left from the whirlwind. I watched them stop by the corral fence and pump clean water at the trough. Zack washed his hands and face, then his whole head. Albert stood over him, working the pump handle at a gentle speed so the water came evenly. I heard Albert say, "Ears, too."

"Yes, sir," Zachary replied.

Then Zack pumped water, and Albert did the same washing up. There was some little thing in that act—something beyond the forgiveness, something greater and nameless—that my sons would never know. My boys have lived so long without a father. I can only hope they have some memories of their own papa. Some cord that can't be cut by the hardness of life or worn away by the soil on his grave. I felt hot. There was a burning behind my eyes, a hard place forming in my throat, and I leaned on the broom with my cheek.

Chess came out the door just then and said, "Miss Savannah has supper on the table, and me and the boys are about to lose our foothold in heaven over having to wait for Albert to say the blessing. Land o' living, what's ailing you?"

"Dirt in my eyes."

"Dirt, eh?" Chess held the door wide for me, and he shook his head as I passed him.

I propped the broom against the wall and sniffed back my tears before I went in. I said right out, "You all save a pullie bone for Zachary."

When Zack entered the room, everyone cheered him.

Charlie said, "We carved you the best, buddy. Beaks and feet—all you can eat."

"Zachary," Savannah said, "you may ask the Lord's blessings on this meal."

Listening to his tiny voice in prayer, a kind of ache came into my chest, one that didn't leave me all during supper. I forgave my sons for not caring about the education I wanted for them. I forgave them, too, for not thinking of the future, not seeing it the way I did. How could they know? No more sense about life than little gray Hunter bumping his mama's belly. I forgave them for busting with energy and thinking they'd already figured out all about things. While Savannah and Albert surely were thinking about Zachary, I was thinking of my own boys. We were plum overflowing with forgiveness at that table.

They piled up plates with chicken, pan-fried steaks, and liver, which were passed around with potatoes bought fresh last week from a wagon out of Phoenix, gravy, vegetables, salad, and Mary Pearl's best biscuits. The first one went to Zachary's place.

Finally, Clover said, "Tell us what it felt like, Zack. Did it feel like jumping on the bed? Well, swallow that bite, and then talk. Tell us what it was like to fly."

Chapter Two

Charlie came to the house with a bucket in his hands and a fearful expression on his face.

"What's that you've got?" I said, thinking he was going to show me some two-headed pollywog or something.

"Mud, Mama," he said. "Nothing but mud." He slapped his hat to the floor and wiped sweat from his head with a sleeve. "From the well."

I put my fingertips against my mouth and stared at the mud like it was filth he was fixing to throw on my bed. I asked, "How far down?" Cold shot through my insides, and the look and smell of that pan of off-colored water I'd pumped the other day seemed as fresh a memory as this mud before me.

"All the way. When we hauled out for bathwater last night, the last of it was dark. I reckoned it'd just gotten stirred up or something, but this is all we're drawing."

"What do we have?"

"Olla's half-full. Creek's dry as a bone. Tucker rode down and back, and he says Little Muddy cattle tank has about two feet of wet silt."

I sat hard on the kitchen chair. We'd wasted our last drops of clear water on bathing and then put it on the garden and under the shade trees. My throat felt like cotton; my tongue was parched. The thought of having no water made me long for it all the more.

I pondered the work I'd been doing, straining buttermilk, and it gave me an idea. I said, "We'll set up a sieve with cheesecloth. Get some grease cans, and we'll tack the cloth on them, start pouring mud through, and then boil it." If a person could even find a driller in this country, it could cost a thousand dollars or more to sink a well.

"That isn't going to water the horses and us, both," Charlie said.

A gust of breeze came just then, rippling through the curtains hanging in the window. "I know it," I said. "Get your brother, and you ride to Maldonado's. See how they're fixed for water. If their tanks are dry, tell them I'll drive the buckboard with two or three barrels in it. We'll fill up from the windmill in the southeast section."

Charlie said, "We thought of that. I already told Gil to go down and check the float, make sure it's opened all the way, so it can start filling the troughs before we get there. I sent Shorty to Majo Vistoso with a bucket to try the spring-water on the animals, since those antelope were using it. Tomorrow I'll go to town and find a driller."

I shook my head. "Let's see what we can do here, first. We'll drill if we have to, but I need to be certain that we have to, before I lay out the money. Hand me that. Go get the boys, and get the buckboard ready."

Mary Pearl was out in the barn, watching Grampa Chess work on a new saddle. I told them what Charlie'd found, then sent her to tell her folks, and to get Esther, along with Zack and Ezra, to help me move my chickens to their place. By the time the children had half the chickens carried up the hill and the buckboard was ready, Shorty rode back with half a bucket of the mineral water from the hot spring. I tried giving a sip to the dogs, but they wouldn't touch it. I let the boys take a sip, tasted it myself, and like to choked. The horses turned away from it, too. We all agreed there would be no saving ourselves or our animals with this stuff. It was worthless for anything except a bath, and even at that, it turned our skins white with crust that had to be rubbed off. Judging by the salty taste, that water couldn't be used even to keep the garden alive.

Thank heavens for our other windmill. Toting water from it would save our lives. It had been a difficult decision to make, but since I'd bought those last two sections, some of my range was so far away, I had to get water to the animals there. It would take about three hours to get down and back from the southeast section of land, where the giant windmill brought up water for the range herd. Three hours, if we took our time, not pushing the horses, for an animal might suddenly die in its tracks in this heat, and I'd had to unhitch a dead horse once. I surely didn't want to have that work to do again.

Charlie rode a paint horse near ahead of the wagon. None of the neighbors had lost water, only us. We talk about water here, rain, acreage, and feed. I remember wondering early last summer whether our well needed to go deeper, as it was only about eighty feet, but the late summer had brought rain, and we never lacked for a drink of water. What we had this year was an empty well full of trouble. Four miles from the windmill, I could see the top of it rising above the trees ahead. Charlie fell quiet. When he stopped in his tracks, he motioned me to stop.

"Whoa," I said, and pulled up the brake. "You hear something?"

"Rider. Coming fast," he said.

I stayed put in the middle of the road. Charlie edged off to the side a little ways. A few seconds more, and we saw the man on horseback. It was Gilbert. He pulled up next to the wagon, and Charlie came from the side of the road. "There's no water there," Gil said. "Somebody's bunged up the pump. Shot all three tanks full of holes. Two dead steers in two of them. The third one looks to be just drained from the holes."

A terrible pain gripped my throat. I said, "Why would anybody—" There was no answer for the question. "We're more than halfway. You think we can get it running and fill these kegs?"

Gilbert said, "Hard to tell. Those tanks are ruined sure."

Charlie said, "Seems to me this is recent, if the dead animals aren't even swelled yet. Like it was just last night or this morning early."

We found the windmill like Gil had described it; its gears had been wrenched out of place with a pry bar of some sort. The chain used to lock it down had been tossed high up, where it had caught on the blades and twisted around the scaffold. The real nightmare of it was in the troughs. Three steel tubs, each big enough for a grown man to have a swim in, stair-stepped down a low hill, one after the other seated on leveled-off ground, set just so that one would overflow into the next, keeping them all full, and any runoff would create a shady, grassy place nearby. It had been a regular oasis before someone ruined it. The two lower tubs had the dead animals in them. The third tub, closest to the windmill itself, had a thick white crust in the bottom. Looked to be salt.

Buzzards circled over us. The boys set about climbing the scaffold to free the chain. They both went up, one on each side, to get a better idea how to pull the chain from the top. I pushed and poked at the pipes below, and near as I could tell, although the pieces were not connected, nothing seemed damaged.

"Stand back, Mama," Charlie called. "I got this chain loose."

I stepped back, and he dropped the chain. The big wheel started to revolve. It swung around on the tower, catching the smallest breeze, and the blades started moving. I heard a shout from on high, Charlie hollering something I couldn't make out, then Gilbert's voice crying loudly, "Gosh almighty, it's going to kill me."

There was a sound like a *whop,* and a hat whipped down from the windmill and landed beyond the scaffold. Gilbert was holding tight to the scaffold right up at the very top. The blades of the huge mill turned in the space right behind his neck. He'd been too high up when the thing let go.

I sucked in my breath sharply as the machine whipped by Gilbert's head. It left only the width of his neck between the scaffold and the moving blades. The tail vane was broken, raised straight up, letting the windmill spin around the tower as it turned. If Gilbert drew back to climb down, the blades would crack him in the head and kill him. At the very least, it would knock him off. Forty feet is a long fall. Too long to survive.

"No," I said, though I don't know which one I called it to. "Hold tight, Gilbert. Hold!"

"I'm coming. Don't move," Charlie said. He edged his way through the wooden rails, close enough to Gilbert to touch his outstretched arm, just out of reach of the turning blades. He held his brother's arm, steadying him against the frame while keeping himself clear of the blades. I watched him grapple for the spinning wheel as it turned faster and faster. Pulling back his hands because of the stinging, he tried again to grab one, then caught it, but it nearly threw him from the scaffold. "Glory, that hurt! Mama," he called. "Can you turn it off from the ground?"

The spoke. I knew I'd been searching for something, but I couldn't immediately figure what was missing. The spoke was a piece of an old wagon wheel that hung from a cable and fit into a notch as high up as my shoulders, above the base of the pump. The frame, when it was caught underneath, pulled up the wind vane and stopped the blades from turning so it could roll around with the wind and not tear itself up. "Hang on, boys," I said. The cable had been jerked and had snapped clear up into the scaffolding, the way a wire will do when it is stretched and broken. The handle was gone. I pulled up my skirts and started climbing up that ladder, studying all the time where the end of the cable might be. I reached for it and climbed higher, then reached for it again. It was snarled tighter than a rat's nest and far out of my reach. I hollered up, "I'll do something, don't worry," but I was worried, plenty.

From where I stood on the ladder, the shaft of metal pipe shuttled up and down in the wooden barrel, about a foot over my head. It was greased and slick. I didn't need anyone to tell me taking hold with my hands would cost me fingers. Higher up, ten feet or so, the pipe connected to another one with a thick band of metal strap and melted lead. I got back to the ground and ran and got a hank of rope from the wagon, then hunted for something that could take the place of the pin. "Hang on, Gilbert!" I called again. I tossed the rope around the moving pipe and pulled it tight, but it just slid in the grease. Next time, I tried lassoing the tangled cable line. It was tied up there, and all it did was creak when I pulled on it and slide the loop off. If I could get something long enough to push against the joint where the pipes met, maybe it would stop.

I pulled the team right up next to the windmill frame and climbed into the wagon. From there, I was only about six feet below the joint. In the bed of the wagon was a five-pound hammer, mixed in with stray hanks of wire and turnbuckle pullers. I took that hammer and beat the top rail right out of its nails. Then, holding it straight up over my head, I leaned into it as the metal joint came down. It nearly sat me down flat. There it came again, and I pushed with all my strength. "Is it slowing, boys?" I hollered.

Time and again, that metal knob beat into the end of the board, and each time I pushed harder. It happened quick and sharp, straining every fiber in me, like birthing pains, coming close to the end and hard. I said, "Wait. I'll try something else."

"No, Mama," Gilbert called. "Just slow it down again. I got it figured. There's enough time between vanes for me to duck out if you can only slow it down. I'll count every second, and be ready to pull my head out."

Then both boys hollered, "Push, Mama, push!" I forced that board upward against the pipe knee, slowing that great wheel. My fingers cramped; my back made a noise. The pipe rose again, and I held my breath. Then down it came again, and I managed to slow it nearly to a stop. I was waiting for a cry, waiting for that horrible *whop* again, followed by the merciless sound of one or both my sons falling to the ground. Down it came again. I gave a loud groan, driving the board with my whole body, holding fierce against it. Straining. Waiting. My arms burned like fire.

I heard Gilbert's voice. "Let up, Mama, before you bust. I'm out."

Charlie gave a whoop of relief. "I'll get the cable untied from here," he called.

I dropped the board. My fingers, useless, formed a curl that was hard to open. I stared upward as my youngest son edged his way down the scaffold. Even from where I was, I could see Gilbert's knees shaking. I had a knot in my side.

When he got to the ground, he was breathing hard, red in the face, and he kept gasping over and over. After a while, he said, "Reckoned you were going to have to buy me a stone, too, Mama."

"Ornery rascal," I said, and squeezed him good and tight. That's why, I reckon, I bought that stone for myself, but no others. Ensuring they wouldn't need one until long after I'm gone. I'm not putting another one of my children in the ground. No sir. I was shaking so hard, my teeth rattled. I said, "Honey, you went and got your hat dirty."

"Yes, ma'am, I did," Gilbert said.

The boys jerked on the gears and shook things back into place, banging on pipes and mashing their fingers. Half an hour of that, and the pump got to hissing, and a minute later, water came from the pipe. It seemed fine. Cool and beautiful. We held our heads under the spit and drank deep and hard. Then we pulled up the wagon and filled the kegs. Charlie found the missing pin when the water started pouring into the whitened first tank. It was corroded, but whole. He rinsed the salt from it, then shut down the windmill. No sense drawing animals to drink their death. No sense rinsing salt into the grass basin we'd made three years ago, and killing it for all time. Though it meant hauling barrels every day, at least we had some water for the house now.

I chucked the reins and headed the wagon homeward, the boys following on their mounts. Charlie tossed Gilbert's hat to him and said, "Never saw India-rubber legs before. Where'd you get them things?"

"Hush," Gil said, beating the hat against his leg and then putting it on his head.

"Reckon you could stretch 'em out? Tie 'em in a knot under the horse, and you won't need a cinch," said Charlie.

"Why don't I tie you in a knot instead?"

"Your hat's got a new yank in it. Reckon it's a goner."

Gilbert cleared his throat, a loud noise. He said, "Just my work hat. Reckon it looks like it's been worked under now."

"Or worked over." After a long silence, Charlie said, "You can have mine."

"You're giving me the new black Stetson?" He sounded hopeful.

Charlie laughed and waited just long enough for me to think he was really going to give his brother his best hat. Then he said, "Well, no. I meant the greasy sombrero Sparky used to wear, that one Flores keeps as a tar bucket. It's black, too, you know."

"Knothead," Gilbert said.

I smiled. Sometimes there isn't any better music than two brothers bickering.

On the road home, I could see a large cloud far, far north of us. It looked dark, but it would be no good anyway. Any storm that forms in the north never brings rain, only dust storms and driving wind. Rain comes from the south. On the southern horizon, there was nothing in the sky but heat shimmers waving in the air.

We spent part of the good water on the horses and animals. I drew up three buckets full of thick gritty water from the well and left them on my front porch. Then I went out to find Chess, and a grease can or three, to begin straining mud. I figured to give the boiled-over water to the animals after this and keep the good in the house. Still, it would take a lot of work to keep a supply going.

I asked Mason to help me keep the fire going under the boiling pot outside. Then I put some lunch on the table and called the boys.

"Where's Charlie?" I said to Chess.

"Down the well with a shovel," he said. "He'll be up directly."

Charlie took a few minutes to beat the dirt off his clothes. Finally, he put his hat on its hook and sat down.

"Doing any good?" I asked, handing him a cup of water.

"Two inches," he said. "I cleared out a foot of mud, and there's two inches of bad water on top of solid rock. Not enough room down there to swing a pick."

Chess said, "You can't dig through that. All you'll do is blunt the shovel. Maybe come evening, some will seep back in. Or we'll buy some dynamite from one of the mining camps. Until then, we'll work on not getting thirsty. First thing after lunch, we'll go back down and get to fixing those water tanks."

We'll be losing those cattle right and left if they have to go a day without a drink, since they're already starved for water. We'd better start pushing the criollos in the section closest to the house toward part of our land that borders the Maldonados' little creek. Early afternoon, Chess took Charlie and Flores back to the windmill. They drove the buckboard, and carried the two empty barrels to fill again. While I strained mud and boiled water, Gilbert rode down to Benson to buy five sticks of dynamite.

Shorty and Gilbert succeeded in wiring up a cap into a single stick of dynamite, then dropped it down the well by the house. We held our ears, waiting for the explosion, then covered our faces and waited for the dust to settle. All it accomplished was to collapse the sides of the well. It took them the rest of the day to dig the rubble out. We were left with worse water than before—until it could settle all night—on top of having a blessed hole nearly six feet wide where it had been only three before.

It's a frightening thing to see quail and bobcats politely drinking side by side from the same little mud puddle, which is all that's left of Cienega Creek. If it rains in the next forty-eight hours, we can go to sleep with easy souls. If it doesn't rain, we are either in God's hands or at the devil's mercy—I don't know which.

May 5, 1906

Gilbert was out this morning early, watching little Hunter prance and play, teaching him not to mind being handled and having his feet messed with. Petting a pony seems like a silly job to an outsider, but not to someone who has had to shoe a horse that doesn't like his feet being touched. We have hauled water until we have—at least for today—some excess, so this morning I plan to wash some clothes, and then try to get a pound of rust off my own hide.

Long ago, Rudolfo Maldonado built me a Mexican-type oven in the yard, and we have a little cooking circle with a table and a shade where we barbecue sometimes. Charlie and Mason are lighting a fire under the soap cauldron for the washing later, as I don't intend to heat the stove and, with it, the kitchen. In the summer, we even make the morning's coffee outside.

All the men around here had strict orders to stay away from the house after breakfast, as I intended a long soak in the tub, which I set up in the kitchen. As I soaked in the cool water, I tried to call to mind all the things that had slid by the wayside while we'd been busy hauling water each day. I had to get Ezra and Zachary back to their schooling, that was one thing. Mary Pearl, too. That girl seems to have slipped away from her lessons, and she is probably thinking I've forgotten all about that theme I asked her to do on the legislative power of government. Well, I was deep in thought, absently scrubbing the bottom of my foot, when a bang made me jump near out of the tub. Something had hit the window in the parlor. Sometimes we get a dove that's lost his mind or his vision or some such, and the poor bird will kill himself against a window. More than half the time, though, they don't die, but lie on the porch, knocked all cattey whompus for a while, then get up and head for home. They leave dusty outlines shaped just like a bird, and it is so pretty a picture, I hate to wash the glass. Sometimes I leave the picture there for a long time.

When there is a good dust picture of a bird on the glass, I wait until the light is just right and then hold a page of thin letter-writing paper to the glass and pencil-line the bird. I have about nine or ten good sketches of birds that seem to be still flying, the way their wings are spread. Well, I was curious to see if the one that had just hit had lived or not, so I got out of the tub and dried off quick, then tipped into the parlor with a quilt wrapped around me in case anyone came in. I opened the back door, and sure enough, there was a dove on the boards, its downy feathers swirling around it like smoke.

I knelt over the bird and got a closer look. I touched it with my fingertips. Then I stretched out its wing a little. I could see a movement in a vein under the wing, and I knew it was still alive. I love how a dove feels. Its feathers were soft and smooth, not like a chicken's, where you can feel the ribs. Of course, we don't mind how they taste, either, but I wasn't planning to eat one that had died this way.

Well, my quilt started to slip down, so I pulled it back into shape, then had to stand up to rearrange it without it falling. I suppose I fanned that senseless dove with the corner of the quilt, for at that second it came to life and flew straight upward, right up between two folds of the wrap. I hollered and flung the quilt off, shaking the bird out of it. There I stood, buck naked in the sunshine, on the back porch, startled by a silly bird. It fluttered wildly, crying in that sad moan doves make, and I heard footsteps at the side of the house, so I knocked the door open, stepping backward. The silly dove flew straight over my head, into the house, and I closed the door fast for my own decency.

My heart was thumping wildly, though I couldn't move for a minute. The bird fluttered through the house, dropping downy feathers like a pillow that had been hit too hard and was losing the stuffing. Someone banged on the back door. "Mama?" a man's voice said. "I heard you yell. What's going on? Are you all right?" It was Charlie.

"I'm fine!" I hollered. "There's a bird in here."

"What?" he said. The door started to open.

"Don't come in! I'm—I'm taking a bath. It's nothing. Just a bird."

"How'd you get a bird in there?" he hollered through the door.

"Oh, Charlie, just go along. I'll tell you after I get dressed!" The dove sailed right past me and lighted on the frame of the door, looking as if it was pleading for escape. It seemed as if it might stay put for a minute, and I got my drawers and a chemise on before it started dashing hell-bent through the house again.

Doves can fly so fast. I've seen one outrace a hawk in flight, darting and turning, sighing with each push of its wings. In my underwear, I tried cornering it, tried shooing it to one end of the room. Now and then, it came to rest, looking fearful and wide-eyed, and I'd creep up on it, getting my hands within inches of it before it would take off for a bedroom or back to the kitchen. Finally, I held up the wet towel I'd used to dry off with after my bath, and when the bird lit on the back of a chair, I flung the towel on it and caught it.

Well, I figured Charlie had left the back porch. Seems to me anybody would have reckoned that if you told your son to go away because you were barely dressed, and just happened to be chasing a bird in the house, too, he'd go away. But no, not one of *my* sons. I pushed the back door, expecting empty desert, planning to open that wet towel and release the dove so he could fly willy-nilly into a tree or something, and standing there in a ring, waiting for a spectacle, were Charlie, Gilbert, Flores, and Chess—and Rudolfo Maldonado.

I let out a yell, and then flapped the bird out of the towel. It lay on the ground, pathetic and wet. The boys all looked sheepish, seeing me in my drawers, and turned their faces. Flores put his hat down in front of his face. Rudolfo, I noticed, took a little longer than the rest to turn away. "Well?" I said. "What in heaven are you all doing here?"

Charlie, still facing the brush, said, "I came to tell you that El Maldonado was on his way over."

"Mama, why were you bathing a dove in the bathtub?" Gilbert asked.

I said, "It wasn't in the tub."

"Well, it's wet. I think you drowned it."

"Good Lord, Gilbert. I wasn't *bathing* the bird."

I heard a strange noise—a vibrating, hissing, fluttering noise. Before me were the backs of five men who were shaking up and down, hands to their faces. Every last one of them was laughing up his sleeve and trying to be polite about it. I picked up the quilt I'd left on the porch and went back in the house, making sure they heard the door shut. Shaking my head, I went to finish getting dressed. Standing at the chest of drawers, I looked into the mirror. My hair was covered with a crown of gray down, like a cap. I looked to be wearing a hat of dove feathers on my wet hair. I'd probably catch lice from this mess.

The chuckling on the back porch had become full-out laughter. "Mama!" Gilbert called. "Your bird is about dead. You want me to call the undertaker?"

"No, no! It's a miracle. Look at that," said Charlie. "Resurrection! You want me to catch him? After a bath, he probably needs a shave and a shoe shine, too."

I opened the window and shouted through, "One of you boys go get me some turpentine, and quit that braying. The rest of you drift on out of here."

Charlie was laughing all the harder. "Mama," he called, "I don't think you can shave him with turpentine."

"Charlie? Do I have to take a switch to you?" I said.

I went to put on my skirt, so at least that half of me would be decent. I wasn't about to get fully dressed until I'd washed my hair again. When there was another knock at the door, some man's long arm reached in with a gallon can of turpentine. I opened the door all the way. Rudolfo's arm was sticking through my doorway; the rest of the no-accounts had vanished.

"Well, I was going to ask Chess to help. Rudolfo, will you do this for me?" I said. "I'm going to hold my head over the rail here and you pour that stuff on it. Try not to get it on the wood."

"Sarah," he said. Then he waited, as if he were about to say something else, and finally he said, "All right, then. *Sí.*"

I bent over the rail. He poured the turpentine all through my hair. I squeezed it and rubbed it until I believed I'd gotten every single hair coated. Then I worked it some more. Finally, I rolled up the hair to the top of my head and held it with one hand as I stood and unbent my back. Rudolfo held the can between us. He tried to smile. His face was dark red. *"¿Suficiente?"* he said.

"Well, I reckon it might take longer to catch lice from a bird than five minutes, but I don't know for sure. The boys said you wanted to see me. Is it urgent, or can you wait until I wash this out?"

"I'll wait," he said.

I nodded and went back inside. I finished the job, hanging my head back over the cold bathwater and scrubbing with lye soap, then rinsing with a pitcherful of clear water.

When I finally got a towel around my hair and wiped my eyes, I was startled to find Rudolfo had been sitting silently on a kitchen chair the entire time. "Why didn't you say something?" I asked. "I didn't know you were inside."

I could hear him breathing. Rudolfo had a strange, hungry look in his eyes, though he seemed to be studying the window curtains or something in that direction. He said, "You left the door open. I thought you meant for me to follow you. Forgive me if I've embarrassed you, *por favor.*"

I suddenly felt uneasy, and I was very aware that I was alone with Rudolfo in the kitchen, wearing only a damp white shimmy from the waist up. "Well, do you want some water? Shall I make some dinner?"

He turned his gaze at me, his eyes sweeping down then up to my own. "Sarah, you have the form of a young woman. So . . ."

I crossed my arms over my breasts. "That's not what you came here to say, *amigo.*"

His face reddened before he spoke. "I came to tell you one of the hands said to me he can find out who ruined your windmill. I told him I'd pay him extra if he's correct. I think he already knows. He wants more money than I offered."

I said, "Paying for information—that feels sort of dirty."

His brows moved, but his face stayed calm. "No worse than beating it out of him. You can't expect every peon to be honest and just confess it to you."

"No, I don't—rightly—expect that. Do you want me to pay it?"

"No. I'm just telling you what I know. *Con permiso,* I'll get back to my work."

I took up the quilt that had started all the fuss and folded it in my arms, holding it high, so I felt a little more covered. "Stay for dinner? It's nearly noon."

"Luz will expect her papa. *Buenos dias.*"

"*Y tu,*" I said.

He left by the back door, where he'd come in. Feathers and down flitted across the porch in a small stirring of breeze from his passing. I touched my hair. The towel had fallen around my shoulders and my hair was already starting to dry in the warm air. It had been a long time since a man had looked at me the way Rudolfo had. Not that I'd wanted for males around the place, but they'd always been family. There was nothing brotherly in Rudolfo's expression, nor in the violet flush of his neck and face.

As I pulled my arms through the sleeves of my blouse, I remembered Jack's arms, and his broad shoulders, and leaning against him, listening to his heart beating. Rudolfo—when I pictured him before me—didn't move me that way, but the memory of loving a man seemed now just a moment past, not years. I stared at my reflection in the mirror over the chest of drawers. My face was flushed, too. Was that passion? For Rudolfo? Did I really want to be Mrs.— *Doña*—Maldonado? Had he awakened something with his dark glances? Or did I just want to be loved again?

With a sigh, I tucked the shirtwaist into my waistband and fastened on the string with its scissors and key. I needed to get outside, get my hair dry in the sun, put it up, and get the boys' dinner on the table. Once I got my hair up, I went to my keepsake box and took out the old daguerreotype of Jack and me, looking formal and starched, right after our wedding. Jack's pocket watch was under the picture. I took it out and opened it. Engraved "With my love" and given to him on our wedding day, it still worked if a person cared to wind it regularly. I held the watch case to my cheek and felt Jack's warmth come through it into my face. If I married Rudolfo, would I always close my eyes and think of Jack?

Chapter Three

First thing, I thought I was dreaming. I rushed outside in the dark, still in my nightdress. It was rain that woke me, but it came from one of those odd desert cloudbursts that cobble up and move off, all the while with clear sky around them. The house was wet. Not a drop had hit the garden. The round corral was soaked and puddled. Half the barn looked darkened and damp, the other half dry as tinder. Soon as the sun came over the hill, the ground had dried. Within an hour of sunrise, hot air stirred around the yard, creating small dust devils, as if it had never been wet. Reckon that was proof enough it was too good even for a dream. I don't know if it was good news or bad, but the well seemed to be about half-full of red-brown water. Surely it's going to come back up.

I rigged up a regular water-sieving machine on the porch. It had a can at the top with a piece of window screen in it to get out pebbles and twigs, which drained into another can, this one with a single layer of cheesecloth. When the water dripped through that, it was thin enough to run, and it was poured into a third can with four layers of cheesecloth and one of hopsacking. The last can was lined with muslin, and the water that came from it, clear but still a bit brown, went into a kettle to be boiled on the pit fire in the yard.

Savannah sent Esther and Mary Pearl to help me with the water preparations. They have water aplenty up there, and Albert's place is higher than mine. I surely can't figure that one, for I thought the lower elevation meant we were closer to the groundwater. I'll ask Charlie if he's read up to anything about water levels in his geology studies. Sure can't figure why it would rise underground.

When I had a two-gallon can full and cooled off from the boiling, I carried it out to the old horses in the round corral to see how they'd take to it. Well, they didn't seem to mind it at all. Then I left the girls to the task of cleaning more water, and took a ride down to Rudolfo Maldonado's place. His oldest daughter, Luz, met me at the gate and called one of the other children to run and fetch their father. I had always thought of her mother, Celia, as a friend. I taught her to speak English after she married Rudolfo, and she taught me better Spanish. It made a peaceful evening when we finally learned enough in each other's *lingua* to be able to find the right word in one or the other, and stop all the silly pointing and acting out. Before Celia died, we spent years sharing recipes, cures for children's ailments, bolts of calico. After Luz and I talked awhile, she took me in the house and brought a tray with a pitcher of water and glass tumblers to drink from.

Luz led me to the gallery, set down the tray, and bowed as if she were a servant, then left me alone. Luz has taken her mother's place running the household. She's the age of my Charlie. The second girl they have, Elsa, has gone to a convent in Tucson. To Elsa, I had been *tía,* an aunt. But to Luz, older and always more somber, I was just another *ganadero* here to speak to her papa.

The adobe room was wide as a church, freshly plastered, with tiles and fine carpet on the floor. The ceilings were fourteen feet overhead, and every wall had windows in two rows high and low, so that breezes pulled in and ruffled the curtains, even though there was no wind outside. One side held three sets of tall, narrow double doors that opened on the courtyard in the center of the house. Rudolfo came in with a little girl tugging at his pant leg. He put his hat on a hook and said something to his smallest daughter, Magdalena. She looked to be about eight years old. She giggled, then left.

"You know I've had some trouble," I said.

Rudolfo poured water in glasses for us both. "*Sí.* The person who did this must be found." He added a dram of whiskey to his water and tipped it toward me, just for a moment. He knew I'd not have it, but did it for politeness' sake. Then he handed me my glass of water and sat before me, crossing a foot over the other knee.

I said, "When Charlie went back to get more water, he thought enough to look for footprints, but he couldn't find any except our own."

"I have *dos caballeros* I don't know well. A couple more I know, but don't trust. All the others, I have talked with. We'll watch, listen to the small noises of the night. We'll discover things in the quiet." He drank about half the glass, then set it on the desk. He smiled. "I'll sort it out for you."

"Magdalena is getting big. Blooming."

"She needs a mother, Sarah. I cannot be a mother to her."

"She's lucky to have sisters, then. I never had sisters. Not until Albert married, and Savannah came along with us from Texas."

"You know what I ask. Not for me alone."

"I know." There was so much more in it, though. Could I love Rudolfo? I believed I could live with him as a wife and be contented. Children are easy to love. I remembered Chess telling me to let go of my boys, and I winced. This man before me would trust me to raise his children, and I'd trust the lives of my own to him. But I'd always wonder, somewhere in the dark, smallest corners of my heart, if the proposal was about the land. Nothing in him tells me that. It was just my own hard heart, I suppose. Still, the combination of our two ranches would make this one of the largest spreads in the county, outside of the Hashknife Outfit.

I said, "I've not had much luck keeping husbands around, Rudolfo. Why would I want to marry you and then in a year or two become *la viuda* Maldonado? I'd rather keep you around as long as possible, *mi amigo.*"

"I could give you anything."

I smiled at him. "Give me your friendship, then."

He sighed, beaten, and turned to sit again at the *escritorio grande.* "Now. Let us talk about cattle and *l'agua.*"

Rudolfo said he thought the Bakers, Wainbridges, and Cujillos would all be willing to round up in June as usual, but push the herd north to Tempe and sell early because of the drought. He said Kansas had been getting plenty of rain and that beef there was going for near-record low prices. He thought it would be a good idea to combine the stock and send some of each of our hands to drive a large herd to the stockyards outside of Phoenix. Rudolfo was going to Tempe in a few days to see what the market was like there, before we go to all that work. Since he speaks plenty of English now, he is going alone.

I asked him what kind of numbers he was talking about, and he said five hundred of his. "I don't think half the herd could make it all the way to Kansas this year," he said. "Getting them past Picacho will be a feat in itself."

"Fine," I said. "Circle east up the river bottom. If there's water in the

Rillito and the San Pedro, they'll make it to Tempe. I'll put in payroll money up front."

"We'll share that, too." Rudolfo moved his head very slowly, nodding. "We *could* wait for rain."

"I'm going broke waiting."

"I know you don't believe in such things, but I know a woman, a *cantadora*, who has said it will be a bad year for this area. We should move them as soon as possible. Tomorrow I'll talk to Baker, decide when to start, since his place is farthest south."

I didn't remind him what he'd just said about believing in superstitions. I said, "If it rains, we'll be all right."

"We can always change our minds. I'm not sure we'll see rain by July."

So it was agreed. Maybe my boys will want to go. Maybe a month of eating dust would make studying books taste better.

Rudolfo saw me to the door. As I went to put on my gloves, he took one from me. For a couple of years, he's been saying things to me about needing a wife, wanting me for the job. Never before has he so much as taken my hand or given me a moment of hesitation in his presence until that day with the feathers in my hair. Holding my leather glove, he pulled the hand of it inside out and kissed the leather, then turned it right side out again. He said, "You will hold a kiss in the palm of your hand. I meant what I said."

I rolled my eyes and put on the glove. The silliness of men confounds me sometimes. "Let me know what you find out as soon as you get back," I said.

I rode home thinking that if we take our cattle to market early, it could make some real trouble for other ranchers in the area, and none of them would be too kindly disposed toward us for the rest of time. I'm thinking maybe it would be worth the investment to set them at a feedlot for two weeks before we sell, especially after that long drive. They'll get there all lean and stringy from the trip. By the time the other herds come in, ours will be fat and sassy, and bring the best price. When I got to the border of my land, I saw another little cloud over the sandy ridge. By the time I got to the yard, it had fiddled out and disappeared. Dry well. Thirsty herd. There was plenty of work to do.

The girls had made good progress, having cleaned near fifteen gallons of water when I got there. Esther said it was coming cleaner straight from the well, too, as if the sediment was settling. But it was so much trouble, she said that I might think about just hauling it from their place. "No," I said. "It might take every last drop of your well, and I'd be to blame. I'm sure the well will come back in." I thanked them for their hard work, and they both laughed, saying it wasn't near as much what they'd do at home, since it was canning season.

Then Mary Pearl said her mother insisted that my family all come to supper tonight, soon as we got cleaned up. Rachel, Rebeccah, and Joshua were home at last from school, and Savannah and the twins were cooking up a storm.

I told her, "We'll bring something, too."

Mary Pearl said, "Mama'll say you shouldn't."

"I know it. Would you girls want to ride to Majo Vistoso? We'll have a bath up there in the spring, and take a jug of clear water to rinse the caliche off." I could see them eyeing each other, working up some kind of excuse. So I added, "You probably have chores to do, though." Why would they want to bathe in that when they had fresh water at home? "Better get along, then." They didn't look too sad about missing the rock-salt bath I'd offered in payment for their hard labor.

I was too tired, myself, to ride all the way to Majo Vistoso. I poured a bit of the dearly won liquid in a pitcher, took the tub, and went to my bedroom, and shut the door, vowing that not even a flock of doves was going to interrupt this bath. My hair still smelled of turpentine. I washed my face with just a trickle of water in the basin, then poured the drippings onto a drooping plant on the windowsill.

My face felt cool. I felt altogether different, and, no, thank you very much, I am quite satisfied not being married. I've got my two boys and Jack's papa, Chess, to take care of, and Shorty, Mason, and Flores to worry about, besides Granny and the rest. Why on earth would I want to wash yet another pair of socks? I kept thinking about Rudolfo going to set up the sale of the herd and about my boys fixing that windmill, and I felt pure lightened of spirit. All we had to do was get this well producing again for the house and things would be all set. I can stand anything but standing still.

Later, as I strolled to Albert's place, I thought about town. Cinco de Mayo celebrations were this week, and they were having a weeklong shindig in Tucson for it. I had planned on spending a few days in town, then riding home with the boys because they'd be done with school. But since they're already here, there was no use in that. April and Morris will have expected us, so I figured I'd better write a letter and explain. With a bit of good fortune, we'll sell my cattle for more than the cost of their feed, and the boys and I will spend some time with my daughter and her family in peace. It'll give me plenty of time to get to know those grandchildren.

May 11, 1906

This morning, a stranger stopped on the horizon above the east end of my ranch and watched this way for a long while before coming in. Time was that would have been enough for me to come to the porch carrying a carbine. Nowadays, I just set it by the door, handy. The rider picked his way down the hill, fording Cienega Creek after letting his horse drink from it. He was in no hurry, and that aspect made me feel in more of a hurry than I'd been in many a day. Finally, he came to the yard, got off his horse, and commenced untying some kind of square bundle off his pack.

I stepped to the sunlight and called out a hallo to him. He looked up like I'd shot off a pistol. He said, "Good day, ma'am," and took off his hat. "Looking for Mrs. Jack H. Elliot. You know the place?" He wiped his forehead with a large handkerchief, then stuffed it back into his breast pocket.

"This is the place," I said.

Then he studied the writing on the package, as if he'd forgotten it as soon as he saw it. At last he said, "Orson Healy, missus. I come here to deliver this from the stagecoach. It's from San Francisco. Marked urgent."

"San Francisco—that'll be from my brother." Harland is an architect in San Francisco, in addition to teaching at a school there. "Well, it's a hot day, Mr. Healy. Will you have some water?" I drew a dipper from the olla. "It's brown, but it's clean. Have you been with the line very long?"

After he drank a spell, he wiped his mouth on his sleeve. "Thank you, ma'am. No, I hain't. Been working my way west since the Spaniards' war let out. Figure to be to Alaska 'fore long." He handed the dipper to me. "Thank you, ma'am."

I told him to wait; then I got four bits from inside the house, where I keep some money under the lamp on the mantel, and gave it to him. I offered him a meal, but he wouldn't stay. He said again that he had to hurry back, but he mounted his horse and rode off at the same tired pace he'd come in at.

The brown paper was many times wrinkled, tied with what appeared to be twenty yards of twine. With a little care, I could save enough of it to use again.

In a large hand was written "To Mrs. Jack H. Elliot, south of Butterfield's Trail, due north from Tombstone, Arizona Territory. Urgently, and with all haste."

I keep a pair of scissors on a string around my waist, along with the keys to my strongbox, which is hidden in the smokehouse. They aren't my good scissors for sewing, but they come in handy for little things. I sat right there on the steps with the package in my lap and cut a knot on the string.

Chess came from the house about then. "What'd you order?" he asked.

I pulled the paper off. "Nothing. It's from Harland and Melissa," I said. It was a picture painting—a really fine one—with a letter from Harland and a firsthand copy of a new *Collier's* magazine. I handed the picture to Chess and began reading aloud.

" 'Dear Folks, there has been an earthquake, and a fire. Most all the city is leveled or smoldering. They are calling it the worst tragedy in all of recorded history.' "

Worse than that hurricane that hit Galveston? Worse than the Civil War? Chess and I locked eyes. I was afraid to say anything for a moment. I don't know what he was thinking. He stared toward the man on the road. "Didn't that feller have any word?"

"He didn't say anything. Just that he's working his way to the Klondike. He wanted to leave here right away," I said.

"That wasn't much of a hurry. Likely someone told him there was quicksand. What's an earthquake, exactly?"

I was already back to reading the letter. "Charlie can tell us. I think it's the ground shaking. Rocks moving and such. Harland says he and Melissa ran through the streets with trunks on their backs, pushing the children in a stolen wheelbarrow. They begged anyone passing to sell them a horse, but even for a thousand dollars, none was to be had. By the time they got to the hills outside town, fire was on their heels. They dropped all their clothes and possessions, carried the children, and ran for their lives. When morning came, he found the picture under his arm, having had neither time nor thought even to drop it. It says this is all that is left of their lives, and he has sent it to me for safekeeping."

Chess held the picture up at arm's length. "Kind of blurry," he said.

We sat stock-still, letting all this go through us. I said, "Well, I can't leave my brother and his family in that kind of fix. We'd better go get them."

Finally, Chess said, "I'll be dogged if it doesn't rain when it pours. You want to leave in the morning?"

I said, "I'd be on a train in two shakes if I knew how to find them. When he wrote this, they were living on a hillside with hundreds of other people. Surely they'll have found a home by now. Likely we'll be getting some word any day." Then I sat up bolt upright with the thought, and said, "Maybe they're coming here."

"Finish the letter," Chess said. "Maybe he says."

"He says, 'Please don't fret for us. We are well, though Melissa is worn to the bone. I know you will want to be on the next train, but please wait until you hear from us. You can't imagine the trouble here, and though we are getting by, we cannot offer you shelter or food, either one. Will write again soon. Give our love to Mama. Faithfully yours, Harland.' Well, I suppose that answers that."

I searched the magazine for the articles and pictures Harland had mentioned. When I found them, my heart slowed and ached. There were printed photographs of what used to be a large city, with smoke rising over it.

There would be no finding Harland's home in that mess. I haven't seen my little brother in ten years, and I long to run to them and help somehow. What a trial to witness our lives to each other in letters, especially when he needs family nearby. I have been truly blest, as the loving arms of my kin have surrounded all the trials I have been through, and I'm ever thankful for that.

I said, "We'll set up beds in the extra room for when they get here." I sat right down and wrote, care of General Delivery, San Francisco, and offered that they come here. I told Harland I'd put them up as long as they needed, or they could have my house in Tucson, or that I'd go to California to help out with things while they got their house back on the ground. I sent one of the hands to catch that poky deliveryman—better yet, pass him—and go clear to the stage depot with my letter and two dollars to make sure it got there as soon as possible.

That evening, we passed Harland's letter and the *Collier's* magazine among the family, which was gathered this time at our house, and we read it aloud word for word until the pages were all feathered and smudged. We all admired the picture painting again, too, trying to sort out just how it came to look like something when held at a distance, but the closer you got to take a good look, the less it resembled anything more than smeared color.

Albert and Savannah scrunched together, reading the same page at the same time. Ezra and Zachary sat at their feet, waiting for bits of the article that Albert would read aloud when it wasn't too terrible for them to hear. Mary Pearl stared at that picture painting all evening, like it was a wonderful thing to her. She was so quiet, even Esther seemed like a chatterbox next to her, and Mary Pearl's usually the talkative one of those two. "Come on into the kitchen with me, Mary Pearl," I said. While we made lemonade, I tried to imagine what my brother and his wife had been through.

"Uncle Harland really painted that?" Mary Pearl asked.

"Yes," I said. "He was always drawing things as a boy. Animals and such."

"Reckon a girl could learn to do that?"

"If she's a mind to, no reason a girl can't learn anything she wants."

Mary Pearl was silent. She and I took lemonade into the parlor and set to pouring cups.

Granny was studying the magazine picture, and she said, "Well, which one of these is Harland's house?"

"I don't know, Mama," I said. "He said it burnt down."

She nodded, then after a long time said, "Did the curtains catch fire in a lamp?"

Albert said, "No. The gas lines exploded. The whole town went down."

Granny nodded again. "Gas lines. Well, I best make them some pickled watermelon rind."

I, know my mama sometimes doesn't see things in the here and now, but it was strange how the first thought in my mind was that the watermelons weren't ripe yet. I twisted my apron in my lap, unable to say a word. Savannah had a catch in her voice when she said, "Mother Prine, they don't have bread to put it on."

Granny said, "Well, I'll bake some bread, too. I can do that much for 'em."

Albert said, "Mama . . ." Then he waited a minute, and finally he said, "Well, they'll like that. You do turn the lightest loaf of bread in the Territory."

Granny just smiled and nodded. I reckon she will probably forget it by morning.

I, too, had this gnawing need to do something for them, to salve their woes. We talked round and round about what to do for them, and it came down to nearly nothing. I'm afraid I've done all I can for now. A simple letter. That makes me fret more than if Harland had written 'Please come, else we perish.' I don't know if I can wire them money without knowing where to send it.

After everyone left, Chess said he was worried we'd never get up in the morning, after staying up until all hours, fretting. I, too, was worried I'd never get to sleep, with so much to think about. In my letter, I'd told Harland and

Melissa to promise the railroad I'd pay their tickets, saying they could come here until things get better. Other than hope they have already planned to come here, all I can do is wait, and that is something I have never got the knack of.

Savannah came over early in the day. First thing she asked was whether we were alone. "Sarah," she said, "will you sit with me a spell?"

"Surely," I said. I went to the kitchen table and pulled out two chairs. I got out some glass tumblers and the clay pitcher of water.

"I'll pour it for you," she said. Savannah reached for the pitcher and poured water into each glass, spilling about half a glass on the table as she poured. A little thing like that, I notice more now than I ever would have before; half a glass of water is a lot to waste. When she held out the glasses of water, her hands trembled, and her eyes were brimming with tears. As she sat, the tears spilled, and she wiped at them with the cuff of her sleeve. "I want to say this quickly," Savannah said, "before any of the children come in." More tears ran down her face, and this time, she didn't wipe them. "Just needed to tell you this before I let them know. I believe we're expecting another baby."

"Oh, Savannah," I said. That explained all about her feeling poorly of late. Savannah, though, is older than I by two years. Time past, usually, for having babies. This one could be difficult, or born sickly. "Are you certain?"

She nodded. "You'd think after doing this ten times, I'd have recognized it. It just isn't quite the same this time. Different from the ones I lost, too."

I finished my glass of water. "You're worried something's not right, then?"

Her face clenched in pain, and she nodded very slowly. "Seems put wrong. And I don't remember any pain with the others, just the nausea and tiredness. I'm worried."

"Oh, honey," I said, and hugged her to my shoulder. "We'll take you to a doctor in town and make sure. He'll put your mind at rest, and you just concentrate on getting through the next few months. A Christmas baby. Won't that be nice?" In my heart, I felt a terrible ache. I didn't think it would be nice, not at all. The dry goods store in town had quit selling the Ladies' Preventatives Savannah and I had kept at our homes since I first discovered them. Supposedly, it's not up to some people's morals anymore to keep from having children every

year by any means other than widowhood. Just like everything else, I reckon
they wear out and need replacing. I'd be afraid to face this, myself. I've lost
enough babies already. Lands sakes alive.

Savannah pulled her hankie from her sleeve and dabbed at her face. "Well,
I do feel better, having told you. I don't want to let on to the children until
quite a bit further along. Just in case—well, the two I lost, you know, I never
told the children about. Didn't want them to fret."

That was Savannah. She would save her children from fear and mourning.
Take it all upon herself. Tears trickled from the corners of my eyes, too. I said,
"How soon can we get you to the doctor? I'll go along."

"Well, so much is happening. I'll be happy to wait until we take Esther and
Josh back to school."

"If it can wait until after my roundup, I'll go along. My boys are going
back, too. I'll stay in town and visit April a spell. Promise me, Savannah, that
you'll say something sooner if you feel something more is ailing you?"

She nodded, sniffed. "I'd better wipe that table. I've got water everywhere."

I took a towel and handed one to her. We worked on it side by side. When
we got it done, I said, "This will be all right, sweetie. You'll see. With the twins
gone teaching, and two at school, you've got plenty of chairs."

She looked as if she would cry again, but she smiled through it, though her
face was red. "Well, I've gotten eight blessings on this earth. I'll take another, as
the Lord provides."

I said, "When mine were little, I felt so rushed and tired. Now I wish I had
nine of them, too." That much, at least, was true. I wouldn't mind having more
children, now that the others were grown and could, like April, be bringing me
grandchildren soon. "Want me to walk you home? I need to stretch my legs a
mite." On the mile of dirt road between our houses, we talked about chickens
and weather and little things. They have a house cat just had a litter in the
pecan house. A hawk circled overhead in the distance.

The kitchen was steamy and sweet-smelling, and rows of quart jars stood like
little soldiers on a rack, cooling. Savannah's daughters were busy canning. White
curtains ruffled at the window. Mine at home were tattered calico—remnants
of a skirt April wore when she was thirteen years old. They'd gotten purely
shabby, but I couldn't make myself take them down. Savannah makes new
kitchen curtains every spring; says it keeps her cheerful. Her children have
grown up fine, and they mind her and Albert better than mine do. Those girls

were chopping and cooking and cleaning as well as any experienced wife might do. Savannah herself is pure blessing to everyone she touches, I thought. The rest of us have done precious little to protect her and show her how we care. Not near what she deserves.

Don't know why this news of hers has left me feeling down, almost as afraid as I felt when she told me of expecting their first baby, Clover, so many years ago. As if it will just make the current troubles of life multiply beyond bearing. Reckon it's enough to put me on my knees tonight, at that. This ranch is calling out for work from every corner and crook. Flores got back yesterday with the new troughs for the south windmill and they're going to get them in today. I haven't heard from Harland, and I can't take Savannah's dilemma for her. Faraway troubles will have to stay far away until I know what I can do.

May 26, 1906

No rain. No word yet from Harland. I'm so torn about their strife. I can't stand not doing something when something needs doing. Not that our days need filling out, for we stay busy hauling water, and every day we count more dead cattle. Rudolfo came home yesterday, and he says the news from Tempe is not good. It's too early to get anything but the lowest prices, and he will not agree to go rounding up the herd yet. I can't do it by myself, that's certain. So I'll have a talk with him later and see if I can convince him to round up now.

The air is dry as tinder and itchy. The prickly pears have curled up and are falling over like heaps of old tortillas. The boys found another three steers with our brand, died of thirst out on the hill. Everyone is touchy, even the dogs. Chess, Mama, Mason Sherrill, all the old folks on this place, snap like wildcats at anyone near them, myself included.

Last night, the sky seemed to open up with thunder and lightning, but it was a dry storm, with nothing but our battered ears to show for it. My head aches like I've been hit with a hammer from listening to thunder most of the night. I have had three large loads of hay brought down from town and stacked so I can feed my animals. It is sorry stuff, and costs dear.

I got my supper cooking in a big pot and some bread rising, then took a ride to Rudolfo's house. All the way there, I added figures, trying to plan how long I can keep on buying hay and dragging water. My old buckboard isn't going to stand up to this hard use forever, either, and a new one would cost at least two hundred dollars. Maybe more now, for it's been near fifteen years I've been using it.

Once again, it was all I could do to get Rudolfo to talk about the reason I'd come. I told him the roundup must be done the first of next month. The cattle can wait no longer. He smiled warmly and motioned me toward a chair. "The Bakers are selling out. I made him an offer on his land. He said he had family to think of, but if no one in his family accepts his price, I will own that land, too. But, for you, there is a simpler solution. The combination of our *rancheros* with Baker's will make this one of the largest holdings in the Territory. Sarah, I have *agua*. Grain and grass. This house is enough for you and your sons. Here, I have more men to do the work, to get us both through this drought. All I own will be yours. I have plans. Grand plans for the future."

"Life . . . ," I began. I was going to say how life had just not dealt me any good hands lately, and how I didn't plan on adding to the commotion by planning a wedding or taking on a husband and five more children. I had come to talk about rounding up our herds. All I said was, "is hard."

"We've been friends a long—at least tell me you'll think of it."

I rubbed my eyes with both hands. Baker was selling out for good? If there was one thing I didn't want to add to my load of things to think about, it was this. Glory, maybe I'd be forced to sell out eventually, too. Maybe I'd be forced to marry Rudolfo just to keep one foot on my land. And then, like other times in the past, I found myself lying to Rudolfo just to avoid hurting his feelings. "All right," I said, "I'll think about it."

Rudolfo grinned broadly. "Will you stay for supper?"

I shook my head. "I've got stew in the oven and bread rising—it'll be over the side by now."

"May I tell my son and daughters you've decided to consider my offer?"

"Oh, Rudolfo, please don't." I watched his face drop in disappointment, almost like a child's. I said, "Only because I don't want them to have—well, expectations either way. I love your girls. I don't want them to be hurt if the answer is no."

"Is the answer already no?"

I fiddled with my hat, then stood abruptly, putting it on my head. "I have to think, is all." I'd already said far too much, is all. Digging myself a hole I'd never be able to back out of. I cleared my throat and adjusted the tie on the hat. "About the herd gathering? When do you want to drive north?"

"Another two weeks before we go. Baker said he'll be ready by then. Some cousin is coming to see the place."

On my way home, I let the horse meander slowly. I had some serious thinking to do. Marry Rudolfo? Lands. He's the best neighbor anyone could want. I tried to picture kissing Rudolfo, loving him the way I loved Jack. I pictured Savannah, too, discovering she is yet again with child. Could I really bear having more children? I missed the times when my small brood was little, and there are times I wish there were eight of them, but to begin over now with diapers and three-day crying jags? And women die in childbeds far more at forty-three than at twenty-three.

I turned the horse off at the cemetery and dismounted, looping the reins around a limb of the jacaranda tree. I tiptoed between the markers and stood in front of the only one I needed to see at that moment. Jack's stone was dusty. The cholla that had sprouted behind it looked withered. I winced as if I'd been stung, and I put a hand over my mouth as a grimace of pain took over my face. A whisper of a breeze tussled at my hair, my skirt, and at the dangling fingers of the cholla. It made a scratching sound against the back of the stone. The corners of my mouth turned down hard against my chin.

There I was, a stickery woman, trying to shade a headstone. Trying to keep all this going for the sake of a memory. And there down the road was Rudolfo, offering me water. My sight was blurred with tears. "Jack?" I said. "What should I—" Then I stopped. I looked down the hill at my house. A warmth ran through me from my toes to my hair. The very ground I stood upon fed life into me. How ridiculous to let Rudolfo make me feel sentimental and weak. To think I'd run to him before I'd hardly dug in for the fight. We weren't under attack. No one was gravely ill. It was all about needing water.

"I'm not licked, yet," I said aloud. It will rain someday. And the well is still putting out. This ranch will go on, even if I sell the whole herd. Even if I have to sell part of the land. Heaven knows I've bought so much in the good years, it wouldn't be as if I were admitting defeat just to unload some of it. I straightened my hat and moved my shoulders around. The sudden call of quail sent a cottontail bouncing across Jack's resting place. He'd been hiding under the cholla as I stood there. There was work to do. I'd best go do it.

I headed for my kitchen. My sons were out working, Chess and Mason Sherrill gone, too. The house was quiet except for a mourning dove sighing from the chimney top. It'd been lean for four summers now, and having the cattle moved out of their regular grazing meant hauling hay and feed would be that much harder. Charlie said he was going to torch off the nopal thorns and let the cows have those.

As I laid my bread dough in three pans, I admired the soft, alive look of it. Making dough in this weather, it all but takes over the kitchen before you can get it cooked. I remember telling my little April a story about a loaf of bread that a farmer's wife forgot to bake, and it grew and grew, until it got up and walked out of the pan, sat down at the table, and demanded to be served like a king.

I took my knife and cut the shape of a crown in the top of each loaf—just like April always wanted ever since I made up that story—to show that dough it would indeed be served in a kingly style. Next time I see April in Tucson, I'll bake her some bread, tell her babies the story, and let them eat the bread with the crown on top.

Chapter Four

I haven't laid eyes on Rudolfo for two days. Maybe I don't need to. Maybe I don't even need to gather my herd, but just wait for the rain. Seems like the well will give about a foot a day, which, along with carrying water from the south well, the neighbors', and straining and boiling some, will keep the hands and the yard stock alive.

My morning passed pleasantly, for Granny and I have a little game going. We sorted our quilt scraps last Christmas and divided up the pieces, and she and I have both pieced a quilt top. We are seeing who can get done first, and whoever does gets to keep both quilts. I've been making a nine-patch with flying geese on every other square, and she's started one of nothing but hexagons. Says she is going to call it "Granny's Garden" because most of the calicoes are flowered. I thought I'd get mine put on a stretcher before she did, as I have a sewing machine Jack bought me, and I keep it oiled up and humming till my feet nearly come off at the ankles. I told her to come use it anytime, but Granny said it would take her longer to learn to use the machine than it would just to run up a quilt top. Well, there hardly comes a time when I don't have a quilt stretched across the ceiling of my parlor, ready to let down to lap height by a rope, but this summer has been a hard one for work. I haven't gotten three rows of blocks together, and I think Granny may have hers nearly done. I've asked her about it, but she just smiles and talks about the weather. Then she asks me how mine's coming, and she grins like a cat with a mouse in its paws when I tell her. I strung my nine-patch squares across the kitchen table this morning and matched up cloth until I liked the result. I was just starting another row when Shorty came up with the mail.

Harland has written again. His letter filled me with such sorrow, I had to carry it to Granny. He says Melissa has taken very ill, and this time, he says, "Sarah, please come quickly." Soon as I finished reading her the letter, I walked across her yard to Albert's place to show it to them. I begged their cast-off clothes to carry to Harland's children. All I can see to do is to go to California and get them.

It will probably take near a fortnight to get to California and back. Chess says he will go along. My boys think I should just wire Harland to come here, and wait. All I can say is that it's been ten years of writing letters to my brother, and never has he said "Please come quickly." Besides, staying here worrying isn't going to put a cloud in the sky or a drop more in the well. Part of me is terrified to leave this trouble behind, and part knows there's not a blessed thing I can do about the weather.

The one thing I can do is fetch Harland and Melissa and their children and get them to a safe place. I'll take Melissa to the hospital in Tucson, and they can surely use my house in town until she gets over what ails her. Then they can come here and stay as long as they like. After supper, I spent a good hour giving the boys instructions as to what to do, depending on what might happen, while I'm gone. Plum wore out their ears. Then I made a list, too, and put it on the wall by the pantry.

A chill seeps up from the land after the sun goes down—a sure sign that the air is still dry, and the rains are yet to begin. The rocking chair on my front porch allows me to see a great deal of the horizon surrounding this place, as the porch turns on a northwest corner. By pulling the chair to the edge, I can watch the stars and moon. It is a place I can think. Pleasant and cool, too, until the time of the summer rains, when it will get dank. I can see the faint orange glow of a lighted window off to the east, at Albert and Savannah's house. Someone there is still awake, too.

I feel for the string around my waist, for the scissors and the key, holding them in my hands without trying to see in the darkness. I know to the very penny what is in that strongbox. Three thousand eight hundred, seventy-six dollars and eleven cents. Cash to last me a year paying wages to the hands, buying dry goods and yard goods, fence wire, and horseshoes. Hard currency, too, for I don't trust paper bills to the termites. I read where someplace a widow hid her insurance money in a coffee can, but when she went for it, it had turned to mold from the damp in her cellar. Well, damp doesn't happen here, though the termites we have would eat a whole man if he stood still long enough to let them. I had to decide what might be needed here, and how much to take to Harland.

Under the candle stand on the end of the shelf behind the stove was a twenty-dollar gold piece, two five-dollar pieces, and six tenpenny bits. After I take out the mercy money for Harland in the morning, I'll put the key to the strongbox under there in case anything happens and the boys need more than what's under the candle stand.

I'll have to take cash, too, for two round-trip tickets, and six more for Harland's family to come here, plus food and medical care. If I wire Harland a thousand dollars from Tucson and hold fifteen hundred here for expenses for six months, there'll be only eight hundred left once I've paid for the tickets and such. Not enough to pay for a new well if we need it. Nothing extra if anyone gets hurt or sick, either. No tuition money for the boys. And all that is if things run smoothly, according to my calculations. The thought crept up on me that I might end up having no choice but to marry Rudolfo. I can't think of that now. I won't think of it. I haven't told him no yet. Reckon I'm feeling cowardly about it. Or maybe I'm not ready to close that door. Best thing I can see is that if everything goes bad, I could sell out to him and move home to Mama's.

A deer came on tiptoes into the yard. They usually won't come this close, afraid of yard dogs. This one stepped warily toward the trough by the gate. It peered all around, and without any sound—it must have made some signal that all was well—it was joined by three little does. They slipped from the shadows across the yard and nosed at the trough, where I knew barely an inch of murky water lay in the bottom. If I got up to draw them a drink, they'd run and probably never return. I let them lap up the rest of the mud, and when they had all they could take of it, they turned and fled as if something frightened them.

I added to my note for the boys' chores to put a bucket and a half of water in the trough each night. The stuff was precious enough, but we still had water, and I won't begrudge a creature a drink. As I changed clothes for bed, all I could think was that what we need is the one thing we couldn't buy with a barrelful of gold eagles—rain.

May 29, 1906

Chess is driving our carriage with me and my trunk, and two extra trunks full of clothes given by Albert and Savannah. Gilbert asked didn't we want him to ride shotgun, but I said that's what I was there for. Underneath a box, inside one of the trunks packed with patched children's underwear, is a packet from my strongbox. Besides that, we have a load of food from Savannah's and my pantries, canned goods, and fresh-baked bread. Seems that's what Savannah and her girls were up doing last night.

In the green light of the sky before dawn, the desert is still and cool. It feels good on my skin, but not on my mind. I suspect when you get to judging the seasons by the feel of the air, and you know it's high time the mornings should be steamy and heavy with rain coming, then when it's just clear and brisk, without a drop of dew, well, it feels wrong. The coyotes were quiet, but out in the open. You can ride right up on one and surprise it, as if they all were drunken from some devilment the night before.

In the back of my mind I hear Chess talking a steady stream about what work needed doing on the ranch. He was saying something about how Charlie has made a good second boss, taking up the reins of Mason Sherrill, and he said I'd be doing my boys a favor to let them jump in and get a taste of the real work they want to do so much. Charlie and Gilbert have always done their share of things, but never without someone setting out the chores like tomorrow's clothes. This time, they'll have to dig in by themselves. He didn't quit talking until we got nearly to the *arroyo grande*, halfway to town.

The horses strained against the load we'd packed, so we got off the wagon and led them up the arroyo. We stopped for some lunch there and straightened up the boards we were keeping in the bottom so the wagon wheels could take hold. After that, we talked over this trip, and saying how urgent it was, reassuring ourselves, I suppose, that it was right for the two of us to go to California, even when the ranch was blowing away.

When we got to town, we went straight to the depot. A train was leaving at six o'clock in the evening, headed west, and the agent said it stopped in Barstow,

California, for half a day. From there, we could take one straight to San Francisco. In two or three days, we'd be there. After we bought tickets and checked on all our extra baggage, I went to make a money transfer at the bank. They could cash money and telegraph the numbers to San Francisco, and then I wouldn't have to travel with all that cash. If Harland got the idea, he could draw from it, too. I sent a thousand dollars. The rest we'd carry.

I've never wired money before, and it was hard for me to pass the cash under that brass grate to a total stranger. I figured I'd rather carry it tied into my petticoat, but Chess said if the train was robbed, we'd never get to California with it. So I passed it through the window and ignored the man behind there, who was telling me it should have been kept in their vault all along. I never did put much trust in bankers, except for April's husband, Morris.

We still had four hours to wait for the train, so we went by my old house in town for a bath, and to see if things were in need of repair. With Albert and Savannah's children living there, I knew some things were kept up, but they are young, and it's never the same as when you own a place. If Harland and Melissa needed this place, why, I'd get it spruced up for them.

What a pure blessing it was to have a bath in a tub alone in a room where all you had to do was pump the water, not tote buckets. Then all you had to do was pull out the cork, not tote more buckets to the back porch—that kind of thing is easy to take lightly until you don't have it. Even so, I used just as little water as I could, thinking every drop that went down the drain could have gotten my chickens by another day.

We left early for the depot, so we could stop and see April and Morris before we left. Their house was on the north side of town, toward the university. The house was blue as a robin's egg, with cream-colored sashes and black shutters, and the white porch was covered with more blue-and-cream gingerbread than I'd ever seen. A peering glass was set into the stained glass on the front door. Stained glass was everywhere, and gingerbread railings, too. I thought she and Morris were only staying in Tucson until the bank got some kind of business done, but surely, to create a palace like this, they must be planning to stay for good. Oh my soul, what a joy that was to me. Our visit was too short, and I longed for her as we drove away.

The train ride started hot. It felt as if the inside of the cars had been heated up. With every breath, I hoped and prayed that Barstow was a place cool and pleasant in the summer. Cooling fans operated in the car, but the air they pulled in from outside was warm, too. It wasn't until we'd been going at least an hour, and the sun got low, that it finally got comfortable. People talked here and there, but Chess and I pretty much stayed quiet. After all, we'd said to each other what we were come for on the way here. Strange how private a conversation can feel when you are out in the middle of the desert, compared to being in a moving train car, hidden behind the bench seats but surrounded by other people who might overhear as well as I could overhear them.

I thought about my quilt waiting for me at home as I pulled out the sewing I intended to do on the train, just mending of clothes we'd all given. My sewing box is an old cigar box. Inside it, there is a little folded pouch where I keep needles; I put that in my lap and took up a spool of white thread, cutting off a length with my teeth. When I went to open the pouch, though, I dropped my spool. Someone had sewn it completely shut with black thread. I could feel the needles still inside, but a tiny seam ran all the way around it. Who would play such a silly joke at a time like this? I took off the knot and pried loose the new stitches. A tiny slip of paper was inside it, along with a ten-dollar gold piece. On the paper was such a tiny handwriting, it almost seemed to be from a newspaper.

We're sorry we don't have more to send, but our new boss is frugal. We traded greenbacks for this coin. I (Charlie) earned eight dollars cutting weeds at the college, and Gilbert gave two he got from delivering milk in town. He didn't have hardly time to do naught but study, so he's going to show off his best medical school stitching, which will be his proof that he did study and would have been a fine addition at any ladies' quilting bee. Our love to our cousins, and good travels, Mama and Grandfather.

He hadn't signed it. English composition had never been one of Charlie's favorite subjects. I smiled at the word *grandfather,* for I'd never heard it used in our house. I'd raised a couple of upstanding fellows, even if they were a touch ornery.

The car swayed on the tracks, and once it slowed down at a small hillside, puffing and churning steam. I wondered if they'd make all the passengers get off to lighten the load while it crested the hill, but Chess said more than likely it was the freight holding us back. A few dozen passengers couldn't weigh near as much as the goods they were hauling. After that hill, the rocking of the train felt like a cradle. I slept a good long time. I dreamed of rain and cool wind. I dreamed of having ice just like the icehouse in town makes, and setting it around the room to cool us, even having the animals all come in the house to cool off. They licked the ice like they do at salt licks, and smiled at me. I woke up, tickled at the pictures in my head of a smiling cow and grinning chickens. It felt purely silly, but it was good to smile.

A porter announced that an evening meal had been prepared and was now ready. The train had a fine new supper car, with waiters in stiff white jackets, tiny tables and chairs fixed to the floor, and food that smelled as good as homemade but didn't taste worth a plug nickel. When we got back to our seats, Chess said, "That there was about the finest dinner I've et since I left the Confederate prison camp."

An old man turned in his seat across from us, smiled, and gave Chess a quick salute. "Sir, did I hear you correctly? You were in the Confederate camp? Which one? Could it have been Andersonville, where my dear brothers died? Bless me. I'm proud to salute a fellow soldier, sir. Perhaps you knew them? William and Charles Brown?"

I held my breath for a few seconds. Chess had spent three weeks before the end of the war in a Kansas prison *for* Confederate soldiers, not the one *run* by them. I sensed him stiffen up all over. I went to looking for my bag and my clutch, expecting Chess to get riled, and then we'd have to change seats so as not to have a two-man reenactment of Gettysburg right there on the train.

"Can't say as I did know anyone by those names," Chess said.

The man leaned forward and whispered, "What was your regiment? Ohio Sixteenth Regulars myself. Corporal Stephen Brown, here. Say, did you know Captain Richard Thomas—what a gentleman he was—fought like three men the day the bloody Johnnies ambushed our whole unit on the road to Vicksburg."

"Yes, I was at Vicksburg. But let's not talk of war in front of the lady," Chess said. "My daughter-in-law, the Widow Elliot." I nodded at the aged Corporal Brown—without smiling. Chess said, "My son was a cavalry officer on the Indian frontier."

Mr. Brown let his jaw hang slack for a second, then nodded. "My deepest apologies, madam."

"Thank you," I said. I hate being introduced as "the widow" anything. I know why Chess said it, but it still catches me up, as if he's talking about someone else. I stared down at my hands. I still wear my wedding band. Someday, I'll take it off, I reckon. A callus keeps it in place. Whether it is the one on my finger or the one on my heart, I couldn't say.

After a while, Mr. Brown took up a newspaper to read, and shortly after that, it slumped over his face. Soft snoring came from under it. I nudged Chess to get his attention, then whispered to him. "Vicksburg indeed. I have to say, Colonel Elliot, you showed amazing calm there. Time was, you'd have finished the job as General Lee meant to do."

"I'm getting older, too. Seen enough fighting. I just want to ride this train and get where we're going. Long as he didn't get insulting, I figured I'd just let it be. War's over."

"I don't reckon I've heard you call me a 'lady' before."

"Well, you don't hear a lot of things I say."

"Some of them I'm better off not hearing."

"Reckon so," he said. Then he leaned into the corner made by the seat back and the windowsill and put his hat over his face. He said, "It was meant as a compliment." Almost as soon as he'd said the last word, he drifted into sleep.

I was surely thankful Chess had come with me. All this time, he's been there for me to count on. I felt a swell of affection for this man, Jack's papa, so I reached over the distance between our knees and patted his arm. He startled and sat up, dropping the hat to his lap. "Just wishing you a good nap," I said. "And thanks."

"Are you so dry for compliments that that's all it took to have you bothering people out of a nap?"

"Ornery old cuss. Take your nap, then," I said.

He settled back in his corner. I took out some sewing I planned to get done on the trip, patching up knees in little britches. Mama always told me to save the mending for home and do some "pretty" when you're in public, some embroidery or tatting lace or such. I wished I'd brought my quilt squares, for I imagine she'll have hers done before I return. Still, I'm on my way to some kind of refugee camp that would be no place for quilting, and Savannah's little boys are hard on the knees of their clothes, so I've got to get these fixed for Harland's children before we get there. I fixed holes in the knees of little pants, reattached pockets to a pinafore apron. Trouble was, with the train switching back and forth and the lights low, setting my eyes on the stitching was hard.

Dry for compliments, he said. Maybe so. Jack's been gone a long time. Even his compliments came few and distant, but they were powerful. Chess didn't have call to be so cranky. Maybe he'd spent all his patience holding himself back from a fistfight. I had to smile at the thought of these two old men going at each other out of some long-carried sense of righteous dignity.

One thing I know from living with Jack is that war, any war, stains a man deep, and nothing can get the stain out. They can wear clothes like a rancher or a banker, but the stains are under there, never far from the surface of their skin. I stared at the whiskered old man opposite me, trying to picture him in a uniform, forty years younger.

I pushed the needle through the cloth again, trying to patch this pair of little pants so that it didn't look like it belonged in the ragbag, and drove the needle straight into my middle finger so hard, I had to tug to get it out again. Blood poured from the stab. I held it to the side so it wouldn't stain my dress or the pants I was fixing. By the time I found a handkerchief, three large drops had hit the floor. I wrapped the finger, but red seeped through the handkerchief, blooming like roses over snow. Just like that, I was back in Jack's hospital room, holding him as blood bloomed on the white sheets, pleading with him not to leave me. I leaned my head against the back of the seat.

Then, I was further back, seeing against the inside of my closed eyes images of myself that I'd purely laid aside—things that were no longer of any use. The word *war* must have caused it. I wasn't the only woman around who had fought a different kind of war. There were no uniforms, no medals, no rank and file. Reveille was a baby's cry—or worse, an Indian raid before dawn. Our battle hymns were lullabies, and field strategy was simply to preserve the living at any cost. I've seen so much bloodshed, I can hardly stand to butcher an animal for food. I make the hired men do it.

I remember the first time I pulled a trigger against a man. I remember the blood on Savannah's sister, Ulyssa Lawrence, and the blood on the ground where those two men who hurt her lay after I'd finished with them. My one regret was that it took so long on foot to get to the rifle that I hadn't been able to prevent their tormenting her. And I remember Savannah's mother dying at the hands of the Comanches so soon after. Then my Papa, buried near San Angelo, Texas, died of an infected bullet wound, and nary one of us have ever been back to the spot.

I unwrapped my finger. The flow had stopped, leaving just a tiny red dot. I squeezed the finger again, forcing more blood out of it. I watched it make a bead, perfectly round and deep red. I never really saw the others I'd killed. In the heat of a battle on horseback, dust obscures your aim so much that you have to hesitate to be sure not to shoot your own horse. Indians always pulled away their dead before anyone could see them. But there had been a man on the road once, threatening my children, holding a pistol to Harland's head, planning to steal Melissa away and abuse her. I suppose that was one I saw up close, eye-to-eye. That one I'd kill over again, too. Thinking back on all of them, there wasn't one I'd undo, given the chance.

That must be different from men fighting a soldier's war, side by side, pushing up some hillside with bullets flying around them like bees. They'd have to believe in something awfully big to go on doing it, I reckon. To shoot, and go on shooting at some man who was following the same orders as you, and who, like Mr. Brown, would salute and shake your hand on a given day forty years hence. A man who could look like you, think like you, who was not ready to rob or kill you any more than you yourself would rob or kill him, just a man with a family and an idea he thought he was serving.

Chess was sleeping rough, fiddling with his hands, twitching like a tired dog. The grinding of the train's big locomotive seemed loud, and just for a moment, Chess was a young man, on his way to a war, and Jack was a little child, younger than Albert and Savannah's boy Zachary. Across from us, Mr. Brown's paper had slid downward, showing his face, eyes closed, mouth open, peaceful. Maybe that was the easy sleep of the ones who claimed victory. Chess rambles about the house so often at night, I don't wake any more. Jack used to do the same thing. Called out, even in his sleep. When he was awake, he often stared into the distance for an hour or more at a time, feeling some kind of huge sadness for all he'd seen and done.

Chess shook himself awake, then settled again. He slept quietly this time. Life in the territories has never been genteel. Men who have been chased away from every lawful place in this country still come here to hide, to steal and kill. Until we get statehood and government of a higher caliber than the outlaws they're supposed to corral, that war will not be over. The sentries, most likely, will never step down. It's a hard place to live. Don't know why I'm bent on all this reminiscing. Must be just the luxury of sitting down for a spell with nothing to do but ride.

I never pictured myself being like Chess, until now. Nor like Jack, neither. Reckon, though, we were two of a pair. He kept going, strong and healthy, as long as he could keep up his battle. I'd known from just about the first time I saw him that he was fighting something inside just as dark and frightening as the Indians and bandits he fought with sword and carbine. I'd asked him to lay it down, quit soldiering, and within a couple of years, he'd been killed in an accident. Maybe we all have to go on fighting our wars to stay alive. I reckon my war will be over when the boys plant that marble stone over me and six feet of dirt. I put the pair of children's trousers back into my carpetbag. Tucking the bag at my feet, I leaned into my own corner.

Savannah's children used to sing a little rhyme: "Niddy-noddy, knitting needles, busybody, butter beetles. When will I meet my fair true love?" When there's a string, or ribbon or such, on a finger, as you unwind, for every time it circles your finger, that's how many years until you find your true love. The point, I suppose, being the faster you can say it, the sooner you are in love, and it's near impossible to say it quickly. Childish nonsense. A true love, though, isn't nonsense. Pure aggravation sometimes. And great joy. I tried to think about Rudolfo, tried to imagine feeling passionately in love with him. But the face that came to mind was Jack's. My handkerchief was short and folded over. It hardly crossed over itself, so love should come this year. I smiled at the silliness of that. If it were supposed to be Rudolfo, well, I'd met him long ago, and if it were Jack, I'd known him and buried him, and—oh, nonsense. Just a child's game.

With my eyes half-closed, I looked down and slowly unwrapped the handkerchief on my finger. The blood had quit running and dried, and this time I left it alone.

Chapter Five

Barstow was anything but the cool mountain town I pictured from the sound of its name. The half-day layover they promised us was not morning to noon, either, like I expected, but truly half a day—nearly twelve hours. We had to change trains, and in less than an hour, the first train pulled out. Trouble was, we were told to stay on board the second one, and so we didn't have the freedom even to mill about the depot. There was no food served, nor toilets opened, for twelve long hours. They urged passengers to stay in their seats, as the railroad could not guarantee our safety in the town, nor would the conductors go get anyone who was not on board when they got ready to pull out.

We spent a long day, hungry and miserable. Folks with children fared far worse, what with the crying and restlessness. A couple of poor mothers, desperate to soothe them and change diapers and such, braved leaving the train, despite the advice, but they managed to get back, none the worse for it. By the time we got moving, I was ready to go up front and shovel coal myself just to get this thing going down the tracks.

Thirty-three hours later, the train stopped for good in a little town called San Jose. The conductor said there were no sound rails farther up, since the earthquake had made all the ground unstable. Anyone going to San Francisco would have to go by stage. Chess and I took stock of all the trunks of clothes and crates of canned food, then decided we'd need a whole stage just for us. We asked the freight agent where we could rent a wagon and team, but he said there weren't any left. Everyone standing and everything rolling was gone west to the disaster area to help.

This was something we hadn't counted on. We needed our own wagon. Still, if we'd tried to drive our own team, it would have taken the better part of ten days to get this far. We parked our lot of crates and trunks on the depot platform, paid two dollars to the depot master to watch it, and promised him a dollar a day if nothing went missing.

Chess said he wanted to get something to eat that didn't taste like thumb soup. I laughed and asked him what that was. "It's where you pour boiled water in your cup, and forget to take your thumb out first. A little salt and pepper, and it's all right if you're hungry enough."

"Lands," I said.

He whispered, "That was about the longest train ride I've been on in fifty years. Leastways, it wasn't in some cattle car." Then he took my arm in a way he's never done before, gentlemanly, and we started walking toward the center of town.

I said, "Reckon there's someone in town still might have a wagon they'd lend?"

"We'll ask around. I'm thinking something else, though. That feller on the train set me to remembering some good-hearted men with a wagon of food coming into the prison. Men were starved, some of them, lots longer than me. Even the guards were starved. The gents trying to pass out the bread were just being kind, but pretty soon someone said he didn't get one, and someone else said he'd got two. Before we knew it, a scuffle broke out, the horses spooked, and the fellows passing the loaves tumbled out, and one of them lost an eye. Other one died, crushed by sick, starving people just wanting something to eat. I'm hungry."

I saw a sign for a restaurant and nodded toward it. "There's a place," I said.

PARTRIDGE HOUSE RESTAURANT it said in big fancy letters. Underneath that it said GOOD FOOD, FAIR PRICES. Two men tipped their hats, then went past us through its doors. Chess shrugged at me and said, "This place looks all right. Let's talk inside, over some grub." He opened the door and then followed me inside. We got a table right away because it was still early in the afternoon.

While we waited for our food to come, Chess talked in a hushed voice. "I want you to listen to me, Sarah. I didn't suspect how bad it was until they said there's no transport to the city. Could be more like a war than anything you've probably ever seen. Most likely dangerous, too, to carry anything that looks like food." The waiter brought us coffee. Chess poured cream and sugar in his and stirred it slowly. He said, "I'm saying we ought to leave that tucker here, for everyone's good. And not at the depot, but in a hotel room. We'll find your brother and his family and bring them here."

I stared at the tablecloth, thinking how pitiless it was to plan to hide food from starving people. I said, "I believe you. But then, it's hard to believe folks would—"

"People get desperate; that's all I'm saying."

Now the waiter came with food and refilled the coffee cups. As the waiter left, I leaned over the table toward Chess. "Think the hotel will let us leave the food in their storeroom?"

"No. I think we should take a room, just like we were living in it."

That went against my grain, and I was bound to argue with him over it. "Pay for a room but not stay there?" Waste money? Now, of all times?

Chess put his hands on the table and leaned toward me. "Look, Sarah. You know what a woman will brave just to change a diaper. Imagine what she'd do to *feed* those babes."

I knew fear, and defending your own, but I'd never seen my children hungry. What worse torture could there be for a mother? I said, "Then I reckon we should take a few clean things for the children to wear and a few apples and those hard cookies. Just as light as possible."

He nodded and said, "I'm already feeling the rain in my bones, and I reckon it could be muddy traveling, and hard. I've seen a town burnt down. It isn't a clean fire, not like a cookstove. Everything turns black, even your skin. Worse than a coal town. Wear the worst clothes you've brought."

We spent the next half hour without another word. Chess finished off his steak and worked on the remainder of his coffee cup. He kept peering around suspiciously, as if he was really afraid of something, and it unsettled me more than I could say.

I was mad as a wet hen that the hotel manager wanted payment in advance for a whole week at a time. He said too many people fleeing the fire had taken advantage of him and he was not given to trust anyone else. It was not until we got everything stacked into the two rooms we took, and paid for two weeks in advance, that I could rest. The traveling money I'd brought that was supposed to last us a month, if needed, was half gone, and we'd barely begun.

When I laid my head down to sleep that night in that paid-for bed, I watched the curtains stir, and I heard something crackling. At first, it frightened me, such an unusual sound, and I leapt up and looked out to see if something was on fire. Rain. Not just a sprinkle, but a gully washer. A river poured down, as if up in heaven someone had tipped a trough right over us. It came without wind or storm or thunder, just rain, flowing straight down. I opened the windows so that the smell of it could perfume the room.

I reckon, the world over, a good deal of human tribulation is connected to water, either too much or too little. The stagecoach would leave at five o'clock in the morning. All I could do for now was shut my eyes. Time enough tomorrow for tomorrow's sorrow.

The next day, during the eleven-hour stagecoach ride, rain drummed on the tin roof and seeped in the walls of the stage. Everything was damp and stuffy inside. The rain quit, and the sun came out between heavy banks of clouds just as we came to the edge of what had been San Francisco. Other people riding with us may have been a bit annoyed, but I had to lift the shade and look out. The fresh air felt good, even if it was damp, compared to the staleness inside the coach, and as the road wound toward the depot through ever-thicker mud, the mules slowed.

The whole scene was too big to see all at once. Curves in the road made it seem as if I were on a merry-go-round, a tableau passing before my eyes. The sad state of what I saw was too much to take in, as if the understanding of it all had to come as slowly as the trip to get here. Chess had tried to tell me, I suppose. My eyes opened wide and my chin wanted to drop. As the stagecoach slowed, other people opened their shades, and we stared like children at a circus. Pitched in the mud, which was itself thicker and more beat-up than I've ever seen, rows of tents or sheds built of every imaginable material covered the near ground like a crust. Soot coated everything and everybody, even horses and dogs scavenging for food. In the distance was a great ruin; smaller, blacker, wider for sure than Pompeii in the pictures I'd seen in books.

Nothing prepares a person for the smell. A blanket of odors hung in the damp air, so thick I could taste it. It was part smoke from a hundred little fires, animal manure soured by rain, and human waste, sharp and sickly. Now and then, something vinegar-y and powerful as rotted wood clung to the inside of my mouth. Then it came to me. It was the rot of death. Surely, though, it was just from animals that had died. Surely they were burying the people.

We got off the stage at the small depot building. The depot platform seemed to be the only dry footing between here and the rest of the world. Hard

to imagine how rain-starved and parched my land at home was. We were surrounded by a group of people clamoring to get on the stage before they'd even
had a chance to change the horses. At one corner, two men shoved and pushed,
cursing each other, trying to be first to climb on, just to ride on top with the
rain-soaked luggage. Soon as they unhitched them, the horses plodded to their
stalls without being led there, exhausted. Two men pulled the fresh team into
place, and within five minutes, they pulled out. I stiffened like a post, standing
on the floorboards, sorting it all. "Harland said they had a tent in the hills, east
of town. The town—what was the town—seems to be mostly west of here."

"We'll start at the east side of it," Chess agreed. He passed me the lighter of
our two carpetbags. We stepped off the platform into the mud. A few steps
away, a ragged pile of feathers was crushed into the mud, trampled and nearly
buried. It was impossible to tell if it had been some lady's fine hat or a chicken.
He said, "Clouds are back. Can't tell where the sun is."

I looked for a shadow to get our bearings and see which way to start walking. After a minute, a cloud shifted, there was a faint lighting of the air, and the
merest shadow appeared in front of us. Without a word, we both headed east-
ward, back to the depot and beyond it. Around the corner of the depot, I saw a
scene I'd never imagined as the stage came in from the south. A ripple of small
foothills swelled like a billowing sheet before us. In the lower land before the
hills, a line of neat army-type tents gave way to a jumble of sheets and tarps,
overturned wagons and tilted boards. It appeared as if some giant child had gotten tired of playing with his toys, dropped them down in the mud, and mashed
them. I drew a deep breath. "Well, there's no way to start but to step up to it,"
I said.

He said, "Manners aside, I reckon. I'll take the lead, and you hold on to me."

The odor of death gave way to the sharp and tangy smell of the outhouse—and the whole hill was an outhouse. A food tent was set up. They were
serving out bowls of something that appeared to be along the lines of Chess's
thumb soup. A man in a police uniform sat at a desk in front of another tent,
talking to people who were filling out papers of some kind. He hollered at us to
come write down who we were searching for and any kind of identification
marks that would be on the bodies. He passed Chess a little paper and a bit of
pencil, and Chess handed it back to me.

As I wrote, Chess said, "Sir, our folks are alive. Do you have a list of live
folks?"

The policeman said, "This tent is for deceased or unknowns only," and he reached over and tore up my paper, an angry look on his face. At first, I felt purely insulted. Then what I saw was a man tired to the bone of his foolish task, probably hungry, too, getting people to write how many freckles their sister's cousin had on her arm or whether their grandpa had three gold teeth or four.

We walked a good two miles, Chess hollering Harland's name, me cutting off the path into tents and between cardboard shacks, asking people face-to-face. At midday, the clouds parted and sunshine brightened the scene, but it only made the vision more ugly. People with carts moved up and down, cross-wise of us, carrying soup in big cisterns that they ladled out at each tent. By the time we came to a little wide place in the tent rows, our clothes were mud-caked to the knees. Every time I stopped moving, my feet sunk into the mire. The sun was going down.

Chess said, "We best start back. We can cut down that row there. Spend the night at the depot at least. How are you getting along?"

"Fair," I said. "Shoes stuck to the ground." I took a deep breath. My face felt hard and cold. "Let's look some more."

He sighed and looked around before he answered. "Down where we came in was all scuttled up. We don't want to go back the way we came and waste time. They're starting evening fires. Reckon there'll be light enough for an hour, before we need to get back to the depot." As he said that, however, the clouds again parted and the sky brightened, giving the appearance of some kind of providential approval. If the clouds stayed open, we might have two hours to search.

On we marched. Babies cried. Dogs barked and fought over scraps. We hollered away like barkers at the street market. Then we made the crest of another small hill. "Lord a mercy me," I said. "Look at that."

The sun was going down into what had to be the Pacific Ocean, and heavy mist made it out all blurred. I wiped my eyes, but it didn't change. In front of the sunset, painted in gold light, was a sprawling ruin of what had been a city. This scene had been hidden from us by the closeness of the hills through which we searched. But from here, it was a picture image right out of that *Collier's* magazine. Some buildings were standing, but most were not. Smoke curled up from places, even after all this time. Some were just a wall or two, with open windows, the sky gaping through them. Whole areas were black and flat, and like animals rummaging through the trash heap at home, people searched through the wreckage, stooped and bending. Over it all, in a far-off bank of clouds that hid half the sun, lightning flickered.

My face felt cool and wet from the mist that clung to us, and when tears spilled from my eyes, they felt warm. The sun settled lower every second, and now the town's remains turned blacker, like silhouette cuttings, against the yellow sky.

Chess stood behind me, watching. He said, "Reckon that's the ocean beyond there?"

"I think so," I said. I shifted my carpetbag to the other hand. It was starting to get mighty heavy.

"Never seen an ocean." After a long time, he said, "We'll find 'em tomorrow."

I took his hand. By the time we got back to the stage depot, we found that about a hundred other people had the same idea of trying to find dry footing for tonight's roost. The depot master was giving every one of them the boot, too. And we hadn't brought gear to sleep out. Hadn't planned on the wet ground, either. Chess tried to talk to the man, but he wouldn't listen. He wasn't letting anyone sleep there, he said, not after what had happened night before last—not putting up with that kind of thing here. This was a decent place, and he was a God-fearing man.

He had a short-barreled shotgun in his hands. The man was dead set on his mission, and we weren't going to find purchase there, any more than the other folks had. We stepped off the platform. The depot master pulled the shutters.

We could see his shadow against them, and then the light went out inside. What did he expect us to do? Go beg a place to lay our heads amongst the poor folks on the hill? Mist was seeping toward the low area where we were. I'd seen fog now and then at home, but never like this. This was like some live thing, creeping forward like a snake, sliding around things and people, filling the air. I began to shiver. We drew ourselves into the darkness, moving toward the stables. The crowd wandered away. A couple of children huddled on the floor, close to the horses. One of them looked up as we came nearer, then held his finger to his lips, begging for silence.

"Look there," Chess whispered. Next to the depot, under a tree, was a coach almost like the one we rode in on, but about half the size. Someone had covered it with a tarp. "Looks like a dry roost, if it's not full of vermin and someone ain't got to it first." Chess peered all about and lifted up the tarpaulin; then he tried the door latch. It gave. He motioned toward it and said, "After you."

I followed him, feeling like I was breaking into someone's house. Repaid by Providence for our sneak-thieving ways, crawling in where we didn't belong, the tarp caught my shoulder and covered me with water and mud, some of which went down my collar. I stepped in, fearful of coming face-to-face with some critter wanting shelter, too.

I heard a racket in the distance that sounded like thunder. Sure enough, after a bit there was a little streak of lightning that lit up nearby, and we could see why this stage was unused. The whole ceiling had fallen in, broken somehow, and the tarpaulin was keeping out the rain. Thankfully, the little box seemed empty except for us and a couple of crickets, which we invited to go hunt for their dinner outside.

I stared into the darkness. Chess made some noise. "What are you up to?" I asked.

"A feast fit for kings, I'd say," he said. "Hold out your hand and I'll give it to you in the paper it's wrapped with. No telling what filth is in the mud we've handled." He put a cookie in one hand and a piece of jerky in the other.

I tried hard, but I just couldn't eat. A drink of water was all I wanted. After a time, I folded the papers over the cookie and meat and put the food back into the bags.

"We'll find 'em," he answered without hearing my question.

Like an echo, I said, "We'll find them. Surely we will."

In the morning, fog covered the earth so densely, it seemed as if those heavy clouds from yesterday had spent the night on the ground with the rest of us. It surely felt as if the sun didn't rise until nearly ten o'clock. By that time, we were as dirty and wet as the refugees on the hill. Chess was slowing like an old clock that wouldn't keep its winding. The commotion all around, the cold, wet air, horrible stench, and walking through mud that seemed to be going uphill no matter which direction we took made it harder with each step to have the breath to call their names. The odd thing was, now that we'd been through the rows and jumbles of tents and shanties a number of times, mostly lost, I might add, it began to take on a sort of order. Leastways we recognized where we'd been and where we hadn't.

"Look yonder," I said, and pointed. We saw a line of folks circled around a large tent with a big red cross painted on the side. I said, "Maybe they'll have a place we can rest. I'm thinking we'd better give up for now, and eat some of these apples. I'm beginning to feel faint from want of food, and I reckon you're not doing much better."

"I'm all right," Chess said. He had a grim stoniness in his eyes. He turned away when I looked toward him.

We went toward the tent. The miraculous smell of coffee came from it.

Chess said, "Cup o' coffee wouldn't hurt."

"I'd take that, too," I said. I was worried about him. With old folks, you can't always tell. They can look spry and fit, and then take sickly on you with no warning, like a little child. Besides the resolution I saw on his face, his movements were slowed and shaky. Chess was looking peaked, and one of his legs was almost dragging.

We moved into the crowd at the tent's doorway. There was a post there so thick with paper messages, it appeared like a feathered board. Just inside the tent, a woman was sobbing. Another woman in a blue getup was pouring coffee into cups.

A man at the entrance was trying to calm some folks wanting to push right in. "Medical cases only," he said three times. "Anyone with fever, come this way. Other complaints, wait right here. If you're waiting for someone, please step to the side. Over there, sir! They are taking names. They have drinking water!"

"Chess," I said, "maybe the coffee is just for the doctors and nurses."

Just as he was about to answer, people shoved between us, four different adults, then a woman leading two children, all flushed and feverish. "Pardon me, so sorry," she said. Just at that second, the littlest child slipped in the mud and fell face-first to the ground. "Help me," the mother cried. The poor child started wailing at the top of her lungs, and the mother picked her up. The other little one slipped from her arms. I took up the child from the ground.

She saw me through the flailing arms of the little one she held. "Oh, bless you. Thank you. Me husband and me mother was both kilt. Me children been a-fever since yestidy, but we coon't get in. Thank you, mum." Then her face turned gray and she swayed under the load in her arms.

Chess held the woman's arm as she clung to the child, and I carried the other babe, who was fighting and thrashing like his sister. We got them in the tent after much loud wailing, the children smearing mud on everything they touched. What a scene it was in there. It was supposed to be a hospital. Instead, it was pure bedlam. How anyone could be better off having come into the place was beyond me.

Canvases, most of them soiled beyond anything I would have wrapped a dead horse in, hung from wooden racks, separating the tent into at least fifty little cloth rooms for people. A tired-looking woman came to us and said, "This way," then kept going without another word. We followed her until another woman in blue tapped the mother on the arm and helped her to sit. Chess and I left the sick three and started for the doorway.

We hadn't gone ten feet when two men passed, carrying a litter between them. I called to them, "I'm looking for Harland or Melissa Prine." The men ignored me. I turned to the main area of the tent. "Prine?" I hollered, hopping up and down, trying to call over the partition.

Someone took my arm and said, "Ma'am, you'll have to wait outside."

"Harland Prine?" I hollered again, though they were pushing me toward the doorway.

From out of the din, a man called, "Here!"

"Harland?" I screamed at the top of my lungs.

A handkerchief fluttered a hundred feet away. "Here!" the voice called again. Chess and I fought our way through the commotion. "Sarah! Are you here? Are you coming?" The man's plaintive call rose above the noise, and a hush came over the room. "Sarah!"

Just beyond another partition, four grimy children sat at the foot of the cot, looking like little wooden eggs in a box. They appeared about as forlorn as any children could. Their eyes were sunken and hollow, their hair matted, faces streaked with mud.

"Harland?" I said.

The man holding the kerchief twisted around to face me. "Sarah?" he said.

I would never have known the man had it not been for my name on his lips. "Harland. Oh Harland!" I took him by the neck and hugged him to me.

He held me to him, shaking, repeating "Oh, oh."

Really softly, I said, "I've brought some apples in the bag. You can feed those babes. How is our poor Melissa?" I asked.

He seemed pained. Shaking his head, he just said, "Sleeping."

I patted her hand, but she didn't waken. I hooked one arm through Chess's elbow and the other through Harland's. "This is my boys' grandpa Chess. This here's Harland. Lands, I can't remember the children's names. Tell Aunt Sarah again, won't you?" The children turned to their father but said nothing.

Chess pulled open the carpetbag and whispered, "Are you hungry?" The children stared off into the distance, as if they were purely addled—scared out of all feelings whatsoever. The littlest one chewed on one of her braids, tattered ribbon and all.

Harland said, "The children? Yes. The boys are Truth"—he pointed to them in line—"Honor, and Story, and that's Blessing. She's her papa's little dolly, aren't you?" He patted the girl's head.

With great ceremony, the tiny girl took the hem of her tattered and filthy skirt and made a perfect curtsy. "My name is Blessing Serafina Elizabeth Prine. Honor doesn't talk anymore. If you need to ask him something, I'll tell you what he means."

Then she turned with her brothers to their first meal in any number of days. Each of them took an apple from my carpetbag, then said their thanks without smiles.

I shuddered at the dirt on their hands, fearful of what they might catch in this place. "How is Melissa? Your letter sounded—" Then I remembered the children sitting there, so in order not to frighten them, I said, "sounded as if you might need some company."

There was a piercing hurt in Harland's eyes. Tears dribbled from the corners, and he wiped at them, unashamed. He said, "Lord in heaven, it's so good to see you, Sarah. I'd given up hope that you got my message."

The oldest boy, Truth, said, "Papa, is she a nurse? Is Mother getting worse?"

"No, son," Harland said over his shoulder. "Mother is not worse. Doctor will come back as soon as he can. He's caring for many people who are sick and hurt."

"Papa," said Blessing, "Honor wants to know if this lady is an angel."

"Yes," Harland said. "Our own angel."

Honor burst into tears. Blessing said, "He wants to know when she's taking Mother away."

Harland knelt and scooped Honor and Blessing into his arms. "Not that kind of angel. She's going to get us all out of here. Wouldn't you like to leave this horrible place and get Mummy to a nice clean bed where she can get well? You can have all the food you can eat. All the food in the world. Now, Truth, just keep an eye out while I talk with your aunt Sarah."

The boy drew himself up as only small boys can, taking on his little shoulders the whole dreadful world that had recently been handed him. I saw in his face a kind of awful fear mixed with pride at his great responsibility to watch over his mother.

Chess nudged the other children from their places on the dirt floor and sat between them, saying, "I'll just rest my bones here with you children. We're all tired out from hunting for you. Did you know we were coming? Bet you four could eat a horse. Look what else we've brought for you. You, too," he said to Truth. "You can eat *and* still watch. Soldiers are allowed food on guard duty, I know that for sure. There's a brave fellow."

The children crowded around him as he opened the carpetbag. He seemed like a little old Santa Claus, handing out cookies to them. Truth had jerky in one hand and two cookies in the other, and ate them back and forth. It made me smile, thinking how I'd always liked something salty with a sweet. The marks of family, just like the conformation of a horse.

Harland said, "Poor hungry little goblins. They wanted some kind of gruel folks're dipping out. The first couple of days, it was all right, but by yesterday it was soured, and I wouldn't let them have it. Ask me, that's how come everyone has got the galloping go-around, drinking that stuff that's not cooked right. I wouldn't let them have it, and at least their stomachs are still whole. I've been trying to get out of here, but I'm afraid to drag the little ones through the crowd. I can't get to the stage, can't get to the bank, or the train. We're stranded. I have to get Melissa to Chicago."

"Trains aren't running," I said. "Tracks are out. What's in Chicago?"

He said, "Medical doctors. Specialists. I—I'm at my wit's end. Any wagon still rolling is being used to cart the dead. I—I just couldn't put them in one of those. I'd lose them all to some wretched pestilence before we got to the edge of town. People in the next cell had been trying to get a stage ticket out of here for two weeks and said they would ask for me. I gave them money for our passage, but they never came back for us. I'm out of cash, and just flat out of ideas. Out of hope, nearly, excepting that maybe you'd come."

I smiled and patted his poor face. His grown-out whiskers made him look a pure heathen. I whispered, "Well, we've brought you a wagonload of hope. I've got a few clean clothes for you, and a little food. There's plenty more in San Jose, but we'll get you there." The noise around us seemed to fade away. Harland put his hand on my shoulder and turned his face toward the ceiling. Without a word, he shook his head, hugged me again. I took Harland's hand and said, "Is Melissa strong enough to be moved?"

"She doesn't seem to be in a lot of pain, although she could barely walk on our way here. She's weak."

"Harland," I said, "you just pull together for a little bit longer. If you want to get her to Chicago, all we have to do is get you all to the stage depot. We'll get her to San Jose and then on the next train east. Now, business. I wired money in your name. You should be able—"

Harland shook his head. "Sarah, I have money. Nothing in my pockets, but plenty on account. A whole roomful of gold won't buy what we need—Melissa to get well." Then he swayed on his feet and held his hands to his head like he was bound to pull all his hair out. His eyes rolling, he sobbed, saying, "You sent more money? I've worked so hard for money. We had the finest of everything. And what is it worth now?"

My poor brother seemed to be headed for pure distraction. I said, "Harland, hold on just a few more hours. I'm here to help. Don't you let go now. There's work to do."

He breathed like a drowning man, as if he was sucking in hope that had been lost. After a spell, he nodded and said, "How soon do we leave?"

Chess had come around the tent pole and now stood next to me. He said, "Fast as we can carry her," and I nodded in agreement.

In the little cell where Melissa lay, Harland circled all the children in his arms, kneeling in the dirt. "Aunt Sarah's going to fix everything. Mother's going to a special place called Chicago, where she can be well. Will you help me take her there? I knew you would, my darling children. What do you say to Aunt Sarah?"

The children obediently mumbled something. Their mouths were full. They didn't look convinced, but they chewed on. All of them were so dirty, I wouldn't have known them from a pack of coyotes.

Truth, true to his name, did not look away from his guard duty. Honor punched him in the arm. Truth shook him off. Staring unflinchingly at his mother, he said, "Is Chicago another name for heaven?"

Harland's hair was standing up almost on end. "No," he said. "Just a hospital." Harland leaned over Melissa and whispered to her she was going to get well. She was so pale, I reckoned she was already gone.

I said, "Don't wake her, Harland." I announced to the children, louder than I needed to, "Now, children, are you ready for some traveling?" Dismay clouded the faces of the older three. The youngest one just stared off.

I hunkered down so I was eye-to-eye with them, smiled, and said, "I know you are exhausted, but you only have to walk a little way. Most of it is riding." They stared at me, wide-eyed, but not as worried as before. I said, "Harland, is anything left you need to collect?"

"My business is gone. The bank will hold my account until we return. I'll send for the cash when we get there. I'll return yours."

I leaned forward and said, "Keep it until you know whether you'll need it."

Harland rubbed his hands through his hair, which didn't do anything for the upstanding way of it. The poor man was haunted. I wanted to clutch him to my shoulder, and pat him like a child, tell him I'd fix everything for him.

Instead, I patted Melissa and felt her head. She was pale, drawn. A touch of fever. "Melissa, honey? If you can sit up, I'll help you get dressed. We'll go get you some food, and you'll feel a lot better." At that, she finally opened her eyes. I clapped my hands softly and said, "All right, that's the spirit. Men and boys, out, out, out! You go see if you can beg, borrow, or steal something to carry her on. Blessing, you stay and help your Mama get her shoes on."

Chess found a stretcher with the help of a nurse. It looked awful, but we covered it with the sheet on Melissa's bed, then gently helped her onto it. We carried her to the stage depot, while the children marched behind, with me bringing up the drag.

The depot master said the coach would return to San Jose as soon as they changed horses. There was no knowing what time of day it would be, but I speculated late afternoon, just as when we'd arrived. To get here, we had paid twenty dollars a head. Leaving cost seventy dollars a seat. There was no clamoring crowd waiting, either. The place seemed deserted. The depot master said the line had raised the rates, and now folks were having to wait. Three other men had already bought tickets. There would not be room for all of us to travel together. We couldn't leave that way.

Two of the men holding tickets were on the platform outside, smoking pipes and talking together. Chess and I explained our situation to them, and they grudgingly sold me their tickets—for seventy-*five* dollars apiece. The third man stepped around back of the building, probably to avoid having to hear me beg for his ticket. Chess followed him for fifteen minutes, telling him every aspect of how my brother's wife was sick and that we'd come all this way to get her. All the man would say was that no one was going to put him aside, not for life or death. We'd have to go in separate coaches or take our chances waiting in the depot all night for the first stage tomorrow.

I had an idea. I said, "Chess, I'll need your help. Lord, forgive me for what I'm about to do, but I'm going to get us a seat by hook or by crook. I'm about to jerk a knot in a snake's tail, and have him thank me for it. The rest of you wait here. I'm going to get this family out of here."

Chess caught my arm. "You carrying that little peashooter?"

"I don't aim to murder for a seat on a stage. At least that's not my *first* strategy."

Chess and I ambled around the side of the building, where we caught sight of the ticket-holding man. We talked louder than we needed to about how the weather was, and the camp, and what a shame it all was.

Then I began a little speech. "Certainly those children we were carrying this morning were pretty bad sick."

Chess stared at me like I'd lost my head, then said, "Well, yes, they were."

"Reckon the doctor said the contagion isn't too bad yet," I fairly hollered.

I saw Chess's eyes brighten, and he gave me a tiny wink when he nodded. "*One* of those children appeared like she wouldn't live through the night."

I saw that fellow step closer to us, listening, acting like he was trying to light his pipe and keep it out of the wind. "Well," I said, "if you had to leave one here, would you leave the sickest child or take that one to the doctor and leave the well?"

"Aw, I'd leave the healthy one to take his chances. Although any doctor would say the quarantine should apply to the lot of 'em. Nope. Take the sick. That's my advice."

"Leastways we did get most of the tickets."

He said, "A person'd surely have their hands full traveling with a lot of diseased children, what with all the coughing and sneezing and vomiting."

Now the man was staring right at us. I waited a bit, then said, "Reckon it's spreading pretty fast. Could be cholera."

Chess shook his head. "Children without handkerchiefs, wiping their noses on everything—it'll be slow traveling if there have to be burials on the way."

This conversation had taken a turn toward the truth, which was making my insides squirm. It'd be just like Providence to pay me back for this yarn spinning with some bitter truth. I felt guilty and shamed. The man started edging away. I hoped Chess could see that I was done with my terrible plot. I said, "It'll be good to get Harland's children to San Jose."

Chess tried not to grin. "Specially after we carried the mother all the way here on a litter."

I couldn't stop my lip from quivering. "She's not contagious. I'm sure of that."

Chess said, "That feller has skedaddled. We can let up now."

A few minutes later, the depot master was calling out the barred window. "Oh, sir! Madam! We've had a cancellation. I can give you the whole coach. Seems that last seat is free."

I walked to his little window. "We'll pay. We didn't ask for charity."

"It's not charity, madam. It's policy. Stage is full at six adults, or seven if they're children. I couldn't turn away a paying passenger, but he booked again for tomorrow. One extra little girl on someone's lap—well, it hardly seems right to make her pay for a ticket. Check your luggage."

I felt low-down as the snake I thought I was fooling. Little Blessing probably could have just sat on my lap without my having concocted this frightening tale. "There isn't any luggage," I said. "These folks have lost all." He nodded, as if he'd heard that story a hundred times.

The trip was miserable in some aspects, and marvelous in others. What kept us going was the idea of heading toward cleanliness, food, and rest. Inside, though, I was ashamed of myself. After a lifetime of trying to teach my children honesty, I repented about sixty times an hour for the whopper I'd told. Reckon I'd have felt worse if I'd used the derringer instead, but not much. I shifted Blessing on my lap, and she clutched my sleeve and put her thumb in her mouth.

I'll need a bigger house. Don't know why these children whom I've never met affect me more deeply than Rudolfo's, even when I've known and helped birth most of them. Reckon it's just the ties that bind.

It wasn't long before the children had fallen deep into sleep. Melissa had not stirred. "Harland," I said, "tell me the rest. The children are asleep."

He looked out the window a long time, and I'd about decided he wasn't going to say a word, when he started to talk. He said, "The first doctor said she was exhausted, that it caused a loss of appetite. She got thinner each day the last month. And she'd been tired and fretful for six months before that. Wakeful at night, consumed by unusual sweats even in a cool room. The second doctor said she was going into the change of life. Said it was 'female hysteria.'"

I shook my head and said, "A woman could have broken bones coming through her skin, and they'd call it female hysteria. Surely it's just the malaise from all this goings-on. She's just worn-out."

He dropped his head to the side. "Ten days ago, another doctor came and examined her. He believes it's cancer. That's when I wrote you. He said the shock and excitement of the last few weeks has aggravated her already-weak condition. Told me the only chance was to get her to specialists. Chicago."

Compared to the ruins of San Francisco, San Jose seemed like heaven on earth—baths, clean sheets, laundry, plenty of good things to eat. I was ever thankful that I'd listened to Chess when he said to pay for a hotel room and leave things here.

I helped Melissa bathe, then washed her hair. She was bones and thin skin, and she slept for several hard hours after the bath. After a day's rest, though, she perked up and sat up in bed, talking to us and the children. I couldn't tell if she knew she was terribly sick. Doctors never tell the person suffering if it's something serious. They say it's better for the sick to keep up believing they will get well. When Harland told her she was going to Chicago to see a specialist, she nodded and passed it off as if he'd told her she was catching a cold. She put on a good brave face for her children, but I could see darkness there behind her eyes, as if she knew. I didn't dare say a word.

Melissa spent every waking hour talking to the children and listening to them tell what they'd endured. All the while they talked, they clambered on the bed beside her. She petted the little boys and kissed them, and as they told of their adventures, she said, "Oh my, how brave! You did? All by yourself? There's my little man. Oh, Blessing, my sweet darling bunny rabbit."

Chess and I tried our level best to convince Harland that there was plenty of room for the children at my house in Tucson or at the ranch. We didn't mention the well running dry, but I expected by the time we got home, the boys would have dug it deeper. Maybe it had rained. Harland insisted on taking them. I took his arm and said, "Do you know what you're doing? It could be so hard on them."

"I'll take a room, and hire a nursemaid. They'll be with their mother. That's the most important thing," he said.

"I had every intention of taking them home with me. You, too, Harland."

Melissa said, "Sarah, you have saved us. We owe you everything. But the children are my little angels. I—I know what I'm facing. I can't do it without them."

That evening, Chess took the last of our cash, went to the depot, and bought them six tickets to Chicago. Their train would leave in the morning. We sorted some clothes that fit everyone, packed all the food they could carry, along with a few extra things like hair combs and shoe buttons. Some bread was still good and had dried, rather than gotten moldy, so I packed that, too.

Next morning, we took them to the depot and put them on board, settling Melissa and the children in their seats. When I hugged Harland one last time, the conductor was calling out, "All aboard!" I pressed my sons' ten-dollar piece into Harland's palm.

"I owe you everything," he said.

"You're my brother," I replied. Then I went down the stairs and stepped off the train. The engine hissed and the whole thing jerked. The sound of the iron wheels squealing against the rails felt as if it pierced my rib cage.

Is this all I can do? Drag them from that disease-ridden tent, buy some tickets, and put them on a train? All that way we'd come, all those weary footsteps through the mud, searching, and in the back of my mind the whole time, I'd figured on them going home with me. Instead, there we were in front of a depot, waving farewell. I could see the face of my brother through the window. Little Blessing peered out, too, and waved her hand slowly, like a mechanical windup doll. Harland was cleaned up and pressed, his face shaved and his hair combed neatly; he seemed like he'd got a second wind. It would have to hold up the six of them. I just wasn't sure he could do it without me.

Chess clasped my hand and said softly, "Leave it be, honey. It's better this way." As their faces disappeared in a cloud of steam, Chess took my arm and pulled me back from the edge of the platform. "We've done what we come for," he said.

I said, "It feels like the job's half-finished."

"It isn't. You did all you could. Let them go now. It's cruel to take children away from their mother, even if they have to watch her die. They did that to me, you know. Your brother's a grown man, and he's got his feet back under him. We've got stock at home dying from thirst, and I'm so tired of the rain here, I can hardly think about the unfairness of the spread of rain on this land. Myself, I could use a drink of something besides water."

"Well," I said, "when we get on that train, you go to the saloon car and have one, with my blessings."

"I bought us tickets for home last evening, too. Leaves at noon."

I looked at the tickets and nearly hollered, for he'd left me precious little time to pack. What Harland's children couldn't wear would fit no one at home, so I put the rest in a crate and told the desk man to send it to the relief society. That left us with just a single carpetbag apiece, filled with our dirty laundry. A couple of minutes before the trip, I opened mine to find my comb, and I nearly fainted from the moldering smell of mud and sweat. It was a good thing Chess had advised me to wear something old and tattered. I took tongs from the fireplace and used them to lift the dress out and put it down the incinerator chute. Except for the comb and a little hand mirror, my bag was empty. Light traveling. I had set my mind to be corralling young ones on this trip, and I felt purely empty-handed—and exhausted.

I slept on the train straight through Barstow. I reckon I slept the whole way from California to Tucson and barely woke when we got to town. As much as the heat in the territories can dredge the life out of a person, I felt revived being close to home. Chess whistled a tune, and when I asked him why he was so cheerful, he said there was no reason not to be. I have to admit I felt the same way. Sleeping in my own bed under my own roof will be a blessing times two.

Driving to our place from Tucson, we stopped at Albert and Savannah's place to tell them the news. We weren't halfway from the bend in the road when I saw someone walking our way. "What's Charlie doing on foot?" Chess asked.

I waved to him. It was Charlie all right, but him a-walking toward us felt wrong. Before too long, we finally come up alongside him and pulled up. He climbed on the back and sat, breathless from running the last little bit. "What're you doing, son?" I asked as Chess chucked the reins and we started moving again.

"Saving watering a thirsty horse. Where's the rest of the folks? I thought Harland and Melissa and the kids were coming back with you," Charlie said. "Gil and I cleared out of our rooms so they'd have a place to stay. We're living in the bunkhouse."

I turned on the seat. Well, at least he wasn't turning out selfish or purely foolish after that leaving-school stunt. "That's generous of you boys. Suppose you can move back in now. What's happened with the water?"

"We've done everything we could figure. We kept on trying to cut the old well deeper. Tried two sticks of dynamite the other day, and this time it opened a little seep. I searched through my geology books, thought I had figured the best place on the whole range for a well, but it came up dry."

"How far down you go?" Chess asked.

"We dug out about twenty more feet. Seems to be the level of the hardpan. Gil's still trying."

"What's in the well?" I asked.

"Enough to drink, but not for the stock. Still no more than a foot a day after that last blast. All that boiling and straining—we couldn't keep up with it and still do the rest of the chores, so we're hauling barrels from the lower quarter for the house and the horses."

Chess swatted at a fly. I stared straight ahead. I don't know why I'd expected it had rained here and that my well was full again. Maybe when you see so much sadness and damp weather as we have, you quit thinking any place is dry and hot. You quit thinking you've got troubles of your own. Maybe you quit thinking at all. Chess finally said, "S'pose it's no sense asking if there's been rain."

Charlie said, "Not a cloud. That big saguaro off the side of the smoke-house has dropped two arms. Lucky no one was nearby when they fell."

We rolled up to Granny's house. My mama was on her front porch, a fan in her hand. She was setting in her old rocker, and wearing a faded cotton dress. She was moving so slow a person could have guessed she was not moving at all, just tipping in the wind. If there'd been wind. The air felt hot and dry, as if someone had opened a stove—a heat that seemed to cook your skin, unless you were under a tree, not moving.

I asked Chess to let me off, and I'd be home after I saw Granny. He drove on to the house with Charlie and our bags. I told her about Savannah's new baby coming. She was having a good day, and asked questions and remembered where I'd gone and all about April's family. "You've done real good, Sarah," she said. "Sakes alive, you have a way of getting things done just like a man." She got up and went into the house.

I followed her. "Well, Mama, I don't have a man to do them for me."

"Me, either. Your boys are home now, though. Look here at my hexagon quilt." She pointed to a chair set at her kitchen table, where the length of patch-work had been spread and admired. "It's nearly six feet in one direction."

"Yes, Mama, it is. You've got some done while I was gone."

"I hired you a driller, and I'll pay for a wind pump. I sold some land."

"Sold some land? Who to? When?"

"The railroad. They just needed it for a passage right. Take a look. They paid in gold. Here. It's for you." She pulled out papers that appeared to be a le-gal quit claim on her homestead and held out a cloth sack full of gold coins she could hardly lift with her little side-bent fingers. As she proceeded to pour out her booty, she fingered each piece. Her face was like a pirate's in a storybook— she was purely tickled with herself. Mama started telling the whole story. While I was gone, a man had come to her house and told her she had a parcel he was interested in for the railroad, and she'd signed her X to his paper without know-ing at all what it said.

They could drive tracks clear up to Granny's doorstep and put her out of the house. The railroad could lay them up to Albert's or my places, straight through the kitchen, and then offer to buy the land at a tenth of the price. While she talked, I looked over that claim, and it seemed sure enough legal.

There was no mistake about the money. It was real. Sixty acres, gone. The name at the top was some attorney's office in Prescott, and nowhere did it say the land would be used for a railroad right-of-way.

After I'd read all of it, I folded the deed back into the sheaf it came from. At last, I took a really slow breath and said, "Mama, let's have some coffee."

"It's too hot for coffee. You'll strangle." She reminds me all the time of things I've been doing since I first married.

"How about some water, then?"

She said, "I've got some lemon conserve one of Savannah's girls made last year. It'd make a lemonade." She fetched a pitcher, and I got the jar of conserve off the top shelf in her pantry. Then she doused cool water from the olla on the back porch in the pitcher, I stirred in the yellow stuff, and we poured us each a cupful. I was amazed at how quick she stepped and how strong she seemed. Not near as frail as some days. As she was pouring, Mama said, "Now don't ever put this in a plain cup. It has to go in the plated kind, or you'll get the tin poison."

"Yes, ma'am. I know." I took a deep drink. "This is good. It feels cool all the way down." I took another long drink, then waited to get hold of my feeling of dread about her land. If there was anything I'd never mess with, it was the railroad. You couldn't trust those men in their fancy woolsey any more than you could a politician in a two-dollar suit. She'd sold her place, and probably ours, too, on some kind of whim. I tapped the folded paper. "Did you have someone read this to you? This deed gives them the top sixty acres by the road. Mama, why did you do this? You know they'll put tracks right through my land and yours, even our houses, if they please."

"Don't you worry. He had a nice honest face. I made him read me the important parts. Gilbert told me how you'd gone and wired a thousand dollars to Harland in California. Now you've got to round up and sell out if you're going to make it through. That's just like you to run throw your last hitch to save someone else. Well, I ain't farming this land, nor ranching, nor doing a thing but setting here getting old. I'm just holding it for you-all to inherit, but if you cain't hold on, what good will that be? So I'm throwing this here hitch for you, just like you done for Harland. After all, they cain't put tracks through *your* land if you don't sell to them. I figure if I sell and no one else does, why, those varmints'll be up a creek without a paddle. You need a well dug."

"Mama."

"Now don't go treating me like I'm some addle-brained child. He offered me twelve hundred, but I bargained him up. I hadn't lived this long without knowing a few things. Just you take this money and get that water in, before you lose everything."

"I still have some cash."

"Not enough to drill a well *and* keep the ranch going."

"Mama, I've heard about doing business with the railroad. They'll stop at nothing to get what they want. Did you ask Albert about this before you did it?"

"I don't need Albert's go-ahead to tell me what to do."

"What did Albert say?"

"Same as you. Threw a fit." She pushed the pile of money toward me. "Fifteen hundred and seventy-five dollars."

"I'm going to write my lawyer in town and see if we can get your land back. Sue them if we have to."

Mama picked up the packet with the deed to a third of her land and held it to her chest with a look on her face of pure determination. "Sarah, you do that, you'll pay the lawyers all of it, and still lose your land, and still not have a drop to drink. You think your papa and I come all this way and suffered and died just so you could give up on account you're too prideful to take money from the railroad? Your boys been digging and hunting, and like to killing themselves trying to water them cattle. Take that and drill a well, or you can't have it. I'll spend it on a purty dress and bonnet if you don't."

There was nothing to do, and no way to argue with her. Sixty acres, gone, just like that. Anybody could have told her I'd figure out something to do without losing our land. The very idea of a railroad track cutting through this property just put my insides plum in a knot. A sackful of knots. I'll have to move in with Mama to protect her from flimflam men. I put my hand on top of Mama's as she moved the last coins, and held it. I said really softly, "Well, Mama, you've got this all reckoned."

She started filling the canvas sack with the money. "The water witch is a-coming from Sonoita day after tomorrow. I sent for 'im myself. Mr. Sherrill is to send down to Douglas for a driller when the time is right. You know Savannah is having none of that, said she won't lay eyes on a sure-enough witch? I told her he's not that kind of witch, and that my grandmama could find water, too, but she's afraid it isn't Christian. This feller's found water up and down the territory. I sent him ten dollars and told him there'd be forty more when we see clear." I could see this was not going to get better before it got worse. I stared into the bottom of the cup, where a little lump of the lemon conserve sat. Mama went on: "I made some butter biscuits this morning. My dog Molly's getting so

fat, she cain't hardly get ahead of her own tracks. We might as well have a few."
She set a pan of biscuits on the table and pulled a jug of molasses down. "You're
looking a mite peaked after that traveling. Did you know Albert's girl Rachel
has got a job with the Mexican government teaching school down to Nogales?
Starts in a few weeks. The other like-alike Rebeccah, she's going to teach in
town. Those girls aren't coming home. Girls ought to come on home. Say,
what's the meaning of you coming here before getting on home?"

I leaned forward in my chair and rubbed my head. I said, "I just came here
first to visit. Remember?"

"Well, my quilt top's near finished," she said real soft. She ate the last of
her biscuit and syrup. Staring out the window, she said, "Albert's girl Mary
Pearl is fixing to buck loose."

"She's that age. Mama? Why don't *you* think about moving in with me?"

"You ever taste cauliflower? We used to have that in soup. Grandmama
would take it right from the garden and break it up in little bits, and put butter
in the soup, too. And top milk. Nothing like cauliflower soup with top milk. I
wonder if it could grow here. We'll know once you get that water in."

Well, she wasn't going to answer me, I could see. I used to think she was
addled when she changed the subject; now I'm wondering if she's just clever.
Land sakes alive, I'm going to lose my mind trying to keep up with her. I took
myself to Savannah's kitchen soon as I left. The afternoon sun was low and the
smells of supper came from the door. "Savannah," I called from the yard. "Your
coffee on yet?"

"What's wrong, honey?" she asked.

We talked about the railroad and what Granny had gone and done. No one
felt right about it, but it was done now. I couldn't let it rest, and finally Savannah said, "Sarah, what ails you? Is there something more?"

I hadn't meant to tell her. I didn't want her to worry. It just came out before I could stop, and I said, "It feels like some kind of evil sign. I had dreams
last night of going out to gather in the herd and finding nothing but a field of
dried cattle bones."

Savannah stirred a pan with a long wooden spoon. "That sounds like a
vision."

Albert just laughed and said, "Well, Sarah, I do believe I've read a story
like that before. Like as not, you better hire the first man comes along named
Ezekiel."

Savannah smiled and pointed at him with the wooden spoon, saying, "Now, Albert, don't be taking the Scriptures lightly," but I knew she wasn't really fussing at him. Truth be told, having a little joke about the drought didn't make me feel better, even though I smiled at the time.

June 11, 1906

The water witch came midmorning, on a mule, with a narrow bedroll and a forked twig tied to his back with a piece of hemp string. I don't know if I'd ever seen a man so dirty and ragged. Looked like he'd been living in the desert for years. Smelled a little like it, too. Of course, after all this time without water, none of the rest of us were wash day–sweet, either. We'd been bathing and washing in water from the mineral spring, and everyone smelled slightly sulfurous. The yard dogs circled him and his mule, low noises coming from their throats, the hair on a ridge down both their backs standing straight up.

"You'd be Mrs. Elliot?" he said from the back of his jenny. He rode without a saddle, sitting on an animal skin tied to the back of the mule with a braided yellow rope. He wore moccasins that still had the hair on them, wrapped over with strips of blue cloth tied right up on his pant legs.

"Yes, I would," I said. "Get down, dogs," I called. Nip and Shiner left off growling at the man and went and sat under the porch in the shade. "And if you're the water finder, I'd also be more'n a bit skeptical. I don't believe in this kind of thing. If *I* was paying you, I'd turn you around right now and have done with it. Science. Geology. That's how to find water, in my book."

He dismounted. "I'll maybe want to see that book. Rewrite it. Where will I find the courteous and generous Mrs. Prine, the lady who sent ten dollars cash to ride all this way?"

"She'll be along."

"I suppose you haven't even got a drink for a tired man? A little water, a little food. Last I heard, that was polite custom even among *Anglos.*"

Felt like my feet took roots. I could barely see his eyes, hidden under a mat of hair and a huge flopping hat, but they pierced their woolly hiding place— the eyes of a badger. Sometimes Chess saw everything that went on here; sometimes he got lost in his leatherwork. Right then, I'd have give anything for him to come from the barn and turn this fellow away. I got rared up to do it myself;

then I saw Nip and Shiner from the corner of my eye. They panted hard, but no saliva dripped from their tongues. We needed water. Maybe, something was telling me, we needed this water man.

The man stood there with the reins in his hands, like he'd turned to stone on the spot, too. After a couple of minutes listening to myself breathe, I said, "I'll fetch you a cup. What's your name, sir?"

"Oh, not 'sir,' Mrs. Elliot. Just Lazrus. Folks call me Lazrus." He smiled, or did something that made his great furry beard move up on the sides of his head.

I leaned my head back a little and studied him, then nodded slowly. "Mr. Lazrus, set yourself on the porch here, and I'll bring you a cup."

"Don't you have a pump inside?"

"Gone dry. Water's in the olla, that water jug hanging in the shade. It's been strained and boiled. Rest is mud."

He showed no surprise, just sat—not on one of the chairs, but right down on the porch floor. Folding his hands across one of his knees, which he'd pulled up, he stared off to the side of the house. I went in and came back quick as I could with a tin cup. I filled it myself with the dipper, not because I was used to taking on for folks, but because I didn't want his hands near the precious little water I'd spent so long making clean. He took the cup. It made me feel nasty when his fingers touched mine.

He pulled off his hat and laid it beside him on the floor, then leaned way back to finish off the water. I went back inside to fetch him some food. I tiptoed across the room and peered out the window; it seemed the fellow hadn't stirred except to put his hat back on his head.

My boys had not moved their things back into the house, since I came home without Harland. They both said they had a mind to once they got done with all their digging, but they have not had a moment to spare, what with hauling water. They spent their days working, and by the time the sun had gone down, they were sound asleep, too exhausted to think about a little thing like where they bunked. If only one of my kin would take a notion to come to the house right now, I'd feel a lot better.

I cut three pieces of bread and covered them each with a big spoonful of apple butter; then I cut hard cheese and smoked ham and put those on the plate, too, along with a tin fork. I went to the pantry, then decided against opening any jars in this heat. I hadn't even lit the stove this morning, and I wasn't fixing to now, so there wouldn't be any cooked eggs or vegetables. As I carried the plate toward the door, I spied my rifle in the corner, and I moved it right up against the doorjamb before I opened the door.

I handed Mr. Lazrus the plate, and again he touched my hands with his. He ate with his fingers, not the fork, and then took another deep drink. He saw me watching him, and he said, "I helped myself to more water. Didn't think you'd mind." Then his eyes narrowed, got fiery and mad. "I didn't touch anything. Your water isn't defiled."

"I didn't say—"

"Yes, you did. I heard exactly what was going through your mind just then."

"Besides being filthy, you're impertinent, Mr. Lazrus."

"Doesn't matter, Mrs. Elliot." He went back to eating. Stuffed half a piece of bread in his mouth, then licked his fingers twice, getting the apple butter that fell on them. They still looked dirty, but now they were shiny, too. "I've discovered a lot of things being dirty, that you don't see, being clean. Anyhow, none of it will matter once you see that water coming up cool and blue. Other folks around got water?"

"Yes. It's only my well that's dried up."

He nodded, chewing. "Just as I thought. Pocket water. Your well is sunk in pocket water, and the real underground pool is below it. Whoever dug it didn't know what they were doing. Miracle it lasted you this long."

It was as if he knew how long we'd been using the well. I said, "We've dug it deeper. It's down a hundred feet. There's nothing but solid rock."

He swept the last crust of bread around the plate and held his mouth against the edge, pushing the crumbs and the bread in like I'd sweep dirt onto a tin plate to dump. He gulped the water, then put the cup on the plate and held them both toward me. I took them. Standing, he brushed himself down, as if he'd made that same gesture often. Dark streaks ran down the front of his clothes. "A hundred feet won't get water in this area," he said. "That was a delicious repast. You're quite the cook."

"You don't have to thank me for it, Mr. Lazrus."

"Oh, I wasn't. You're the one to be thanking me. In fact, most folks, if they want it bad enough, will pay just about anything for a well." He stepped one foot closer.

I dropped the dishes. The plate shattered and the cup rolled across the porch. I reached behind me and shoved the door open, taking up the rifle with my left hand. I had it pointed at him before he could blink. "Ride on out of here," I said. "Mount up and go, or I swear you'll be sorry you ever showed your face on this land."

He smiled again, lifted his hat. "No reason for that now, ma'am. I see that I've said the wrong thing. Misspoke myself there. A workman is worthy of his hire, is all."

"Well, so far all I've seen is eating, and that's free. When I see a man working, I will pay him."

His beard rose at the edges again, and he made a strange noise that took me a minute to decide was a laughing sound. He said, "I'll need to see the lay of your land. See if you've even got water on it. You have anyone who can show me around? Twelve days, I don't find water, you owe me nothing. If I do, the fee is fifty dollars."

"Twelve days? Why's it take so long? I reckoned you'd just do some kind of incantation and water would bubble up from the dry ground."

"Mrs. Elliot, you have no concept of my work. And I want to know this mysterious Mrs. Prine exists, and that she has forty more dollars, since it seems I'm doing the work for someone named Mrs. Elliot. In the meantime, you have to feed me. Breakfast and supper. I do not eat at noon. Clogs up the nervous system. That's the bargain. Take it or leave it."

"Nervous system? Well, get to work. The boys will be in shortly, and they'll take you around. Not many people can earn fifty dollars in twelve days, and I—"

"It's a deal, then. Send for the drilling rig tomorrow. Usually takes them more than a week to get it moved someplace. I can recommend two drillers if you don't know one already, and don't worry about my sleeping arrangements. I make do."

Well, I hadn't given a speck of worry to his sleeping arrangements, because I hadn't figured this would take a fortnight to do. I reckon Mama had no idea what she'd sent for when she wrote to this coot. He stepped off the porch and pulled the twig from his back. It wasn't anything special, just a fork broken off a mesquite tree, something we've got growing like weeds. He held it in his hands, the middle of the fork pointing into the air, put it over his head, then turned in a circle. He eyed the sun, watching this way and that.

I wondered if Savannah was right, if this was indeed some kind of sorcery. It gave me the pure shivers to watch him. He held the branch out in front of his chest and commenced walking around in circles, and the circles got bigger each time, until finally he went over to the well. He looked in it, shook his head, and moved on. I picked up the pieces of the broken plate and put them in the metal can where we burned trash. That was one way to save on wash water.

I had no intention of paying a driller to come until I knew there'd be something for him to drill. I went and told Mama the man she sent for was here, and she was excited. She came over, but he was nowhere around, so she handed me a piece of paper with forty dollars folded inside it. "Mama," I said, "I didn't send all my money to Harland. I still have some in my till." Still she said I wasn't to be ornery about it but take the money as she meant to give it. I decided all I could do was to give it back to her some other time. I still mean to sell out half the stock, and that'll be enough to last me a while until we can do otherwise.

Well, for the next three days, that man hovered around the place, always with that piece of mesquite in his hands, over near the garden, up by the road, off where the rocks rose in the back, and even in the barn. Charlie and Gilbert went with him all over the land. I think they were glad to be done with digging, especially when there was nothing to show for their work but blistered hands and sore backs. Part of a year in school had softened up their skins, and every night I gave them each a bowl of carbolic acid and water to soak their hands in, so they didn't turn septic from the blisters.

Chapter Six

Albert had come over to my place to meet the water witch, along with his boys, Clover, Josh, Ezra, and Zack, but Mr. Lazrus had disappeared. So each day after that when I drove the flatbed to Albert's to fill a barrel for my chickens and dogs, he would tease me that I'd imagined Mr. Lazrus up after dreaming about bleached animal bones. Savannah called me in, handed me a plate of food, and I sat with them at the noon table. While I was eating, Albert said, "I told you to name the fellow in the dream Ezekiel. He was the one called up the dry bones. You've got Lazarus in the wrong story."

I said, "I think he's nothing but a lunatic."

"Oh, Albert," Savannah said with a sigh. "We shouldn't be meddling with witchcraft. You go over there, find him, and send him away. But be careful. Take the Bible with you, and find something shaped like a cross and hold it up toward him. If he's really a witch, he'll run from it."

"Well," I told her, "it doesn't seem like he's doing anything besides getting the lay of the land. He didn't say anything like incantations. And he says his name Lazrus, just two syllables. I don't think he's magic. He's rude. He stinks. He eats with his fingers, and he rides a mule sitting on a puma skin. If there's any witching being done, it doesn't show."

"Still," Savannah said, "you don't know what he's doing through the night. He could be up howling under the full moon."

"Mama!" all of Savannah's children said at once. Even Albert said it. Albert gaped at her. He said, "Sweetheart, you've surprised us. Howling under the moon?"

"Well, I've read about such things," Savannah said. "He could be a wizard or sorcerer. Anyone who can get a mule to wear a catamount skin! We must stay watchful for Satan's minions."

All their children glanced back and forth to each other, but they didn't say a thing. No one I know would question Savannah's Scripture reading. To think she'd read about sorcery amazed me as much as it did her family. She said, "Really, Sarah, I'd feel better if you came and slept here until he's gone. Or just send him away. I wish Mother Prine hadn't called on him. He's so—"

"Stinky?" Zack said.

The children, grown and young, all clucked under their breaths, trying not to laugh aloud at the supper table, which was not allowed. I had to smile, too. I said, "Well, I am purely tired of my boys following him around over hill and yon. And he does disappear at nightfall, and there's no sign of water, not a drop."

Savannah put her hands to her face. "Oh my soul, I can hardly sleep at night knowing he's abroad on the land. At the very least," she said, "he could be some sort of vagabond with *intentions*. We have girls here. Albert, won't you send him on his way?"

Seeing Savannah so concerned made me feel as if I had to defend the dirty old vagabond. I didn't want her to be worried. Seems I'd have noticed if he'd had goat's feet and a tail. She was truly frightened. I wanted her to know I'd be as careful as I could. I said, "Savannah, from now on, before I let him eat, I'm going to have Mason Sherrill bless the food and consecrate everything he touches. If there's something wrong with Mr. Lazrus, he won't stand for it, and will run off on his own. Don't forget, honey, Mama says it's not witchery. It's just a talent, and even her grandmama had the gift. I'm sure it'll be all right, but we'll do that, just in case."

"Everyone here will pray about it, too, morning and evening, as long as that man is about," Savannah said. I saw her girls nod quickly, agreeing. Josh did, too. Clover didn't move, but the little boys looked at each other like they'd been given second helpings of boiled turnips.

I patted Savannah's arm and said, "Let's all pray for rain, too. Likely all I really need is a good rain to fill up the well, get it going again."

Then we talked about Granny selling off part of her land. Albert said he agreed with me it was a terrible thing to sell to the railroad, but he didn't seem near as upset as I was. "Albert," I said, "I just don't want Granny to get cheated out of her land."

He said, "She really doesn't use her quarter section of land except for the garden next to the house. The boys here do all the hoeing and weeding, and the girls plant it for her and gather. What we need to do is get Granny to live in with one of us."

"She won't come easy," I said. "Talking her into anything might be difficult. Unless, of course, you're a man from the railroad. I have more empty space than you all. Gil and Charlie moved to the bunkhouse to make room for Harland and Melissa. Since they didn't come, it's just Chess and I."

Savannah said, "Rachel and Rebeccah will go to their teaching jobs this fall. Josh and Esther will be at school. It'll be so quiet here, and we'll have an extra room."

Even with half their children gone, Savannah and Albert will still have Clover, Ezra, Zachary, and Mary Pearl. I smiled at the little fellows and said, "You two better start making more ruckus. Your older sisters were so noisy that now they're going away at teaching, your mama thinks the house is empty." They chuckled. I said, "Well, I won't argue that Granny'd be happy here. We can just let her know either place she chooses, she's welcome."

Albert sighed and set his fork down. "It's a nice dilemma to have, two families both wanting their granny to live with them. There *are* people turned out by children when they can't do for themselves anymore. Maybe she'll spend time with both."

Clover said, "Sort of like the rich folks in town who go up the Catalina Trail to the mountains for the summer. Part of the year with us, part with Aunt Sarah."

Savannah said, "We'd better ask Mother Prine. I believe she already needs to be with somebody all the time, to make sure she's safe. That sort of thing."

That sort of thing, and selling your land to the railroad. We talked awhile longer, and eventually Albert made me feel better about the land deal that our mama had made. Still, I'll wait for Mr. Baramon to write back whether the sale is legal and binding, and whether it means the tracks are going straight through Granny's parlor.

Ezra and Zack followed me home. I planned to have them explore some poetry and percentages. "Your mama says she's kept you up on your schooling," I said. Both boys nodded and I caught them eyeing each other. You can never guess what may be going on in the minds of little boys, but it doesn't pay to let them out of your sight very long. So while we walked to my house, I explained about percentages and what they were. Then I told Ezra to take out his slingshot, and we lined up a row of ten pebbles on the top rail of my front gate. "That's a hundred percent," I said. As he shot them down, we figured what percent he had taken down and what was left.

Zachary asked if you always had to start with ten for it to work, and when I said no, he wanted to know if you had fourteen and shot two, what percent that would be. So we had to do that one in the dirt with a stick. It took some explaining, but after about three times, I think they both understood it. Then I told them I planned to continue lessons down at the pool where the Cienega runs under some rocks and a ridge.

They shouted for joy while we walked down to the stream's edge, where there wasn't any flowing water, although still plenty of mud. Up a little farther, we thrashed out the brush growing at the edge of the pool. It was more shallow than I'd ever seen it, but it still might draw snakes at the edge. The only thing we chased out was a little striped racer. Then I let them get in. I'd just taken off my shoes and put my feet in the water when I felt more than saw someone move nearby.

It was a small figure, sitting, arms about the knees and head tucked low. Mary Pearl. She might have been crying or sleeping—I couldn't tell which. "Mary Pearl," I said quietly, "what are you doing?"

She raised her head, looked toward me through the leaves only for a moment, then stared straight ahead. She definitely was not crying, but she looked angry. "Just trying to be by myself for ten blessed minutes," she said. "I just want to be alone."

"I see," I said. "Well, you come here for privacy, and here I am bringing these rascals to break up your thinking time. I wanted to let them cool off a bit. We'll be gone in a few minutes." I turned away, trying, much as I could while being only five or six feet away, to ignore her. The boys played and splashed. The water was warm, but having their summer overalls wet would cool them off, and the playing would wear them out, both good measures for little boys.

"Aunt Sarah?" Mary Pearl said. She'd come no closer. Wasn't even looking in my direction. She watched Ezra and Zachary as if they were just animals gamboling in the water. Spoke as if I weren't there, too, the way I talk to Jack sometimes. "Why would they do such a thing? I'm so embarrassed. I'd like to die."

I said, "What are you talking about?"

"Mama and Papa. I—it's horrible. I can never go to town—if people find out."

I turned to face her, though she still faced the water from her vantage point. "What have they done?" I asked.

"Mama said you knew already."

"Knew what? Oh. Are you talking about the baby?"

Mary Pearl shuddered. She turned her face as if she had to study something on the ground. I saw then the hard blush on her neck. "How could they?" she said angrily.

I put my shoes back on, leaving them unbuttoned, and walked around the brush until I could sit next to her. The boys hollered and I waved at them so they'd know I hadn't left, and they went back to playing. I said, really soft, under my breath, "You figure you've got enough brothers?"

"It isn't that. You know. It's not decent."

I reckon to a girl Mary Pearl's age, the idea of her parents having more children might seem, well, irregular. But this was more personal, I believed. Mary Pearl herself had only just found out the truth about marriage and what it meant to share a bed with someone. And she was right: Folks in town might talk or say something low-down about the family. To a lot of busybodies, a new baby coming to parents with a son as grown as Clover was proof of a lack of restraint and good manners. I said, "Well, it's a good thing we don't live in town, so we don't have to hear folks' ridiculous chatter."

She glared at me. "Just because we don't hear don't mean they aren't saying it."

"Since when do you care a flip about gossip?" I picked out some pebbles at my feet and ran them back and forth from one hand to the other. "It's not the gossip that's needling you. It's the whole idea of your parents—"

"They're old!"

"No, they're not."

She crossed her arms and stiffened her back, staring again to where the boys were playing. "They should be like you. Just be smart and be single. Before Elsa left for the convent, she told me her parents each had their own bedroom."

Well, that closed my mouth for a moment. It would do no good to argue or try to explain life to a girl already head up about the idea of her parents' nesting habits. After awhile, I said, "Maybe I want to be like them. Did you think of that?"

"That is disgusting."

I threw my handful of pebbles into the pond at the water's edge. "I remember feeling that way when I first learned about it. Eventually, you get over being sickened by the thought. Then you get curious. After awhile, you sort of look forward to it."

She breathed loudly, her face deep crimson. "I prayed all morning never, ever, to do that."

I said, "When it's the right man, you'll quit praying that. Until then, keep it up. You've lived around animals all your life, Mary Pearl. You can't make me believe you are that shocked and surprised. Say, you want to come stay a few days? The boys are in the bunkhouse; it'd just be you and I and Grampa Chess."

"I don't ever want to go home again. I can't stand to look at them."

It hurt to hear the bitterness in her voice. I said, "Well, that's probably temporary, too. Ezra! You fellows get on home now. Tell your papa you found out what fifteen percent of fourteen is, and that Mary Pearl is staying the night at my place." Ezra and Zack got out of the pond after a few more splashes toward each other. They went up the road toward home; then I locked arms with Mary Pearl and we strolled up to the house.

Suppertime, Lazrus showed up late, taking a chair so far removed from the table, he hardly seemed to be seated with us. With Mary Pearl at the table, he was surly and quiet, and he kept glancing at her with those beady little eyes. Mason Sherrill blessed the food good and long, so it was near stone-cold, but it got done in a way that would have made Savannah proud. Soon as he'd eaten a chicken wing and a spoonful of squash, Lazrus muttered, "'Scuse me," and left.

The rest of us finished our meal in peace, talking about what a good thing it would be if he truly did find us water. All the while, I was thinking about what a blessing it would be to see the last of him. After supper, Charlie wanted a haircut, and then I did Gilbert's, too. Mary Pearl offered to sweep out the kitchen as we trimmed. I wrapped an old sheet around Gil's shoulders to catch hair, just as I'd done with Charlie. When we were done, I took the sheet outside to shake it out. With one snap of the cloth, there was no one standing there, and with the next, Mr. Lazrus was standing in front of me. I caught my breath with a sound.

"Hello," he said. "Crept right up on you."

I frowned at him. "Yes, you did." I realized he was eyeing the scissors and the sheet in my hands. If he thought I was going to cut into that vermin-crawling nest of hair on him, he was going to have to think again. Nevertheless, he kept staring at them.

After a bit, he said, "We'll be going to the west tomorrow."

"Fine," I said.

"Did you send for the drill?"

"You haven't pointed out any water to me."

"Send for them tomorrow. I'll be ready to dig in a couple more days, and the rig needs to be ready. Tell them to bring only twelve-foot pipes."

"Everything comes in twelves for you?"

He smiled. "Yes, ma'am, it does. Works out that way. Twelve days. Twelve years. Earth goes around the sun in twelve months."

"Twelve apostles."

"Oh, yes. The sermon on the mashed potatoes this evening. Very effective."

"My brother's wife thinks you are a sorcerer."

At that, Lazrus laughed aloud. "Oh," he said, "I haven't laughed like that in a long, long time."

"Mr. Lazrus?"

"Yes, ma'am?"

"Do you bathe? Ever?"

"Not when my host is short on water. My business is *finding* water, which naturally means there isn't any to spare where I'm at."

I said, "Well, in your line of work, I suppose that passes for an excuse. Nevertheless, it's amazing what you can do with a bucketful. I have hauled a hundred gallons today for the stock, and there's some in that barrel yet. There's a washtub in the barn and homemade soap on the back porch. Use it. Or you'll be having your meals outside, downwind."

"Mrs. Elliot, if you're trying to insult me to get rid of me, I assure you I'll not leave without my forty dollars. I won't take it until I've earned it. And I won't have earned it until you produce the drilling rig. Good evening."

It'd be hard to say why I felt a bit sorry to have hurt his feelings. Still, I asked my boys to sleep at the house that night. In the middle of the summer, as if the heat just cannot leave the land, the sun goes down late, and it stays fairly light past nine o'clock at night, so there is plenty of time for chores after supper. Last month, Chess and I moved our beds to the back porch. Ever since Lazrus has been here, I just cannot make myself lie in mine, and have gone back to sleeping inside. With the men home, though, it felt fine to be out in the cool night air. We were good and crowded, with a blanket up between men and women, so Mary Pearl could have her privacy.

Late into the night, I awoke with a start. Mountain lion, screeching in the night. They sound like a human being, half screaming, half moaning. A chill moved through me. The boys mumbled. Chess said he'd hunt in the morning and see if it took down one of our animals. The cat had probably come down from the mountains, searching for water just like the rest of the critters. What made me wonder, worry even, was that Nip and Shiner were under the house; they didn't growl or even come out. It wasn't like them to ignore so much as a prairie dog, much less a puma growling. It could be near the barn. In the dark, with all the little hills and cliffs around here, the sound travels, so the puma could be half a mile away, or it could be at the barn door. The yard cats usually slept in the barn, and Pillbox and Hunter were in there, too. Rose was out in the pasture with old Dan and the other retired horses.

Suddenly, in a burst of noise that made me let out my breath with relief, the two dogs came barreling from under the house, barking and snarling. Now we were all awake. I heard the cry again, more distant now. Chess called the dogs back. It was still dark. He went back to bed. In just a few minutes, he was snoring again. Nip and Shiner prowled outside the house, grumbling and growling, as if they were planning to stay extra vigilant, having been caught off guard before. I got up and made some coffee, then sat myself on the porch, my rifle across my lap, and watched the sun come up.

While I sat there, first thing I planned was to chase that Lazrus off my land at daybreak. If I didn't get a well, I knew I'd better make a list of everything I had to sell. The land, of course. Maybe Rudolfo would buy a lease. There were still eighty and some years left on a couple of them. Then there were between four and six hundred head of cattle, and the horses, probably four dozen if we rounded up the wild ones from out beyond Majo Vistoso. Yet it would take an ocean underground to keep things going if it didn't rain. There was the south windmill! I could build a house there. I heard a dog growl beneath my feet. "Shiner," I whispered. "Come here, girl."

Shiner slipped from under the porch and looked suspiciously at me. Then her tail began to wag. I don't know how anyone can get by without a good old dog. This dog is really the second Shiner I've had. I named her after her mama, who was a pup from my dog Twobuddy. I tapped my lap, and she came and sat beside my chair. I petted and scratched behind her ears. She lay down and went back to sleep.

I tried not to let myself think about Mary Pearl and her shock at the revelation that her mother was expecting another baby. But that's about like trying not to think about a cricket chirping, the more you don't think about it, the louder it gets. Those were long ago days, before I knew what went on between a man and a woman. I felt a flush rise on my own face. A breeze stirred my hair, and I pulled the long braid that hung down my back to the front and loosened the hair from it. Then I put the back of my hand against my lips and remembered Jack kissing me. Strange how I rarely even noticed the mustache, although it was a good-size one. Reckon I was a long ways down the road from girlish embarrassment. Not far enough down that road not to feel the desire I used to know, that was for certain. I shook out my hair and flung it back behind me. Pure lonely, sometimes. Surrounded by people and lonely for the love of a singular man. The quiet talk in the night, when you've both wakened and can't sleep. The arm across your ribs, or your knees bumping into another set of knees if he's turned the other way.

About the time the sky went from indigo to green, I took the long stick I use to check for rattlesnakes, and walked up the rise to our little graveyard, with Shiner on my heels. The one blessing about this time of day is the weather. It is cool and dry. No breeze, but the morning bristles with doves and quail waking up and hunting seeds, rustling in the brush, calling to each other. Shiner followed me partway but then got to chasing a lizard and ran off toward the creekbed. I felt wide-awake but drained, as if my heart had dried out like my land.

I walked among my people, lying there, and I took joy in remembering them. I always save visiting Jack for the last, so I can spend some time. A cholla has sprouted behind his headstone, and it had three soft yellow flowers on it this morning. Such an odd plant. It's about the worst thing on the range for riding through, man or beast, but the flowers are delicate and lacy, and just beautiful. They smell nice, too. I suppose I ought to pull that thing out before it takes over the whole cemetery, but I reckon I'll wait until it is done blooming. At least Jack might like to look up at it now and then.

I knelt before his grave and smiled, leaning on the stick. "Jack," I said aloud, "I miss you sorely. The day isn't begun, but I'm already plum wore out. All I'd hoped to do this summer was look forward to April and Morris and their children visiting. Instead, I wrote them to stay put. The well has gone dry, Jack. The cattle are near dead of the drought, and five chickens died yesterday of heat. I need you home. Granny has gone and hired a lunatic, who's stealing her money to run around here looking like John the Baptist come to life. Even calls himself Lazrus, like he was some kind of preacher, and I *know* that's not his real name. *And* she's sold sixty acres to the railroad to pay for a well for me. Never in my life would I have asked anyone to sell that much land for me. I told Mama to get it back, and I'll make do, but she won't hear of it. Lands, Jack, I'm tired. Wish you'd just come on home."

A quail swooped up onto a wooden cross a few feet away. It was one of those soldiers' graves. The poor man's name is about gone. I'd better paint it again before I forget it and can't read it any longer.

"Where's the other one?" a voice said. I near about jumped up in the air. Lazrus stood not six feet in front of me, square on, like he'd been there the whole time, but I never saw him. He said, "There was another girl. You've got one buried here, but the age is wrong. Not the one living with you now, either. There's an older girl. She's gone, then, not dead."

I was shaking so, my teeth rattled. "What the devil are you doing out here? You just come to scare the living breath right out of me?"

"Moved away? Married maybe. Yes, she's old enough to marry. That's it."

"How do you come to know so much about my family?"

"As I said, you learn more dirty than you do clean. It puts a touch on things."

I was thinking it puts a stench on things, but I only said, "Who are you?"

"Lazrus. *God's* Lazrus. Come to life again to walk in the desert. Almost like John the Baptist. You were right."

I tried to calm my breathing. "What are you doing out here?"

"Where should I sleep but among friends?"

"These aren't your friends."

He cast his arms about. "Over there, five men of different names. Little wooden crosses. Strangers who died close by, no doubt. Here's a Maldonado, and a Cujillo, both from down the road about two miles. This one, this was your baby. Big marble stone with two angels guarding her little bonesies. Suzanne Elliot. Just a baby. So sad. You can still feel the curve of her little head in your hands, smell the womb's fragrance on her little neck. Sometimes you cup your hands and remember holding her head, feeling the hair on it, softer than a fairy's whisper."

I pulled the snake stick in front of me. I wondered if I could thrash him enough to beat the pain into him that he was putting on me. "Get away from here," I said. "Get off this place, away from me, before I whip you."

He pointed with his hat. "There, you've got a young man name of Reed. Wasn't that your name long ago? Rabbitbrush growing next to the stone. Yes, I see very well. You cared for him, and he let you down. So you relegate him to the far corner, and you aren't come to seek his opinions, because they don't matter, and maybe they never did. But here? This is *his* grave. Here, it's so trampled, nothing grows. The dirt by it has been ground to powder beneath your feet. The rocks line up like the soldier he was. Captain John Edward Harrison Elliot. Lot of money to carve a name that pretentious in marble."

I wanted to crush that snake's head of his. Put out those beady eyes staring at me from his horrible hair. I said, "Get off my land. Get out of here, and don't you ever come back. Don't you even breathe the air over—"

"Over him? It's always been him, hasn't it? More than anyone else."

I whipped the stick and swung it at him so fast and hard it sang in the air, aiming straight for his head. If it had caught him, I'm sure I'd like to have killed him with it. He snatched the stick from the air faster than I could react, and jerked it toward himself, pulling me with it. I gasped as he wrenched it from me and tossed it down. He was no more than a forearm away, and he smelled stale and peppery and rank. He was breathing quickly, and he peered into my eyes. He said, "Yes. It was him. You still haven't grown tired of him, even if all you do is stare at the stone."

I took a step backward, and then another. Then I turned, and ran to the house. As I ran, I couldn't stop a groan coming from my insides, and I reckon if I'd had a pistol in my pocket, I'd have turned and used it.

Chess said, "Coffee on yet? I'll get some kindling and start the stove for you. Goldurn, you look peaked."

I was trembling so hard, my teeth clattered, and I had to hold the back of a chair to steady myself. "Chess," I whispered, "I want to run that water witch off. I don't care if we never get the well. I don't care if I have to sell everything I own. We'll get someone else to find a spot. The driller, he could do it, maybe, or Charlie. Anyone can find water if they've learned how." It wasn't often I felt inclined toward murder.

Chess blinked a couple of times. Then he said, "Where've you been, Sarah?"

"Out to the graveyard. He jumped out of the bushes at me. Like he takes fun in scaring the daylights out of me."

By then, Mary Pearl had heard us talking, and she came into the room, rubbing her eyes and trying to waken.

Chess said, "Damn fool. What'd he say?"

I caught a sound in my throat, folded my arms across my middle. "Nothing. Started naming off the headstones and acting like he knew every one of them. He—he knew about April—leastways, that I had an older daughter and that she was gone from home."

He stared off a minute, then said, "Well, the boys likely told him. It's nothing."

I let out a deep sigh, which felt so good, I needed to sit down. "The *boys* told him. Of course. It's not like he can read things beyond, or see people's thoughts."

"They're gone to the outhouse, both of 'em," Mary Pearl added to our conversation. "They'll be coming right in," she said with a shrug.

Chess shook his head. "Sarah, you're letting Miss Savannah's worries about that rascal being a spook get you plum turned around. That old boy just enjoys making folks think he's something special. Probably had a good knock in the head once, and now he's a mite off-kilter."

"More than a little. I want him gone anyway." That crazed lunatic had rattled something deep in my core, things that I don't like to stir up.

Chess put his hand on my shoulder and patted it. He said, "All right. I'll find him and send him packing. Can we have a bite to eat first?"

"Lord, that's right. He'll be coming in for breakfast."

"Boys will, too. You get them alone when he's outside, ask them if they mentioned April. You'll see. It's nothing. Now, let's get the stove going so it can cool down before the air gets too hot to breathe. I'm going to ride out and see if I find any tracks of that mountain cat."

I made pan steaks and gravy and biscuits. I even opened a jar of peaches, put a little sugar on them, and warmed them in the oven, in honor of my gladness that Mr. Lazrus was having his last meal with us. He showed his face, too, five minutes after the boys got here, and he acted like nothing in the world had passed between us.

Only, he did come in carrying my long stick, saying, "Look here what I've found. Mrs. Elliot, you ought to carry something like this when you go walking. It's good for chasing off reptiles."

Charlie prayed over the food, taking the honors because Mr. Sherrill was feeling poorly this morning and had stayed in his bed back in the bunkhouse.

Just as soon as he'd said the amen, Chess started eating. He pointed with his first biscuit at Mr. Lazrus. "You know, Lazrus," he said, "I get the surefire picture that you have gone to school quite a bit."

"That so?" Mr. Lazrus said. He held a steak tight in one fist and was chewing at the bone end, cutting marrow out with his teeth.

"Nobody around here says the word *reptiles*. Must be you learned that from some eastern college."

Lazrus sat stiffly upright. Then he pointed at Chess with the steak. "Well, sir, you've found me out. A product of civilized society, born and bred for the finer things of life." He laughed menacingly. "Which I enjoy even now. Why, is there anything finer than Mrs. Elliot's biscuits and a good steak? Not a hotel in Paris serves such food." He licked each of his fingers, smacking his lips, showing his whole tongue, and making a big show of the process.

"You've been to Paris?" Gilbert said.

I gave him a look. I didn't want to get this varmint engaged in a long conversation full of his lies and deceits. And my sons didn't know about what had gone on in the graveyard before breakfast. I wanted the boys to hurry up and eat, and get out the door. I want to watch Chess and me giving Lazrus a boot in the britches. I plotted in my head exactly the words I'd use to send him flying.

Lazrus looked accusingly toward me, nodded, and said, "I see your point, Mrs. Elliot. Enough dillydallying. It *is* high time we got about our business. And you have endured my company long enough. Hurry up, boys. When you lads have done eating, you'll find me up on the sandy rise, waiting your escort. That drilling rig should be in this afternoon, and I'll be here to tell them where to start." He rose, putting on his hat.

"You've found water?" I asked. I jumped to my feet. I couldn't help the look on my face. If there really was water to be had, my ranch might be saved.

"Of course. I came here to find water, and find it I did. It *is* the eleventh day."

Chess stood up, too. "Then where're you off to?"

"A secondary site. It is always a good idea. As I've discussed with Mrs. Elliot, it is possible to drill mistakenly into a pocket that won't last, or is brackish. Most everything hereabouts runs to alkali to one degree or another. Your boy Charles there said he'd show me the mineral spring. Too bad about that being so close. I'd never put a secondary site there, but it is good to see it, so I can judge how far it runs. That way, we don't waste either time or money."

With that, he went out the door. The five of us ringed the table, looking at one another. I said really softly, "Did you boys tell him you have a sister?"

Charlie seemed startled. "No, Mama, I didn't," he said.

"Me, either," said Gil. "I wanted him to tell about Paris. But what was all that other he was talking about?"

I started pulling plates toward me, and covered the biscuits with a clean dish towel. "He makes like he can read minds. Pretends things. Ever so often, he hits on something. You know, if you guess heads or tails and flip a coin enough times, once in awhile you'll come up right. When we've got water, he is going to be gone, and none too soon."

Chess watched the man through the window, glowering. He said, "Make sure you boys don't give him any more information about our family than you may have already. Let your mama rest easy."

Gilbert said, "Well, Mama, if it makes you feel any better, we don't like him, either. We've been trying to accommodate him, on account of needing the water. Charlie and I both think he's a coot."

Charlie nodded and pulled another biscuit from under the cloth. "We'll just ride to Majo Vistoso and back. Should be back by noon."

I said, "When you get back, go around to Granny's place, and your cousins', and tell them he's found water. Reckon everyone will want to come watch the drill."

When there was no one in the house but Mary Pearl and me, she said, "Aunt Sarah, that man scares me, real deep inside."

I bit my lip. "You ought to start carrying that knife again. You've quit for a while." I knew Savannah had probably asked Mary Pearl to leave it off. Although I've tried very hard not to go against their child raising, I believe Savannah might agree with this, and I'll tell her I pushed Mary Pearl to carry it for her own safety. If she were my daughter, she'd tote a loaded gun, too.

Chapter Seven

In the late afternoon of the twenty first day of June, a ten-pair team of mules came down our road, pulling a tremendous rig loaded with rows and rows of steel pipes. The wagon was so large, at first I could barely make out the wagoner driving it. As this monstrous thing came closer, the dogs went to barking like they were going to turn inside out. All the hands and everyone else came a-running. On the back was a steam-motorized drilling rig, clanking and thundering. When they got closer, I also saw a brand-new windmill, near ten feet across, with two sets of wooden vanes screwed to metal shanks, one inside the other.

Sitting right up front with the driver, like she had the reins to the whole kit, was Granny. My tiny little mama riding up there, proud as a hen on a set of hatched-out chicks. They stopped moving right in front of me, and the man helped her to climb down. I said aloud to anyone who could hear me, "Well, I didn't order all this. My order was supposed to be a drill and hand pump."

My mama nudged me with her elbow. "Ain't that a beauty?" she said. "Like to cost the whole amount, but that is the finest windmill money can buy. Steel plates behind the wood, and if one breaks, why, you just send up a man with a piece of wood and an iron peg."

My mouth hung open. I said, "Mama, you ordered this? Without asking me?"

"Well, it's a present. I don't need your permission to give a present."

It is a blessed thing, a joy I can't describe, to look on a powerful gift such as this. Something that represents a sacrifice from someone else, or an effort far exceeding what I'd feel was normal, is so beyond my expectations, it touches my deepest soul. My throat tightened up and I felt something swell in my chest. "No," I said. "Reckon you don't." My eyes burned, and I had to hold on to my head for a few seconds. Then I put my hands down and said, "To me, a present is a nice feather pillow or a new apron. Mama, this is way overgenerous. It has cost you sixty acres of land. It's too big and too fine, and—"

"Well, then you just mind your manners and say thank you."

"Thank you, Mama." I went to put my arms around her, but she was grinning as she headed out to inspect the great machine. I pulled my apron over my eyes and went inside for a while so no one could see me crying. Then I had a little drink of water and soothed my silliness.

Here came my sons, saying Mr. Lazrus was behind them about a quarter mile. I didn't ask why they'd come so far ahead. To me, keeping distance between yourself and that lunatic was always a good plan.

There was plenty to do, drawing water from the last of the barrels for the team of mules and the men accompanying it. Lazrus's mule came ambling down the trail off the sandy cliff like he had nothing but time. The man running the drilling team had already asked to know where they were to set up, but I'd told him we were waiting on that fellow coming. One of the men said, "Oh, it's old Lazrus. Yep, he'll find water for you, ma'am. Strange character, but he's got the touch."

Well, that strange character waved and called hello to the drilling men, then kept on a-riding right through the yard and toward the hill behind the house. He rode that mule up the slope to the only flat spot on it, a rock slab at least ten feet wide, part of it sinking into the dirt at one side. He got off the mule, pulled the mesquite limb from his back—the limb, I saw, was not even the same one he'd come here with, but much different in size—and held it out in front of himself, then pointed it straight down at the rock.

Lazrus knelt slowly, bending lower and lower, until the point of the stick touched the rock. Then he pulled something white from his baggy shirt and drew a big cross at the point where it touched. Holding both arms out and up, he called, "Come to me, all ye who thirst! Behold! I smote the rock, and the waters gush forth." I searched the little crowd for Savannah. Thankfully, she was not here to witness the blasphemy. If there truly was water under that slab of rock, I didn't want Savannah to declare it was not fit to drink because a madman had discovered it. All my relatives and the drilling men busted out with cheering and clapping, like he'd made a speech. I didn't clap. I just put my fists against my hips and waited for him to pull some kind of shenanigan. Yet he just put his arms down and very calmly walked straight toward me.

Lazrus said, "Mrs. Elliot, it will take them the rest of the day to set up. If they commence drilling at daybreak tomorrow, you will have water by nightfall, as long as the bore doesn't break, and they've brought pipe for three hundred and twenty or thirty feet. Twelve days, just as I promised. Order your men to build you a foundation for the tank, and get the concrete hardened by then, or you'll not be able to hold the water coming from this well."

I said, "You have gone and spent eleven days searching every inch of my land. If the water was this close, why didn't you say so? You had to have picked this spot the very first day."

"Just because it is close doesn't mean it's best, but now I've confirmed it. In fact, this is probably your only chance at fresh water. You're far too close to the mineral spring. That, too, explains the formations holding water that you had used for these past years. Your previous well was an underground cistern holding ought but rainwater."

It seemed to make sense, even coming from him. "Well," I said, "I'll pay you, and you can be on your way."

"Not until we see the well bringing forth life. If you drink of my well, you will never thirst again." Two flies buzzed over Lazrus's face and settled on his beard. He paid no attention, just kept staring into my eyes like there was something new there. "Your salvation awaits, a hundred seventy feet from the surface."

I decided to ignore the last comment and concentrate on the money I owed him, which meant getting him out of here. "That is fair of you," I said. "Especially after we haven't exactly gotten along."

"Not this trip," he said. "Some of our journeys have been more pleasant than others."

There was no telling what he meant by that. I said, "Reckon I better see to the tank, like you say." I started walking away, then turned. "A hundred and seventy feet, you reckon?"

"Or a hundred and eighty. Between the two. Of course, they'll sink an extra fifteen feet of pipe so as to reach below the slump. There's a natural curve in water, you see. Pipe's got to go deeper; otherwise, it'll dry the slump and you won't reach the pool."

"That is twice the depth of my other well. If there is nothing there, my mother has paid for a mighty deep privy."

He said, "And you will owe me nothing. Nevertheless, when you see it, you will have your faith restored, and you may thank me profusely with supplication and fanfare."

I put my fists against my hips. "*If* I see it, I will pay you the rest of your fifty-dollar fee, without fanfare or supplication. And, if, as you say, it comes in fresh, between a hundred seventy and a hundred eighty feet, I think you should be obliged to *use* it."

His eyes narrowed, and he actually stepped back away from me. "What do you mean, Mrs. Elliot?"

"I mean a thorough coating of clean water inside and out. I saw you mark that stone. It was a piece of soap you used. I don't care if you eat it for supper later, but I will have the boys set up a tub in the barn and fetch together some extra duds. You'll get in it and take a brush and scrape at least an inch of topsoil and rust off you. Then I'll feed you a last time, pay you, and you'll get on out of here—and don't come back."

"You always did like to get the best of a man, didn't you?"

"You wouldn't know."

"I know your heart. I hear your thoughts."

"Hogwash. You're just good at guessing. A woman living alone with grown sons, naturally she'd have been married. Chances are, she'd have loved a man. Chances are that she'd have buried at least one child. You didn't hear anything. You just speculated and got close to the target, that's all. You're not a prophet. You're nothing but a low-down gambler. That's how I know you'll take the wager."

"I will not bathe in your water."

"Then I'll pay you the remaining forty dollars and you can ride out anytime."

"You're a cruel, hard woman."

"Well, I had all the kind generosity scared plum out of me this morning at dawn."

He roared with laughter. "Lord," he called to the sky, his hands over his head, "verily, 'tis better to live in a corner of a cattle stall than in a wide tent with a contentious woman!"

I spun on one heel and walked away from him. Let him roar and bellow. Let him screech through the night, pretending to be a puma. If I see hide or hair of that horrible man after tomorrow night, I'll let some air through him with buckshot from my short-barreled varmint gun.

Chapter Eight

June 22, 1906

Last night, I kept a pistol under my pillow and the shotgun straight out next to me in bed, and put Shiner at one end of the porch and Nip at the other end, but at least I had some solid sleep. During the night, I saw Jack riding down the slope toward home. He was waving and calling, holding his hat in his hand. The boys were little again, and April just a girl. Suzanne not even born, nor the boy baby who never took a breath nor had a name. It all seemed so real. Even *in* my dream I asked myself if it *was* a dream, but no, there came Jack, and all was restored to right.

"Jack! Supper is ready!" I called. I ran toward him, and he leapt from the saddle and ran toward me, too, his arms open to sweep me into them. "Look," he said, "I've brought you sweet water to drink!" I reached for him. My finger-tips touched his shirt. At that touch, I awoke, panting from running so hard. I stared at the ceiling boards for a minute until I knew where I was. Trying not to move, I tipped my head enough to see the dogs sound asleep by the edges of the porch. Chess snored. The screens kept the mosquitoes off, though I could hear a couple of them whining. The moon was bright near to daylight. A nighthawk burbled. Another one called back.

I had a cotton sheet pulled over me, but nothing hanging on the cord. I folded my hands over the top of it and rubbed the frayed and ragged edge with my thumb. It was one of the embroidered ones Savannah had made for Jack and me years ago, a wedding present. An old sheet, nearly threadbare. Perfect for summer sleeping. Almost.

That time, I'd almost touched him. I felt a tear slide down the side of my face, and I turned on one side so it soaked into the pillowcase. I dismissed thoughts of Lazrus startling me, then thought for a moment about Rudolfo's marriage proposal. I dismissed him just as easily, though with a bit of guilt. There'll never be another Jack Elliot. That, I knew for sure. "Jack," I whispered, "supper's ready. Water's plenty. Come home." Likely, I will go through my days like my mama, alone by fate and choice. I remember Mason Sherrill used to court Granny, every Tuesday evening. He'd play her songs on his guitar, and she'd make him cookies. They did that for five or six years, and then up and quit one day. Reckon it was just over. I lay still, listening to the night sounds. When I'd touched Jack in my dream, I was almost in his arms again. Tears wet the hair at my temples. When the sky faded from black to green, I breathed a sigh and got up to see the dawn. Getting out of bed is a good way to leave your troubles behind.

It is the best time of all, that blessed few minutes before sunrise. A woman can have some time utterly to herself, without someone needing her. The night animals go to their holes, and the dove and quail are still asleep. Men with fields to plow and miles to ride are still deep in sleep. It is a time to take out a woman's cares and tend them, to uncover the aches and dust them off gently, with affection and tenderness, not brusquely, the way Lazrus had in the cemetery.

I looked over my life and fingered the pains of it, the many scars upon my heart. Then I sorted through the other times, the almost times, when something terrible might have happened but was kept away. Like Gilbert on the windmill, or old times past, when Albert was hit in the side of the head by an arrow, but only hurt skin-deep, and lived to tell about it. I stared into the distance until my eyes hurt, keeping away the dreams by reliving the real.

By the dim light of dawn, I collected eggs in my apron, then got back to the house to feed the work crew. By the time I got the dishes done, they'd started the machine boring through the rock. My hired hands, my boys, my brother and his boys, all rushed to the work of putting a tank together with rock and concrete and sand. Albert told them to build the walls a full three feet thick, and we managed to settle it pretty close to the hole, so it should practically fill itself, unless we want to use the hand pump on the side. It was a torment getting it built while staying clear of the drillers, but they were used to it, and they told us to keep on.

Clover and Charlie hauled rock and mixed mortar with Flores and Shorty.

While Chess helped them set stones, Joshua and Gilbert set to puzzling out the construction of the huge windmill. Its span was bigger than the one in the south pasture, and fully twice the size of the older one I have out front of the house. Mason put up that windmill years ago, after Jack had it sent from Oklahoma.

The sound of the drilling machine hammering through rock filled the air like something solid. All day, the drillers shoveled wood and coal into the steam engine, and four times we had to send to Albert's with a water barrel to get more water to put in the big drum of the motorized bit. Albert's little boys never got tired of looking at it and darting around it. I tried to stay in the house, and I got nearly half my quilt top done, but every hour or so I went out and watched, too.

Toward six o'clock, I took some stewed meat with vegetables, fruit, jam, and bread to the men doing the work. They let up for just a little bit to eat, but then went on with drilling after just fifteen minutes or so. By that time, the big tank Albert had built was drying and solid-looking, and Mary Pearl had the job of going round and round it, trickling water over the top and sides so the lime cement didn't crack.

There was no sign of Lazrus, and he'd never missed a supper yet. Maybe he was so sure they'd find water, he'd gone off, just decided he'd get his money in the morning and then disappear into the desert he'd come from. I washed all the dishes in water brought from Albert's well. By eight o'clock, Rachel, Rebeccah, and Esther had come from Albert's. Even more surprising, Savannah had come with them. They brought sugar cookies for everyone, great hand-size ones, which the men and boys wolfed down. After Savannah handed out the last cookie, she sat on my porch with me.

I was too tired to talk, so we just sat and fanned for a spell. Out of the blue, Savannah said, "Well, even if that water man is as heathen and sinful as they come, I believe the Lord can draw a straight line with a crooked stick. You need water, and if he—Lazrus—can point it out, that is our straight line."

"Good," I said. "I'm glad you didn't say it would be cursed and alkali. I'm still worried it's going to be just a dry hole."

She leaned toward me and said, "You know, honey, there *was* a while I was hoping it would be dry, just to show that man out to be a liar and a lunatic. Then I realized how unfair that would be to you. I'm truly sorry I wished it. Please forgive me."

"No harm," I said. "I don't suppose you hid any of those cookies, did you?"

She smiled. "I know men and cookies. Look here." She pulled up the basket sitting at her feet and took off the bottom layer of a checkered towel. There were six more cookies under there, and she and I ate them, three apiece. She had a little jar of apple cider in there, too, and we also had that, taking turns sharing it. I believe Savannah Prine makes the best apple cider in the county. She and I sat and pieced my quilt for a spell.

With Savannah pinning up and me stitching on the machine, we got two more rows up in jig time. Then we went to the porch again to get some night air. I had just leaned my head against the back of the porch rocker and shut my eyes, when there was a loud cracking sound, and the drilling machine made a terrible whine that had us holding our ears. Savannah and I sprang from our seats and hurried toward the drill. The men holding chains under the scaffold moaned and threw down their tools as they walked away from the rig. I ran toward them, calling "What happened?" again and again to anyone who'd listen. Savannah was behind me until I passed her girls.

The foreman mopped his brow with his sleeve and threw his hat angrily into the dirt. "Suffering angels above. Pull that son of a—oh, sorry, ma'am—pull it up, boys. Sweet Mary and Joseph—sorry, ma'am. A goddamn hundred-dollar drill bit. Sorry, ma'am. Solid rock—and blasted—that Lazrus better be right—suffering. Damn. Can't cuss with all these women around. Pardon me, ladies, but would you please go in the house and let us finish this work?"

Savannah took off toward the house as fast as she could go, pushing her daughters in front of her. Instead of following her, I stepped right toward him. I get purely tired of some men thinking work gets greased with cussing, and the more cussing, the better the work. The foreman was a stumpy barrel of a man. I knew he was flying mad, although no more disgusted than I was. "Listen," I said, "don't you have another drill bit?"

"Yes, lady, but it's the eight-incher. We've put a six-inch shaft all the way down. Using the great one means drilling the whole suffering length of it again."

"Mr. Lazrus said to *start* with the eight-inch hammer. I heard him tell you."

"I know my business, lady. I know what needs doing, and how it gets done."

"Well, I'm not paying you to drill twice just because you had to do it your way first," I said, picking up my skirts and going to the house. Savannah and her girls were waiting inside. Candle bugs and dusty black flickers gathered at the window, along with the usual flank of mosquitoes. A couple of them had gotten in from somewhere and were dancing around the lamp globe. After a minute of listening to the commotion outside, I caught Savannah's eye and said, "It feels like we're all waiting the birth of a baby."

"Only the men are in labor," Mary Pearl piped in. With quick glances all around, the girls all laughed.

Savannah said, "No wonder the Lord gave that chore to women. The language of those men!"

After about a half hour, we heard the hammering start again. I had reckoned the men were going to quit and go to bed, but it appeared like they planned to drill after dark. That pounding was making me feel as if my skin skittered around on my bones, and I wanted to leave, if only I'd had somewhere to go. Savannah said it made noise all the way to their house. I felt anxious, believing that someone or something could creep up behind me and I'd never hear it. Thank goodness Chess and my boys were home. With the boys around, there'd be several more sets of eyes watching for that Lazrus. Mary Pearl asked Savannah if she could stay the night here, on our sleeping porch, and wait for the water. Savannah told her she could, and then Savannah and the other girls started for home with a lantern.

Mary Pearl and I got two lanterns and walked out to the drill to watch awhile. At ten o'clock, the drill was still going. Seemed they planned to work the night through. I fired up the stove again and made a pot of coffee in the big gallon pot I use for roundup coffee. It took near an hour to make because of the size of the pot. By the light of the moon, we hauled the coffeepot and a string of tin cups looped by their handles out to the drillers.

Rudolfo and his son Oscar had come, too, and my male kith and kin were enjoying the show. "How far down is it?" I asked the man who seemed to be the boss. I had to holler it again before he understood.

"Ninety-six feet," he said. "Damnedest thing I ever saw—scuse me, ma'am—the way the big one will cut through it like butter. Usually, you got a rock like this to start with, the little one's the way to go."

I put my hands around my mouth and hollered, "Any sign of water?"

"No, lady."

Mary Pearl and I stood with the men, watching. From the corner of my eye, I spotted Rudolfo. He disappeared; then he was right next to me. The noise was so loud, I could tell he was trying to talk, but I heard only every few words he said. "Sarah? . . . *Qiero hablar . . . la verdad.* . . . I must tell you the truth. . . ." Rudolfo's face was troubled. Mary Pearl glared at him.

One of the drillers called out, "One hundred feet!" People didn't say anything, but they did sit up and take notice.

I shouted to Rudolfo, "Let's talk later," and handed him a cup of coffee. I was tired. Rattled, too, from listening to that engine chewing through rock. Rudolfo looked into the coffee cup as if something was really on his mind, but I didn't want to leave again. And with my boys and Albert all around, I didn't want to wander off in the night with Rudolfo, no matter how long we'd been friends. I hadn't said a word to them about his proposal, and I didn't plan to until I was good and ready.

Another man called, "Hundred and thirty." I turned, and Rudolfo had gone. I swatted a mosquito that had lighted on my arm. At least the night had cooled off, though we still were sweating. The men shoveling were plum ragged. "A hundred sixty feet!" came the call. Now all the folks stood and moved a little closer. "Hundred sixty-five. Sixty-six. Seventy-two . . . seventy-eight. Hundred seventy-nine—cut it off! Here it comes!"

Water bubbled from the machine's blowpipe. They stopped the steam engine and unhooked the chains. The drill hammer pulled up, and with it came a fountain of water. I rushed toward it. It ran off the rock and down the slope. The ground fairly hissed as the water touched it. It ran straight toward me. I knelt right there in the dirt and scooped it up, gravel, twigs, and cool, sweet mud, and held it under my nose. Sweet water. Oh Lord, sweet, good, cool water.

People around me cheered and shouted, whooping and stomping. Everyone jumped and hollered. I stood in the center of them, howling with delight, like a child. Without any notion that he'd been nearby, I suddenly saw Rudolfo. He swept me up in his arms, and before I knew what was happening, he kissed me.

I reckon I was so happy about the water, so exhausted and happy, that I kissed him back. The commotion went on around us, and though I don't think it was more than a second or two, it was a sure-enough kiss. He let me down, and I held my fingers to my lips, shocked at myself. His eyes looked warm and sad, though, not happy. Then he vanished into the crowd, and I was swept into the celebration. We shook hands all around and slapped one another's shoulders until we were raw. I never came upon Rudolfo again. He'd gone home, I reckon.

The men had lowered 228 feet of pipe as the hammer sank into the ground—nineteen of the twelve-foot lengths piled on the wagon. The top four feet made a connection to the windmill scaffold. The water stopped running out of the hole, but the smell of it was as good as a clean sheet just off the line, better than a cake in the oven, sweeter than pulled candy at Christmas. Everyone lined up and tossed out their coffee, holding the cups under the spigot, filling them with that good water.

When everyone got quiet, the Irishman held his cup in the air and said, "To the saints who watched over this drilling, and the dear Virgin for letting me keep me temper, and to Lazrus, that water-witching son of a gun. Finally, to the dear lady of this house, long may this well serve you and yours, and may every drop that comes from it bring health and wealth and happiness!" He upended the cup, letting it drizzle down his face and darken his shirt in streaks. "Sweet Mother, that is the most wonderful water I've tasted this side of the ocean. Drink up!"

We drank and drank that water, like it had come from heaven. Indeed, I thought, watching all these people reveling in my good fortune, it nearly did. Without some kind of outside guidance, how could that crazy varmint Lazrus know the things he knows? It was long past midnight. It was the twenty-third of June. Twelve days after he'd arrived.

The noise went on around me, and for a minute, I was alone. I felt embarrassed at what I'd done. At the liberties Rudolfo had taken, right here in front of my family. I was mortified at the thought of my sons having seen that kiss, and I knew right then that I didn't love him. It meant no more than if I'd been holding a puppy or a chicken in my arms; when the water came, I'd have kissed them, too. Poor Rudolfo. I didn't love him, and now I'd gone and kissed him. I was going to have to do some long talking to explain.

In just a few more minutes, they put out the lights, and all those fellows from the drilling company bedded down on blankets in the yard. My boys went up to the sleeping porch; the rest of Albert's bunch headed for home. I glanced at the clock as I put out the last lantern. It was three o'clock in the morning. The hour of teething babies and birthing foals. The hour when fevers broke and wells broke through. Three in the morning had never come my way without some blessing attached to it. I nodded at the mantel clock, wound it for the day ahead, and went to bed, so thankful that my gratitude included Lazrus, too.

I awoke to the sound of Nip growling low in his throat. He didn't bark, the way he does when there is some kind of danger close by, but kept on growling, telling me he was worried and sensed something was out of order. I tried to stay awake and listen for strange sounds, but my arms and legs seemed to be stitched to the bed itself. The next thing I knew, the sun was full up, and people began rousing.

The drilling men shared some breakfast with us, then packed up and were gone soon after, along with a very large stack of Granny's gold coins. I felt like a thief, paying them money that my mama had put into my hands. I vowed to myself that I would repay her for it soon as I could get her to understand my reasons and take the money.

I spent the morning doing washing that had gone waiting, hauling the tub and wringer out to the well. By afternoon, the boys finally got the windmill together and had it mounted and all. Chess pulled the pin and, with just the lightest little breeze, it started turning, filling the tank Albert had built, the water channeling through a pipe in the side. What a heavenly sound, that of water running.

I felt as if I'd been given a whole new life, as if nothing could go wrong now or ever again. I stared for a long time at the water running into the tank, clean as it could be, and a pretty pale green color. I'd better get to hauling some of this water to my horses and other critters. I'll get the chickens back to the coop, take up house again. As long as we have water, the world will right itself. I turned around, and nearly ran right slam into Lazrus. I gasped and put my hands to my face.

"How many feet down?" Lazrus asked.

"A hundred and seventy-nine. Just like you said. I'll get your hundred dollars, and you can get along home."

"That's all? You told me I'd have to be soaked in that water. Thought that was why you brought the washtub—for the baptism service."

I put my hands on my hips. "Mr. Lazrus, I'm tired. Drink your fill. As for the rest, I don't care if you take a bath or not. I thank you for the work, and I'm glad to pay you a bounty on it. It's a fine well, and good water, and that is enough for me."

"What is man that thou art mindful of him? What does it matter if I live in the dust I shall become?"

"It doesn't. But if you're so quick to quote the Bible, read the Psalms. 'You are not called to uncleanliness, but are judged by the cleanness of your hands.' And yours, Mr. Lazrus, are nastier than—"

"Oh, madam, let us not trade insults again. I'd forgotten your learning and letters. You're missing a great opportunity, and I've decided you're ready to see me clean and shaven. But if you'll fetch my payment, I'll be on my way."

I just closed my mouth and went to the house to get the money. I came from my bedroom, and was shocked to find him standing right there in the parlor. "Here you go," I said, holding forth an envelope.

"What's the matter? Do I make you . . . nervous?"

"You make me aggravated. I've put a hundred dollars in there. Have a good journey, and godspeed on your way to wherever you're bound."

His beard rose on the sides, like he was grinning under there. "Perhaps you should suffer more anticipation. Perhaps I'll return someday and take you up on it, the bath and all. That'll be something to ponder."

I didn't move. Neither did he. After a little bit, he raised the envelope to his forehead and clicked his heels together, as sharp a salute as Jack ever made, stuffed the money into the front of his old shirt, and walked out the door. So like a soldier, that stride. He's so terrible and mysterious and crazy, why does every new thing I know about him rattle me clean to the bones?

I will keep my bowie knife sharpened, and the shotgun loaded with double-ought shot, just on the prospect of his visiting again. And get another dog, a bigger, meaner one. And put guineas and geese in the yard, the snappy kind that will chase a person and bite the hide off him. Maybe I'll ring the house with chollas and tarantulas, and train a three-headed sidewinder to guard the porch in back. Catch that puma and chain it to the front door for a watch-mountain lion. That's how much I'd look forward to that lunatic showing his rusty hide around here again all right.

Chapter Nine

Every morning since the well came in, I have awakened with the feeling of Christmas, just happy as a little lizard to have all that good water. Happy, too, to be rid of Lazrus, and looking forward to a future without him lurking about.

It's been nearly a week since I kissed Rudolfo. Daily, hourly, I suppose, I have searched my soul and mind to see if there were something I was not being honest about with my own self. Was there some desire, some secret longing, that Rudolfo alone could answer? And daily, even when I allowed myself to think of him in very personal ways, the answer was always no. I decided that I'd need to talk to him, and tell him what the kiss meant to me, which, sad enough, was more about water than about him.

Still, with him on my mind, it wasn't much surprise to see Rudolfo tying up at my porch rail as I poured milk into a bowl of flapjack makings at sunup. Charlie came around the back of the house, where he'd been washing up, at the same moment. He greeted Rudolfo, but though Charlie's voice sounded cheery, his eyes held suspicion.

I turned my attention first to my son. "Charlie, coffee's ready."

"Mama, Mr. Sherrill is bad again."

"I'll see to him soon as breakfast is done. Rudolfo? You coming in?"

Well, he joined us for flapjacks and steaks and drained the last of the coffeepot. I was thinking about taking a steak to Mason Sherrill, with some top-milk gravy, just letting my mind wander, when Chess and the boys got up from the table to leave. Rudolfo stayed behind, lingering, silent. Then he asked how the well was working, and after the health of everyone we knew. He brushed sweat from his brow.

We both waited, and then at the same time, we said each other's names. Then we laughed. He was fidgeting in his chair, the way the boys do when I scold them for something. Suddenly, Rudolfo didn't look any different from the way he had when I first met him. At that thought, I smiled again. "You wanted to say something to me the other night?" I asked.

Rudolfo didn't smile. He said, "*Sí.*" He looked into the bottom of the coffee cup. Reckon if I was polite society, I'd have jumped to make another potful, but we were just past six of a morning and it was nearly ninety degrees in the house already, and I'd let the stove go too cold to boil more water. I didn't expect to heat it up again, and I *did* expect him to be friend enough to know that. But, to my surprise, Rudolfo pulled a silver flask from his pocket and poured some liquid into the coffee cup.

And then he told me a long tale of how he'd started asking around for anyone who knew what had happened to my south windmill and the tanks there. One of his hired hands then confessed that he'd gotten drunk one night, and hearing how his boss wanted to marry the woman with the adjoining lands, the man thought he was doing his boss a favor, ruining my tanks, so I'd have to marry Rudolfo to stay in business.

Rudolfo got so angry with the fellow, he beat him, he said. Not just a little, either, but enough to teach him a lesson. The trouble was, after Rudolfo hit him, he fell backward against a post. My friend hung his head and said, "*El hombre . . . es muerto.*"

Dead? Rudolfo killed the man? I chewed on my lip. The wind blew, and half a dozen tumbleweeds passed by the window. Not that I wasn't mad enough to have done that myself. I didn't know what to say, so I said nothing. Rudolfo said, "I never meant to kill him. He hit his head, and didn't get up."

He and I both stared at the floor, as if we'd find some answer there. I didn't know what to say. I didn't know if this made Rudolfo a hero to me, or a murderer. "Did he have any family?" I asked at last. "What did you do with him?"

"*¿Familia?* No one knows. We buried him. I felt I had to tell you."

A gust of wind pushed another tumbleweed across the yard. A couple of quail darted from its path. This man across the table from me had not tasted the liquor in his cup. I stood and stacked plates, my back to him.

Rudolfo said, "I want to take care of you, Sarah. Let me. I will make you a good husband. I will watch out for you. Your herds. Our land will be the biggest—"

"I'm not looking to get married, that's all. You saying you killed a man for my sake, that doesn't make for a romantic proposal."

"I feel very bad about this . . . thing that has happened. The man who did that thought it was good. You see, my thoughts are for your welfare. We both know the strength it takes to live on this land. And, Sarah, I ask you, think of the children. They need you. I need you. We can put this all in the past, forget about it. It won't matter."

"Rudolfo—"

"You see, Sarah, I have plans for the future. I want to run for governor. With you at my side."

Governor? Me at his side? Well, those words set my kettle boiling. Is that what this is about? Him needing a wife so he can go off and do politics? Why, I'd have more use for a man who went and held up a bank. If I married him, he'd have the land. The cattle. Water rights to my part of this dribble we call Cienega Creek, not to mention a new well. *And* someone to comb his children's hair and tie their bows, so he could dote on them and have their photographs put in the newspaper, and buy and sell cattle from his beautiful *oficina* at the capitol.

He stood then, heading for the door, and he said, "I need a wife. I'm asking you. But I will not ask you again. This . . . incident, it will not be spoken of again. When you make a decision, come to me like the old friends we are."

There are probably women all over this territory who would think that was as fine an offer as a person could have. I said, "Rudolfo, I have work to do."

In the bunkhouse, Mason was sleeping soundly, mouth open, snoring. I had cut up the last steak into little bits and made pan gravy for him, filling it with the steak, then poured it all over a piece of hearty bread, which I knew Mason was fond of. I left the plate by his bed with a towel across it and went to get some chores done.

While I worked, I reckoned I should have felt sorry for the misintentioned dead man who'd tried to ruin my windmill. But because of his untimely passing on, I could be forgiven for not wanting Rudolfo, and I didn't have to explain to anyone, not even him. It would spare his pride if he were to believe the rest of his life that my refusal was about that man who died. That sorry hombre likely got his desserts, too, for if he'd been found to have ruined a water tank and windmill and got hauled down to the sheriff in Cochise County, he'd have been hung that same afternoon. He wouldn't be doing Rudolfo any more favors. And I was free.

I walked home through a wind so stiff, I had to carry my hat in my hands. Hard wind and hot is no relief. It simply blasts your sweaty skin and clothes with dust, puts grit in your teeth. Chess once told me he'd gotten hit in the head by a lizard on the wind. I laughed and told him he'd better mind carrying too many tall tales in his pocket before they made a hole. He insisted it hit slap dab on his hat and knocked it off. Even showed me a little line shaped like the shadow of a lizard in the dust of his hat. Though we have a new well, we are not free of the drought, and the stifling thickness of the air has not brought any rain with it. Yesterday, a paloverde tree out by the barn just fell in half in a hot gust, and I thought nothing on earth could dry up a paloverde. They've got a tap root that reaches near to China, and can't be pulled out with a team of four mules.

The day was beginning to heat up something miserable. Until the rains come, we will all be wishing for winter. The round corral is close enough to the barn to haul in hay and water without much trouble, and we've gotten pretty handy at keeping the fifty-gallon barrel in the back of the flatbed. But the metal trough out there is in the sun, and gets hot enough to make coffee if water is left in it. It was near empty, and needing cleaning, so I dumped it over and took care of that. I dragged it under a stand of trees and brush, where it won't get as hot as it would out in the sun. I plan to get up all my old horses and keep them up here, where I can take care of them without having to search for them. I'm going to have Shorty and the boys build a lean-to over the trough today or to-morrow. And we'll all start hunting the retired horses.

About that time, Mason came along and said he was feeling better and had heard the racket I was making. He told me I'd surely have snakes getting in the trough, putting it near the brush. So he and I built some stilts and cut grease cans into slivers, then turned those upside down under the legs to keep the snakes out. It looked to me as if it should work pretty well. I filled the trough with a bucket from the big barrels, thinking to myself we'd done a good morning's work.

While I did that, Charlie and Chess rode south to Baker's spread to see when they expected to start gathering in their herd. Rudolfo has been saying he was going to organize everything, but he just puts it off. Something's got under his saddle blanket. Whether it's me that's the bur I can't tell. Any rate, they are going direct to Baker's and see what he's got planned. If we start from the ranchers near Patagonia and drove each bunch this way, by the time we get them combined, it won't mean any double back.

Gil and I rode out to the east pasture, hunting for my five old horses, that are no longer part of the working remuda. I rode a buckskin named Pally, and we took our time picking through the rocks and brush. After about an hour, I spotted one I was looking for—old Dan, a draft horse near eighteen hands, and he has got to be nearly thirty years old. He hardly moves, and I have expected to find his bones out there any day. His big nose has turned white, like an old man's hair. He's a good old horse, and as long as he is not ailing, I sure don't mind spreading him a sheaf of hay and a can of oats. Then there's Maize, a horse named after the grain, because he's kind of yellow-colored. Not much horse to look at now, but in his day, he could almost ride out from under you, cornering calves nearly faster than a dog. Best cutting horse on the place. All I had to do was catch sight of Maize and whistle, and he'd come following. That's how good a horse he was.

The rest of the riding stock is part of the remuda, the bunch of horses we use for everyday work. I usually take Pally or Stubs or Baldy, as they are my favorites. Stubs is one of Rose's colts. Rose is an all-around quarter horse. None of her offspring have been half the ride she was.

After I found Maize, I led him and Dan up to the round corral. Then I stayed in the corral, petting Rose awhile. I put some fly ointment on her face around her eyes and nose. She had a scratch on a flank from some kind of thorn, and I put some balm on that, too. Rose nickered and pushed her head against my back. Gilbert had built a first-rate shade over the water trough, and after he finished it up, he spent a while looking at the feet of all the old horses.

Rose bumped me with her nose and I scratched her between the ears. "You old sweetie," I said. When I was a girl and we'd first come here, I often spent a gentle afternoon sitting on her bare back and stretching full out, with my head on her rump, just lying there as she ambled around grazing. I used to spend hours staring at the sky or clouds, thinking about things. Now she is fat and a little stiff from not moving too much, and she's got a foot that hurts her at times where she got a bruise in the frog. That happened a long time ago. Maybe horses get rheumatism like old folks. When she saw I was going to brush her and tend her a little, she just lapped it up like a puppy. I stroked her all over, and she murmured and twitched her sides as if it tickled.

Then Gil and I went to the barn for Pillbox and Hunter. We led the mama into the round corral, and the colt followed at her side. What a wonder a baby is. Human or animal, I never fail to see the miracle of a new life. I put a cord around his neck that is a special one I braided from old cotton rags, bits of shirts and things. It is really soft for him to wear for a while as he gets used to something being on his neck. Then I rubbed his little legs and back, slow and gentle, until he quit fidgeting and stood still for it.

Gilbert said, "Mama, you want me to take the saddle off your ride for you?" He was busy stroking little Hunter, and spoke quietly. "Guess I should be doing some real work instead."

"No, I reckon I'll do it," I said. "Gentling that colt is real work, too. You've got your hands full there." I gave Pillbox an apple. I'd just turned to take the rig off Pally and turn him into the west corral when I heard hooves.

"Aunt Sarah!" a voice called. It had been in the back of my mind that Mary Pearl should be along anytime. She came up to the corral fence, her legs stretched around the horse's bare back. Mary Pearl said, "Granny Prine sent me to fetch you, Aunt Sarah. I think you'd better come. She's all head up, saying, 'Ernest is home. Ernest is home.'"

"Ernest's home?"

"Some boy just came walking up the road and knocked on the door. He's not old enough to be Uncle Ernest. I don't think he is much older than me, but he's tall."

I cupped my hands over my eyes to shade them so I could look her in the face, then said, "Granny thinks it's my brother?"

"Yes, ma'am. They're in our parlor right this minute."

"Lands sakes alive. Your Granny is going to start taking in roomers next. Gilbert?" I called. "You want to come see?"

"Go ahead, Mama. I'll get Charlie and be up there after a bit."

Mary Pearl clucked to her horse and turned him around as I got into my saddle.

We rode on a little ways, and about halfway there, Mary Pearl turned and said, "I saw you kissing El Maldonado."

I drew in my breath and stopped the horse. Flat out didn't know what to say, so I figured the hard honest truth would be the best. I said, "Well, that was a foolish thing I did. I had to explain to him that I didn't mean anything by it. Just got all tied up in happiness about the water coming in. He didn't take it too well. I'm afraid he thinks I care for him."

"Do you?" The tone of her voice was more angry than curious.

"Not like you're thinking. He's a good neighbor and I trust him. But I don't want to marry him."

She rearranged her hat—some old beat-up thing of her brother's—pulling it low in front, then fiddled with a thread at the hem of her skirt. "I don't want to marry anybody."

"That's all right." At least she wasn't looking to run off with some vaquero. I clucked to the horse. "Does everybody else know I did that?"

Mary Pearl laughed under her breath. "You sound like one of my sisters, caught writing a letter to a boy in town. I don't know if anyone else saw or not. Maybe not." She started her mount moving up the road, and I rode half a length behind.

Well, it would serve me right, I suppose. Proof, one more time, that any little thing a person does can be called to her name and have to be accounted for down the line. I'd really let myself go that night, what with all the tiredness and the excitement. "Well, maybe not," I said. "Are you still coming over to stay for a while?"

"Soon as I get the wash in off the line. It's my turn folding. I should be there before long. This boy coming along put off my chores for a bit." Mary Pearl straightened her hat again, trying to get it to suit her, and said, "Poor Granny is sure this fellow is Uncle Ernest. Wouldn't he be a grown man, though?"

I said, "Yes, he would. He's older than I am."

"She's getting addle-headed. Worse than usual." She picked at a thread on her pocket, twisting it around her finger. Mary Pearl's tiny hands reminded me of Granny's.

"Granny has just seen too much, and her mind just can't hold any more. Anything new comes along just won't go in."

"I know that feeling. Like Latin. Declining nouns always makes my head feel like it's full of cotton lint. I fall asleep."

I laughed. We were safely away from the subject of my errant kiss—away from her discomfort on the subject of men and women—safely into Latin nouns. I said, "Maybe Granny Prine feels like that, trying to figure out some things. Here's a new one for you: *efficiunt clarum studio.* Tell me what that is, tomorrow." I pretended not to see Mary Pearl roll her eyes, nor to hear the sound of her teeth clicking. We passed the gate into the yard and tied up at the rail by the porch. I took off my riding gloves and folded them into my waistband. "Let's get a look at this hombre. See what *this* one wants."

Well, there *was* a boy sitting there in the parlor with all the family gathered around. And he *was* the spitting image of Ernest, at the age when Ernest lost his leg from the knee down while we were traveling. Indians had circled us around, and after they damaged all the people they could, they stole Papa's horses. I reckon they stole my mama's mind, too, because a few days later, Papa died of infection from his wounds, and Granny has never been the same since. Everyone got quiet as Mary Pearl and I came in. I looked at the boy and at Granny beaming at him, her eyes glistening. Albert seemed confused, Savannah puzzled.

The boy himself was having a fine time, his hands loaded up with pound cake and a glass of milk. And had no idea how to manage them both in his lap and talk, too. Albert cleared his throat and said, "Sarah, this here fellow says his name is Ernest William Prine, Jr."

"How do?" I said. He didn't stand up, nor even nod. Not a lick of manners.

"I do rightly well, ma'am," he said, talking while trying to swallow a large bite of cake. He crossed his legs, putting one foot on a knee. He took a noisy swig of the milk and let a little air back up from his throat. "Ahh. Durn-burnit, that's good cake." He cast about as if he was addressing everyone, then said, "Truth be told, I go by my middle name, which is William—Willie. Willie, that's it. I'm shore pleased to make ya'll's acquaintances, after being told so much about you and all. Jus' call me Willie. Ma shore sets a store by all of ya'll. She truly does. So when I come of age, I says to her, I says, 'Ma, high time I set out to find my kin out in the territories and take up being part of the family.'"

Albert leaned on his elbows. "And your mother's Christian name would be?"

"Well, y'all knows her! Mrs. Ernest W. Prine. Her first name's Lulu—er, Felicity, I mean, but she goes by Lulu. That's it, Mrs. Felicity Lulu-bell Prine."

Albert sat back in his chair. Savannah glanced at me. I raised my brows but didn't say anything. Savannah said, "Esther, please fetch Aunt Sarah a piece of that cake, and something to drink."

Esther left to do it, leaving a chair empty next to Savannah, who patted the seat and motioned me over. Granny was clapping her little hands together, tucked up at her neck. She kept repeating, "Ernest's home. My boy's come home."

"Er you Aint Sair?" the boy asked. When I nodded, he said, "Well, I shore heard about you, yes. Mama said to pay you special mind. I figure to learn to shoot, and ride, and he'p you out. You know, real cowboyin'. Wrangling cows and all. Riding and roping and shooting up the town. Got m' boots."

He unfolded his long legs and wagged his feet back and forth, stretching them toward the center of the room. He was wearing the most amazing Mexican bullfight-wedding-fandango boots I have ever seen. They had to come from one of the big stores in town that sells to dudes in bowler hats, eastern blowhards who like to wear cut and tooled leather boots under a black three-piece suit. They were short stoves—barely came to midcalf on him—and he had his pants legs tucked into the tops of them. Anyone riding through the chaparral more than two feet would learn real fast not to do that.

Albert's second boy, Joshua, pursed his lips and said, "Well, you're all set, then. Those are sure enough some boots." Clover nodded. No one said a word. Esther came back with cake.

I took it, thanked her, and said, "Will you be staying, Ernest?"

"Yes'm. Yonder with Granny," the boy said, "and, Aint Sair, everyone calls me Willie. Isn't that a cowboy name, Willie? Else I figure to change it to Jesse or Frank."

I said, "Willie's as good a name as any. Granny's got her hands full already. She doesn't need to be cooking and washing for you. She's staying with me regularly now. Why don't you come on over, with me and my boys? We're fixing to start gathering up the neighbors' herds. Cattle work. Could use another hand."

"Oh no," Granny said. "No, I want him home, honey. Home with me for a while. I'm going to make him some buttermilk pie. It's so good to have him back."

Willie grinned like a dog with a piece of meat in its mouth. "I'm pleased to stay there, too. I don't take up too much space, do I, Granny? Still, I'd shore like to go rounding up. Figure to start right in cowboyin'."

Just then, Charlie and Gil came in. Charlie took off his hat and said, "Afternoon, Aunt Savannah, Uncle Albert, Granny. Mama, Mr. Baker is putting off again. Now says they'll start come Wednesday. They're still collecting hands. Here's why, too. Baker says he's got someone to take over the payments. After the roundup, whatever money is made is to be sent to this address, care of Denver, Colorado." He pulled a square of paper out of his chest pocket and handed it to me.

I took the paper and stared at it. Selling out. Lands. I knew the drought was bad, but I was guilty of not seeing how my neighbors were faring. I hadn't even offered the Bakers some help. Now they'd be gone, and no telling who'd come take their place. Good neighbors are worth keeping. I should have done more.

Willie said, "Tracking, that's something to get the knack of, too. Why, I read about the West in ever' dime novel I could find. A-sitting under the picture of naked Dutch Ora Lee. She's a-hanging over the bar in a saloon back home, place name of Skeet's."

Savannah gasped, along with Rachel, Rebeccah, and Esther. Mary Pearl just made a face of disgust. Albert, Josh, and Clover frowned. Savanna said, "Charles, Gilbert, this is your cousin Willie. His name is Ernest William Prine, Junior."

My boys stared at him. After a bit, Charlie said, "Pleased to meet you. Name's Charles Elliot. This here's my baby brother, Don Quixote."

Gilbert shot him a look and scrunched down his eyebrows. "Gil," he said. Then he nervously shook hands with Willie—Ernest junior.

Willie's face showed his every thought, and he said, "Donkey Hotie?" Gilbert said again, "Gil. Gilbert. Call me Gil."

Every chair in the room was taken, but Clover and Josh stood up. Clove said, "You boys take a seat. Any of that cake left, Esther Sue?"

"*I'll* go look," said Mary Pearl. "I've done nothing but sit around all day." We all knew that was never true about Mary Pearl, but her saying that was just her telling us how odd everything felt to her, too.

Silence hung in the room like a blanket had been dropped on us. Willie gobbled cake and nodded, now and then gulped milk, then wiped his face with his sleeve. He fished in his pocket, took out a little bag, pulled it open, and gingerly lifted out a slip of paper. He chuckled, saying, "Time for a little smoke to settle it down."

Albert stood. "Not in this house. We don't abide tobacco."

The boy looked from face to face, a kind of dare in his expression, as if he expected one of Albert's or my children to take his side or declare him clear of the rules because he was a newcomer. Not seeing a soul willing to put in a word for him, the smile left him, and he sullenly poured the grains of tobacco back into the pouch, putting the paper in on top of it. "At's all right," he said. "It can wait." He grinned again, but this time it was forced and odd-looking.

Granny got up from her chair and said, "I'm going to go home and put on a little dinner for you, honey. You come on home when you finish visiting."

The boy shook his head and looked around the room at us after she left.

Looking him square in the eye, I felt like I was seeing my brother, young, skinny. I said, "Well, Ernest—that is, Willie—why don't you tell us about yourself. Why you've come all this way when we've never heard about you before."

He nodded, then nodded again, like he was hearing his own thoughts. Finally, he said, "I sure do b'lieve I owe you that much. You never heard o' me and I didn't hear of you 'til lately. You see, Ma and me, we was down-and-out, you might say. So one day after she told me about you folks out here, she up and left. She done that before, but she usually come home a day or two later. Didn't have no way to know if her troubles caught up with her or not. I waited near two weeks and then I lit out. I figured if I had some people, if they knew about me, maybe they'd want me, since she didn't anymore. If you want me to go, I'll just head on down the road."

I caught sight of both my boys' faces. Charlie, in particular, looked as if the boy had been trying to sell him a wooden horse. But I could see how he looked like my brother as plain as day. I said, "Willie, are you being chased by someone? Some law looking for you?"

"No'm." He looked toward Albert and said, "No, sir." His lower lip stuck out, making him look for all the world like Ezra when he's on a pout. "Nobody looking me at all. I ain't asking y'all to take me in like some freeloader. I work for my supper."

Savannah said, "Well, you may stay, young man."

Albert added, "We look out for family." I suppose that meant Albert had come to the same conclusion I had.

"I don't know nothing except city living," the boy said. "But I'll try."

"If you're willing to lend a hand," Gilbert said, "there's always work to do."

"Thank you, folks. Thank you much. Well, Granny's fixing me some dinner. I'll mosey over there and wait." At the door, he swept up a bundle tied in a ratty cloth with coarse string. His kit. I hadn't noticed it when I came in. He let the screen door slam. We listened for his high-heeled boots to clear the porch floorboards. When we heard the crunch of the sand and gravel, Clover let out a long, low whistle.

"Mercy," said Savannah.

Albert said, "He does look like Ernest. And that kid has to be six feet tall, but I bet he's not more than fifteen years old."

Charlie said, "You ever see anything like those boots?"

Josh laughed and said, "And the size of 'em?"

Gilbert said, "Why, that critter'd be tall if he didn't have so much turned off for foot." The boys all laughed softly.

I said, "Well, the person I'm worried about is Granny, having him over there, and no one else watching what's going on. And Ernest? If he had a son, don't you think he'd've told us? If he knew, that is?" We all sat and thought awhile.

Albert said, "Wasn't Felicity living somewhere east—Saint Louis or Memphis or someplace? What I want to know is, what got into this kid all of a sudden for him to come clear across the country wearing a two-bit set of clothes and a pair of hundred-dollar boots."

"Maybe," Clover said, "maybe he's heard something from the army about Uncle Ernest coming home. Or maybe he figures he'll stand to inherit something."

Then I said, "Well, I'm pretty sure from the looks of him that he's Ernest's boy. Still and all, no matter the reason he's here, it isn't right for Granny to have to do for him." What was really going through my mind was that family or no, we don't know what kind of person he is, except that he was born and raised by Felicity—Miss *Lulu*. The state Granny's in, she really believes he's our brother, not our nephew.

"Savannah, Albert," I said, "I want that boy over at my place. This time, I'm going to be stubborn. I know you'd watch over Granny as good as I would, or better. But this rapscallion will be better off if he's away from your girls, and where my fellows can keep him in their sights. Even if we have to drag him everywhere we go. We've just got to convince Granny of it." Here I'd made a standing promise to be five miles south in two days, helping my neighbors gather a herd, just like they'd help with mine, and the only solution I could come up with was to have Mama and Willie both stay at my place. I had been planning to get my boys back to the big house when we were done at Baker's. Now they'd both have to take the remaining room, or stay in the bunkhouse.

I said my good-days to Savannah's family, and then Charlie, Gilbert, and I followed Willie's footsteps to my mama's little house. My boys told me in quiet voices that they'd stay in the bunkhouse for now, and would help with getting Willie broke in. I smiled when Gilbert said that. "Like he's a colt."

"Mustang, more likely," Charlie said. "I'll stack Granny some firewood here while you cobble up something." Gilbert nodded. The two stayed outside.

I spent twenty minutes helping my mama fix a dinner for Willie, all the while talking a blue streak about how I needed her to come live at my place. Willie sat and watched the whole time, now and then saying something about how hungry he was, how long it had been since he'd had a square meal. Mama finally turned around and said, "Sarah, it ain't like you to wheedle. What's the matter?"

"Nothing's the matter," I said. "But Albert and Savannah have a houseful, and now my boys are living in the bunkhouse. You'd be here all alone. My house is empty as a tin can, and I'd just like Willie and you to come stay a couple of nights. Plenty of time to talk."

Granny called out the window, "Charlie, Gilbert, you two sit down there and have a bite. Always a plate for you at this table."

"Thanks, Granny," they both said. It didn't matter to those boys that they'd just had cake; they could always eat a meal.

She said to me, "Have some of this corn bread. You're wasting away."

Willie stopped eating for a minute and chewed, staring across the room as if he was listening to something. He swallowed, making a noise. I still spoke toward my mama, although I meant for him to hear it. "Besides, I need the help. We're about to go bust with hauling water to the stock, even though the new well works fine. And roundup's coming. Yesterday, I just about met myself coming the other way."

She said, "Well, that's true enough. Don't know why you'd want me sitting there collecting dust, but you need Ernest. All this while, we've had to do without him, and there's plenty of work to be done. Papa would want him to lend a hand. As long as he's home, he can just start right in making up for lost time. Ernest? Your sister needs us up to the house. Finish up, and then pack your duds. We'll go visit a spell."

"Yes'm, Granny," he said, and gave a flapping little mock salute like he was a soldier. Then he laughed.

Granny seemed satisfied, and she said, "I'll wash the dishes, and Ernest, you harness Belle. Reckon you'll drive, too." Gilbert and Charlie took off for home. Well, after a while—with me overseeing something he apparently had never done before—Willie got Mama's mule Belle in her traces and drove the little old buggy to the front porch. When all was said and done, though, I decided if we were to get to my house alive, I'd better be the one driving.

At my place, Willie waited while I unloaded Charlie's books and keepsakes from the shelves and moved them to Gilbert's room. I checked the bureau for anything left behind, then pronounced it ready for Willie to move in. He flung his kit in the corner and bounded onto the bed, crossing his legs and grinning at the ceiling. Then I reckon he saw me frowning, for he sat up suddenly and said, "Time for resting later. You just show me what work you want done, and I'll get after it for you."

Granny put a dress on a nail behind the door in April's old room and set her nearly flat carpetbag on the short table by the window. I could tell she didn't plan to stay long. Maybe, though, this would be sort of a trial, a breaking-in period. Later on, I'll try to convince her to stay permanently. Then she sat in the chair by the window and folded her hands. She closed her eyes, and a pleasant, rested smile came to her face.

The boy followed me from room to room as I moved things, all the while looking this way and that with his eyes bugged out, like he was seeing something just crazy. "Aint Sair?" Willie said to me. "How quick can we get to learning me the farm? Got to be ready for when Pa gets home."

"First thing," I said, "a farm is where you grow crops—wheat, corn. This is a ranch. We run cattle and horses. At times, it's slow and lazy, and other times you'll work yourself off at the knees for days on end. We call our neighbors friends, except for the Wainbridges. That old man killed three of my dogs on my own land for no reason five years ago, and he hasn't said he's sorry yet. While you're here, you'll be expected to tote your load as best you're able. And to get more able as time goes by."

"Golly jee-hozuz, I didn't mean—I . . . I come a long way to get here."

I wasn't mad at him. I was careful to make my words sound friendly but sincere. "Well, I know that. Another thing—we don't abide cussing, particularly in the house. No tobacco, no cussing, no spitting. Wash your hands and face before meals. Everything else will come a little at a time."

He kicked at the floor, drawing a scuffed circle. Then he said, "I was just a-wondering where you keep the guns."

"Put up," I said. "Why?"

"I done read where everyone out west totes iron. Only I don't see any."

I wanted to ask where he'd read that. Likely in another dime novel whilst sitting under a naked portrait of some other harlot. Granny came in and asked me to fetch her some water to make lemonade for Ernest. I wondered if lemonade would salve what he was wanting. She was bound and determined to feed and water him like a pet dog.

Well, we just got him sat in front of some lemonade, when along came Savannah's girls Esther and Mary Pearl, carrying a basket between them. They came up to the porch, and Esther said, "Mama sent over this stack of Clover's and Josh's clothes. Thought maybe Willie could find something that fits."

I watched him closely. He was eyeing those girls, and what I saw on his face wasn't any brotherly kind of affection. I said, "Tell your *cousins* thank you, Willie. These girls are your blood relatives. Just like sisters." Usually, I get a notion about a person right off. Could I have been wrong? I decided right then to keep a close eye on him. Not that he'd done anything, just because I couldn't figure him.

"Never had no sisters. Thanks *to* you, ladies," he said. "But I brought my own duds. Well, it's what I got on. Maybe a new shirt or two wouldn't hurt. What's that you're carrying?" He dipped his head at Mary Pearl.

She said, "Basket. Like Esther said."

"Naw. I mean that there."

Mary Pearl looked down at herself. Esther was wearing a full pinafore tied over her dress for doing housework. Mary Pearl had a half apron tied at the waist. She shrugged. "Reckon I don't know what you mean," she said.

Willie grinned and made a noise low in his throat. "Like the Irish pirate queen. A dagger at the belt."

Forevermore! The boy read more than dime novels. Mary Pearl was explaining something to him about the hunting knife she keeps in a leather holster at her waist. I sat listening to the explanation, and tried to figure this boy. Savannah wants her girls to grow up genteel, and at the same time, she knows this is a hard land. Esther is too mild to arm herself, and she clings to her mother's teachings. She leaned forward, listening to Mary Pearl, a troubled expression on her face. Mary Pearl would defend herself or another, and is all around a whole lot more use, to boot. What was going through my mind was the startling thing Willie'd said. A wastrel he might be, but a well-read one at least.

"What year did you do in school, Willie?" I asked.

"Ma'am?"

"What year, that you'd know about an Irish pirate queen?"

He grinned, looking foolish—just exactly the way I remembered my brother Ernest looking when he was about to play a joke on someone. "I been to school some." He turned back to Mary Pearl and said, "You don't know how to use that, do you?"

Esther caught Mary Pearl's eye, and it looked as if she was trying to say something with her worried expression.

Mary Pearl said, "I been known to stick a fence post some." Then Mary Pearl peered at Willie from the corner of her eye while she said to me, "Mama wants us home to finish helping with the canning. We're only doing eighteen quarts today, so if you want me to, Aunt Sarah, I'll run some of Ezra's schoolbooks over after supper tonight." She smiled, all dimples and beguiling. Mary Pearl is about as smart as a razor, and she has a little rascalness in her blood, too.

She was laughing to herself, I could see, thinking what Willie was about to step into.

I nodded. Let her laugh. A girl can be too smart for her own good. Old Willie was still just grinning, looking from me to Granny and then to the girls. He hadn't caught her little mean grin, thought she was just being polite. All the while, I could feel myself setting a course for him, this pushy stranger, this trespasser, cocky and grinning, looking like my brother, and as young and full of himself as Ernest senior always was. No telling why he'd really come here, but no denying he was family. That alone settled it: No Prines living under my roof were going to reach accountability without geometry, Latin and poetry, geography and stellar navigation, United States history, and at least a passing knowledge of Greco-Roman art forms. I'd schooled my boys and Savannah's children up through their college exams, those that were old enough, straight from my bookshelf. Every one of them got in, too. My shelf of books was in there waiting for him. This boy would have to pass muster, just like the rest.

He grinned at me. I smiled right back, too. First thing I planned to do was judge how far he'd gone. A first-class education, that's what he's about to get. "Welcome to the family," I said. "There's some responsibility for you, and some fine blessings."

"School, too? Ya'll're nice folks," Willie said.

Mary Pearl giggled and touched Esther's arm, turning to go.

I said, "Get along home, chickens." Mary Pearl laughed louder, not even trying to hide her glee. When the sound of the girls' feet on the porch had faded, I said to Willie, "Now, don't be ashamed. Tell the truth. How far have you gone in school? We believe in normal education here. Makes a man out of you."

"I just want to larn to rope an' ride an' stuff."

"Well, we'll teach you that, and a whole lot more. Right now, we've got our hands full with the summer chores and an early roundup because of the drought. Come fall, when the work's all done, you'll be doing school lessons to prepare for college. Manners, morals, too. How's that sound to you?"

Willie stared at me like I'd just hit him with a wet dishrag. He stared at my mama for a long while, then down at his hands. He picked at his fingernails, rubbed his nose. He said, "I couldn't go to college. That's for city boys in starched collars. I'm ignorant as they come."

"Not if you stay here," I said. "If you are family, and you seem to be, then you have a right to become a gentleman. A real gentleman."

He rubbed his calloused hands against his pant legs.

Mama nodded, as if she thoroughly agreed with me. "Sarah, do you have any blue thread?" she asked.

With Willie come to stay, Albert and Savannah withdrew their permission for Mary Pearl to live at my house, for the time being. She could come and go as much as she wanted to, chores permitting, but she was not to spend the night until he'd been there at least a week and seemed "settled in."

Willie followed me like a motherless calf. He asked questions about everything from why a brown hen lays white eggs and a black hen lays brown to how to tell one snake from another. I showed him Caesar, the six-foot-long bull snake that lives in the garden. "It'll scare you sometimes, seeing him draped through the beans, if you aren't looking for him," I said. "Here's how a rattler's head looks, and he's got a tail like this." I drew in the dirt with a stick. "Don't ever touch one without seeing the tail, and don't kill him if he doesn't have a rattle. Old Caesar there keeps the pocket mice from ruining the garden. One time, we had one get in and eat so much, he couldn't get back through the fence. After that, Caesar came for lunch one day, and we are pleased to let him stay."

"Gol-durn," he said, rubbing his chin. "A snake to watch the garden. You reckon I can touch it?"

"Maybe. Sometimes you can find him feeling sleepy. If he's feeling his oats, he'll still bite you. You just won't die from it. One time, he got caught in a tomato string and I had to hold his head with one hand and clip the string off with these scissors. He wrapped clear around my arm up to the shoulder. Soon as I got the string off him, I turned him loose, and he took off for some shade."

He slapped his hat against his leg and said, "God Almighty!"

We had a discussion then about why a person shouldn't plant cucumbers and gourds in the same garden. At everything he saw, Willie was wide-eyed with wonder. He was also clumsy, and just as likely to step on a pepper plant as to pull a weed. When he watered the garden, he washed out roots of things. Willie needed a mother as if he'd never had one. I never saw a boy so eager to learn new things yet so bitterly upset when he was corrected. One aspect of him would make a fine college student, and the other might cause him to give up before he'd half started. I reckoned I'd seen evidence aplenty of that trait in the family line already.

After supper, Gilbert told me that Willie'd been looking at his set of ivory

.44's, and admiring them without bothering to see if they were loaded or not. I told him just to take the bullets out, as he doesn't carry that set anyway.

Underlying everything was his hunger for guns, seemed like. And his wearisome picking at me to say if I'd ever shot someone. "That was in the old days," I told him. "Indian Wars. There's no law against defending yourself, but there's a lot more to know about handling a gun than how to draw a pistol. Mostly, it's how not to get yourself in that fix in the first place." When he asked me if I had ever been shot, that was the last I could take. I gave him an hour-long lecture about what you do not say to a lady under any circumstances, top of which are items about personal health. I reckon he'd learned more than he'd bargained for that afternoon, but he quit pestering me about personal things. That night, Charlie told me Willie'd been after him about shooting, too.

Chapter Ten

The next morning, I made Willie go with Gilbert and Charlie out to the range. While they were down by Baker's place, they found a hank of good rope, some wire twists, and pliers where somebody had dropped them. Gilbert and Willie spent the better part of three hours tracking down the owner of the tools.

Willie came to me after that, thirsty and hot. "Why'n tarnation," he said, "did I have to waste the whole morning doing that? Gilbert told me he'd learn me to shoot a rifle this morning, and the whole durn-burned time we chased around, taking stuff to people. Then he tells me he's got work to do, and to go home." He took off his fancy boots and banged them on the floor, dumping half a cup of sand from each one.

First thing I wanted to do, naturally, was box his ears straight to Texas. But I took hold of myself, set down right by him, and said, "Willie, a man is known by two things, the people he rides with and the value of his word. This family has a reputation for being straight-up. That's who you're riding with. A man who is honest about a piece of wire will be honest about a horse, about his money, and about his life. Someone who'd steal something as silly as a wire might just steal a whole lot more."

"That's about the stupidest thing I heard, ever."

"You ride with us, you do like us."

I saw him bristling up again. "Tarnation."

I smiled, and nodded. "Sometimes it's a lot more trouble to do the right thing."

He grinned. Then he said, "Aint Sair, this being a rancher is pure work."

"Yes, it is. Now," I said, "another part of living by your word is taking up what you put down, not leaving something of yours that interferes with someone else." I pointed to the two piles of sand on the kitchen floor.

"How's that interfering with anybody?"

"I spent half an hour cleaning this floor."

He jerked his head. "It weren't dirty to begin with. You wasted your time."

"That's because I don't let long-legged jaspers dump their boots here. Take that little broom and brush that outside." He did as he was told, screwing his lips around as if he'd been a green horse with a new bit in his mouth. But he did it. While he swept, I said, "You know, your aunt Savannah says sand and sin are one and the same. Tolerate a little, and soon it'll be a lot."

He held the broom in his hands, peering at it as if it were strange. "What? Does it grow? Sand?"

"It does in the Territories," I said, laughing, "like weeds. Here's some lemonade for you. Did Charlie tell you where he was going this afternoon?"

"Down to that big house. I reckon that old Mex is one mean son of a gun."

"Who's that?"

"Old man Maldaraedo."

"Don't know how you figure that. The Maldonados have been our friends for two decades."

"I seen him take a horse halter to a fellow and slap him out of a saddle."

I said, "Well, what did the man do before that?"

"He was just trying to get the stubborn thing to move. Kicked him with some of them Mexican spurs. I like those kind with all the jingle. Big old stars with about a hundred spikes."

"I better not see any Mexican spurs on this place, or I'll chase off the fellow wearing 'em, too. Nothing but a little spit would wear something like that."

My mama was snoozing in the rocker on the porch. When I said that, she suddenly came awake and hollered, "Sarah Agnes, did I just hear you cuss?"

"No, ma'am," I said. "No more than usual, anyhow." Willie laughed.

Granny said, "I'm going yonder to Savannah's house, where the air is cleaner," and she took off like the wind.

I started up the road, caught up to her, and took Granny's arm. "Willie!

I'm going with Granny to Aunt Savannah's," I called. "When you get that kindling split and stacked, you can just take it easy."

I talked about Willie on the way with my mama. Long as I left out the part of him being Ernest's son, instead of Ernest himself, she seemed to have a pretty good idea of how he acted. Willie was a kind of boy I'd never known before. The day had gone well, but sometimes when I tried to talk straight to him, he'd get his back up or get a wounded look on his face. When I'd go gentle with him, he'd sometimes get ornery or say something rude. I didn't mention that to her. Just seemed like something I couldn't prove nor ask about. But I kept hearing in my memory him saying how his mother had run off and left him. Even a mother like Felicity was still a mother, I suppose.

Granny stayed in the kitchen, where the girls washed clothes in five big tubs. I went outside to where Savannah was hanging things on the line. Savannah and I speculated about Willie, whether he was the type to grow up to become an outlaw or some kind of hellfire–Holy Ghost preacher. I laughed and said, "Maybe both."

Poor Savannah has been ailing a little with this baby she's expecting. Her feet keep swelling up on her. She says she has trouble sleeping, and some back pain that doesn't seem warranted from a strain. That makes me worry for her, since that was exactly how I felt when I had that boy baby who never drew a breath.

They'd hired Flores's wife, Conciliada, to help them when the work was overwhelming. Other times, Conciliada went to watch out for Granny and cook her some meals now and then. She was out in the yard, too, and came from behind a white sheet when she heard us talking. "Señora Elliot!" she called. "I hear we are to be cousins. I am so happy."

Savannah looked toward me over her shoulder. Clothespins stuck from her mouth as she rearranged a shirttail on the line. I looked at Savannah, then to Conciliada. I said, "Cousins? How will that be?"

Conciliada said, "Doña Celia Maldonado was my cousin. May she rest in peace. If you marry her husband, won't we be relatives?"

The clothespins fell from Savannah's lips. She stared at me.

I said, "I don't have any plans to marry Rudolfo Maldonado." I felt myself flush dark red, and sweat broke out on my face. Maybe more than one person *had* seen that foolish kiss.

Savannah said, "Did he propose to you?"

"Yes," I said. "I told him no." Conciliada looked a little sad. I said, "I'm not ready to get married again. He's a nice fellow and all." Even as I said it, I felt doubts about him being so nice. He'd always been a friend, but that business of the man he'd killed over tearing up my windmill still bothered me. It wasn't that justice in the territories hadn't come in the form of a ten-cent slug of lead before. I just couldn't put my finger on what I didn't like. The more earnest he seemed about wanting to marry me, the more my heart seemed to be pulling me away from Rudolfo.

Well, I'd no sooner gotten the last pin screwed down over a dishrag when an owl, mottled white and brown and big as a house cat, sailed past us just a few feet overhead. In these parts, it's more common to see hawks of a dozen varieties in the sky than not. What you hardly ever see in the daylight is a barn owl. Its wings cut through the air in complete silence, ghostly, as if it were just imaginary.

Conciliada's eyes grew round and fear clutched her. She made the sign of the cross three times in a row. Then she said, "*No mas trabajo. ¡Acabado!*" And she turned and ran from the yard, saying something fast and low. She disappeared down the road toward Granny's place. Farther up is where she and Flores have a little house.

I turned to Savannah. My sister-in-law held absolutely no toleration for superstitions that touched on heathenness. I didn't say anything about the owl and how I'd heard from Shorty that the old-time Mexicans believed it only flew in the daytime to carry a message of death. Good thing we were all Methodists. I said, "I don't know what got into her, but I'm not marrying Rudolfo."

July 8, 1906

Each and every Sunday since we moved here, except for one when she was giving birth, Savannah has put on a black starched dress and a white bonnet, and she teaches anyone who will listen a Sunday school lesson. Folks come for miles. It is a nice time. Once in awhile, folks stay for supper, which is potluck, but mostly it is just us, and still a fine way to spend an afternoon.

Sundays in their house begin and end with regular feeding and watering chores, but no gardening or mending. Once Sunday School is completed with long, quiet prayers, the Sabbath is observed by doing needlepoint and quiet reading, and no laughing out loud.

I asked Savannah once, as she insisted the Lord's Day was for rest, how did she figure to rest, what with fixing meals for ten people three times a day—more if my bunch came—on top of teaching Sunday School to all the children in the county. But she said there wasn't any way to get around it that she could see. Even if all the food was served cold, someone still had to put it on a plate, then wash up afterward.

Savannah said that the rest must be of a different kind. Animals still had to eat. Cows must be milked. She said she depended on the Lord for inner peace and didn't worry about the other kind. Reckon we work so hard that when I look for peace behind closed eyes, I tend to fall asleep. I knew what she meant, though. I always found mine on the hill under the jacaranda tree.

We finished our meal today and pushed back our chairs, talking about heading for their wide front porch, lazy as lizards in the afternoon heat. Flores's wife, Conciliada was there, helping cook and clean, and Rachel and Rebeccah had already washed most of the dishes. Esther and Mary Pearl were drying them. The twins went to get their books from the parlor. Savannah and I linked arms and went to the porch. Albert smiled at us and patted the chair next to him for his wife. Joshua, who was sitting on a long wooden bench under the shade of a bougainvillea, moaned, putting his head in his hands. He called out, "Conciliada? Did you put something new in the tamales?"

Conciliada came ambling over, hands on her hips. "No, Señor Josh. The same. You didn't like them?"

Josh leaned forward, rubbing at sweat gathering in a rush on his face. "Oh glory. I'm sick." Josh wrenched his hands at his middle. Then he faced us, wide-eyed, and suddenly headed for the backyard.

Conciliada was worried. "I'm sure it's not the food, *señoras y señors*. I cooked fresh today *los tamales*."

Several minutes later, he came back, weakly holding the porch rail. "You all please excuse me. I'm just going to sit on the back porch and sip some water. I'm feeling scoury, too; need to be nearer the privy."

"No one else feeling poorly?" Savannah asked. "Well, thank goodness for that. Must be Josh got hold of something."

Charlie said, "Or something just got hold of him."

I turned to Savannah and said, "Now, there's a hundred other things to give a boy the scours. Let's just hope he got some sour milk or something. He'll be all right."

Clove shook his head. "Aunt Sarah," he said, "if Josh is up to drinking curdled milk, he deserves what he's getting." Clover went and put his head in the front door. He called over his shoulder, "He's not in here. I can hear him back by the outhouse. Doing the coyote love call."

Savannah sighed and rolled her eyes. "Son, please!"

We left Josh his privacy on the back porch, and the rest of us settled in chairs on the front. I handed Willie one of my boys' favorite books, *Treasure Island*. Told him to sit still and read, as we were observing the Lord's Day, too. He cut his eyes this way. Nevertheless, he started reading it, and before long, there was no sound from him but the turning of pages and a nervous throat clearing, a sound I'd heard him make before. We lolled away the day reading and napping, the girls and Savannah doing needlework.

Gilbert offered to stay with Josh, saying he'd watch the "old tyke" so Savannah and Albert could rest, and that he'd call if Josh seemed seriously ill. Charlie, Willie, Granny, Chess, and I ambled home. Our day of rest would still end with our feeding and watering, and that had to be done before dark.

That night, I wound the clock, turned out the lamps in the parlor, and checked in Granny's room just in case she'd left a candle lit. The breeze that came in the windows was cool. It felt good, but it was more proof of how dry the sky was. Night settled into the house, and the only light came from the back porch, where Charlie was sharpening a knife, and from the kitchen, where Chess pushed a threadbare rag over the worktable. He said, "How's our boy Josh?"

"Same, I reckon," I said.

Chess was quiet for a while; then he said, "I know why you did that, asking that boy to come here."

"You mean Willie?" I was really proud of the way Willie had stuck his nose deep into that book all afternoon.

"Surely. He's a tinhorn, but I don't think he'd mean your mama any harm. He still wearing them Mexican boots like a fandango dancer?"

"Wouldn't Ernest have told me if he had a son? I've got two dozen letters in there, and not word one about a boy. Specially a smart-alecky one like this."

"Thought you should know this. Yesterday, he says to me he wants to quick-draw a pistol. Found that old revolver you keep behind the sugar jar in the kitchen, then went outside while you were gone to Albert's place. He killed two fence posts and Old Bitsy."

"My best settin' hen?"

He nodded. "Through the gut, so she wasn't fit to eat, either."

"Well. Why'd it take you so long to tell me?"

"I told him to be a man, and tell you himself. Told him every way there was. I was hoping he'd do it; then I decided this morning during Miss Savannah's prayers that if he wouldn't tell you, then I'd have to. I scolded him. Only good it did was now he steers clear of me."

"He didn't tell me. I thought we were getting along pretty well." I stared at the table Chess was working on. His rag went around in circles, a scattering of bread crumbs next to it. In the dim light, Chess couldn't make out the top of the table.

Chess nodded. "Where're our boys?"

"Gilbert's sitting with Josh. Charlie's putting an edge on a couple of blades. He'll be along directly. Reckon we'll take Willie gathering with us. Maybe he can fill Josh's boots, but I doubt it. I declare, if it's not one thing, it's two."

Chess said, "He'd never fill 'em. Josh's boots are working boots. Not enough fancy folderol for that fellow."

Chess sounded purely crotchety. I patted his shoulder and said, "Get some rest."

Well, next morning, I walked back to Savannah and Albert's house just after sunup. I went to see how the boys had managed, if anyone else took sick, and to get Gilbert to work with Hunter for a few minutes. He is a real good hand with horses. Gilbert told me his poor cousin had run to the outhouse every ten minutes or so until midnight, when the lower part of his innards started working double time, too. Josh had slept on the porch, leaning at the edge, boots on, so he could run.

Gilbert said during the night he awoke several times to check on Josh, and felt his cousin's head for a fever, but he never noticed one. Gil said Josh and he were talking and Josh said he'd 've sworn there were bugs in his cup. "Then," Gilbert said, "Josh asked for well water instead of from the olla, and he fell hard to sleep this morning. I had some pancakes and eggs and a beefsteak. I went out to the porch again, and old Josh was in the rocking chair, covered with a blanket, snoring like a beehive." Gilbert picked at his teeth with a twig. "I said to him he'd missed some good eating, but if it wasn't going to stay put, it was a waste of good food to feed him."

"Well," I said, "you boys are so kindhearted, it makes a mother proud."

"Can't figure it, though. If it was something in the food, the rest of us would be sick by now." He rolled his eyes at me, and said, "Old Josh said he was going to help load the wagon, and I told him to stay here, or I'd lay into him."

Along came Clove and Charlie with extra cups of coffee for their brothers. Josh took his, looking suspiciously at it. "Maybe it'll taste like something more than yesterday's bathwater," he said, and sipped slowly. "Lands sakes, Charlie. Glad you put a little coffee in this cup of sugar."

Charlie laughed and said, "Clove said you liked it sweet. Just trying to be obliging."

Clover said, "Make it sticky enough, maybe you'll stay in the saddle."

Josh moaned, and it turned into sort of a growl. "Thanks."

"You boys enjoy your coffee. It's going to be a long day," I said. "And Joshua, don't you even think about coming to work today. You just get well."

"Yes 'm, Aunt Sarah. I'm going to bed. Yonder comes my replacement, fellows." Willie was walking toward the house. He had a lariat in his hands and was swinging a loop beside his leg as he came, making figures in it. He had his hat pushed down so low, he could hardly see out from under it.

Savannah and I started packing up food she was sending to the gathering. All the girls were busy helping in the kitchen. They are always generous with the pecan cookies and doughnuts and fried peach pies. Savannah stood near me at their kitchen worktable. She said, "Girls, you all go carry those baskets to Aunt Sarah's house." She laid her hand on my arm gently for just a moment. "Go along now. We'll be right behind. It'll be a nice walk. No need to rig up a buggy for some cookies."

It was taking her a long time to put on shoes. Leaning back on the bench, I put my head against the wall and closed my eyes. Although I do not approve of, and generally do not engage in, eavesdropping, I could hear the boys talking on the porch clear as if they were in the room. They weren't trying to be particularly quiet, and I wasn't trying to listen. I just heard it. Gilbert said, "Lord a mercy. It's taking me, too."

"What's that?" Charlie asked.

"The scours that Josh's been suffering. My gut feels like the entrails are about to become outtrails."

"Isn't there some epidemic that does that?" Charlie asked.

Gilbert moaned. Then he said, "Yep. But there's never been cholera in Arizona Territory. Too hot in the summer and too cold in the winter."

I leaned through the open window and said, "I heard that, Gilbert. You sick?"

"Yes, ma'am. I'm afraid so. Oh, oh—" And he dashed toward the outhouse.

When he came back, he walked slowly, and planted himself on the side of the porch, his feet hanging off. Charlie said, "Think you can ride anyway? Everything's packed, and the horses are saddled."

I told him, "I don't want you out riding in this heat if you're going to suffer like Josh. Him, either. You'll both have a heart spell if you take the scours in the sun. Charlie, you and Clove hitch the buggy for Savannah. She's tired."

Charlie called back, "Gil can ride home with you and Aunt Savannah."

Savannah appeared at the door at that moment. Suddenly, Ezra stomped down the stairs and ran into the room, waving wildly with one hand, the other hand over his mouth. He made a straight line for the kitchen door. After several minutes, he came back and flopped into his mama's reading chair. He said, "Mama, my whole breakfast just went down the side of the house." He closed his eyes. "I'm gonna die."

Loud voices came from the front porch: a man yelling, a second, higher voice shouting in return. Then there was scuffling and a loud bang, and the door swung open. In came Clover, snarled around and dragging Willie. Willie was dark red in the face, clenching with all his strength to Clover's large elbow, which was crooked around his neck. Willie kicked wildly, and Clover gave him a quick boot to the backside and, flexing his arm, jerked his head. He said, "Settle your oats, boy. This isn't over yet. We're going to let them decide what to do with you."

"What is going on?" Albert asked. "Clove?" Ezra opened his eyes and watched, unmoved. Gilbert hadn't moved from the porch, either. He just frowned and rubbed his temple with one hand.

"Joshua!" Clover called. "Joshua Prine, get yourself out of bed and come handle this. You get the first lick at him." Clover hauled Willie by his head back out the door. Savannah, Albert, and I followed, watching. The girls lined up behind us.

I'd learned long ago not to get between the boys when they got to scuffling. It hardly took more than a blink of an eye to set them brawling, but if I got myself worked into it, why, I'd just be stoking up a good mad when they'd already have bruised each other's eyes, then gone fishing together to celebrate what fun it all was. It was probably time Willie found his place in this family, if he was planning to stay. This was the shortest path to it. Besides that, the only way to find out what had lit a fire under Clove—usually so somber and quiet, the boys called him "old man"—was to watch. So we watched.

Willie squirmed and roared, saying, "Let me go, you big dumb shifter."

Clover squeezed harder, clenching him like a bear. Grunting and dark in the face, Willie struggled in his arms, throwing his legs out, trying to kick again. His bright-colored boots had been dragged through the dirt, so the pointed toes had lost all their color. Clover's old work boots were heavy, and with every move Willie made, Clover landed a boot print on Willie's backside. Clove said, "I told you to hold still. Take your medicine, runt."

Willie hacked, then squawked out, "I told *you,* sod buster, get your paws off me."

"Shut up, boy, before I give you the licking you deserve. Brother Joshua, are you coming?" Willie squirmed and grunted, pulling and puffing, trying to push a hand between Clover's arm and his own neck.

Josh called out from the back room, "I ain't dressed."

The three boys yelled, "No one cares!" In a moment, Joshua appeared in the doorway in his short union suit. Savannah's girls all gasped and rolled their eyes. They murmured little noises about how boys just had no modesty whatsoever. Even poor sick Ezra pushed himself between the girls' skirts and came outside to watch.

Clove dragged Willie toward the edge of the porch and said, "You fellas come here and take a look. Just come on. It isn't cold, Josh. Hurry up. It's going to make you get well right now. You'll take a swing at him when you find out what I just saw this fella doing." He tumbled to the front steps with Willie, and once there, he loosened his hold, so that Willie fell to his knees and spun head over heels down the steps.

"Now, Zachary," Clove said, "reach up to the olla and draw yourself a big dip of water. Don't drink it. Just draw it." Zack did as he was told. With a confused look on his face, he climbed onto a chair, then the rail, and pulled the scoop from the clay pot hanging from a rope. While he did, Clove continued. "Since we got up yesterday, none of us has seen that water pot in broad daylight. It's too high to look into without a particular reason. Till I just did, after what I saw. Got a dipper, Zack? Dump it on the boards."

Zack looked around and said, "Waste water? Papa'll holler at us." Then he turned to Albert. His papa raised his eyebrows in a question, then nodded. Zack threw down the water. Bits of paper and scattered brown leaves, some rolled up, dark and dingy—old cigarette leavings—that had been floating in the cup swirled on the porch in gray water; it sank through the boards, leaving the shreds posed like so many dead bugs.

Charlie dropped his jaw and said, "Oh for— Blast his hide. Look at this!"

"Tobacco cigarettes. How many are in there?" Josh asked, and started untying the rope that held the olla under the eaves while the other cousins watched in silence.

Clover said, "I went to get my horse. I was just walking up from the barn, and he was puffing like a locomotive. Then he takes it and pitches it right into the jug."

When Josh got the water pot down so he could see inside, he said, "It's a cesspool in there! That clodhopper must have been doing this for a week. Lord, it stinks."

By that time, the boys had plum forgotten the rest of us were there, and we sort of backed up against the wall. Charlie made eyes at Joshua and motioned toward Willie, who was standing there at the foot of the steps with a startled look on his face, his arms curved outward from his middle. Charlie said, "He looks thirsty."

Then the fight was on. Sick or not, dressed or not, Josh, Ezra, Gilbert, and Clover pinned Willie to the dirt and gravel. Even Zachary got into it. Willie fought for all he was worth, but there was no moving the weight of the bunch on top of him.

Charlie stood over him with the three-gallon jug. He said, "You look like you could use a drink, boy." He started pouring the water in Willie's face. "Drink up. Had enough? Have some more. It's been so nice of you to share what you had with us, and we'd like to help you to a taste of it, too." He dumped the last of it with a big splash. The boys let Willie up. He was coughing and spluttering and cursing each of them. "Now," Charlie said, "smell this jug, boys. What do you think? My guess, it's ruined."

Gilbert put his nose over the jug's mouth and gagged. He said, "That's what I tasted. Oh no—" He ran toward the outhouse again.

Josh snatched the jug and threw it against the ground, cracking it in a dozen pieces. Then he said, "There goes three whole dollars. We've lost a whole day, sick on account of someone's stupid, careless— I say someone's first three days' pay is going to the cost of a new olla, ain't that right, Willie Prine? Or do you want another drink?"

Willie backed up, his face redder than I'd ever seen a person's look. He shouted, "No one bothered to tell me the pot was for water. I figured it was to keep bears out of the trash. Sodbusters. Cow shucks. Lousy shifters. Can't take a little tobacco without curling up and dying, that's what. Must have livers like a girl, that's what."

Albert had moved around him, and he suddenly took Willie by the back of his collar and hoisted him. For a man with grown boys, Albert was still in his prime and strong as an oak tree. Albert said, "Young man, stop right in your tracks, and hold your tongue. All this time I've let you go on, being new and all. It's time you and I had a talk. Out in the barn. There'll be no more talk like that in front of my family. Now you come with me and take your licks like a man. Then you straighten up and stop acting like you're being put-upon just because we expect you to act decent. They had *cause* to be sorely mad at you, boy. You just have to learn a lesson from it. Let's go." Albert started pulling on Willie's collar, moving toward the barn.

"You ain't a gonna whip me!" Willie said. He jerked his arms loose and freed his neck from Albert's grasp.

"In the barn. Right now," Albert said, pointing.

Willie put up hands like a prizefighter, fists waving in front of his face. "Come on, farmer. You can't whip me. You can't make me stay here."

Albert glowered at him, his own face darkening. He said, "Willie? I don't plan to make you stay here. Nevertheless, if you're going to stay here, you're going to abide by our rules. And you're going to take the whipping that you earned." Albert strode to the barn without another word. Willie breathed through his mouth, loud enough to hear, his eyes cutting back and forth, not at us, but like he was weighing things in his mind.

Well, I could hardly believe it, but that six-foot-tall boy let himself be strapped three sound smacks by his uncle. There were any number of reasons I had figured he'd never put up with it. No sign in that boy that he'd ever followed a rule in his life. He just walked out there behind Albert and took it. Never saw the like. I believe I'll have to speculate on that for quite a while.

Willie came up to the porch, staring hard at the dirt, his hair and clothes bearing the looks of the scuffle earlier. "I'm sorry, folks. I didn't never see anyone drinking outta that jug. Didn't know what it was for." I don't think any of his cousins cared for his apology, but I wanted to believe him. I reckon any boy needs to know where the fence is, and he'd just found it.

Chapter Eleven

Willie gave work a fair start, trying to make amends. At half past four the next morning he crawled out of bed after I'd called him only once, then went out with Charlie and Gil to feed stock. All the boys who'd drunk from the tobacco water had been drinking clean water again and seemed to have recovered.

Having Granny and Willie staying here and my boys gone from the house sure made things seem strange. It was as if I'd exchanged families with someone else. Granny puttered around, quiet most of the time; then she'd do something like leave a measuring cup of the front porch, forgetting why she'd taken it there in the first place. Willie was noisy and clumsy, catching his long-toed boots on every chair and table leg without fail. That's another reason I believed he was lying, saying he was nineteen years old. Both my fellows spent a couple of years being clumsy when they grew so fast. But by nineteen, my boys had found their feet.

The boys had left their gear at the bunkhouse, and I figured I'd no choice but to let them. In that, there was little difference from having them away at college. But the brittle air around my supper table the night before had worn on me. I'd tried asking them to let up on Willie a little, and they'd agreed to it, but I don't think they give him a minute's peace.

When the boys returned from their chores, we had our breakfast, and Granny insisted she'd do the dishes so we could get to work. "After all," she said, "the rest of my day is just setting and rocking. Roll that quilt down, Sarah, before you leave for the roundup. Think I'll do a piece on it."

I pulled the ropes. The quilt came down into place. It was her Granny's Garden piece. She'd gotten it so far finished that it was put in layers, pinned to the quilt frame, and ready for the process of quilting to begin. I smoothed its surface, admiring the many little pieces that made a pattern under my hands. I said, "We're going to work the colt for a bit before we head down to Baker's place."

My mama paid no attention, just went about gathering her scissors, thread, and thimbles. Then she set up her chair and pulled up an empty one next to her. She patiently threaded two needles. She'd work with one until it was gone, then the other, and then rethread them both. The extra chair, though, was a sad tug at my heart. Anytime we worked a quilt, it was the thing to do to set out an empty chair. It was for the missing woman. The friend who might call, just as you'd sat to quilt, and who might bring a loaf of bread, lend a hand, do a square. As I watched her concentrate on her tiny, even stitches, every one of them a bare eighth of an inch between, I sensed the empty chair was for me, and it filled me with an uneasy longing.

There are times I miss the things I haven't done in my life. The things Savannah is so good at doing, like taking up the empty chair. Like wrangling all those children into good-minded human beings. My three have gone, it seems to me, like a whirlwind. April runs off soon as the door opened, Charlie balks at my every word, and Gilbert just seems happy to flit from one chore to the next without a thought for the future at all.

As I stood there in the doorway, looking at my mama, needle just whipping like a tiny silver dart, that empty chair told me I'd have to make time for more. Not as if I didn't work enough, but somehow there had to be an extra hour in the day that I could spend with her. I felt as if my mama needed me more than she used to, and that no matter what else I got done, I was not taking care of that need.

The men and I went to the barn and worked on getting Pillbox and Hunter out to the corral. Gilbert started in talking to the horses, and after a time, Pillbox let him get his hands on Hunter. He petted the colt all over, lifting his feet one at a time, stroking his back. The third time he touched Hunter's back leg, the colt lifted it without any tugging. Gilbert held the little hoof in his hand for a second and tapped on it with his fingers. He was teaching the horse about getting shod—not to wiggle, and not to be afraid of something hitting his foot. All the while, the look on my youngest son's face was purely spiritual. He was a natural horseman.

Pretty soon, Pillbox'd had all she could take of Gil messing with her baby, and she squealed. That meant it was time to saddle our rides, pack a little food, and fill canteens. The boys said they'd do the horse work while I wrapped them each a sandwich, so I headed for the house.

I meant to go to Savannah's and fetch some more pies the girls had made, so I told them I'd need the wagon hitched, too. Before long, I handed the three boys their lunches. They left, leading an extra horse for me to use when I got there later. I also planned to see if Mary Pearl would be allowed to come stay with me for a bit, now that Willie was fitting in. Maybe having her around would take away some of the strangeness that seemed to have taken up residence with me. I was glad to care for my mama, and Willie seemed to be doing better, but I still felt lonesome. Felt like I'd been uprooted.

As I headed for Savannah's house, just to give myself time to think on things, I drove down a path we rarely used—a circle to the north side—where the land rose a little steeper. Besides, it would cut to the acreage that Mama had now deeded away to the railroad. I could see if anything had been laid there, like fence wire or tracks. I often rode the coyote trails around my land, instead of the roads. Seemed if you wanted to see things clear, you had to get them in a different light. When I got to the last little hill overlooking Granny's old place and Albert and Savannah's, I put on the brake and stepped out.

I took a walk up on the ridge. Standing on top there, I looked into the desert for a long spell, watching for any new post or the least little sign that it no longer belonged in our family. The quiet was what startled me. Quail are never quiet during the summer. Woodpeckers, bees, all kinds of critters make noise the livelong day. But here, I didn't see or hear a sign of life. Not a coyote. Not a bird. First thing I thought of was that a mountain lion might be near. Waiting, hunting, while everything else fled. This kind of silence wasn't about birds and critters hunkering down for a storm coming. Before rain, the quail run around in a panic, warning one another about every drop until it gets too thick to see, and then they have to run and hide. The sure thing was, if nothing was stirring, something had scared them.

As I turned to head back down the slope to the wagon, something moved. It was an awful feeling—wishing I had a pistol in my pocket like the old days, but knowing I couldn't reach the rifle under the seat in the wagon. I stopped breathing, trying to pick out where I had seen the shadow move a second earlier. Wild burros and other critters move around the desert all the time. I was worried to take a step until I knew what it was. I held my breath. Behind a stand of brushy ironwood and fallen mesquite, where a finger cholla had grown near to the top of it, a large dark form moved again.

The animal snorted. Not a horse. A mule. It stepped from behind the brush a little, cropping at something on the ground. It was a large black animal. A puma skin was tied to its back. The claptrap fixed to the skin made it unmistakable. The animal belonged to the water witch. I searched the area all around it. Even sniffed the air for the reek of Lazrus. The only thing moving was the mule, which was eating; the only smell the sweetness of coming rain.

I looked in every direction. A lizard whipped out of the weeds at my feet. Turning around again, I ran down the slope too quickly, startling my horse. I half-expected Lazrus to appear out of the very air, the way he'd done before. When I got on the buckboard, I still thought he'd spring up before me. I loosed the brake and snapped the reins harder than needed, jerked the wagon out of its shadow, and made tracks for Savannah's house.

Albert insisted on driving back with me to make sure everything was all right. I told him I was wanting someone to stay with Granny while we worked the herd. Well, Mary Pearl had her heart set on riding out with us and working, and the two little boys together could be more trouble than they'd solve, so Savannah decided to ride back with me and spend the day helping Granny work her quilt. As we drove the short way back to my place, Savannah put her hand on my arm. "You take good care, with that heathen around here."

"I will," I said. "Chess is going to be out in the barn most of the day. Are you afraid to stay with Granny?"

"Not if you leave me a shooter," Savannah said.

"Why, Savannah! Are you telling me you'd let a vent through Lazrus's hide?" I meant it to lighten the mood, but Savannah was having no cheering up. She glowered, first at me, then at the land around us, as if she expected him behind any bush, peering at us. She wanted him to see the intent on her face.

Savannah said, "If I find it's him writing love letters that have got my girls in a stir, I'll let a vent so's a jackrabbit could jump through sideways."

Her talk startled me. It wasn't like Savannah to let a vent in anyone. "Who's in a stir?" I asked quietly.

Savannah lowered her voice and said, "Nearly every day, Mary Pearl finds a note pinned at the windowsill. She and Esther sleep on the top floor. Someone is putting up a ladder at night, right at their bedroom window. Rachel and Rebeccah swoon over the notes, too, trying to guess which one of the hands in these parts is so educated to write that way. They have long talks about it, discussing what sort of romantic notion has got him mucking stalls when he could be doing something grander with his fancy words. Truth is, there is no name on any note, neither for whom it is meant nor from whom it comes. Each girl imagines it is addressed to her, although they'd never say that to me. I know my girls, and I know what's going on." Then Savannah raised her voice and nearly shouted, "It's a sorry, indecent way to go courting, and I'd never let one of my girls have any truck with the kind of sneak-thieving hooligan who'd do it. Never. Not as long as I have breath!"

Savannah had never spoken like that before. It was as close to a vow as she'd ever made in public, and vows were sacred things to Savannah Lawrence Prine, not tossed to the wind without thought. This one, hollered right out, was meant for someone to hear. We talked more about why she thought Lazrus was writing the notes. He'd said something to Chess about having been educated, but I couldn't put him together with paper and quills and love notes to young girls. It just didn't make sense. Of course, then I remembered the person we were talking about, and then I had to agree with her.

While Savannah said good morning to Granny and took a seat in the empty chair at the quilt frame, I got my old rifle from behind the bedroom door. I took an extra box of ready-load bullets to put in my saddlebag. I stopped in the parlor. Making sure the chamber was empty, I sighted in, aiming at the nail on the wall that held a string behind a picture.

Granny looked up from her stitching. "What're you fixing to shoot?" she asked.

"Varmint," I said. "If I see one. There's been a two-legged one sniffing around. Lazrus. I saw his mule across the crick. Savannah thinks he's nosing around there. If you feel the need, my kitchen pistol is on the top shelf in the pantry, next to the grease can that's got the candle wax in it. Loaded. Remember it kicks like a mule."

Without looking up, my mama said, "Makes you purty jumpy, don't he?"

Savannah said, "The man is pure evil."

Granny suddenly stopped her sewing, looked directly at me, and said, "You leave me that firing piece, I'll make sure he gets the message."

I laughed. "Mama! You never shot a gun at a man in your life."

"Yes, I did. I never told you, but I did once. As a girl. Reckon I ain't lost the knack. Never was no dead shot like you, but I can do it justice." She turned from me to Savannah and back, nodding. "It ain't something you forget how to do."

Savannah held a needle at arm's length and pushed the thread through its eye, making a knot faster than I could have even found the ends. She had a stern look on her face, but, as I'd seen her do many times, she smiled through her fierce determination. She said, "What hymn shall we sing first?" And that was the end of our talking about the prospects of two ladies needing powder and lead to get through the morning.

By the time I got to the Bakers' place, work was in full swing, and plenty of dust hung in the air. It was good to leave my troubles hanging on the Bakers' front gate and think of nothing but moving cattle. There's strength in the solitude of work. Hot or not, dust and wind and every other torment, hard work is still peace compared to what can worry a person on the inside. On the back of that horse, I could leave behind thinking of my mama getting old, my brother Harland and his sad predicament, Lazrus tormenting me, and even Rudolfo.

Baker had a couple of Spanish dandies working for him. They weren't much use, but in this kind of work, a good horse that knews its job could have a sack of potatoes in the saddle and still get it done. Willie did his share of sitting and watching and waving his hat when the cattle got too close to him. He fell off his horse at least twice that I knew of, and maybe more I didn't. Watching him, I wondered how long it would take him to get planted in that saddle. Reckon it'll depend on how much he wants it.

We didn't slow down for lunch, just ate in the saddle. The afternoon was long and torturously hot. One of those Spanish fellows got in a fix with his horse and ended up in a thicket of cholla. He was a sorry sight, and his hide was going to smart for a few days. Plus, that accident took him and his brother off work more than an hour while the brother went to pulling thorns with a pair of pliers. Still, I'd never known a gathering without someone getting stove up one way or another.

We had made good progress by the time the dinner bell started ringing in the evening. My boys and I had just cornered a little bunch of five and were pushing them toward the holding fence when we heard it. Willie whooped loudly and let out a curse, saying "Let's go, boys!" It caused the lead steer to dodge, and my pony took after him. I could still hear the boys, but I was too far away to do more than listen. I waved the loop in my right hand and turned that steer back to the bunch.

Charlie told Willie to hush, said that cussing insulted the cattle. Willie laughed at that. So Gilbert told him it rankled the horses, and Willie laughed all the harder. While he was laughing, Charlie snicked a quirt behind Willie's back onto the flank of the pony he was on, and in a snap, Willie was riding nothing but dry sagebrush. Willie cussed the horse, cussed the ground he landed on, cussed the rock that scuffed his fancy boots, and cussed the cattle, too, for good measure. "Told you to watch it," Charlie said to him. "That horse took all the insults he could, and left you high in the sky."

Willie looked like he was just about to cuss Charlie, too, when all of a sudden he stopped, thought a minute, and said, "Hey. That horse don't understand English."

Charlie told him the horse understood English *and* Spanish, and even some Hungarian and French, because it had been bought at an international horse auction and it had picked up all those languages from the other horses there. Willie scratched his head, but he didn't open his mouth the rest of the way to the fence.

When we got the bunch through the opening in the fence, we turned off to the house. The smell coming from the supper tables was heavy with pies and sweets, mixed with the scent of roasted meat and chicken. Stepping out of the saddle after a day like we'd had sometimes mades me feel I could barely walk. My legs would swing all cattey whompus and my shoulders always wanted to sway as if I was still riding. Willie took off ahead of us to get to the chow line. He scuffled through a little pack of chickens, sending them squawking out of the way of his fandango boots.

My sons and I took our places in the line of men, plates in hand. When Willie figures out about the horse's English, he'll be mad all over again. Well, he's busting to act like he's lived here all his life. Reckon if he had, it wouldn't be so confusing to him. I said to my sons, "You boys see that you don't ride him so hard he bucks and runs the other way. There's a limit to what a boy can change about himself in a day." They both muttered something about it needing a lifetime to change Willie.

Mrs. Baker had set out a load of good food on some planks laid on sawhorses, and there was plenty to go around. It looked like she was cleaning out her larder and garden both, what with the spread of pickles and preserves tucked in between all the meats and fritters and such. I felt sorry I'd not spent more time with her. I hardly knew this woman, and now she was leaving. I couldn't for the life of me remember her first name, and when I passed her, she gave me little more than the nod she gave the men.

As we gathered around the planks loaded with food, all we talked about was how the rain's so late this year. There were fellows from Cochise County come to help, and vaqueros from Sonora, too, working for Rudolfo. Most owned their spreads, large and small. No one else had lost a well as I had, but we are all holding our breath, saying prayers, hoping and wishing for rain. I suspect we are all wondering who'll be the next one to call it quits and sell off.

The sun was dipping into the trough between two hills as the boys and I headed home to do the sundown chores. This far into the summer, that meant it was around eight o'clock. Willie dawdled behind us about three lengths.

"Well," I said, "when do you two figure to move back to the house?"

Charlie made a little face. "Mama, we're kinda enjoying the bunkhouse."

"Not enjoying, exactly," Gilbert said.

I said, "Well, what, exactly?"

Gil turned to his brother. "Old Charlie and I have been talking about maybe building up a little house. There's all this land. Maybe it wouldn't hurt to have a second house on it? Then the ranch would be a regular compound. Maybe you wouldn't mind?"

"What's wrong with the house we've got?"

"Not a thing," Charlie said. "Truth is, Mama, we're leaning toward *glad* Willie's there. Gives you someone to get after besides us. I was just wanting a place of my own. Don Quixote said he'll help me build it as long as he can sleep there now and again."

Gilbert said, "You better remember my name, or you'll lose the only help you got that knows which is the working end of the hammer."

My son wanted a house of his own. I wondered if the name Esperanza was going to come into this discussion. I said, "You want me to deed you boys each a share right now? Divide your inheritance?"

Charlie was silent a long while. Then he said, "Hadn't thought of that."

I said, "Well, have you thought about who's going to cook your three squares?" I wondered if all mothers feel like their children have sprouted wings and are too eager to use them before they've learned how hard the ground is. I thought of Pillbox, hiding Hunter from me, who meant him no harm, and felt a sad smile inside. I pulled my horse next to Charlie's. I said, "Reckon we need to sit down one of these nights and talk about the future. Sleep where you please till we get it sorted out." I thought for a moment he might say something more, but he just smiled.

About the time we passed the Maldonado place, Charlie said, "Mama, there's something else I've been thinking about."

From where we sat, Maldonado's place was cheery with light from inside. Savory air came from the place. Rudolfo had worked with us at Baker's all day, but his daughters would still fix food for their household. I said, "You've seen the folly of your ways, I reckon, and are going to go back to school?"

He said, "No, ma'am. I was thinking about getting married."

I took a deep breath, trying not to let him hear it.

Gil said, "Well, have you got a girl picked out? You'll need one of those, too. They aren't just lying around like old horseshoe nails."

"Her name is Miss Esperanza Von Bracht." Charlie's voice was steady and clear, not the least bit hesitant when he said her name.

"I see," I said. I settled my hat at a different angle. Now Charlie was thinking of marrying, without a hoot-down-a-hole idea what it meant. My hat felt as if it didn't fit me anymore. I nudged it down at little.

He said, "I want you to meet her. I'd like to know what you think of her."

I pushed my hat up in front. "You want my opinion or simply my approval?"

"Well . . . both."

"Fair enough," I said. I took off my hat and fussed with the inside of the brim liner. I said, "What do *you* think of her?"

"She's a real nice girl," Charlie said. "Real nice. Kind of pretty in a way."

"Do you know the family? Met her folks and all? Is that name Mexican?"

"And German."

I gave the tired horse a little nudge. "How do you plan to support a wife?"

"Thought I'd run cattle."

I smiled. "Own some land, do you?" I teased.

"Mama," Charlie said, "it doesn't have to get complicated. I just thought I'd buy some stock of my own, put them with yours, and we'd—"

"That doesn't sound like an invitation a girl with half a mind would take," I said.

Gilbert laughed and said, "She means, knothead, that a hen wants her own roost. You can't bring a wife to Mama's place. You got to build your own. Say, you were going to make me help you build it, and then get *married*? If that isn't the double-crossingest thing I heard ever. Where'm I going to bunk?"

Charlie said, "Well, Miss Von Bracht wouldn't mind if you stayed there."

I grinned and put my hat back in place. Whatever adjusting it needed had worked, and it sat fine now. I said, "You'd better learn something about women before long. A wife wants her own house, and one that doesn't get it, why, you'd be better to live in a turned-over boxcar than put her in the kitchen with your mother. Or, worse yet, have your kid brother picking at her cooking."

Gil said, "If it *was* upside down, I believe the iron wheels would get hot enough in the summer that she could save on firewood, and bake your tortillas right on the plates."

I laughed, saying, "Gilbert? Do you have a sweetheart, too? Reckon we could have a double wedding." I surely can't imagine Gilbert married. A puppy in a top hat.

"Haven't asked her to yet," he said.

It took a few minutes for words to come to me. For a moment, I was lost in a whirlwind, not able to see my sons clearly, just as it had been on Savannah's porch in the whirlwind. My voice trembled a bit when I said, "Maybe those girls will want to marry college men. You best not spend the whole summer without a trip or two to town. Maybe they'd like to see you now and then, too. After we get the work done, you better ride to town and pay your respects to their folks."

Charlie whooped out a shout, spurred his horse, and took off, with his brother fast in his tracks, making his own noise. I was left riding beside Willie. I said, "Reckon you've got a girl back home, too?"

"Not to speak of."

"Well, that's one left home, then. There's time enough for that," I said.

"I'll get all the girls I want. Soon's I get me some money." Willie kicked hard at his horse and bolted up to ride with the boys. My horse followed without my urging, just wanting to be part of the parade.

Willie followed me to the house, where Chess was snoozing in my rocking chair. Granny had gone to bed. Savannah had returned home before dark. In the lamplight, Willie and I barely kicked off our boots, then sprawled on our bunks on the sleeping porch. I didn't remember my head hitting the pillow. Probably fell asleep somewhere between the words *good* and *night*.

July 11, 1906

The dawn was cool and clear. We took care of a stack of flapjacks and sorghum with beefsteaks and coffee. As good as the cool morning felt to our skins, it meant only one thing to me: no chance of rain. "Willie?" I called. "Come on outside, and I'll show you how to throw a loop before we go."

He'd no sooner crossed the ground toward me when we saw Zack and Ezra coming down the road together, bareback, on a huge plow horse they've got named Big Boy. Big Boy is about the size of my old Dan. The little fellows waved when they saw us in the yard.

Suddenly, Ezra shouted, "Whoa, whoa! Stop, stop, stop!" He jumped right down off the horse while it was still moving. Big Boy plodded onward toward us, unaware. We stared in Ezra's direction, waiting to see whether we should come running or not.

"Well, what'd you find, knothead?" Zack yelled over his shoulder from the moving horse.

Ezra picked up a stone, held it to the sky, and rolled it around between two fingers. He hollered, "Shooter. For marbles. Almost round, too." He popped the pebble in the air a few times. "Yep, it's a good'n." He grinned from ear to ear and put the stone in his pocket, running toward us. "Old horse is deaf," Ezra said. "Mary Pearl is on her way over after she finishes prissing around in the mirror. Mama said *we* was to help out over here before she tans us for life." Big Boy kept moving at the same tired pace. Zack looked like a flea on the animal's back.

"Well, what were you up to?" Charlie asked.

"Not doing nothin'," Zack said, hopping off Big Boy and landing with a thud as he hit the ground. He stepped in front of the seventeen-hand horse and grabbed hold of his halter. Big Boy stopped amiably and went to cropping at some grass among the weeds at the yard fence. The little boys didn't bother tying him; he was never hard to catch, and not given to wandering far from anything green he could nibble. Zack stuck his hands in his pockets. Hard to believe a little boy could look like a day's worth of play and dirty roughhousing by half past five in the morning. He was wearing overalls with no shirt, and he looked like a ragamuffin under his shaggy head of hair. "We positively wasn't doing nothing but having some fun, and Mama says she's got another tired spell and we're aggravating her."

I said, "Well, fancy that. Playing marbles again?"

Ezra said, "Papa fusses at us if we fight, and Mama fusses if we play. Esther says we stink when we just both had a bath two days ago, and Clove says 'Get out of the way before you get your arm tore off in that machine,' so we figure"— he stepped toward Willie and glared brazenly up at him—"to run away from home and live at Aunt Sarah's place." Ezra made a face at Willie, as if he saw in the six-foot-and-some boy something that was more akin to himself than any adult.

"Yeah," echoed Zack. "Ain't no harm in playing marbles here. Even if you use your fists now and then to see who won."

"Well, you're just in time for roping lesson," I said. "You two varmints want to be the calf or the bulldogger?"

"Calf!" Ezra put his forefingers to the sides of his head and cut around in circles, trying to hook Zack with the horns he was pretending to have. "Moo-oove, you mule-headed, lank-legged sodbuster. I'm a gonna poke you in the . . . noggin!" Zack fidgeted, swatting at Ezra. The two of them eyed each other for a minute, then nodded.

Willie watched them for a bit, then said, " 'Ere up to something."

"Don't mind them," I said. "We'll use a barrel."

Ezra and Zack smoothed themselves a marble ring in the dust outside the fence, and were silent, studying their play like some hard-core gamblers leaning over a bad hand of cards.

I took a hank of rope from my shoulder. "Willie," I said, "take a turn at this riata. Hold near the *honda*, let it loose a little, and then roll your hand around and around over your head." I talked like I was gentling a colt. I said, "See how this is made? Not one you'd tie up something with or go cutting without thinking twice. A good rope is expensive. Look here how I've got it in my hand. Turning it over like this." I let fly with the lariat. It went over the barrel; then I started pulling it toward me. "If you're on your horse, you dally this quick around the horn. If you're on the ground, you've got to have another hand throw him."

I handed Willie the rope. He swung, and swung some more. I told him to try without thinking about it so much. When Willie managed to get a loop over it, we all cheered him, and he caught it pretty regular after that.

Then my boys went to feed and saddle up for the day's work. Willie followed them into the barn. I went to see the old horses. I petted and coaxed my old bunch to the trough, checked all their feet while they drank. Before any time at all, I heard shouting coming from the barn. First it was a cobbled-up noise, then Charlie's voice saying, "Leave it alone! Get on out of here before I pin you to the wall with it!"

Willie came scooting out of the barn, red in the face, beating his hat against his leg as he walked. He turned around and shouted back toward the building, "I 'as just trying to help. Do it yer own way, then. I can't do nothin' to please yer damn hides."

"Willie!" I said. "Hand me that bucket. No sense getting underfoot."

"I weren't under foot. He asked me to toss him the line and I did, but he didn't say which'n." He lifted the bucket of oats and held it toward me and I took it. The boy said, "I didn't mean to hit him with that thing."

"What thing was that?" I'd hear from Charlie about it.

"Oh, it was nothing," Willie said. He climbed up on the fence rail and hung on with his elbows, then said, "You know, I'm getting pretty dang good at riding. Say, Aint Sair, you s'pose I could learn me to ride one o' *them* horses? They look pretty tame."

"This bunch is old. Not working anymore, except the colt, and he's too young."

"That'n there, he looks all right." Willie pointed to Pillbox.

"That's the mare that's nursing the colt."

"I like the looks of it."

"You wouldn't like the ride. She's full of vinegar." I said, "There're three dozen horses on this ranch you can ride. Take your pick, and try your saddle on one. Best not lay as much as a handkerchief on one of these."

Here came Charlie with a black eye, Gilbert behind him, leading our mounts. Gilbert said, "*He* coming with us?"

"What hit your eye?" I asked Charlie.

"I asked him for a tether and he threw me the hay rig. Hook and all." Willie said he was sorry for knocking him in the head with the cast-iron hay hook. Charlie nodded, and that was that between boys.

When we slowed to eat our packed lunches, Mary Pearl and I happened to be near Charlie and Willie. Gilbert had ridden with one of those Spaniard fellows after some stock down a gully. "You'll be a pretty good hand in no time," Charlie said to Willie.

"Show me how to draw a pistol, then," Willie said. "Don't I need to carry a pistol?"

Charlie looked from Willie to me and back again. Then he said, "Well, I don't carry one. Neither does Mama nor Grampa Chess. We keep rifles in the house for varmints. A shotgun for quail or dove hunting. Now and then, we have one in a wagon, I reckon, for putting down a horse or something wounded badly. What you want a pistol for?"

"Well, just like this here. To see if I can. Besides, what's a cow—I mean, hand, without a gun to tote?"

"One who's busy earning his pay," I said. "I don't mind you plugging some tin cans tonight after chores. But go off to the west and aim toward the mountains. Any other direction, and it's not safe."

"Well, I wouldn't aim at *nobody*," Willie said.

Charlie flicked the brim of Willie's hat with his fingertip. "It's not what you're aiming at, bud, it's what you hit if you *don't* hit what you're aiming at. Day or two, I'll get Mama's old pistol and a few shells. You go to the trash and find us three or four tin cans. Square enough?" Willie nodded with that wide-eyed, half-scared, half-eager look he has, and we went back to work. I never have seen a boy as old as that who acted like such a little kid. Don't know how long it'll take to get some sand in him.

Mrs. Baker laid out a spread that made yesterday's feast look as if it had been just a practice run. She must have been up all night baking pies, and turning out roasted meat all day long in the heat, to spread a board like the one we had for supper. Work was done, and while we ate, the Bakers told everyone their thanks and said how they'd be moving on by the end of the week, leaving hired men to work the cattle for the rest of us. Rudolfo made a speech, too, about what great friends and neighbors they'd been. Made me feel sad I hardly knew these folks.

Rudolfo knew pretty much everyone from San Simon to Quartzite and Naco to Holbrook. I got to thinking it was no wonder he thought he could be governor, the way he could go on, as if hearing himself talk was the best music there was.

Chapter Twelve

I woke before sunup. Laid there listening to Chess and Willie breathing. Somewhere up on the hills, a band of coyotes was celebrating finding something to eat. I hope and pray it isn't another steer. Gilbert said he saw a single footprint yesterday with five toes. Wolves or coyotes leave a print like a dog, four toes with claws. The big cats leave five toes and no claw marks.

There was a faint whiff of javelina. No smell of rain. The sky was clear, but the moon was down already, and the stars themselves looked tired, dusty. Granny was up when I made coffee. I took our morning coffee out to the front porch, along with a quilt for her to wrap in, then waited the sunrise, breathing in the only cool air we'd have all day. I made a list of everything I needed to get done today. Chess and Willie stumbled in at the same time I went to refill my cup.

I fixed everyone breakfast and then sent them off to work. If someone didn't wash some clothes, we'd be reduced to wearing barrels next. Reckon it'd be purely selfish of anyone to have enough clothes they could go a week without washing. There was nothing for it but to drag out the washtubs, set up the wringer cranked onto the kitchen table, and start hauling water. Since I don't do ironing in the summertime, for fear of roasting myself to death, it didn't take too long just to hang things on the line and then take them down. In this heat, one load will dry pretty near before the next one is washed.

While I did that work, Granny took down my big yellow crockery bowl and started breaking eggs into it. She worked away without making a sound, and by the time I turned to look, she had made enough doughnuts for the Sixth Cavalry. She said she was counting on me taking some to the boys. I could already picture them wolfing down the sweets like it was their last meal. But, for the most part, she was making them because they'd always been Ernest's favorite thing.

I just finished hanging out the last load of washing, and Granny and I were having some water and a couple of those doughnuts each, when Albert's boy Josh got there. Josh had ridden up to get mail, and he'd brought a letter from Mr. Baramon. In a lot of hundred-dollar words, he said he didn't have a blessed idea who had bought up the land of my mama's, but it did seem to be a railroad, as rail companies had been "engaging in transactions" in that area. He said he would personally have to lay eyes on the agreement to do any more than that. And, of course, there was a bill from him for ten dollars for that opinion. Well, I'd known right along it would cost me, but I was hoping at least for the money I'd get something. That's the trouble with lawyers. It's not like they shoe a horse or hammer you a single blessed nail; you have to pay them just for thinking.

Granny was talking on and on, and I didn't hear a word of it. She asked me something, and I let out a sigh. I said, "I'm sorry, Mama. What was that? Didn't I already rinse those?"

She turned the crank on the wringer with one hand, feeding a pair of man's pants through it from the washtub sitting on the table into the rinse tub set on the floor. Mama said, "Still got soap in the corners. That boy's pants are so tall, they're hard to get clean." Somehow, she'd gotten a pair of Clover's old trousers, probably meant for Willie to use. "You're being a flibbertigibbet lately. Leave that alone about the railroad and the money. What's done is done."

I just opened my mouth to ask her what she thought I was doing badly when there was the sound of hooves outside, and heavy steps on the porch. The door opened without a knock. It was Willie. "Morning, Granny. Aint Sair? Me and Charlie and Gil was working down by the mud tank, you know."

"The Little Muddy?" I said.

"Yep, that's it. Little Muddy. Mr. Baker said as how he's promised to leave some fence at his boundary on that side to the new owner. Anyway, we was putting up some poles to keep the cows out on account of it's gone dry, and Gilbert says we're out of number twenty-threes. All he's got out there is eighteens and twenties."

I puzzled over that a minute. Granny went to hang that last pair of pants outside, paying no attention to Willie and me. Willie went on. "I looked high and low in the barn. There wasn't a single sack of twenty-threes, and he said they was all up by the tool rack, a-hanging on a nail."

"Sack of twenty-three what?" I asked.

"Number twenty-three postholes. He said he came out there with a sack of eighteens and some twenties, but he was pure out of number twenty-three postholes."

"They sent you for postholes?"

"Yes'm. To put up the fence."

I reckon something must have happened where my sons decided they'd get more work done with Willie gone than with him helping. It took me some fast talking to get him settled once I told him what the boys were up to. He was mad enough that he got red in the face, and looked like he did yesterday when I fussed at him and he nearly cried.

"I hate those two. I just hate 'em," he said.

"You've got to not take it so hard," I said. "Son, they don't mean any harm in it. They're just yanking a knot in your tail."

"They got no right. I'm trying my best."

"I know you are. You're doing fine."

"They hated me the minute I come here."

"No, they didn't. If they hated you, they'd ignore you. They wouldn't bother pulling your leg. Here's what you'll do. Your Granny's just emptied a whole flour sack making these." I pulled up a plate of doughnuts, moved the towel, and watched his eyes nearly pop from his head. "Have yourself a few. Then you take this sack with you, and tell them you had some fine doughnuts after hunting for the postholes. You toss the sack to 'em and say you brought them some number-nine doughnut holes instead."

He said, "Doughnuts don't have holes."

"That's right." I waited while he thought on it.

The side of Willie's face wrinkled up, and then he laughed in a kind of halted shout, slapping the table. "Number-nine doughnut holes." He pushed a whole doughnut into his mouth at once.

"You know how bad you felt hunting postholes? Well, Charlie and Gil think that's a joke, but I guarantee those two take their doughnuts plenty serious. It isn't going to be funny to them when the joke is turned around, now is it?"

Willie swallowed hard, licking his fingers at the same time. He picked up another doughnut, turned it this way and that, admiring the sugar that coated the brown crust of it. "I like it here, Aint Sair," he said, and bit half of it off. "I sure do like it here."

A few minutes later, I watched him ride away, his hat tipped down near to his nose, the empty flour sack held forth. I pictured my boys' faces and smiled. It wouldn't hurt to turn the tables on them once in a while. Willie was surely fighting an uphill battle all around. This would just be a level spot for him to remember now and then.

Granny wouldn't let up then, wanting me to help her finish off her quilt. I had a hundred and one things to do, and that wasn't one of them, but I figured I'd spare an hour. It'd be good to get off my feet a little before I took to the rest of the days' chores.

We wheeled the quilt down to a good working height, then tied off the cord to a piece of ironwood that Albert had found rolling down Cienega Creek one day. It had turned in the water until it was smooth, and felt nice to handle, and it was heavy as a piece of iron. I keep it to hold the door ajar when there's a breeze.

Pulling down a quilt is like opening a package. All you see is the white underneath, and then as soon as you get it down, there are all the colors. We pulled up chairs and took up stitching where we'd set it aside last time. We worked on it for quite a while without saying a word. I'd learned long ago not to say to Granny how pretty it was, for she'd fuss. I used to think I was showing too much pride and boasting, but I have figured out it's just that she's embarrassed to take a compliment.

Granny stood up, kind of stiff, and rubbed her back. "I've got to go check the sheets. See if they're dry," she said, and left for a bit. Then she came and stood right behind my shoulder, watched me take several stitches. When I came to tie off the short thread, she said, "On those white squares, I aim to do a cornflower."

"That'll be fine," I said.

She fingered the pattern of little hexagons. She said, "You know, this boy ain't really Ernest."

I turned to her with a start, but she'd already disappeared into the kitchen. I got up and followed her, feeling sheepish. She kept on straight through the kitchen to her bedroom. I said, "We all thought you didn't know. Willie is Ernest's son. Not Ernest himself."

"Ernest had his leg took off in Texas." Granny was standing over the rug in her little bedroom, staring hard at something on the ceiling.

I said, "Yes, Mama. I remember."

"That like to killed me. I wished they'd a cut off mine instead."

I remembered that day. I remembered having to help hold him down. Then, just that quick, instead of my brother, I pictured that it was one of my sons I was holding down, listening to him scream for mercy. I was the mama, standing in her place. After I caught my breath, I said, "That must have been a horror for you."

She rocked back and forth on her feet a little. Then she turned and stared out the window. The curtain sagged. Not a breath of air stirred, out or in. Granny said, "Rain would be nice. It ain't rained since last Tuesday."

It hadn't rained since last January. I took her hand in mine. It was so bony, so small. It's a wonder to me she can do the things she does, she seems so frail. I said, "Sometimes I wish I could take the pain off you like you wanted to take the pain off him." I watched her face for some glimmer of recognition, but she was lost in memories. "Did you know my boys are fixing to marry? Both of them told me they have sweethearts."

"That boy's out there teasing that dog of yours. The one with the flop ear."

Just that quick, she'd come back to the here and now. I went to the porch to get a look at Willie and Nip. I called, "Willie? Why aren't you down to help the boys?"

"Watch this, Aint Sair. I can make like I'm throwing something, and this stupid dog will run after nothing, ever' time."

When he got to the porch, I said, "What are you doing?"

"Being tricky. It's a joke."

"Dogs don't take to jokes. They like it one way or t'other, no fooling around. That dog will work for you until he can hardly walk, and still fight a bobcat to save your hide. He'll eat what you feed him, and not kill a chicken if it wasn't enough. All that dog knows is honesty. Cheating the dog will turn it bad, and it'll think being trustworthy isn't worth the trouble. What you're teaching the dog is that you can't be trusted."

"I'm getting dang tired of being lectured all the livelong day."

"I know. You get those bags of feed stacked yet?"

"I want to go riding. Try some shooting. Charlie says I got to ask if'n it's all right, like I was a little kid."

"Well, it's dinnertime." He shrugged and looked away. Sometimes, it was hard to separate Willie from his father—my brother Ernest. When I wasn't seeing a resemblance, I could picture Willie as a drifter I'd turn off the place without much to-do. I said, "We've got plenty of work to do, so I'm going to say this plain and straight up. I run this place. Not a chicken lays an egg I don't know about. Not a horse gets ridden or a nail gets driven without my say-so. I don't know what's got under your blanket this afternoon, but you best mind your tongue, or you can go talk to your Uncle Albert again."

He bristled up like a cat in a lightning storm. "You know? My *pa's* a-coming *home.* I come here to meet up with him and be cowboys."

"That's another thing. A cowboy is nothing but trash stuck to a saddle. Rustlers, drunkards, no-accounts. You want to call yourself a hand, a rider, or a puncher, or whatever else, that's fine, but I don't hire *cowboys,* nor tolerate the sort."

He turned red in the face and stepped off the porch, scuffing one of his bright-colored boots. He walked a few steps, then turned and shouted, "When my pa gets here, he's the boss o' this place, and him and me's gonna be in charge here, and you'll see who's slapping the tar outta who." As he whipped around and stomped off, I saw him wipe quickly at his face with his hand.

Most half-grown boys have got the size of a man, trying to act as grown as they look, and the heart of a five-year-old, all emotion and no sense until they hit at least twenty. That kid was in the hardest part of a boy's life, and no more idea what to do with himself than a moth flying into a fire. As, I imagine, a boy raised by that gal Felicity would be. Chances are he got away with any kind of hooliganism he wanted with her. Maybe that's why he'd let a man tell him what for, but no one else. Lands, maybe he thinks all women are like his mother.

Mary Pearl came up and said she'd met Willie heading toward their house. He asked her if her folks would let him live at their place. I said, "Well, he's acting pretty mettlesome all of a sudden. Come and have dinner with us. What did you tell him?"

"I said he'd have to ask for himself. Then he said there'd be room enough for him and both his folks in Granny's old house, and they could just all take up living there until they took over the big place. What's that mean?"

"Lord, that Felicity. She never could get it through her head it was the pecan farm that Ernest had helped to buy." We Prine children had put our money together to buy those trees after Papa died, and we'd lost everything we had to Comanche Indians. I was no more than seventeen when we did that. Albert and Savannah worked the farm all that time because I up and married

Jimmy. Harland worked there while he was a boy, but he went off to school. A full quarter of the money that bought those trees was Ernest's, yet by rights, it belonged to Albert and Savannah and their children.

Picturing Felicity Prine having a say in decisions on Albert's pecan farm made me want to choke. Mary Pearl looked troubled. "You mean, he owns part of Mama and Papa's land? Our farm?" She set plates out and started cutting a pan of corn bread. "Here comes Charlie."

"Ernest helped buy the trees. He never worked the land a single day. Your folks have the homestead and deed. I'm no lawyer, but I know for certain they've got it. If they wanted to share, it would be out of obligation. Ernest never wanted any part of it."

I told my sons what Willie had said. "It's that Felicity. She put him up to it."

"You reckon she'll be along next?" Charlie asked.

"Lord a mercy," I said.

Gilbert said, "We could be knee-deep in manure, and it hasn't *started* to cure."

Willie, though, had come empty-handed. Had not written to a soul nor received any mail. If Felicity was fast on his heels, or just waiting for Ernest to arrive to "take over," it didn't seem likely she'd be biding her time very far afield. The boy stayed gone a couple of hours, and about the time we'd rest had a couple of hours' siesta, he came on back, acting like nothing had gone on before. I'll be the first one to drop a grudge, but not when it's left up in the air like that. I always want some words said that make it clear we're on even ground again. Willie just went to the barn and stacked up the oats like I'd asked him, whistling and smiling as he worked.

Late in the afternoon, I called him to the house and said, "We're heading to Maldonado's in a couple of days. It'll be more of the same, but probably take a week, and we'll be sleeping over some nights. It's a big spread. You'll have to hold your own alongside men who've been doing it all their lives." From the corner of my eye, I saw my mama sit back at her quilt and run her fingers over it, tracing the red pathways on the white background.

Willie called, "I get to pick my own horse?"

"You get to pick one of mine to ride."

"And ride 'im all day?"

Only someone who'd never been in a saddle for fourteen hours straight would say it with that kind of anticipation. "All the livelong day. Now come on up here. You've got to learn something every hand knows, because if you ask someone to do it for you when you're off with that bunch of men, they'll call you a sissy and a baby, and they'll never let you forget it. Remember, these are men used to doing for themselves, and they won't make exception for you."

"All right, sure. What is it?" he asked, following me into the house. "Howdy, Granny. What is it I got to do, Aint Sair?"

I went to Mama's sewing kit in the parlor and came back with everything he needed. "Here," I said, "sew this button back onto your shirt."

July 19, 1906

Mr. Baker's wife left this morning with a flatbed wagon loaded up heavy. Jim Baker rode as far as my place to wave her off. He had a worried look on his face, watching her leave. Said to me that she was supposed to wait for him in Tucson, though he'd be surprised to find her there, as he expected she probably wouldn't stop until she gots to Oklahoma Territory and her folks' place. Then he said Rudolfo had come to him and insisted he sell him his land. The price Rudolfo offered was not ten cents on the dollar what it was worth. Jim had felt like he'd run flat selling out for half, and didn't want to sell for a tenth. I told him, "Well, it's your land. No one's forcing you to sell it."

He said, "Maldonado said he wouldn't keep the offer open if this other buyer doesn't take it. I really have to sell to someone." He took off his hat for a moment and wiped his brow with his sleeve. He watched his wife disappear at the bend, then turned and went back to watch the cows until it was time to push them north with the rest of ours.

I told Chess I'd sure love to take up Baker's land. He's got 6,400 acres, direction of Sonoita, about half of it real fine. He has a cross-cut canal off a little branch of the San Pedro River, and though it is barely trickling, in better years it will serve fine. Chess and I set to figuring if there's any way we can get that land. We've probably got, when prices are up, close to a hundred thousand dollars worth of stock and land. But we've got barely enough cash to keep food in the house and hay on the ground for six months if rain doesn't set the natural grass. There's just no extra around. Lands, it torments me to see that grassland lost. I always figured my best investment was putting all our money back into the place, but that theory has worked against me this time.

Then, for the first time since we came here over twenty years ago, I pictured what would happen if I had to sell out, too. Granny'd already went and sold a big part of her section to the railroad. Maybe if things got bad enough, and the railroad man came along and waved a stack of greenbacks under my nose, I might be tempted to take it, too. I reckon if the Lord wanted me to have Baker's land, I'd have managed to save more money. I couldn't even pay for my own well.

Chess got kicked by a horse this morning, and while his leg isn't broken, it's bruised blue and real touchy to walk on, so in the afternoon he helped mostly with the cooking. That's all right by me, as he is a right good cook. When we have our roundup, I believe half the boys come on account of the barbeque we have at the end.

I went to the garden to put some water on the choked-looking squash and beans and onions. I don't think my tomatoes are going to make a single one this year. If it weren't for my preserves, I'd have little or nothing to set before my neighbors when it comes my time to provide the hungry drovers with a meal. The chilies are starting to come to life, though, setting little green thumbs that make my mouth water just expecting what will come of them in a couple of months.

July 20, 1906

We were just finishing breakfast when there came a wagon moving slow down the road, and a man riding next to it in a uniform. Charlie and Gilbert, even Mason, had joined us. Charlie saw them from the window first, and said, "Looks like a drummer of some kind. No, that there's some kind of uniform. And there comes Uncle Albert's two-seater after them a ways, with the cousins following."

I've about had my fill of characters coming down the pike wanting something. The first thing going through my mind was that this would be the railroad men, coming to take possession of Mama's place, and just naturally be needing a right-of-way through my chicken coop, and the parlor, too. "Charlie, the shotgun is by the back door," I said. He went after it and out the back. I saw Willie's eyes bug right out of his head as I took up my rifle from behind the front door and dropped it over one arm before I went out. Chess, Mama, and, of course, Willie and Gil followed like ducks as I walked toward the wagon and rider. Charlie would be coming up the side, just in case.

At the side of the round corral, the man on horseback held up a hand to stop the wagon, military-style. Instead of riding the rest of the way toward us, he dismounted, held his reins to the wagoner, and walked. He was gray-haired, but he didn't seem old. Not, at least, as old as Chess, but weathered pretty good. He was heavyset and solid, rather than being tall and lean like the soldier I used to know quite well, and he stood only half a head taller than me. He had brown eyes sunk under permanent squint lines, and a soldier's gait. He doffed his hat and made a little bow. "I've been told by the family up the road that you are Mrs. Elliot. Am I come to the right place?"

"Yes," I said.

"Sergeant Major Udell Hanna, United States Army, ma'am. On a packet for burial. I bring you the condolences of the President of the United States of America, along with all the worldly goods and remains of Corporal Ernest William Prine, Sixth Cav, Arizona Rough Riders. This soldier's last letter, unsent, was addressed care of Mrs. Sarah Elliot. And so this box is sent to the care of the same Mrs. Elliot."

"That'd be me," I said. "I'm his sister."

"He had a stack of letters from you, ma'am. Little else."

My letters? Yes, we'd all sent our notes to him, and I'd written Mama's words for her on a slip of paper, then added my thoughts, and I'd mailed them. It would seem like they were all my letters.

The man was still talking. "It seemed fitting to the colonel to return the remains to your care. May I extend my *own* sincere condolences, ma'am?"

At that moment, Granny started toward the wagon, moving faster than I'd seen her move in many a day. Albert's rig pulled up beside it just before Granny got to the wagon. She stood at the foot and stared in for a long while. Savannah and Albert spoke to her, then came toward the yard. We all waited, stuck in our places, until Granny at last bowed her head and turned aside. The uniformed man nodded to the wagoner, and he proceeded slowly to the yard, all the while with Granny walking beside, holding the side of the wagon.

They stopped at the porch, and we gathered around. Someone remembered to whistle to Charlie that all was well, so he joined us. I read the paper the man had handed me. My brother Ernest, his remains at least, sent in care of me. I'd known it all along, but it shot through me that it was better before I had proof. Better to keep the hope going for our mama, even when I didn't believe. "See that tree yonder, the one with the flowers on it?" I said to the driver. Then I turned back to the soldier. "We'll set him down there. First, though, you come in and have something to drink. Your driver, too."

"Thank you, ma'am," said the driver, "but I'll stay with the wagon awhile yet."

By that time, Albert and Savannah's brood had joined us, and we were a somber little crowd in my parlor. Willie looked purely shocked and dismayed. He never said a word, didn't go to the wagon, didn't make a sound. Just followed me into the house like a hurt puppy. When I tried to put a comforting hand on his shoulder, though, he pulled away. Standing just out of my reach, his eyes disbelieving, his chin taut, he looked from one of us to the other accusingly, breathing hard. Willie fidgeted with his hat, then slapped it back on his head and took off through the house and out to the back porch. I heard the screen door's familiar old creak and then the bang as it shut.

The man stood with his hat in his hands while everyone else came in. He cleared his throat twice, and said, "Udell Hanna, Mrs. Elliot. U.S. Army, master sergeant, retired. At your service."

Savannah and the girls wept softly, except for Mary Pearl, who stood at the window, staring after Willie. Albert sat on the floor by Granny, talking softly to her. I went to the pump with a pitcher and started working the handle. "Mr. Hanna," I said over my shoulder, "I've had a little experience with the army. How is it they've got a master sergeant running errands like this?"

He said, "It's my last mission, ma'am. I've retired, but I was coming this way. Things, well, after the war, they're less formal. I told the colonel I'd be heading this way, and he asked me to bring this last soldier home. We all knew of those Arizona boys. Rough Riders, they called them. I told the colonel I'd be proud to see him to his rest."

"You were heading this way?"

"Yes, ma'am. The rest of the stuff in that wagon is personal possessions. Got some land to look at, and maybe set up my farm like I did before the war. Mrs. Elliot, you folks got the telegram, didn't you?"

"No, we didn't get a telegram."

Mr. Hanna's face fell. "I'm sorry. It was never our intention to spring something like this on the family. They sent telegrams."

I said, "I'm sure they did. I know the army, as I was married to it for quite a while. Likely it'll come day after tomorrow, or next week, or maybe next year. Did you know my brother at all?" Granny suddenly got up from her seat and went outside again. I watched her through the window as she walked back to the wagon. Willie was beside her.

Mr. Hanna said, "No, I'm sorry to say. My brigade was behind San Juan while those boys were under fire. Corporal Prine was the smithy when we weren't fighting, and I knew of him that way. Heard he was good at his job. I— I wish I could say more."

Albert said, "Sergeant Hanna, do you know how he died?"

"Yellow fever. It ran through the garrison down there every few weeks. Took three-fourths of the casualties. If I never see another tropic island, it's all right with me."

Albert nodded. He said, "Reckon we'd better cobble up a little service, and do it quick."

Mr. Hanna took the water I handed him. After he drained the cup, he said, "There was a little patch of mud where we interred all the men we could, near Santiago. What the army's done, now that they're strictly occupation, is located the families of as many as they could, and dug them up to be shipped home. It'll be all right, if you want to wait a spell."

Granny came in just then. She looked purely stricken. "My boy," she said. "My boy's gone."

I'd always missed Ernest. Missed the way he could take a simple thing that everyone had seen, but talk about it in a way that made it silly and more fun. I hadn't seen him since a Thanksgiving years ago, when my children were small. Mary Pearl was just over a year old last time I saw Ernest. Lands, it had to be at least fifteen years. Still, seeing how hard Mama was taking it, I had to hold up for her sake.

"Folks," Mr. Hanna said, "thanks for the water. I don't want to intrude on your family. My son and I will wait outside until you decide where you want us to dig."

Just then, Willie came crashing in, looking wild-eyed and red-faced. He stood, hunched over, his arms to his sides like he was fending off blows from all directions. He hollered, "That ain't my pa. My pa is coming after me. Ma told me last time he wrote he was coming to get me, and we're going to take over the land the family was keeping care of, which *we* owned. He's coming home! You're a bald-faced liar. That ain't him."

Everyone in the room backed up a bit. Albert said, "Son, we know you're upset. But you can't go calling a man a liar when it's obvious he isn't."

"He *is* a liar!"

"Willie!" I said. "Hush. Come here, son. Sit down and get hold of yourself." I didn't want him making Mama more upset than she was, and I sure didn't want him to start some other kind of row right there in the parlor. You could call a man a lot of things without getting more than a bloody nose for it, but "horse thief" or "liar" was another matter. No one would have stopped Udell Hanna from knocking some sense into the boy.

Yet Mr. Hanna only held up his hands. "What's your name, boy?" he said quietly.

"Willie. *Ernest William Prine, Junior*—but I goes by Willie."

Mr. Hanna motioned toward the door with one hand. "Come on out there with me, Willie. I'll tell you what I know was said about your pa. I didn't know him personally, but others spoke highly of him. Always saying he was a good man. I'm sure he *wanted* to come get you."

Willie pulled off his hat and threw it across the room with all the force he could muster. It sailed over a table and landed against the wall, nearly sending a lamp to the floor, except for Clove catching it. "He didn't know me at all. My ma made up those lies. I knew it all along. Telling me he was coming home to get me." Willie was starting to cry. Big embarrassing tears streaked down his red face. " 'N even she threw me out."

The man-sized boy stomped toward the door in his battered fancy boots, strings and strips of colored leather and yarn dangling off them like the leg feathers on a chicken. He nearly tore the door off its hinges as he left the house. It hung open, no longer swinging shut on its own. Savannah's girls began weeping louder then. Mary Pearl just looked mad.

"I'm sorry, Mr. Hanna," I said.

"He's taking it hard, is all. It's understandable," the man said. "I lost my own pa when I was twenty. I remember."

I nodded. "I was seventeen," I said.

Chess came in the door Willie had just left swinging. He tried to close it, fiddling with the latch. He said, "I told Tucker and Flores to dig us a grave. Hope you don't mind where. I had them dig next to Mr. Reed."

A few seconds passed while we waited to see if anyone would say a word against that plan. "It's all right, then," I said. "Mr. Hanna? Did you say that was your son out there, the driver? Why don't you tell him to come on in and rest a spell while we get ready?"

"He'd probably like that," he said. "I'll stay with the wagon while he does. Thank you, ma'am. Folks, I'm truly sorry you didn't get the telegram first. Would have saved the commotion, I believe."

When he left, Savannah said, "Why wouldn't he just call his son into the house?"

Peering through the window glass, I watched them exchange places on the wagon seat. I said, "Orders, most likely. Someone watches the coffin at all times until it is delivered."

The boy who stepped inside was a taller, thinner version of the father. "Pop said you didn't get the notice. Our apologies, folks," he said. "Name's Aubrey Hanna. We've brought three men home, and this is the last one. We'll help with the burying."

"It's a fine thing you're doing, Aubrey," I said.

Mary Pearl had started for the kitchen when Aubrey came in the door. Savannah saw her, and said, "Mary Pearl, will you please fetch Mr. Hanna some water?"

Mary Pearl's face grew sullen, like she was feeling pecked at, having to fetch first one thing and another for people. I was about to offer to get it, when we heard a loud crack outside. Albert was out the door in a second, with us on his heels, and there on the porch floor, sprawled and holding his right foot up almost to his chest, was Willie. He was groaning. My porch rail was cracked and splintered, making a big V in the middle.

"That does it," Albert yelled, swooping at Willie, his arms waving. Well, Albert gave him a tongue-lashing that sent him running, and I might have been worried he'd go on to his Granny's or Albert's house and do some damage, but he just went off into the desert.

Clover and Josh were right on Willie's heels, hollering at him not to go off that way and get lost. Willie took to running, and Clove said, "I'll trail him a ways back and make sure we don't have to send out a search party before the funeral."

Mary Pearl ignored all the fuss; she just took a big tin cup full of water and held it toward Aubrey. I watched something snap between them as loud to me as the breaking of the porch railing had been. That boy Aubrey took the cup and froze solid, staring at Mary Pearl's face like he'd never seen a girl before. He turned dark red in the neck and ears, then tried to say thank you, but no sound came out. He took a drink from the cup, choked a little, and nearly dropped it.

Mary Pearl herself stiffened up when she saw him blushing. I declare, she all but sneered at the boy. He tried to take another drink, and choked on it, which set him to coughing. I saw her pause at the doorway to the kitchen and turn her head ever so slightly, then keep on going.

Well, there's no one around that would say Albert and Savannah don't have a passel of fine-looking girls. Not a one of them, to my mind, is near the beauty

Savannah was as a girl, except Mary Pearl. She is the spitting image of Savannah's sister Ulyssa. Ulyssa was the most beautiful of the four Lawrence girls. Where any one of them was pretty enough, she could have sat for a portrait. Ulyssa was purely lovely, the kind of face only conjured up in poetry and books. Mary Pearl has her outdone.

It appeared that no one else noticed but me. They were all out on the porch by then, fretting over the cracked railing. To me, there was so much going on, what Granny distracted and Willie acting a fool, and the dry lightning coming from Miss Mary Pearl Prine, that I didn't have any room left to fret over the railing. Aubrey was still trying to drink his water, and he seemed to be having a terrible time with it. At last, he turned it up and drained it. Since I was the only one in the room but him, he said to me, "Thank you, ma'am. Will you thank . . . her for me, too? Please?"

I nodded.

"Thank you." He put his hat on his head, and it went on backward, so he had to set it again. He said, "I'd better get going, help Pop take that up to the hill. See if they'll need help with the digging." He quit moving again, frozen stiff in the hundred-degree heat. Sweat dripped from his temples, and he mopped it with his forearm.

"Well," I said, "you go ahead, then. We'll be along when we've changed into proper mourning clothes."

"Yes, ma'am. You will thank that girl for the water, won't you?"

"Yes, I will," I said.

A while later, we gathered around yet another open grave on the rise above my house. This graveyard had a simple beginning long ago. Jimmy Reed was the first one here. I kept the horse that killed him for a couple of years, then sold him in an auction lot. I never would let anyone ride him after that. Albert and Jack and Rudolfo Maldonado fought Apaches right here, along with some men from the Sixth Cavalry. Ever since that time, Albert's face has sloped a little to one side. Rudolfo's brother Ruben was killed, and he was buried here. The soldiers that didn't live through it went in next to Ruben. Now Ernest would lie next to Jimmy, my first husband, who built my house with his own two hands. I remembered watching him work so hard at it, and feeling so excited and proud. I don't mourn for him much anymore, just a little regret.

Jimmy was the first one here. Jack was the last, until now. We'd had a long respite from grave digging. For that, we could be at least a little thankful. As long as I didn't look at Jack's grave, I could get through without crying. If I so much as looked in the direction where he was, I'd not be able to carry on and have it be Ernest's burial and not Jack's all over again. One thing I'd learned from all the burying I'd attended was that sometimes it's hard to pay attention. Burying someone you know will set your mind down some distant trail, as the one you're really on is too painful to view.

So we all sang "On Jordan's Stormy Banks," and we tried to tell ourselves he's on the other side. I know in time I'll come to think of him that way, the same as all the others, but that kind of thinking doesn't come quick. At times, it's better to think of exactly what is happening right in front of you every second, rather than going through things from the past in your mind. It's the only way I can keep standing.

Granny stared into the grave, silent and gray-faced. I reckon she was all done with crying. The rest of the family shed some tears, though, even Mr. Hanna, and he asked if he could say a prayer, too. He was real kind about Ernest, and prayed for him to have peace and comfort in the bosom of Abraham. Willie slipped around outside the rest of us, although there was plenty of room for him to stand beside anyone he chose to. He just couldn't bring himself to stand still and listen. Finally, men got on both sides of the box, holding on to ropes stretched underneath it, and they went to lower it carefully into the grave.

Willie started fidgeting, and pretty soon he was calling out, "No! Don't put him down there. No, no, no! Don't bury my pa!" He threw himself down on the pile of dirt and looked over the edge at the top of the coffin. When they started pushing the dirt in, he tried to hold it back, scoop it from the edges with his hands, and keep it from going in. He was hollering and crying just like a little child.

Granny was the one who surprised me then. She went over to Willie and pulled on his sleeve, saying just as loud as she could, "Get up from there. You got no call to go acting a spectacle. Have some respect for your papa, and act like he'd want to see you behave, standing up like a man. Get on up, and stand. I'll tell you right now that ain't the worst you're *going* to feel, you live long enough. Wipe your clothes off, and do your crying on your feet. It'll kill you doing this."

"Leave me alone," Willie sobbed.

Granny held on to his sleeve. "It's going to kill you if'n you don't stand up."

"I want to die."

"No, you don't. You want to live, and that's why you're fretting that someone *else* died. You just better do as I say." She jerked at his sleeve, and the boy stood.

I took hold of his arm, and for just a second he rested his head on my shoulder, but then something came over him and he pulled away. Willie tumbled down the hill and out through the fence that bounds the graveyard, scuffing his fancy boots, flinging his arms and legs about him, wild, like spokes on a wheel, heading toward my barn.

Well, there hadn't been enough warning to have the neighbors come in and bring potluck for us, so we pulled together our own funeral supper. Rachel went out to the barn to get Willie, but she said he didn't want any dinner. The Hannas stayed and ate with us, too. Udell told us more about the war, and what he knew of Ernest's service before the war, which was all pretty much the same as letters I'd gotten. Granny went to lie down and nap in the bedroom. After awhile, Albert and Savannah left in their buggy.

My sons and Albert's took the little boys out to play some catch, Chess and Mason took up chairs on the front porch to sleep off their lunch, and the girls went to the back porch, where we had hopsack strung. They went out there to talk about whatever young girls talk about, I suppose. They probably had little feeling for an uncle they didn't remember ever meeting. I wish April could be here, too.

In the quiet parlor, I pointed to an empty place on the settee, then sat in my rocking chair. I said, "Where are you from, Mr. Hanna, originally? You said you were coming this way—are you here to stay?"

He sat himself down, and Aubrey took a place beside him. He said, "I was born and raised in Wyoming Territory, but I'm tired of the wind and cold and the prairie. One thing I decided when I joined the army was that I was going to find someplace that suited my family better when I got done. Not much luck so far. I didn't care for the lowlands I came through in the South. Swampland and mosquitoes was most all I saw there. And Texas is, well, Texas. I figure to keep south and cut through the territories, away from where it snows come winter, and if I don't find a place suitable for ranching, I'll keep going to California. I've been told that south of here, toward Mexico, is some pretty country."

"Most all this territory is fit for ranching, but it's been dry lately."

Mr. Hanna smiled. "Does it snow here?"

"Some," I said. "Not enough to stay through the day, but it dusts the plants with white now and then. Five years ago, we had three or four inches on the ground, but it was gone in two days. When I was a girl, up in Cottonwood

Springs, it snowed plenty up there." His son looked around, that sort of half-disguised boredom on his face that I know in my own boys. Aubrey's gaze lingered on the door to the back porch, where the girls' voices sounded like little birds playing. One of the girls was on the summer bed with her legs drawn up, and a sheaf of white petticoats was showing under her black skirt, as if the owner didn't know what a daring pose it made from our viewpoint. "Aubrey," I said, "do you play baseball? The boys'll give you a pretty good game."

Aubrey looked to his father, who dipped his head toward the front door. The boy looked longingly toward the back porch, where the girls were still talking, then at the front door. Reluctantly he stood and went to join the baseball game.

Mr. Hanna said, "A relation of ours wrote they were selling out. Said he'd give me better than the price he paid for it. He's not a close relative, so I'm not buying without seeing it. Thought we'd take a look before we head farther west."

"Who is that?" I said.

"Jim Baker. He sent a map, and when I saw it had your name on it, what with the army business, I felt it was too much a coincidence, more like a kind of message. Reckon I at least ought to go by and see it."

Seemed like I should be saying something nice and neighborly. All that came out was, "It's a fair place, and with some luck, if your water holds, you can make it work."

He seemed to be studying about something. I was thinking about the little strongbox I keep buried in the smokehouse, and how much cash was in there. I wished I'd offered Baker something as a down payment. Or taken a mortgage at the bank. I could have had all that piece. I could have paid it off next year. Then common sense got hold of me, and I felt myself settle down. I'd forgotten about what I owed Mama, the railroad, and everything. "Seems to be providential, you taking it," I said.

"How's that?"

"As you said, you were coming here anyway. Do you have more family that will be joining you?"

"No. Just Aubrey and myself. My wife, she . . . she was killed in an accident. While I was in Cuba. She hated the snow, you see."

"I'm truly sorry, Mr. Hanna."

"My other children are gone, too. But Aubrey's a real good hand, and he's willing to help get the ranch started."

Lord a mercy. What a loss he's had. I had to think of other things before I got wrapped up in our shared grief. I said, "What do you expect to run? About half Baker's land is pretty rocky, more than this. But he's got some nice flatland where he raises feed grain and hay, and a riverbed that runs most of the time."

"I've seen a lot of dry riverbeds coming this way. Folks have told me some of them *never* have actually run water."

I smiled and said, "That's Arizona Territory for you. You'll need a tough-footed, light breed to take those rocks, or you'll be forever dragging them out of the thick. I'd advise you don't try pure longhorn in there. Too muley. We've got an Angus mix, brindled, that's pretty sturdy. A bunch of longhorn crossed with the new Hereford and some natives. Best all-around breed for this area is still criollo. Come up from Mexico, and they can eat near anything. We were planning to thin the herd, and I wouldn't mind selling you a few for a good price. Save me driving some of them north."

He looked a little puzzled, then smiled, shaking his head. "Well, I planned on merinos."

"Merinos. Is that French?"

"I think they're Italian or Greek, or from one of those places. Not sure where they started. But I know they take the heat. I hear they're thriving in Australia. They'll do all right on the rocks. They're pretty light-footed for a sheep."

I stopped rocking the chair and looked from the floor in front of me to the stove and back again, letting that sink in. I said real slowly, "You fixing to run sheep?"

"Going to try," he said. "Grew up on a sheep outfit. It's what I know. And there's hardly none here. Should be a wide-open market. There's just nothing like a sheepskin coat when the winter wind blows."

"You could have trouble," I said, "doing that."

He stiffened in his chair. "Raising sheep?" he said.

That's why he didn't want to live in Texas, I reckon. Now he might be bringing the sheep and cattle war to Arizona. I saw him straighten up, ready for some kind of argument. He knew what I was thinking, and he knew I read him, too. I had no claim to that land, nor to what walked on it. I was done fretting about that. So I laughed and said, "Selling coats in Arizona Territory. Mr. Hanna, it makes no difference to me what you raise. There's good sheep country up on the Mogollon, but I don't know of any down here. You'll spend your livelong day watching out for mountain lion and coyote, not to mention javelina, wolves, wild curs, and bobcat. You'll have to fence the whole range, and probably plant your pastures. You've got eagles and owls that can steal a full-grown house cat, so they can probably lift a lamb. Then there's the rattlesnakes. Can a sheep take a snakebite?"

"I've never seen one live through it."

I just nodded. I was trying to figure if this fellow was a tinhorn or just stupid. "Leastways you won't have the truck with rustlers that we've got."

We talked awhile longer, and had another piece of apple pie each, too. I told him about my well running dry, and what it took to get a new one in. Finally, Mr. Hanna picked up his hat. "I believe we'd better be moving on now," he said. "I'd like to get there before dark."

I stood, then said, "You're only an hour's ride out. Is Mr. Baker expecting you? Stop at the Maldonado place on the way. Look for him there. It's where they've got the herd waiting."

"All I have is a map, and an address in Denver, Colorado, to send a wire to if I decide to take the place."

I got up and headed toward the kitchen, remembering the array of pantry goods Mrs. Baker had fed the hands. "You'll need some things, then. I believe the Bakers cleaned out everything for the picnic they held." I made him hold a little wooden crate, and I fixed him up with some flour and coffee, a jar of sourdough starter, salt and sugar, a jar of peaches, and one of red chili. I put in the rest of the biscuits from the morning's meal, too, and a leftover cooked beefsteak wrapped in brown paper. On top, I set an empty grease can, wadded up some more paper in it, then laid in half a dozen fresh eggs. I said, "No sense going hungry."

Mr. Hanna said, "This is too generous. It's—it's real nice of you, Mrs. Elliot. Much obliged. We'll repay—"

"There's no need to repay."

He carried the box to his wagon. The boys had quit their ball game, and Aubrey was sleeping stretched out in the back, where Ernest's coffin had been. He woke with a start. Mr. Hanna took off his campaign hat, opened a trunk, pulled out a Montana peak, and put it on his head. He laid his army hat in the trunk and turned back to me. He smiled, his face real warm and sincere. "That feels good. My duty's done, and I'm back to living the life I ought."

"Farewell, Mr. Hanna," I said. "Thank you again for bringing my brother's remains home. You both drop by anytime. Good luck."

Mr. Hanna and his boy rode off, the boy and man sitting side by side now, with the horse tied on in back. They just looked like a man and his son, instead of a military detachment. Seemed like decent people. I wasn't going to begrudge a man for raising sheep, although I reckon I'd never actually laid eyes on a sure-enough sheep outside of a farm and ranch supply catalog. Figured if I couldn't have Baker's land, I'd like somebody decent to have it. Didn't know why I felt a sort of wicked gladness that Rudolfo wasn't going to swallow that land up with his. And I wondered if he'd tried, and why it didn't work. Wondered a whole lot of things about Rudolfo, watching Udell and Aubrey Hanna drive down the road.

Chapter Thirteen

The air smelled of lightning, and the breeze from the south carried a scent of wet greasewood. All the signs were good that we'd get rain before the day was through. Rudolfo had set the day after tomorrow as the time to begin the roundup, so we had time to catch up around my house. I was on my way to the kitchen with a load of eggs caught up in my apron when Willie came to me. He'd been gone most of the day to Albert's place. He was holding a piece of paper, folded square.

"I wrote and told Ma that Pa is dead," Willie said. "I aim to carry this letter to the mail myself." He had probably said something about his family life, or lack of, to Albert and Savannah. Savannah, being always kindly and good, probably told him it would be doing the right thing, telling his mother about his papa's death. Myself, however, not being nearly so kindly and not even trying most times to be good, I was happy enough to let things be as they were. I shuddered deep inside, but I tried not to let on to Willie. That floozy woman might come on the next train. Consternation!

I kept moving, not looking him in the eye, and said, "It's a fine thing that you can read and write that well."

"They make you. Police come and bounce you on your head if they catch you truant."

"It's two hours to the station—a long piece, and easy to get turned around. Do you want someone to ride with you?" I asked.

"I ain't no little kid." He sneered when he said it.

"No, you aren't a little kid. Do you have money for the postage? Might cost near a dollar to send."

"That much? Well, I got a couple dollars left. But I'm going. Right now."

I looked at the ridge of thunderclouds looming to the south. They looked like high mountains, sheer and steep, with overhanging snow across their tops. "This late in the day? Best wait. A storm's coming. Could be a real buster." I headed for the house.

He followed hard on my heels, twisting the paper between his hands. Willie's face went pale and he said, "Lightning and thunder?"

"To wake Elijah. Get that door for me, will you?"

"What about tomorrow, then?" he asked. He held the door open. "Tomorrow's soon enough."

I saw the look in his eyes and wondered if it was just the noise of thunder or truly the danger that frightened him. I started setting the eggs in a bowl, moving the last three from yesterday to the table so I could put them on top. Concentrating hard on the eggs I was arranging, I said, "How old are you, Willie?"

I glanced up when I heard him draw a deep breath. He'd puffed his chest like a toad and said, "Nineteen."

I stayed busy, arranging things on the pantry shelves, talking like it was just a stray thought. "I know boys. Most nineteen-year-olds need a shave once a week or so. You think you might have stretched that a little? Maybe more like sixteen? Fifteen?"

"Seventeen!"

"Same age as Mary Pearl," I said. "Only, she was a baby when your folks married. I'd say fifteen is closer."

"Seventeen come January."

If he didn't look so much like Ernest, I'd have believed him, for Felicity might have hidden a baby, along with the other claptrap she'd told my brother before they married. And I suppose there was the possibility that Felicity had lied to the boy about his age for one reason or another. I turned to him and said, "You want me to draw you a map—for tomorrow morning—to Marsh's Station depot, where the mail is picked up?"

"Reckon so." He looked for all his life as if he was about to bust out crying again. He turned away, and his hands went to his face and down again. I missed Ernest, too, in a new way, different from just hoping he was off in some war and hadn't written in awhile. I'd long missed my own father, buried in San Angelo, but I'd lived with him, and been told stories by him. Willie was grieving for a papa he'd never known. The boy was missing a straw man, a landowning rancher stuffed for him by Felicity's pretense.

I acted like I didn't notice his quick tears, fetched a piece of paper, and opened a jar of ink, dipping the pen. He watched as I worked hard on the trail markers, noting the saguaro with two arms down and two arms up, like a Bar Double U branding iron. I said, "If it rains in the evening, sometimes it goes on into the morning, but it will quit by noon. If that happens, don't leave tomorrow while it's raining, but wait until noon. The littlest rain here can bring a flash flood, drowning everything in its path, and there's no earthly way to speculate what direction it'll go. Then you'll have to wait another day. There's really no rush, is there?" I held the map toward him.

"Reckon I'll wait to go in the morning, when it ain't thundering. If you think that's right, Aint Sair."

I let down my guard a little as his face softened. The desperation was gone, and he became a little boy in a big body. "I'm glad you're feeling better." I started pulling dishes for lunch fixings. I said, "I'll tell you, Willie, you've been living here just like a son to me all this time. I want you to know you're welcome to stay. If your mama comes, though, she'll want you to go live with her, wherever she decides to put down. It isn't likely to be this ranch, because she tried it before and didn't like living here."

"Sure enough? She been here?"

"Long time ago. Came to visit just after Ernest and she married. But the wildness—she was nervous. Your papa said she was used to being more civilized."

A slight sneer crossed his face and a grunt came from his throat.

"I need you to carry that box there to Aunt Savannah's. You want the rest of that loaf of raisin bread? You can eat it on the way."

"All right," he said.

Willie didn't come home that night, but I had no worry. No doubt Savannah had merely added a plate to their table. I rounded up my boys for supper, and it was good to talk with them and Chess about the ranch, peaceful, as Willie had always added some slight, raw element of strain. We talked of the drought and cattle; then we talked of April's family coming, and of Harland's family problem. Charlie said he'd been down to the south windmill and had put a padlock on the cover of the gearbox. Gilbert read aloud rates for hoof stock from the newspaper. That evening, I got to admiring my sons' knowledge of things. From my rocker, I purely set them in a different light, there by the oil lamps, and saw cattlemen, grown in ways I hadn't appreciated. One so like his papa, it nearly pained my heart to hear his voice. The other, well, I don't know who he takes after.

As the sun went down, Gilbert got down his guitar, tuned up, and played a little. Chess tapped his foot, and we sang some old songs. Granny smiled the whole time, and her hands came together now and then, as if she might clap to the tune, but rather than keep on, she clutched them, as if she'd reached into the air before her and clasped some memory to herself.

The boys said they'd sleep at the house tonight. Before I drifted off behind the sheet hung on the porch, a good, sweet feeling of peace came to me. Chess, Charlie, Gilbert, and my mama were so near. The men's voices were my lullaby. Trouble was far away.

Jack rode up to the fence out front and hollered, "Sarah! I'm off to find Geronimo." The sky around him was a strange green color, like a china plate I saw once.

"Leave him be!" I called back. "Stay here with me. The boys need you. The boys need a father!"

"The army won't wait," he said. He wheeled his horse around and spurred it hard, so the animal jumped before it put front hooves to the ground.

"Jack!" I called. The sound of my voice echoed in my head and I woke, sitting up on my cot, one arm stretched out. I held my breath for a moment, waiting to see if I'd awakened anyone else. There was no change in the rhythms of sleep on the porch, except for Nip, who raised his head and peered at me curiously. I held back the sheet and studied the darkness for a spell, noting the shapes of my boys.

I have been mama and papa both to them, with Chess's help. Don't know if I can do it again with Willie. Nothing's been the same with him since we buried Ernest. More and more, there was lightning shooting from his eyes, defiant and sassy, like a just-caught spring-season mustang.

We figured Willie went up to the station from Albert's, since he didn't come by here for breakfast. It wasn't good manners not to come by first. Gil and Charlie went to doing chores. I had barely got the chickens fed when Ezra came dragging up, scuffing his bare feet in the gravel. I declare, that boy must have feet hard as a hoof. He was hauling a hopsack bag that looked heavy. From the kitchen window, I watched him approach my house. When he got closer, I saw there were tear streaks on his dirty face. He rubbed his nose clear up his entire arm, then stepped onto my porch and sat.

As I watched, he made his hands into fists and wadded them into his eyes. Then he dragged his heavy bag between his bare feet and opened it. His little shoulders raised and lowered as if he'd given a sigh, his face hidden in the bag. My curiosity had stretched as far as it was going to, so I went out to the porch. "What've you got there, Ezra?" I asked.

He kept his face in the sack and said, "Hidey, Aunt Sarah. M'rocks. Mama says I can't keep 'em no more. Account of Willie got in 'em and made a mess."

"Isn't he kind of a big boy to be fiddling with your rock collection?"

"It waren't these. He got in my secret ones. Now Mama says I have to throw 'em all back in the desert, where I found 'em. I been collecting these rocks all my whole life, since I was a kid. We have to be *nice* to him! I told Mama I was running away from home. Can I live here with you?"

I said, "Well, honey, sure you can. Show me the rocks."

I thought he'd turn the bag up on the porch and dump them, but instead, he carefully pulled out his treasures one at a time. He named each one, saying, "This here's a spoon rock and this here's a egg. This one's a mouse's ear, see that? Shaped just like a tiny ear. This is a corn rock, on account of it's just like a grain of corn. Here's another egg, but it's got a blue thing in it. Here's a one with sparkles in it."

"And what's that, makes it sparkle?" I asked.

Ezra's eyes lit up. "Mica?" He grinned. "Here's a griddle cake and a pudding rock with a bubble just like a custard, and here's a little man." He pulled out a piece of caliche that had arms and a head on a body shape. After awhile, he had rows and rows of them. Ezra sighed. "Can you keep 'em here for me? It took me a lifetime to collect all this."

"You can leave them here," I said. "But what about those others? What secret rocks did you have?"

He squirmed around in his loose overalls, which were easily large enough to put another boy or two in there with him, and finally stood up and reached deep into a pocket. He pulled forth more stones. Tiny wedge-shaped arrowheads.

"Mama said it was a sin to touch 'em. Said I waren't to bring a Indian arrow in the house. I knew I wasn't supposed to keep 'em, but I found 'em whilst I was looking for marbles and such."

I looked at the little weapons in his palms. "That one there goes to that piece there," I said. "They're all broken."

"That jackass Willie busted ever' one. We was all teasing some, and Josh said how Willie looked like a string bean. I showed him my arrows to make him feel better, and he took ever' one and, *crk-crk-crk*, snapped 'em like string beans."

Each of the little points had a match, the perfectly shaped stones destroyed. Without touching them, I said, "Why were these a secret?"

"I told you. Mama said I couldn't keep 'em. I had 'em hid under my mattress and I showed *him*. He broke them all with a pliers and threw 'em out the window, and when I hollered, Mama found out. I got scolded within a inch of my life. Aunt Sarah, I want to live here with you. Nobody wants me there anymore."

"I know you know what these are," I said. "Let me tell you why your mama doesn't want them in the house." So I told Ezra things that Savannah and I have never told our children about how we watched Savannah's mother die at the hands of Indians. How we saw those arrows pierce people and animals and take lives. The old days are not so long ago that we've forgotten the sounds of Indian attack, and what death hangs on those little pointed stones. It would be no different if he were keeping spent bullets from a battlefield to admire.

When my tale was done, Ezra leaned forward, elbows on knees. He scratched his head, and then, putting the arrowheads on the floorboards next to him, he scooped all his other rocks back into the sack. Then he picked up the arrowheads again, made a fist, and flung them out into the yard. One fell short, landing near the house, and he ran to it and tossed it as hard as he could. He turned to me. "Are we having school today?"

"No. It's roundup time."

"Do you mind if I run away to here some other day? If I'm the only otherest one that knows about that stuff, Mama'll feel better having me around to take care of her."

"I think she will," I said. "But you won't have to tell her that you know. If you just give her a look with your eyes, she'll see it. Want me to keep the other rocks?"

"No. It was just them others Mama said to throw away. I'm allowed these. But I'm going to put them somewhere so old Boots can't see 'em ever again." He scampered down the road. Shiner followed him, making a racket, and awhile later he came home carrying a beef bone.

Well, it was time for lunch, so I took Granny a plate and we talked awhile, watching the chickens in the yard. She said she planned to go back to her little house and get some sweeping done, as long as I was going to be out riding all day for a while. I told her to do what she cared to and then have someone take her to Rudolfo's house for supper, as there'd be big doings each night. Granny said, "The girls yonder have baked pies till it looks like a county fair over there."

"Mama?" said Gilbert from behind me. He held his hat in his hands. "Mama, it's Mr. Sherrill. I found him just now. Thought he was asleep in his bunk, but he wasn't breathing. He's . . . he's gone."

I held the arms of the rocking chair. Oh, dear old Mason. I had expected this and yet not expected it. Not now. I was stunned out of speech. We'd all miss him. There was no one to write to; we were his only family. How many days must death swirl around us? Granny started humming, some old hymn loudly. "Is it bad?" I asked at last.

"No," Gilbert said. "Not so far. But I asked Shorty to ride down and see if the Hannas or anyone at Maldonado's can help us get him buried today."

The dogs told us of someone coming up the road, from the south. The first person I saw was Udell Hanna, sitting atop his coffin-carrying wagon. Strange enough, the sight of him made me feel more at ease. He and Chess and the boys went to get Mason Sherrill and build him a box while I took my mama in the wagon to fetch our relatives. She wouldn't go before she'd changed into her faded gray shirtwaist and skirt.

As we drove, Granny said to me, "Seems I'll wear black all my days, now on."

I said, "I thought you didn't care for Mr. Sherrill anymore."

"I never said that I didn't care for him. I said I weren't about to marry him. That's a different thing. We had an opposition."

"'An opposition'?" I tugged the reins. "About what?"

"Do you remember that calico cat we had? The one that sat on the portmanteau all the time?"

"Mama, we didn't ever have a calico cat."

"Her name was Biscuits. I wish I had her back." Granny stayed in the wagon while I talked to Esther, who ran inside to fetch her mother.

Savannah called her family, and they said they'd be along directly. It took nearly three hours for the men to dig the grave. The clay layer under the caliche was so hard and dried out, they had to cleave it loose with picks and then scoop it. Thunder pealed across the land as we laid that box down. Heavy clouds loomed over us, taunting but dry.

Unlike Ernest's burial, which seemed planned out and nicely done in comparison, Mason Sherrill's was hasty and simple. I realized, as Albert said words over the mound of dirt, that for this funeral, I had had no trouble paying attention. Mason had meant so much to me when we were younger—those days when Jack and the U.S. Army wandered the hills and deserts. Before Chess came, there had been only Mason Sherrill. He taught Gilbert to play the guitar. Taught Charlie to throw a lasso. Conciliada and Flores crossed themselves as Shorty and Aubrey began shoveling gravel and clods of hard clay onto the coffin. It beat like a drum as the soil rained down upon it.

Dry thunder. Will it ever quit and just rain?

Udell Hanna came to me. He said, "Mrs. Elliot? Will you walk a spell with me?"

My mind was numb. The air smelled of earth and men's sweat. The rest of the family was already sifting toward home. Walk a spell? But since he was aimed toward the house and I wanted to get in, I said, "Yes."

After we got near the porch, Mr. Hanna said, "I'm surely sorry for your trouble."

"Thank you. Will you have some lemonade?" Then, the very minute I said those words, a thousand tears rose to my eyes. Mr. Sherrill had been here with me through everything. He was the only top hand I've had on this place. Oh, this blessed heat. This hideous drought. It was taking everyone and everything away. Granny might be next. Just like Mason, found slept out some morning. Tomorrow morning. Or maybe Chess. Even Albert or I. None of us could own tomorrow.

I poured out my tears, sitting in the shade of my front porch. Udell Hanna sat beside me. He said nothing. He did nothing. He just stayed there. After awhile, I wiped my face with a handkerchief. "I'm sorry," I said, "to go on like that."

"Not at all," he replied. "I can see he meant a lot to you folks."

"It's not that he was more important than my brother. I know you didn't see me cry for him. Mason's been part of my family, living right here more than twenty years."

"I figure folks got to mourn as it comes. I've done enough of my own to learn not to judge another's. If you all don't make it down to Maldonado's tomorrow, I'm sure he'll understand." Rudolfo had not come. That was the first time I'd thought of him.

Udell said, "I'm no cowhand, but I'll stand in your stead."

I smiled, at least as much as I could. After awhile, something caught my eye in the distance, up by the graveyard. There was Mary Pearl, holding a canteen and pouring from it. Aubrey held a tin cup gratefully, while the other men holding shovels were already drinking from cups. I said, "The world keeps on turning."

His eyes followed my gaze and he saw his son take another cup of water from Mary Pearl. "Faster every year," Udell said. "Aubrey and I—can we lend you a hand with work? I mean, are you going to need help to take up what Mr. Sherrill did?"

"No," I said. "Mostly what he did was long ago." I drew a deep breath. A hard pain shot down through my lungs. I knew that old ache so well, as if it were a companion I'd lost sight of and then recognized the moment it returned. Mason had always been more than a hired hand. "Last few years, he's been more or less retired."

Shiner moseyed up to the porch just then, and Udell held his hand toward the dog, who came to him for some ear scratching and got a good dose of it. He looked up at me and said, "Well, are you . . ." at the very moment I began to say he and his son should stay to supper. We tried again, both talking over each other's words.

The supper table was full that evening. Mary Pearl stayed, too. Granny went to bed early. Willie ate his supper, then went out on the porch, where he smoked some cigarettes, sitting there in the dark by himself. It was a nice evening, though we didn't have music or readings. We talked about the drought and the cattle turning to jerky where they stood, dried to the bone. Before nightfall, the Hannas left for home. My boys slept at the house again, instead of in the bunkhouse.

July 25, 1906

At first light, my mama was rocking in her chair on the porch. When I came to her, she asked me who I wanted to see, and did I bring any gloves for her to wear, for under no circumstances would she go riding without her gloves. Looking in through the window, I could see her kerosene lamp was lit; it was set on a table right under the curtains. She followed me when I went to move it, complaining about gloves the whole way.

The cotton curtain felt hot to the touch when I lifted it away and blew out the lamp. She had turned the wick up tall, and the chimney was black with tar. A few minutes more and the house could have gone up. "Lands, Mama," I said, "you've got to be more careful with the lamp."

"Well," she said, "Ernest's coming home, and he needs some light."

"Ernest is gone. We buried him days ago. He's already come home."

"He'll need some light to see by."

I said, "I'm going to the gathering at the Maldonados' place today. Why don't you work in the parlor and"—I looked around the room—"finish your quilt?"

She looked toward the ceiling, though we were in the kitchen. "It's all done," she said. "Is it going to rain?"

"Eventually."

"*Eventually?* Where'd you learn a word like that? You're putting on airs again, Sarah Agnes. Fix those trees out by the wagon; let the dogs sleep under."

"Mama—" I couldn't go on. She was back on the wagon train that had brought us out here. Traveling through the winter rain from Texas to the Territories. The trip where I met Captain Jack Elliot. "I'm going to start breakfast," I said. "Let's have some coffee."

I made sure Chess would be handy to keep an eye on Granny, and I sent Mary Pearl home to see if Rachel or Rebeccah would come to the house and quilt with Granny until she felt right again.

On the way to Maldonado's, Mary Pearl rode beside me, while the boys went on up ahead. I asked her if she'd mind staying at my place regularly now. I was troubled about keeping an eye on my mama. She said, "I'll tell Mama you need me. I'm so tired of putting up pickles. Honestly, I smell like a cucumber." A little farther on, she said, "There's a chance those two little outlaws may be sent with me."

"More the better. Long as they stay out of trouble, we'll manage."

Mary Pearl and I joined the men in the gathering. To say we worked ourselves to the bone would have been too blessed nice a picture. Rudolfo and his family, with his old, old papa as *hacendado,* own twice the land and cattle I do. For four days, we sweated under the sun and prayed with every breath for rain, having to stop nearly every hour to rest horses and men alike. It did rain some, but it was just a spurt here and there. Black clouds would gather and off in the distance thunder sounded like dynamite blasting, but nothing came our way.

Early this morning, from behind us, came a loud whoop and a score of men's voices cheered and hollered. We turned quickly and saw Willie Prine bunched up on a saddle, nearly ten feet in the air, as his horse spooked. He came down still in place, and the horse let loose another couple of bucks before settling. I joined in the cheers.

Out on the range that reached south near to Benson, the hands kept count of the dogies they gathered. A second count was kept of the drought-stricken dead cattle, lying sprawled, haired leather and dried meat stuck to their bones, baked hard by the sun. That tally was over twenty. There'd been years past that a loss like that would have put me in the ground. What remained to be discovered was whether that would be my lot this year. Though these cattle belonged to the Maldonados, I still felt like I was dragging on the inside, thinking about how many of mine must be out there, too.

Willie stayed to himself mostly. Ate his weight every meal. My boys worked themselves stiff, and kept with the men. Mary Pearl rode with me some in the mornings and helped me fetching and cooking with the Maldonado girls all the long, hot afternoon. When the sun got low in the evenings, we girls rode home and slept on the porch with Granny and Esther, leaving the men to their bedrolls on the hard ground. They'd all sleep out with the cattle, guarding, talking, being part of it. Sweet Esther set baths for us every day. There was no need to heat the water, for our skins fairly steamed as we got in.

This evening in Rudolfo's plaza, we all lingered over second helpings of green-corn tamales and beans, tomatoes with chili and onions, with crumbled *queso* over everything. A couple of the men played some melodies, one with a guitar and one with a harmonic mouth organ. Aubrey came to me, standing in the small yellow light from a kerosene lantern, and tipped his hat. "Mrs. Elliot? Pa sent me for the mail this morning, ma'am, and this came for you." He had a letter in his hand. His eyes went for a second toward Mary Pearl, who was seated on a board next to Gilbert and a couple of the other hands.

Gilbert was talking and they were all laughing. Aubrey smiled and offered the letter.

"Thank you," I said. It was from Harland. "Obliged."

"Not at all, ma'am." He stirred around a bit, then said, "I don't mind at all."

I knew he was hoping I'd say, "Go on and sit with her, then," or something like it. But nice boy or no, Mary Pearl is only seventeen, and she's got college to do before any boy except her cousins is sitting with her.

Aubrey said, "There was a letter for Willie. I gave it to him. Hope that's all right."

"Do you remember who it was from?"

"Another Mrs. Prine. From Saint Louis, Missouri. You-all have folks all over, I suspect. Ma'am." He tipped his hat again, then disappeared over by the bunch of men. So Willie had gotten a letter from his mother. Nothing to do but wait until he tells us what she says.

It was a near torment trying to read Harland's letter by the light of the fire and a few lanterns hanging on poles. I got through it, and my heart sank. I read it slowly again. Then I put the letter in my shirt, as I had no pockets in the clothes I was wearing. It felt uncomfortable and heavy in there.

The sleepy cattle made soothing calls, nudging one another, asleep on their feet. Usually, I loved that sound, but tonight, there was no peace in their lowing. The day's dust settled. The lanterns drew candle bugs and wigglers, a few flying ants. I found my boys and Mary Pearl and told them it was time to head homeward.

Riding together was a comfort, for there was no moon yet. Distant lightning skittered in the south. Charlie and Gilbert took the lead, and Mary Pearl, Willie, and I followed behind. Our horses took a pace near as slow as walking. Charlie asked would I mind if the boys all cleaned up on the front porch and the girls in back, so they could strip down and be quick about it.

I was just about to answer him, when a great bird fluttered up from the side of the roadway. An owl. It had been sitting in a greasewood bush, and it sailed overhead like a haunt, silent and whitish. All our mounts were nervous, but Willie's horse spooked and bucked. Rearing and churning, it kicked out behind while he held on. After about five good lunges, the horse stopped and Willie jerked the reins tight, turning the animal in a small circle.

"Good job," Charlie said. "You stuck to him."

"Dang-blasted, pin-eared, cattywhompus old nag," Willie said.

I said, "Willie, that's the last of any cussing I want to hear from you. Listen, fellows—and Mary Pearl, you, too—Aubrey Hanna brought me a letter from your uncle Harland. Melissa is asking for Granny and won't be comforted. Harland's asking that we take Granny to Chicago. It's Aunt Melissa's last wish." I already knew I would go. Gathering or no, I expected to spend the night packing. I said, "I figure to have Granny ready tomorrow. Willie, I'm not counting you out, but you did just send a letter to your mama, and you need to stay and see if she answers it. I'd like someone else to come along, but I don't know who we could spare."

The boys said they could see to our gathering without me there. Mary Pearl was silent. I don't know if she was hoping I'd overlook her, or hoping to go. I believed that girl would love to see a big city like Chicago. She might be the one who could go with Granny and me. "What do you think, Mary Pearl?" I asked.

"Me? Well, Mama's wishing I was home helping with the canning, but the last of it will be done in a day or two. Rachel and Becca have teaching positions that they'll go to pretty soon. Esther is going to her first term at the university next month. All I'd be doing at home would be watching Ezra and Zack. I reckon they could spare me, if Mama says."

"Mama," said Gilbert. "I think you ought not to go all that way without one of us fellows. Why don't you wait just two or three more days? Then I'll go along with you."

"Big-city boy," said Charlie.

Gilbert shot him a look. "Then *you* go. Take my new hat. You'll be escorting two ladies."

Charlie gave a snort and said, "Your head's too thick. It'll ride on my collar."

"Stuff some of that wadding you got in your head down around your ears. That'll hold it," Gilbert said.

"Boys," I said. "Your aunt is dying. I know you all don't remember her, but your granny cared for her since she was a little child, younger than Zachary is now. I'm too tired for any teasing or foolishness. Just talk straight."

"I'll go," said Mary Pearl. No one else spoke. Fine, then. She'll be the one.

Mary Pearl and I washed up in the dark. Esther brought us clean nightgowns and a lantern. I saw her face, and she looked like a spark was rising inside her. While I was brushing my hair, she and Mary Pearl put their heads together and twittered like little chickens; then they came to me.

Mary Pearl nudged her sister with an elbow. "Tell her," Mary Pearl whispered.

Esther said, "Is Mary Pearl really going to Chicago with you, Aunt Sarah?" Mary Pearl stomped her bare foot. "No, I meant tell *your* secret."

Esther dipped her head and said, "I've got a secret admirer."

I backed up, newly reminded of Savannah's dread of this "secret" lover. "Well, do *you* know who it is?"

"No," she said. "I found another note for me right here, on the door to the chicken coop, and one nailed on the back porch rail. I can tell by the writing it's the same fellow. He wrote me a poem." She gleamed and put her hands on her face—the same way Savannah, her mother, used to do when we were girls.

Lord, I remember feeling that way myself, but I don't remember my April acting that way. It struck me how much I'd missed of my girl's growing up, being harried by work and raising my other children. It also struck me that I don't know much of how to tell a girl to act. Surely I didn't do everything right as a girl. Yet I do know how my two grown boys are, and I do remember the name Esperanza in the margin of a science book. I had boys figured out better than I knew girls. "Well," I said, "don't encourage him, and that'll get him to come forward sooner. Nothing like desperation to make a young fellow start worrying you might not have noticed him."

Esther giggled. Mary Pearl said, "I think he's got to be a knothead. How's he expecting to be invited to supper if he's going to play silly games?"

"Oh, but this," Esther said, "is so romantic. Who could it be?"

Behind us, I could hear the boys yawning noisily, crawling into their bunks, and I motioned the girls toward our beds on the sleeping porch. I said, "Look around you and figure who's here you'd like it to be. There's not a one of these sorry old cowhands I'd want to see you lassoed by. Esther Prine shouldn't settle for less than a top hand. My top hand is Charlie, and he's your cousin. Maldonado's top man is Card Verdez, and he's got an Apache wife and seven children. That doesn't leave many worth having who aren't family. Reckon it might be a joke. Now, let's get some sleep."

Esther's face fell. "A joke? Well, it's not a very nice one."

Mary Pearl made a noise in her throat. "If it is, then it don't amount to nothing. If it ain't, he'll come forward. Seems simple enough to me."

Mary Pearl's stubborn refusal to mind her grammar sometimes tatters my patience. I blew out the light and we settled in. Granny snored. An owl called—maybe the one who'd flown at us on the road. After a little bit, Esther said, "It's still romantic."

Well, I didn't mean to hurt the girl's feelings, but I don't think a secret admirer's letter means anything except that somebody around here has bad manners.

Chapter Fourteen

July 26, 1906

"Sarah, get up. There's trouble."

I opened my eyes. Granny stood over me, wrapped in only her nightgown. She was carrying a shovel, and there was a smear of something dark across her arm. The sounds of people sleeping made me whisper. I said, "What is it, Mama?"

"Rattlesnake got your best horse."

"What, Mama? A snake?" I jumped from the bed and followed her. She was already through the house and opening the kitchen door before I could shake the sleep off and find my shoes. "Mama?" I called.

I managed to snag my kitchen pistol off the top pantry shelf as I chased after her. In the parlor, the little clock pinged four times just as I got out to the front porch. The morning air was cool and already greening in the east. The moon was up, too, and though it was only two-thirds waxen, it brightened the ground. Granny was using the shovel like a cane, headed for the round pasture. I heard the sounds of troubled horses snorting and stomping the ground, pawing and grunting.

I called for Granny loudly, but she didn't stop until she had climbed through the rails and was standing by the water trough. She turned and waited impatiently for me, one hand on her hip. When I got through the rails, too, she said, "Look here. I killed it, the sorry devil. Killed, but too late. I won't abide a rattlesnake. And now old Rose is going to die."

I gasped. I could just make out Rose by the white on her nose, standing far away from Pillbox and Hunter and old Dan. An old paint named Ringer had been added to the retiree's corral, too, and I couldn't see him or Maize at all over in the shadows. I called out, "Rose? Sugar, sugar," and held out my hands as if I'd remembered to bring sugar. Rose didn't move, just nickered softly. Then she squealed. Pillbox whinnied loudly right behind me, which made me jump in my skin. She pushed herself between us and Hunter, skittering around and around him as he tried to see what was going on.

Granny said again, "Look here," pointing. At her feet was a six- or seven-foot-long rattlesnake in two pieces. The business half of it was still writhing on the ground, wound up in some brittlebrush that grew next to the trough. She said, "I couldn't sleep. Having bad dreams some nights lately. Heard a snake, so I fetched the shovel from your shed. It was too late, though. I saw it bite your horse, and she stomped around trying to shake it off. I stepped on his tail and chopped off his head."

"Mercy, Mama. You stepped on his—you stepped on its tail? Did you see where he bit her?"

"That right pastern. Go yonder and see it. Like as not, she'll be dead by sunup."

Only on the leg? I felt the fear leave me, as if it had weighed a hundred pounds. I went toward Rose and she shied away from me. She didn't wear a halter, so I had nothing to catch hold of. I grabbed a handful of mane and tugged her head down. Talking low all the while, I felt Rose's face. A determined rattlesnake will bite more than once, contrary to what people think. There was no swelling on her nose. Most often, a horse will be nibbling something and catch a rattler with their nose and suffocate from swelling in less than an hour. There on her leg, just like Granny had said, was a bloody smear and swelling, and Rose had the leg pulled up, not allowing it to bear any weight. Granny came up behind me and waited while I talked and petted Rose. The horse nuzzled my leg, where I usually have a pocket on my aprons, hoping for a piece of apple or sugar. "It's all right, girl. You are going to be sore, but it's not a fatal one." Finally, I said, "Mama? How did you hear a snake all the way out here from the back porch?"

"Told you. I dreamed it. I just hate a snake."

"I do, too."

"Reckon I'm getting old. Can't sleep at night sometimes. When I do, I have bad dreams, and so I got the shovel." Granny said, "Reckon you'll put her down?"

"Don't you think we can wait? She might make it," I said.

"That horse is old anyway. Just eating up food. Not earning her keep."

"If she lives, she can go on eating all she wants," I said.

Granny nodded. "Just like some old people around. More trouble than they're worth, but you keep on feeding 'em." She patted my arm.

"Did you really step on that snake?"

"Well, I did at that. That devil made me so mad. The very gall of that nasty old— I just didn't give him time to turn around. Snakes'll just kill everything you love." Granny leaned the shovel toward me and I took it. I jabbed at the squirming half of the snake a couple of times for good measure. Then I put my arm around Mama's bony shoulders. Years ago, Granny had sung to my littlest brother, holding him in a quilt while he died of snakebite. Somewhere, buried in the desert between New Mexico Territory and San Angelo, Texas, is a little grave with a child in it, not seven years old. The boy Albert named his first son, Clover, after. With little Clover, a sister I never knew named Harriet, Papa, and now Ernest, Granny has put a lot of her people in the ground. I have, too. A stillborn boy, little Suzy, Jimmy, then Jack. Now Mason Sherrill. It's a wonder any of us wear anything but black all our days.

I put some sulphur in a poultice on Rose's leg. Then Granny and I sat on the edge of the trough, talking, watching Rose to see how she'd do. Granny held the shovel again, leaning toward it. The moon sank in the sky. I told her about Harland's letter and Melissa's wish to see her. Granny was clear as the dawn. Not a bit confused. I was amazed, for she seemed perfectly able to go on a trip all by herself, excepting that it wouldn't be proper. I asked her which of us she'd like to take along, mentioning myself, of course, and Mary Pearl.

She shook her head. She thought Mary Pearl was too young. "And you," she said, "have to mind this horse. And see to your cutting out the herd and selling them off."

When I was silent for a while, she asked what I was thinking. I said, "Just that I didn't know whether you knew what was going on around here. You've seemed a little troubled the last few days."

"Well, I miss my children that's buried. And your papa. And them others."

"I know it," I said. "I worry about you, is all."

Granny said, "I'm lucky I've got a girl that will. Albert and Savannah are fine children, but they've got a houseful and plenty of worries of their own. It's hard for you, without a girl to worry about you, isn't it?"

"I have April—she's in Tucson—and the boys."

She puckered up her lips and gave a little whistle. "Tucson's a day's hard ride. Too far. The boys are going to marry and go off, or find a war somewhere to die in."

"Lord, Mama." Just like that, my heart welled up and tears spilled from my eyes. "Don't say such a thing."

"Don't go to leaking, now," she said. "Chop that thing up good, before it hurts someone else." I took the shovel, pitched that snake's head over the fence, and then dug a little hole and buried it. We could feel the heat of the day begin before the sun crested the hill. Noises and movements of people waking came from the house. With *both* Granny and me gone, no one would question, as which they might have if only one of us had been out of bed this early. I checked Rose's bandage again, then loosened it so it wouldn't cut off the blood by swelling against the rags. I had a hard time getting it fixed just right, so it wouldn't slide down.

Granny followed me every step while I worked, watching silently, the way she used to follow Papa and talk with him when I was little. After I got done fixing the poultice a second time, Granny said, "I reckon I'll take Clover and Joshua with me. Charlie's your top hand, and you can't spare him. That little Willie, I can't rightly trust. He's Ernest's boy, but he's not much like us. You need Gilbert here, too. There's plenty of work to be done. Albert's boy Clover runs the farm and knows all the machinery, but harvest's a couple of months away. They're just digging rows and berms and such. They can spare that for a month and still get it done. Those two ought to be able to catch an old lady if she gets out of the fence."

I couldn't believe what I was hearing, and feeling. I was hurt. It was my place to go with her. I had a bag packed. "Don't you want me to go?"

"You've got work here."

"Nor Mary Pearl?"

"She's a good girl, but most of the time she's not paying attention. She'd likely be thunderstruck in a big city. Two addled females would be more than one young man could handle."

I said, "You've got this all thought out. As if you knew it before I told you."

"Been up, thinking. Then I took a nap. Then I killed a snake. 'Bout time for breakfast."

What could I do but agree with that? "Yes, ma'am," I said. I hooked arms with her and we strolled to the house in our nightgowns. I'll wash the snake's blood out of her sleeve before she leaves for Chicago.

July 27, 1906

Before she left this morning, I took advantage of my mama's return to the here and now by having another talk with her. I explained to her how much easier it was to keep an eye on Willie if she was at my house. She, of course, knew that was folderol, and she asked why I didn't just come out and say that she was not mindful enough to live alone anymore. "Well," I said, "because I didn't want to hurt your feelings."

She chuckled to herself. Then she said, "I'm tired and I'm lonely and my mind wanders. Got pure spoilt being here at your place them days, and if you don't mind having an old nuisance around, I'd be kindly obliged to stay here. I have a hard time sleeping at night and a hard time staying awake in the day. Being old is harder work than I thought it would be, that's all. It'd be easier if you were to tend to the lamps and things."

So we made a plan, she and I. I'm going up to Granny's house and close it down for good. If my boys take back their rooms, like as not I'll be needing to build on a little by the end of summer. If the cattle sell for a fair price, we'll come out all right and be able to afford that. I haven't added a room on this house in ten years, and I do love the idea of spreading it notch or two.

Clover borrowed my old-fashioned brougham to drive Granny to town, where they'll take a train to Chicago. Joshua rode beside them on a mare. Watching them go was harder than leaving my family behind with a dry well when Chess and I ran off to find Harland in California. Being the one doing something is always so much easier than being the one waiting. Watching them disappear beyond the horizon, I got so full of sadness and lonesomeness, I felt ashamed and quit staring at the road.

I set off to take on the day's burden. It followed much as the day before, except at noon Rudolfo called to everyone and we prayed for rain. One thing I'd started to notice was that where all the cows ran on open rangeland, his brand outnumbered everyone else's two to one. That beat-up land was barely holding my stock, and he had twice as many, eating up everything in sight and starving all of them. Rudolfo was praying because he'd lost so many head.

Charlie came to me after all that praying and said, "He should have culled his herd and sold off part last year, and we'd all have fared better."

"El Maldonado would say you're too young to question an old rancher."

"Well, Mama, you've taught us all our lives to question. I'm seeing land that's grazed off so bad, it's overrun with tumbleweeds where there ought to be natural forage. On one ridge Flores and I rode, the tumbleweeds and thistle were piled up twelve feet high, like nothing I've ever seen in my life."

I pulled my horse close to his. "If that's going on," I said, "I'm going to speak to Rudolfo about cutting down his herd with this sale, and not send so many of ours. They'll do better without the competition."

I didn't see Willie but once all day. Mary Pearl, too, stayed busy, and when we all limped home at the end of the day, Willie stayed with the cowhands and didn't follow us. Maybe Rudolfo would put him to work there. Nothing like good hard-won rest on the hard ground to straighten out a boy. That was the end of it for the Maldonado herd. They'd just be kept in place with Baker's and Cujillo's and the few strays of mine, and then we'd move over to my spread and start combing the hills. All of us could use a day off to tend gear and such.

The next day, Willie came along right after breakfast. He got off his horse at the porch. I said to him, "I heard you got a letter. Did you hear from your mama?"

"I didn't get no letters."

"Are you saying what I heard was a lie?"

"Saying I didn't get no letters. Not from nobody. No *damn* body."

"Willie? This morning, I want you out helping Charlie in the barn. We've got to clear out some tack in the back stalls and make room for when the gathering here at our place starts."

He said, "Why'nt you put them horses in the pen? Good enough for the others."

"Because what I'm putting in the barn are bunks for men, not horses. Just to have ready if someone wants to use them."

His bottom lip stuck out as he said, "All you do is try to work me to the bone."

I declare, that boy flashes hot and cold faster than I can keep up. I said, "You told me you want to learn ranching. Hard work won't kill you. Sloth will."

Willie moved toward the horse, then stopped and turned. He said, "I been worked by that old Mex till I'm done in. Learn ranching? And 'What year in school you done?' Always trying to make like I'm the ignorantest cuss ever born. Everybody here looks at me like they scraped off their boot and there *I* was. You and them others just sit around conjuring up claptrap for me to do. I'm going out to do some shooting." He flipped a pistol from behind his back, where he had stuck it in his belt. Twirled it on a finger.

"Where'd you get that? That's not one of ours. No one's trying to make you look ignorant," I said. "Put that away. Sit here a spell and let's have a talk. You need to make some things right with your cousin Ezra." I reached for him, my arms outstretched.

Something frightening came into Willie's face, so I let him be. "Look at that," he said, twirling the pistol again.

If that had been one of my boys, he would not have been able to sit for a week, talking to me like that. There's something violent inside that boy that I didn't want to stir up. I don't aim to go hand to hand with a man who's a foot taller than me. I *sure* don't aim to call down a boy with evil in his eyes, especially one toting a loaded pistol.

I thought he'd gone off to the desert somewhere, angry, but a little while later, Willie was in the yard, playing quick-draw pulls from his belt, aiming at the barn without a care in the world for the animals that were inside there, or the people who might be working in it, too.

"Come on up to the house," I said. "We've got some talking to do."

Willie said, "I'm busy."

"I'm not going to ask you again, boy. You can just go to bed tonight without supper. See if your attitude is a little gentler in the morning."

I'd just closed the door when I heard a dog yelp. I went to the window. Nip was slinking away from Willie, who had just crossed his path. He ran to the porch and hid beneath it. Now I would go at him. Nobody hurts my animals. I picked up my snake stick and commenced following him, calling out, "Willie Prine! Get your no-account *self* back to this house. Turn around right now and come home. I'm going to give you the licking you just earned."

He turned around, the pistol still in his hand, and he twirled it again on his finger. He stared at me hard. "Home? Leave me alone," he said. "Leave me the hell alone."

I was dumbstruck. I never in my life had felt so muddled and angry all at once. If that'd been a stranger, I might have left fly with a load of buckshot at him. Wouldn't have felt one bit sad if it'd hit him. If it'd been someone threatening my kinfolk, I'd not have given him time to threaten twice. Never in all my days would a member of my family have said such a thing and acted so threatening when called on it. Reckon the end of it, too, was that I was afraid of someone that slept under my own roof.

A hot breath of air rustled some leaves off the bushes nearby. Thunder tumbled across the sky. Willie went on his way, on foot, over the sandy ridge. I went back and coaxed Nip from under the porch with a piece of cheese, then felt of him all over, looking for broken bones. When I let him go and the cheese was all gone, he went back under the porch and stayed.

I started walking just to let off steam. Then I decided the only thing to do was to talk with each person in the family who needed to know and explain what had just happened. This went against my grain worse than anything, because that's the root of gossip, to go carrying tales from one person to the next without saying it in front of the boy. Then I remembered that dangerous look in his eyes and the thought that his mean streak might come out worse with time. We were going to have to take that pistol away from that boy. I kept walking and made a big loop, headed to Savannah's. I figured either something had happened at Rudolfo's overnight or that Felicity had written something that set Willie off.

We worked a long day, pulling in cattle from the south hills and counting more now with my brand. The Lazy Bar E brand was not hard to spot, and it was easier for me to be closer to home, since there was less travel time. Willie showed up, but he stayed away from us all, working either by himself or alongside a couple of the drifters Rudolfo had hired to help.

Someone had bunged up my south windmill again. Not as bad this time, as far as real damage. They'd broken open the lock and put rocks on the gears, which came out just as easy. But there was that white powder in the troughs, and two dead antelopes next to it, along with a bull I couldn't identify, and the half-eaten corpse of a javelina. I closed down the gear works and shut off the water.

Well, I'd barely gotten through and put my gloves back on, when a shiver ran up my spine. I took one step toward my pony and slid my rifle from the scabbard as quietly as I could. I heard the movement more clearly this time. "Step out!" I called, and chambered a shell. "Come out of those bushes, or the next twig that snaps, I'll shoot."

"So violent, my dear lady. Why art thou so ferocious? Could'st it be that Diana endowed thee with the huntress's skill but a murderess's heart?" said a voice I knew like I knew my own mother's.

"Lazrus, you lunatic, step out here."

He came forward, hands before him, like some prayerful supplicant. "I live only to do your bidding."

"You the one who's poisoned my water?"

The cocky look left him. He jerked his head toward the windmill. "Poisoned?"

"You telling me you didn't see the dead animals all around?"

"I only just arrived, Mrs. Elliot, drawn by the electric aura of your presence. Jehoshaphat! I thought it was simply dry and you'd need me to find another. The water!" He seemed to have forgotten I was holding him at gunpoint, and he darted toward the tanks. "Oh!" he roared. "Thunder and lightning! Mephistopheles and Beelzebub!" He grabbed up a handful of the white powder and held it close to his face, grimacing, sniffing, eyeing it as if he were trying to foresee something through it. "What plague! Vile rogue that did this. Show me the villain that procured this substance, and I'll tear his liver out through his eyes." He shook the fistful of stuff toward the sky. The powder filtered down and settled on his beard. Lazrus whirled around, his trappings loose in the wind, and faced me. "What of the water source? Was this put into the well itself, or merely scattered here?"

I hadn't even considered that. "I don't know," I said. "Are you telling me you didn't do this?"

"I have never lied to you, madam. I have brought you truth you will not hear, but I do not lie. Never, ever, would I defile the nectar of life. To destroy water is to destroy creation. Show me to the pump!"

I pointed with the tip of the rifle to the very obvious windmill. "Yonder."

He hurried to the windmill pipe and deftly removed the cover, then brushed away some gravel and pulled the pin so that it began to move very slowly. After a few seconds, a stream of crystal water ran over the fouled tanks. Lazrus sprang right into the tank and leaned over the pipe. He straightened up then and whipped his tunic over his head. Standing right in the trough, he sniffed over the waterspout, then bent and drank deeply from it. If it had been poisoned, he'd be drinking his death.

"Stop," I said.

He gulped more and then stood, a broad grin spreading across his face as water dribbled from the corners of his mouth. His grizzled beard was now wet in streaks, white-powdered in streaks, and something that looked like leaves was snarled in it. "The well is fine," he said. "The troughs, however, are tainted with ratsbane and caustic potash."

"Are you sure?" I shuddered down into my boots. He was standing knee-deep in the deadly stuff.

"I know water, dear one. I'm touched by your sentiment. Your care for my welfare." He turned and faced me, water dripping from his beard to his bare chest.

"My concern was that if you poisoned my well, I didn't want to see you die from it if I could watch you hang instead."

"Vitriol pours from your lips like the water from this pipe." He looked toward the sky and raised his hands. "Is this the woman sent me? How shall I live with her?"

"What are you doing here, if you didn't come to ruin the water?"

"I told you. Thought you'd need another well."

"Lazrus, I'm telling you one last time to get off my property. If I see you slipping around, if anyone sees or even thinks they see you, we are going to haul you to Tucson and put you in jail. And that will be their second option. You won't like the first one."

"Mrs. Elliot, say you believe me about the water? I'd never do this to water." There was earnestness in his voice.

I watched him carefully. And I did believe him. But I wasn't sure if I should allow the scallywag a single moment of hope. I wanted him gone. He turned toward me again, his face open and pleading. On his bare chest were several long and old scars, three of which looked to be bullet wounds. They were laced with newer scars, some still dark and purple. Lazrus smiled. The sun gleamed on the scars. His eyes glared. He said, "Your eyes cut me to the heart. Oh torpid stream, sleep ever more, for she is removed from your grasp."

I looked into his eyes. Time slowed and everything took on a strange quiet. I heard my own breathing. "You did this," I said.

He stepped out of the trough, coming toward me. Lazrus roared. "No! I'm covered in innocent blood, Sarah." He was brawny as a young man.

I moved backward, realizing this could be my one chance to get him to choose to leave me alone. I said, "I see you hiding back there, watching to see what happens, the way a person watches the suffering he caused. You poisoned my well. Your presence here marks you guilty, in my book. I found you here when I discovered it ruined. You want me to believe you didn't poison my water, there's only one choice. Get off this place. Don't come back."

His features dropped as a look of utter defeat came over him. "But I love you." Tears streamed from his eyes, making dark, wet furrows in his beard.

These met with the ones created by the water. "You don't believe I did this, do you?"

Tears filled my eyes. I looked straight at him and lied. "Yes, I do."

"To verify my innocence to you, once more I shall become yet another soul banished from Eden." Lazrus looked at me one more time, hard. "Vesuvius!" At that last, his old mule came from the brush and ambled to his side. He leapt upon the animal, then groaned and said, "Oh, it is a more terrible thing I do now than I have ever done. The only way I can now have your faith is to abandon your presence forever. What curses the gods heap upon the condemned! Vesuvius? Carry us hence!" He whipped that mule and rode off in a cloud of dust.

I was shed of Lazrus! And it had happened by his own choice.

I reckon with enough anger, a woman can pretty much be strong as a man. As hard as it was to waste the new troughs and all, I shot holes in both of them. When the water was drained, I lassoed the rim bracing of one and had the horse pull it loose. Then I wrestled it up myself and turned it clear over. If I ever do catch the snake that did this, there'll be the devil to pay.

By twilight, my count was live stock 190, dead 28—a poor percentage. As we gathered in my yard, where Chess and Savannah and all their girls had laid the tables swaying down with food, I made everybody listen while I told them about my meeting with Lazrus and what he'd said was in my tanks.

Soon as the men got ready to settle, Gilbert pulled out his guitar and Shorty played a mouth harp. The night was peaceful. I went to pet my old horses and Hunter, who was sporting around the ring as Pillbox ate. I climbed through the rails and found myself a perch on the top one. Rudolfo came looking for me. He stood silent nearby for a long time. I knew he was there, but I kept on studying my horses. "Sarah?" he said.

"Yes?" I replied.

"This thing which has happened, maybe it was *predestinado.*"

I said, "*¿Para qué?*"

"Perhaps it is meant for us to be together. Your herd is depleted. That is, if you are faced with losing everything, it can all be saved. Marry me. Marry me and share all that I have. You will live here forever and will not worry about money or cattle the rest of your life. I'm a rich man, Sarah. More than you know. I have land in Mexico, too. Fine horses in Vera Cruz. Things are changing in Mexico. I tell you so you will know this is not a foolish offer. I will be a rich man, whether I sit in the throne of the *gobernador* or not. You will not be sorry."

"Rudolfo," I said, though I didn't really know what I would say next. I didn't feel desperate. Not broken, yet. Not ready to just give over because there wasn't any choice. My gathering of the herd wasn't done. Surely the rest of them were out there somewhere. I was just tired. I'd had the last word with Lazrus, finally. A small victory. I was almost startled when Rudolfo's hand closed over mine on the rail. I didn't pull away. I didn't feel anything for him, but I didn't pull away.

Chapter Fifteen

If there was a time the earth could have burst into flame by its own heat, this summer would have been it. The whole of my ranch felt like one enormous stove top, heated and waiting. Then this morning I saw a rolling cloud, looking heavy and dark, growing high into the sky toward the south. For weeks, I had watched clouds form over distant ridges, seen rain fall, waving like a blue sheet stretched from the sky to the ground, smelled lightning snapping, hungered for the music of thunder. Barely a drop had hit ground that I own, as if it had been singled out to be scorched dry until nothing remained but sand and scorpions. It was an odd time of day for a thunderstorm, but this one was coming straight for us. Hallelujah. Rain at last.

Under the darkening sky, I fed the chickens and then put out breakfast for my family. Every pulse of my heart sang a song in my ears: rain at last, rain at last. The other side of the same coin was that it would be a poor day to gather cattle. They'd be spooky, same as the horses, and we'd have a terrible time moving them. I talked it over with Chess and the boys, and we decided to postpone our sorting and gathering yet another day. Charlie rode south to help picket the combined herds. I thought he'd be back soon, but he's taking a long time. Probably going as far down as the Hannas' place, since they seem determined to help out and are real neighborly.

Over the last couple of days, a dreadful anticipation about Rose has crowded my mind. She's not getting well soon enough—off her feed but drinking water. Just as Mason's death was not really a surprise, I expected at any time to look out and see her down. If Pillbox or the others get close, she hobbles away, determined to do her suffering in solitude.

After breakfast I asked Mary Pearl and Esther to help me clear out Granny's house and do some washing. When we got my mama's place emptied and closed the door, I turned away so as not to feel the tug of letting go. Then the girls and I started the iron wash kettle going at my place. It sure was nice having so much help. Ezra and Zachary tumbled in and out, underfoot, but not really trouble, as every time they got near, I gave them something to carry somewhere or another.

Chess and Gilbert were in the barn. On a ranch there's always a loose stirrup, a blanket with a tear that will blister a horse's back, or some such that needs tending. Willie took a hammer and nails and went up on the roof, looking for loose places in the tin sheets. Now and then he made a racket, fixing them down to get ready for the coming storm.

In about an hour, we had all the clothes on the lines. The breeze picked up but that hollow, dank feeling before a storm didn't come. The way it sometimes rained in patches like a crazy quilt, it could be raining at Maldonado's and not here. I caught a whiff of ashes, as if the hired hands were burning trash by the bunkhouse, and in this wind, there's no good to come of that. I went to tell them to douse the fire, but their fires were cold out. The burning smell got stronger; wood and something dirty, like a log full of termite holes and sand accidentally put in a campfire.

Suddenly, the wind stopped and the air felt so still and hot, it pained me to breathe. Mosquitoes descended upon every live thing. I stood near the bunkhouse and watched as the dark cloud moved upon us like a blanket pulled on a giant-size bed. It still looked like a dust storm, growing without wind. It carried something vinegary and sharp-tasting in it. The air filled with dust and acid; it burned our eyes. Chess and Gilbert left their work in the barn. Gilbert said, "Mama, we told Shorty and Flores to get home and see to their families. Just in case this is some tail-spinner of a storm."

As miserable as that hot wind had been a few minutes before, this terrible stillness seemed to suck the air from the lights. I put my fists on my hips and studied this approaching shadow that looked like a biblical plague. All at once, a gust of air slapped my skirt against the door post and stung my face with hot sand. Mary Pearl and Esther went hurrying inside with damp clothes they'd taken from the line. I hollered, "Willie! Can you see anything from up there?"

"Smoke, Aint Sair."

The word tolled in my heart, so terrible I couldn't say it. It consumed me and my power of speech, as if my voice was in its awesome path. Wildfire. "Come on down. Get in the house, Willie." I watched him climb from the roof, then I took another look at the sky before I opened the door. Willie and I dashed inside just as the blanket of smoke descended. The acid smell eked its way through every crook in the boards so the air indoors was near hard to breathe as that outside. Outside the windows the world had turned to a mist of grayish brown in all directions.

Fire had taken Jack from me. A fire he had gone into, not away from. Charlie had ridden south to Udell Hanna's place. Toward the fire.

Chess said, "You girls better get up the road to home right away."

Mary Pearl's large eyes grew even larger, but she took Esther's hand and said, "We'll stay and help you. We'll clear brush and get the dogs inside."

I said, "I'm riding down to the Hannas'. Make sure everything's all right with Charlie. He went to set picket——"

Chess threw his hat down, saying, "No, ma'am. He'll be helping out if they need it. You'll hear what he knows soon as he gets back, but you *aren't* going there even if I have to tie you up to keep you here. I've seen a prairie fire before. Brush and trees, dry sage and greasewood that'll go up like kerosene bombs surround us. Tumbleweeds in a fire roll like moving torches, and we've got more of 'em than I ever saw in fifty years in Texas. There's plenty of men there to see to the Hannas."

I made a fist and pressed my lips against my tight fingers, pushing back the panic that made me want to scream. I said, "All right. We're going to stay here and draw water and save this house. You all fetch every bucket and jug you can find. Wrap something around your face you can wet down. Gilbert, you and Will fetch every rake and hoe we've got from the barn."

Chess, Gilbert, and Willie went to scraping a line in the yard clear of brush while we poured water in a ring, eight feet wide, about twenty feet out from the house. I moved like a machine, thankful that Chess was there shouting commands and it wasn't left to me. With every creaking noise of the pump handle, I whispered a thank-you for our well and the bountiful water that flowed from it. Even for Lazrus, who'd found it. Another prayer that the water would hold out, that the fire would jump us and all our neighbors and friends.

Staying busy kept me from picturing my oldest son riding toward the range fire.

The air darkened to the pitch of night; the wind quit. Without a breeze to stir and thin it, the brown smoke strangled us. Most every breath I took, I coughed. We got rid of the kerchiefs and put heavy, wet dishrags on our faces to breathe through, and still it burned our throats. I pumped water until my arms would barely move, filling jar after jar, then handing them to the girls to haul and pour. Then we changed places, one of the girls taking over the pumping while the other girl and I hauled water.

I had just passed Chess another bucketful, when he dropped it and pushed me back into the house. "That sound," he said. "Get in the house."

I listened hard, though my ears felt as if they were full of cotton lint. There it was. A faint, distant rumbling, growing louder.

"Thunder!" Mary Pearl said.

Esther clapped her hands, saying, "Rain! It will put out the fire."

Chess shook his head. "It ain't thunder. Get the mattresses. Get as far into the middle of the house as you can. Pull them mattresses, boys. Get, get!"

All those cattle had been waiting down by Rudolfo's *hacienda* to be driven north. A thousand head at least, waiting for more of mine to be pulled in. Jim Baker's herd was there along with whatever number the Cujillos had added. On my range, I figured there should be another five hundred at one end, almost that many in the eastern section, loose and wandering and scared by the flames or the smoke or the black sky. The noise was the resounding hooves of two thousand head of longhorn and criollo, wild and rank as a desert whirlwind themselves, barreling toward this house.

This house had stood through hail and flood. It had always seemed like a good, soundly built house. I shooed the girls toward the bedrooms. The front door flew open and a man, black from head to toe, stumbled in and took off his hat. Charlie! "Ma!" he called. "Hanna's lost his place and everything with it. It's at Maldonado's south border now and the wind is stirring it this way. I've out-run some steers, and the others are going every which way, some right into the fire. There's no place to run."

Esther sobbed and said, "Aunt Sarah, what about your cellar?"

Charlie shook his head. "If they bring down the house, you'll be buried alive."

At last, I found my voice, and it was a shout. "We'll stay right here," I said. "Get this furniture into the near corner of my bedroom. There are more walls between that area and the south. Make a bridge out of the armoire and surround the outer walls with furniture. Push it against the window. Use the iron frames off the beds. Put the mattresses all in the center and we'll hide in the middle of that. Come on, son."

Charlie grabbed his hat, shaking his head. "I'm going to try to turn them away from here. You all do what you can." He vanished without closing the door. Gilbert and Willie bolted out behind him before I could tell them to stay inside and hide.

"You boys get back here!" I ran to the front door and stood on the porch, screaming, "Charles Elliot! Willie! Gilbert! Get in here! Boys!" Chess grabbed my arm hard. "Let me go get those boys," I said, coughing.

Chess didn't talk, just jerked me in the door and closed it, then shoved me toward the mattress fort the girls were making. My mouth opened, but I couldn't make a sound. My boys! Running toward their deaths. I stood there blinking, watching Esther fret, and Mary Pearl, all grim and business, stacking furniture. I felt as lost as my mama looks sometimes. Maybe this was what it took to send me over yonder, into the distance, where I don't have to feel this way, all scattered and tormented inside.

Mary Pearl said to Esther, "Mama and Papa will be safe. The sandy cliff at the creekbed will stop the cattle. The fire can jump it, but those steers can't."

We turned over anything that could make a barricade, cobbling a little fortress out of my bedroom. The armoire went up against the window, and Mary Pearl was smart enough to take all the pictures and mirrors off the wall. She was scared, but she wasn't crying. Esther sobbed aloud. We climbed in and pulled the mattresses around. A gust of wind rattled the window glass. There was the rumbling again. This time, we could hear cattle bellowing, howling their fear and terror and pain as they stumbled over each other and were trampled and gored and crushed. Chess bolted back to the bedroom and into our nest of mattresses. The ground shook. The sound came closer and closer, until a tremendous roar seemed to roll over the top of us. They were right outside the wall. Dust puffed through the walls and the furniture rattled. In another room, something fell to the floor and broke. Mary Pearl hissed between her teeth and said, "Aunt Sarah, I think I left your yellow milk pitcher on a chair."

Charlie and Gilbert and Willie. Shorty and Flores. All my neighbors, all my family. And poor Rose, Dan, and Maize. Ringer and the others. Little Hunter. Touchy little Pillbox. Nip and Shiner. Four or five cats, good mousers all. Thirty chickens and four geese. My poor animals. What a sorry, sorry way to die. On the skin of my eyelids, I saw Charlie, looking blackened and strange, smelling of fire smoke, with that ring of white where his hat had been. Just like Jack. I'd held Jack's head, whispered that I loved him, and smelled that smoke. Just before he died, I had touched his burned hair. It crumbled into my hands. Surely, surely, Providence would not allow a son to die like his father, torn asunder by exploding debris in a fire. Surely, Charlie would know when it was time to run. No herd of cattle was worth my son dying. And he would watch out for his brother. Surely.

When it got quiet, Chess decided to slip out and chance a look outside. He went to the porch and called the dogs. He called Willie, then hollered for anyone who was out there to come to the house. It was terrible, hearing that lonesome calling, not even a dog to answer him. The air was sooty brown and silent. This little house seemed like a lost twig at the bottom of a well. We were helpless ants clinging to the twig.

Another rumble started but then died down. The cattle were lost, dazed, running in bunches here and there. At least there was that. They were *not* in a massive flank two thousand strong, surging like a tide toward this house. Though the small groups could kill, they might be easier to turn. Just as they'd come close but not destroyed this house. I heard men outside, men whooping and whistling, shouting for their lives, trying to control the terrified animals.

Then it was quiet. A deep, thick quiet, as dark as the sky outside, but definitely *not* filled with maddened cattle. I stood up in the midst of our ring of mattresses. "I'm going to go outside and look," I said. When I returned to them, I said, "I think we should get these girls home now. It'll be safer." Albert and Savannah have a house that's mostly rock. It's across the creek, and the sides of the creekbed will form a natural turn for the fire and the crazed cattle. All we have to do is get there.

After ten minutes of silence, Chess said he agreed. It would be safer by far to be up by Albert's place. I pulled back a mattress so the girls could step out. My chest hurt—maybe from the strain of breathing through the wet rag, or maybe my heart was going to seize up and quit. Dirt in the house hung in the air as if it were suspended, as if the whirlwind that had hit Savannah's porch that day had come back and taken up camp. We were covered with silt.

Chess and I took rifles from behind doors, as well as all the shells we could carry. If we came upon a roving bunch, taking down two or three lead steers could form a little ridge. The others would go around and we'd be spared. The air outside was still heavy and thick to breathe, and a wave of my hand made it move in curls around me. The outbuildings, whose outlines I could see faintly in the smoke, were standing and whole. I heard chickens fussing and the speckled rooster crowing.

Chess pulled two saddles from the racks and I carried the blankets and pads. Mary Pearl said, "Don't worry about my saddle, Grampa. Esther and I can ride bareback on Duende." Esther stared at her, holding her hand over her mouth.

"All right," I said. "But I want a saddle. I'll get one of the cutting horses. I've got work to do after we get you girls home." I wanted my whole rig so I could keep that rifle handy. Without it, I couldn't imagine what would be our fate if we met up with a bunch of criollo on the tear, but a good cow horse and a rifle would give me at least a chance to keep them away from the girls.

Rose, the other old horses, and little Hunter clustered at the wall of the barn that made part of the round corral. That fence was stout as could be and parts of it had iron bars, too. Much of it was unseen in the smoke, but from the looks of things when we got closer to it, the cattle had moved against it, but the fence had held. The horses inside were safe, both young and old.

We made our way around that toward the rest of my riding stock, the ones we'd moved away from the barn and penned on the east side for the roundup. When at last we got to them, the horses shied away until Chess and I pulled the dishrags down to our necks. It felt like forever, trying to saddle the horses, breathing air so thick with smoke that it puffed in and out of our mouths like we'd been smoking tobacco. We heard a shout: Gilbert's voice. Chess called him to the barn.

Gil was out of breath and almost as black as his brother had been. "We need help, Grampa," he said.

Chess said, "Sarah, I'm going with the boys. You take the girls home. If you run into bunches of strays, just run *with* them until you can turn off. If they're coming right at you, shoot as many as you can."

"Girls," I said to Esther and Mary Pearl, "I'm going to get you home and come back for these horses. You find me a place for them there while I'm gone."

"Bring 'em now, Aunt Sarah," Mary Pearl said. "Please bring them. I'll help you, and it will take less time in the long run." The sun was a ball of orange in the amber-brown sky. Everything glowed yellowish, like the sulphur on Rose's leg, but at the same time had lost its true color. The whole world was dim, like a picture in a newspaper, and yellowed, like the paper was old. The sun was close to level with my house, yet it seemed to be staying there, impaled against the void that was neither sky nor ground.

"Help me get them caught, then," I said. We slipped a loop over Pillbox and another over Hunter, who got real agitated at it. By just opening the gate to the round corral and leading the two, the others would follow on a normal day. On this day, I felt I needed to cover the horses' eyes and tie them all. Esther held the reins while Mary Pearl helped me get them all rigged. We rode carefully up a road so familiar to me, I could have done it blindfolded. I tried to give Baldy his head, but he kept leaning off to the left, then tossing his head and yanking the reins. We tried to go slowly, considering Rose's leg. Behind me, Mary Pearl and Esther sat on Mary Pearl's thoroughbred stallion, a young horse, full of more beans than sense, and he fidgeted and twisted the whole way, too. I listened so hard for the sound of hooves that the cottony feeling came back in my ears.

When we got to the house, Savannah called out and bustled the girls inside, where their older sisters surrounded them with kisses and hugs. I left the saddle and rig on Baldy. It wouldn't hurt him to wear it for a little while. I turned off my string and led Pillbox and Hunter, still kicking and fearful, to Albert's barn. Ringer, Maize, and Dan dragged themselves behind. Sweat broke out on my face when I saw Dan's lead was hanging in the dirt. Rose had dropped off. She knew to follow, but Rose was hurt, and you couldn't count on a horse in pain to behave rightly.

I went toward the barn door and hollered, "Rose? Rosie, sugar, sugar! Come on and get some sugar, Rose." This time, I dipped into the bag of sugar they kept by the door for their animals. It was just some that had gotten dirty or wet or spilled in the house, but plenty fine for a horse to eat. I held it in my hand and stepped through the door, trying to see Rose's shape in the brown smoke. "Rose! Sugar for you!"

The sun turned deeper orange, bloody-looking. The sulphurous sky moved like some great monster, ribbons of grays and browns and yellows flowing behind it. A shape moved in the smoke, and I smiled, thinking, there she is. A man stepped forward. Albert. He said, "Sarah, come on in the house. The girls are telling how they hid in the bed folds."

"Rose didn't come," I said. "She's nursing a snakebite." If she didn't just drop off here in the yard, she probably never left the corral.

"Poor old thing." He just looked at me and nodded, waiting. I started toward the house with him, thinking that Rose would be safe if she'd stayed behind in the corral. That corral fence was like a fortress against the wild cattle. Then I stopped in my tracks. "But the gate's open," I said. "I left the gate open because I thought I had them all."

"Sarah," was all Albert got out of his mouth. I took hold of a hank of Baldy's mane and jumped on his back without touching the stirrup. For a moment, I was surprised I could still do that—it'd been so long. As I pushed him toward the red sun, Albert called out, "You can't save them all, Sarah. Don't risk your own neck." He said more too, I'm sure, although the same cottony quiet filled my ears and I no longer heard him by the time the shadows of their house and buildings vanished behind me in the smoke.

The smoke near my place lay close to the ground. The whole of the sky had gone a different red-brown tinge, and the sun had vanished. Surely, it hadn't already set and left the sky stained with this ocher light. Then like some kind of miracle vision, the smoke parted and stars showed through. A black velvet sky hung like a curtain behind the ocher-colored smoke. I reined in Baldy and cut around the barn, hopping off as he came to a stop, like we'd just dallied a calf with a rope. For one full minute, I stood looking at what spread before me, unable to move.

The smoke had settled and lowered because the fire had come clear across four miles and was at the hill behind where the new windmill stood like a guard post. It was a ghost of a guard post, for its blades were gone and the splintered metal spokes of them stuck out like a spider's legs.

Beyond the house, men were shouting, and I saw riders, hats over their heads, driving terrified cattle over a ridge where the ground smoldered. The sound of burning, crackling wood filled the air. The fire had come to my land like a disease, eating all it touched. Flames in a line, jagged as courses on a map, flickered and lapped at the ground and the very stones. The leading edge of it looked small. So small to have caused all this! There were patches behind it where nothing was burned. I saw a mesquite tree explode like it had dynamite in it. Then I remembered that tree and how it had been thirty or more feet at the top. Everything was all out of perspective. The flame wasn't small at all. It was taller than the house. Taller than the windmill. Wafts of new smoke, driven forward by the wind, came toward me. The fume was black, chalky, and more bitter than before, stiff and strong, instead of being brown and blanketing.

I searched the yard. "Rose!" I called. "Rose, come here." I whistled, then called again. I pushed open the barn door, and a flock of pigeons and doves whirled around inside but stayed up in the rafters. Bats flew through the open door. I couldn't see the corral. In fact, I couldn't see more than six feet ahead. I listened for her but heard nothing. Maybe she'd gotten out after all and had wandered out the open gate, away from the path of the fire.

I made my way to the round corral. I called again, and this time a horse gave a snort. Keeping the rails in sight, I stepped away from the edge but walked the circle. There she was, at the far end by the trough. She nickered when I touched her. She nudged me, but I hadn't thought to bring sugar. I tugged at her mane. "Come on, Rose," I said. Without a halter, all I could hope was that she'd follow me. She made a grunt deep in her throat. Rose's leg was badly swollen, held at a angle. Part of the bandage had come undone and was dragging behind her, filthy and tangled. "Come, now. Don't be ornery." Black clouds engulfed us. I couldn't see the horse, although I felt her with my hands.

I hurried to the barn and got the cotton-wrapped training bridle and got it over her ears and nose. I looped a rein in the chin buckle and yanked. Rose stood her ground, planting her front feet. The air grew dead still, silent, and heavy, as if steam had come from the scorched land, like when you're ironing a damp shirt. I pulled again, not gently, jerking her head, then pushed and slapped and punched on her behind. She kicked out at me with the hurt leg and let out a horrible squeal, then fell to the ground and thrashed. She kicked and wallowed and screamed, then twisted herself upright again. On her feet but rollicking and mad, she wouldn't let me near her at all.

I saw fire overwhelm the chicken coop. The little building burst open with flame. Sparks and ash, still glowing, showered through the air. Feathers puffed from it like they'd been blown from a pillow, and the oily dark smell of burnt feathers added to the smoke. Half a dozen pitiful chickens flapped away from the fireball, their bodies like torches. They fell in seconds and lay still. All around the yard, greasewood bushes that we'd let grow wild now exploded like the torches Chess had said they'd be. Tumbleweeds shot across the yard like rolling cannonballs of fire. They looked alive, as if they were purposely propelling themselves to do havoc with their fiery heads as they met up with a shed, then the bunkhouse. As other tumbleweeds piled up behind them, flames shot up the sides of the wooden buildings. The bunkhouse windows went red and then shot out showers of blades.

Rose's face was close. I could see a reflection of the red line of fire in her eyeballs. She rolled them wide and held her head high, snorting her distress. When I reached for her, she wrenched away, stumbling. I reached again, and this time she bit my arm. Not in twenty years had Rose bitten anyone but my brother Ernest, and he'd deserved it.

Now the smoke was lower. I could see over the top of it. The bunkhouse window openings had smoke pouring from them. It streamed upward, as if forced from the building. A new sweep of thick brown came over the lowered layer of black smoke, and the world was lost again. The thickened air went from black to bronze to orange and glowed all around, so that there were no shadows in any direction. I was adrift in the orange glow. No day or night. Barely up or down. Rose bucked and disappeared.

If I had ever in my life had a dream this terrible, I would have taken *myself* to a lunatic asylum and asked them to lock me up and operate on me to take this picture out of my brains. I started walking, hands out, hoping to find the fence rails and not the open gate. "Rose!" I shouted about every third step. I found her at last. She reared and stumbled again, then got up quickly and ran, shrieking as she stepped down on the sore leg. Her suffering was pitiful. And she seemed so afraid of me. If I couldn't get her out of the corral, she would burn to her death. There was one last, good thing I could do for her.

With my hands stretching forward, I hurried for the fence, where I had tied Baldy, my saddle and rig still across his back. The first solid thing I touched was a piece of metal jutting out from the railing right at the level of my eye. It had been left screwed out from the force of a stampeding bunch of cattle. At my feet was a dead longhorn steer, lying just beyond the rail, and where they'd pushed against the fence, a metal brace had turned in its socket and now stuck out like a sword, waiting for me to walk right into it and be blinded.

I used the rail to make my way toward the barn. A house cat screeched and darted in front of my feet. I found Baldy's white rump and talked to him while I patted my way around him. Taking my rifle from the scabbard, I turned and listened. Hooves. One animal—and small. An antelope, tinier than little Hunter, sprang from the smoke and darted back and forth across the yard. It turned sharply, leapt over something, and then vanished into the smoke.

My chest hurt. Rose squealed. I hefted the rifle and ratcheted a shell into the chamber. By the time I found Rose, the corral fence was on fire. The barn would go next, and it was huge. The fire was already sucking air in my direction, pulling grit and ash toward me. The house was upwind of the barn, and every piece of timber in it was dry and aged and ready to explode with flames. Baldy was fighting his tether. There was little time left.

The air cleared a bit and I saw across the corral. Rose was tromping in a circle, pivoting on her back legs, stumbling and breathing hard. For a second, I wished her heart would give out. It wouldn't take much fright, surely. Her back feet were snarled in the dangling bandage, for all intents and purposes hobbling her to the middle of the corral.

Fire danced along the corral bars. A tumbleweed popped through the lower rails and sailed toward her as it broke apart, showering her back legs with sparks. Part of the bandage began to smolder. She let out an awful cry. Baldy snorted and kicked at the corral post where he was tied.

"I'm sorry, Rose," I said. "I promise you, old friend, you're *not* going to burn to death." I lifted the rifle to my cheek. Rose's eyes rolled in their sockets and she snorted. Spittle flew from her mouth. The air cleared even more. The fire was closer, the smoke lower to the ground. I made that *X* from one eye to the other ear, getting a fix. She jerked her head and I aimed again. She tossed and then jimmied around on her sore leg. I had to move to another angle to get a line on her. It had to be fast—the last good thing I could do for her—over in an instant. One shot.

Water blurred my vision. "Rose, hold still," I said. "You're not going to burn. I promise." I aimed carefully, then pulled back on the hammer. Rose lowered her head and looked at me out of one eye, its depths full of fear and confusion and sadness. I wiped my eyes, unable to see the end of the barrel. "Hold still," I whispered. She did. Still as a post. It was a clear shot. But there was so much water in the way, I couldn't see. Water splattered Rose's face with dark pocks. Water hit my face and hands and my shoulders. I eased the hammer into its cradle and held forth my left hand while I lowered the rifle.

It was raining.

The metal on the burning fence rails hissed and steamed. The fence posts smoked gray, then white—white as a steaming kettle in the winter. Rain fell on the fence, the ground, the barn. Rose was wearing a blanket of water; halfway down, her back was darkened and wet. She shook her withers and grunted. I stood stock-still.

The rain blurred everything, but cleared, it, too. I could see the house from where I was. It was still standing. The old well, useless now, had survived. The barn was whole. We'd lost the bunkhouse, a shed full of tools, and the chicken coop. Thirty chickens, four geese, and whatever stock had burned or trampled themselves to death. I couldn't think yet about my family. Baldy was gone. He'd shaken himself loose and taken off.

Rose was still skittish, but she let me stroke her and untangle the torn cloth from her back legs. She murmured as I took the bandage off and threw it down. She put her head on my back and nuzzled my neck. Cool rain pelted us. Drops big as a quail's egg smacked our faces and shoulders. Freed of the tormenting bandage and the terror of fire, Rose let me pull her halter and lead her into the barn without any fight at all. I cut her a sheaf of hay and poured a scoop of oats in her box.

When I got in the house, the rain began falling harder and the wind blew water in heavy gusts against the house. It sounded like the old army band drummers all warming up at once, with no cadence at all. Every drop clattered on the tin metal roof. I opened the windows and let the fresh air in. The breeze smelled of ash. Cool and damp, it made me shiver a little. I was soaked to the skin and smelled of smoke, my clothes browned with ash and dust.

From my bedroom, the clock chimed. It was half past ten—the end of an eternal day, one that had begun at five in the morning. I heard hooves. In the din of the rain on the roof and distant thunder, I tried to decipher whether it were horse or cow. Was it one animal? No, two. Light, like a horse? Heavy, sodden, like a bull. I looked out the window, but I saw nothing but a gray sheet of rain. Maybe it wasn't the bull. Could have been poor Baldy, confused and scared.

I lit a lamp and carried it to the front porch. Trying to peer through the curtain of rain, I hoped that some member of my family might be nearby and would see the light and come. I called out, but there was no answer. I waited, watching the rain fall, swelling and thinning, then returning with force, until my eyes burned and my head ached. Then I took the lamp and went inside.

For the very first time since I'd first entered this house more than twenty-five years ago, I was utterly and completely alone in it. It was a different feeling from times when everyone was just busy working and would be home for supper. This was being alone and feeling like they might never come back: hollow.

In the middle of the parlor floor, I knelt on the ash-laden braided-rag rug and bowed my head, thankful to be alive but mightily afraid of the truths tomorrow would bring. My whole body shook so hard, my teeth chattered, and it seemed like I could do nothing to stop it. I only knew I had lived and saved one sick old horse.

It was silent outside. No coyotes, no nighthawks, and, thankfully, no crazed, running livestock. I must have slept, for next I heard the clock chime three times. The distant sound of a horse and buggy coming closer startled me. Then there was a bump on the front porch, followed by footsteps. The door opened without a knock, and the draft it pulled caused my lamp to go right out. Savannah and Albert ran to me, a lantern swinging from Albert's hand. Savannah held me and squeezed me, smudging her clean lavender dress with the filth on my clothes. My brother wrapped his arms around the two of us. He said, "Sarah, we found Baldy running scared, without a rider."

"We were so worried about you," Savannah said. She finally pulled back and held my shoulders, staring hard at my face, as if she could not see me clearly.

"Everyone all right at your place?"

"Yes, yes," Savannah said, dabbing at her tears.

Albert said, "Come on home with us, Sarah."

"No. I'm going to go look for my boys and Chess at sunup. They've been out there all night."

Savannah kissed my head as if I were a child. "They're probably snug inside Rudolfo's house. You come on, and I'll fix you a bath and a cup of coffee. A good meal and some sleep, that's what you need. Albert will find the boys for you, first light. They're in the Lord's hands. You're so exhausted. Isn't she exhausted, Albert? Sarah, come home with us."

Savannah has always felt like she has a heavenly guard around her. I couldn't say to her I felt that, besides the Lord's hands, sometimes my rascals needed me watching over them, too. I said, "I don't know where Willie is, either."

She smiled and said, "Snoring on our parlor floor. Albert found him in Granny's empty house and told him to come sleep in a bed at least. He wouldn't go upstairs, but he fell asleep in the parlor. We just let him lay. Now come, honey."

I left a note for anyone who might come to my place, and in a daze, I rode in Albert's buggy to his house, took a warm bath with sweet soap instead of lye soap, and put on one of Savannah's nightdresses. She put before me a full meal she had warmed on a plate, but I couldn't eat. Savannah stayed with me and we talked until the sky lightened. We spoke only of the ones we knew were safe, here at this house, in their barn, in their rooms, or by now on their way to Chicago. I couldn't even bring myself to tell her about my dead chickens. The morning sky was the wrong color, a dim gray, as if it were winter, instead of the usual faded green of summer dawn. Savannah and I had a good start fixing breakfast by the time their family gathered. Then it took only a little while to get Baldy from their barn and head back to my house so I could put on some work clothes and find out what was left of my life.

Chapter Sixteen

As if Savannah had indeed known from some other-natural source, I found my sons, along with Chess, at Rudolfo's spread. When I laid eyes on them from a distance and summed up what I could see—that none of them was game in the legs or busted up, or burned or gored, but helping others—I all but cried from relief. I ran to each of them in turn.

Rudolfo saw me coming and ran to my side. He looked worn and weary. He held his arms wide, and for a moment, I felt myself being drawn into them. At the last second, he lowered his arms and said, "Ah, Sarah. You live." He crossed himself.

"I'm glad you're all right," I said. "We don't need more orphans in this valley."

They had transformed the Maldonado hacienda into a hospital for man and beast alike. The Maldonados and Cujillos and nearly two dozen nieces and nephews ranging from six to twenty years old, along with El Rudolfo himself, nursed the hurt, trampled, burned, and poked. Rudolfo's daughters cooked meals and washed clothes.

One of the men from the Cujillo ranch had a broken leg, and we sent him to Benson in a buckboard driven by another of the men. The rest were banged, bruised, and coughing. Gilbert coughed so much, it really had me worried, but he said he'd just gotten a lungful of smoke and the cough would go away. There was a weakness in my bones, and the smell of smoke lingered. The air looked clear, but it pained the lights to draw it in deeply. Shorty was all but stopped from doing anything else, with the effort it took him to breathe.

Rudolfo called together the hands and anyone who was interested to listen and discuss what we would all do. Soon as we were able, we'd begin gathering the cattle again, with everyone working at once, sweeping as far as we could past Hanna's place and west toward Cujillo's. Then on the drive north, the direction we speculated most of the lost cows would have gone, extra men would go along and try to pick up as many as they could along the way. If we all pulled together, we'd get our herds to Tucson and split the money afterward. A mean job had to be done before anything else, and it would not be easy. Soon as our meeting was done, men wandered on horseback to find any cattle that were badly injured and suffering, and put them down. The valleys rang with gunfire. I suspect Willie, who'd come to Maldonado's with Savannah and Albert, was putting in his first truly useful day here, happy to make use of his new-learned knack with a pistol.

I stayed with Luz and Savannah's girls, carrying food and bathwater. We set up bunks all around the open-air plaza in the center of their house, then draped blankets over the vigas for shade. Outside the plaza, we built an outdoor *baño*. Through it, we funneled tired ash-covered men all day. We washed and dried clothes on a line and passed them out. Anything that fit fairly well got worn by the next man needing duds, no matter who'd come in wearing them.

Neighbors came from all around. Albert, Savannah, their girls, and the little boys all hauled water, made lunches, carried and fetched. Everyone I knew was there, except the Wainbridges. I mentioned to Albert that it was possible Cole and Dustin Wainbridge might have burned up in their house. While I wouldn't miss them a bit, I still wouldn't wish that on anyone. The two brothers had homesteaded, and both had lost wives. One had died giving birth. Rumor had it the other one ran away. It wouldn't have surprised me to find she was buried under the front porch.

One of Rudolfo's men rode over to the Wainbridge place to see how they'd fared. He came back an hour later, saying they were at home and that not a blade of grass on the Wainbridge land had been lost. Cattle with the Lazy Bar E, my brand, and the Angle Slash brand of the Maldonado herd waited beyond a fence there. Once some hands were tended to and rested, they'd have to go get them.

Midafternoon, I saw a fellow sitting on the adobe yard fence, blackened and hatless, right out in the sun. He was liable to go sun-crazed doing that, and likely already was, sitting there like a stone statue. I took the pail and dipper and carried it to him.

Holding out the dipper of water, I said, "You ought not to be sitting in the sun like this. Have some water, and come in under the shade."

"Mrs. Elliot, I think Aubrey is going to die." It was Mr. Hanna—so filthy, I'd never have known him.

I said, "Rudolfo told me everyone but Shorty was just beat-up some. Where is your boy?"

"They've got him in the house. He's burnt clear up one side of his head. They're giving him liquor for the pain, but I've seen less than that take a man down in the war. He's got a bad fever."

Someday, maybe some doctor will find out what fever comes from and cure it. Maybe Gilbert. I patted Mr. Hanna's shoulder. "Have some water," I said, "and take me to him. I'll make sure he gets cared for."

"There isn't anything to be done. I've seen him."

"Yes, there is. We'll make him compresses with soda ash and tea. My mother treated a little girl with that once, and she lived a long time after that. Married my brother and had four children." I was thinking of Melissa, now married to my brother Harland. Jack had pulled her from the fire, and my mama cared for her all her life.

He asked, "Where are you going to get tea out here?"

"Well," I said, "my sister-in-law gave me some last Christmas. Truth is, I don't care for it as much as coffee, and there's plenty left. There's sage tea, too, growing wild. If we can find some that's not burnt black, we can stew the leaves."

"Show me what to do. I'll try anything. I'll cart him to a doctor, if there's one to be found."

The best cure for sadness is doing something. I put out my hand, motioning for him to come, and said, "Rudolfo has sent one of the boys to town to see if the doc will come out here. We'll have him take a look. What you've got to do in the meantime is see to Aubrey and get him patched up. Don't be sitting out here in the sun without a hat."

Aubrey had a deep burn from the top of his head down one side of his face and wrapping nearly around his neck, then down the opposite shoulder. He was in some pain, but the main symptom I could see was that he was drunk. Rudolfo's daughter Magdalena had been giving him homemade tequila in a gourd, and he'd had enough to stupor a horse.

The Maldonados had no tea. I could hardly send someone to find it at my house. That could take hours, when I knew exactly what shelf it was on. So, with some help from Gilbert, we loaded Aubrey in a buckboard and drove him to my place, where I fixed him a tidy bunk on the sleeping porch.

I found the wooden box of tea and started the stove going so I could make a wet, warm poultice of boiled tea leaves, while Gilbert covered a cool wet cloth with soda ash. We put on the tea poultice for an hour, then the soda one. I rinsed his face, pouring the warm tea from the pan over Aubrey's burned skin while Gil made a fresh poultice of tea leaves and started again. Mr. Hanna watched and said he could take a try at it. Luckily, the boy fell asleep except when we lifted one poultice and changed it for another one.

Gilbert said he'd go back and lend a hand gathering cows, and be home in the evening to help. I told him not to worry, that I'd be here, and I let Mr. Hanna take a spell. While he put on the poultice of leaves, I went in the house and tried to set some things aright. I couldn't move the armoire or the beds myself, but I turned the tables and chairs back on their feet and pulled the mattresses onto the beds.

Mr. Hanna came in while Aubrey slept, and we put the other things in their places. He took the broom and swept one room while I took a second one and started in the parlor, and when I washed some dishes, he was there wiping them right next to me. He never once shunned a chore, the way some men would, as if they only intended to dig a trench or plant a seed, but all the rest of any kind of work was for women to handle. When we went back to check on Aubrey, I said, "Thank you, Mr. Hanna, for your help."

He peered at Aubrey, analyzing every breath our patient drew. After we tended the poultices again, I hauled all the bedsheets that had been dropped on the floor out to the porch. Anything that had laid on the floor all night would have to be shaken out to make sure no spiders and scorpions were inside them, then washed. I went to haul my soap cauldron from the shed to the fire pit right next to the house.

First thing I knew, Mr. Hanna came and lifted it right up, taking all the weight of it. "Where'll you have it?" he asked.

"It sits under the adobe ramada, where I usually stir the soap. Yonder." I pointed. The brush shade had burned and gone, but the four adobe posts of the ramada stood. I kicked up the stones a little, checking for anything with more than four legs, then set to raising up a little fire pit. When I got some kindling set, he took a flint from his pocket and tapped it, lit the fire, and turned the rod so the big cauldron of water moved over the flame. One minute you'd get more fire than you needed; the next, the wood was wet. We upturned the woodpile, searching for dryer staves, then got some going. He put some wetter wood around the sides so it could dry from the heat. It would take some time for it to boil, so we headed back to the house and I made us a plate of biscuits and beans.

I sat in the rocking chair on the porch, watching as Mr. Hanna gently poured warm tea on his son's blistered face. While he was doing it, he said, "Mrs. Elliot? How did you make out? I see the house is standing, but I admit I didn't notice much else."

"Not so bad as some," I said. "Lost a chicken coop and all my chicks. A brand-new windmill. Both my dogs. Of course, I don't know about the cattle. My stock horses and some old ones are all up the road except one, and that'n's all right. And your place? Those little sheep—did you save the stock?"

"Not a one left. Every last dime I had, roasted in the pasture like they were stuck in a trap there. It wasn't bad enough that every night some wild animal would take down one or two, but there's not a one left. Nor a wall standing."

"Not the house? Not anything?"

"No, ma'am."

For a long time, there was no sound but the dribbling of tea. I looked toward the graveyard on the hill, and the blackened branches that had been a shady jacaranda tree. They looked like ugly fingers clawing at the sky. "Listen," I said, "it's raining again."

"Day late," he said.

Water began to course off the roof. Aubrey groaned. He whispered something, then called, "Ma? Callie? Mama?"

Mr. Hanna said, "That's my wife and daughter. They died together." Then he dropped his head to his hands.

Aubrey said, "Mama? I'm sick, Mama."

I leaned over Aubrey and whispered to him. "You keep still now, son. I know it hurts, but it's going to get well. Try to sleep. That's it. Sleep." I told Mr. Hanna I believed poor Aubrey had succumbed more to the tequila than to the burn on him. His skin already seemed a little better. After just a few hours, his burn was not as fiery red and open.

"I've buried my wife and seven children. If this boy dies—"

I said, "He's not going to die. You need food and sleep yourself."

He nodded, then said, "I suppose we all do." The rain stopped, but the air was full of water, and a bright-colored rainbow circled the sky like pretty ribbons. The sun was angled low and the clouds broke. Broken pieces of a second rainbow wove in and out of the vapors higher up. Glancing light pierced the gray clouds like rays from heaven, the way the old painters used to picture God touching people on earth. I'd seen those pictures in books, and I wondered if the painters ever came to the territories. It must shine like that all over the world for some Italian man to have seen it three hundred years ago and put it down with paint. It also occurred to me that maybe God *was* touching the earth. Like the rain—a day late, I'd say.

I dug through my shelves and opened some jarred flat beans and some corn relish. In my bread bin, a loaf sat, waiting, but covered with dust. Well, I just shook it off and then cut off the dirty part, and it wasn't bad inside, just stale. Every plate I owned was dirty, so I poured the beans in coffee cups and piled the relish on the bread, and we ate it together. It tasted like the best Christmas dinner.

Mr. Hanna stretched himself out next to his boy and fell right to sleep. I meant to get up and start washing up the dishes. At least I'd have hot water in the kitchen. But first, I'd just listen to the rain. Be thankful for the rain.

I woke up an hour later with a crick in my neck from sleeping with my head bent. The rain had quit and the air was damp but cool. If there'd a been no one there but me, I'd have stopped and admired the pretty sky for a while. A little sleep had changed my attitude with the Almighty. Maybe there was some truth in those paintings at that. I wondered at the beauty of it, feeling new strength in my bones. There was much to do, and I was determined to sleep in a bed and eat off clean plates.

Mr. Hanna was sleeping near his son, and though it was time to change his dressings again, I decided rest would do them a world of good, so I slipped into the house.

I'd gotten a load of plates clean and stacked when I heard voices. My menfolk had bathed at Rudolfo's house and were wearing some poor-fitting clothes, walking slowly. Directly behind them came Shiner. It's odd, how relieved I was to see my family, but how touched I was to see that old dog following them home. Willie was not with them. Must have stayed there, no doubt eating his weight in Luz's fresh, hot tortillas. But seeing these three, it was hard not to cry. I pushed with my fingertips against my chin, forcing the tears away.

Charlie was the first one on the porch. He nodded to Mr. Hanna. "How's the old man there?" he asked.

Mr. Hanna said, "I think he's asleep. Your ma says he'll live."

Chess reached the porch by then. He said, "If she says so, he'll live. She's pretty stubborn. You all 'scuse me, I'm going to go in and put my feet up."

I poured some more tea in a bowl and took the can of soda ash under my arm. When Chess opened the door, I said, "Stubborn woman passing through," and smiled, and he held the door for me.

Charlie and Gil pulled up some old chairs we keep on the porch, then sat by Aubrey's cot. Charlie said, "Mr. Hanna, did you hear how he came to be in this shape?"

Mr. Hanna said, "No. I was chasing the fire line at one side and thought he was behind me. I lost him in the smoke."

Charlie said, "Story has it that he came upon one of those wild bunches of rampaging steer. They were bearing down on Gilbert. Aubrey cut in front of them, but they twisted and forced his horse right up against a barbwire fence we were trying to cut so they could run from the fire. By the time Aubrey's horse got untangled, it ran off and tossed him into heavy brush. We had to put the horse down."

Gilbert took up the story from there. "The brush was aflame. See that, where his neck is so bad? It was the kerchief he had on to keep out the smoke. It had dried and a spark caught. It went up like a firecracker. Still burning when he ran from the brush."

"Lord a mercy," I said.

"Here," Gilbert said, then reached in his pocket. Pulling out a folded packet of paper, he said, "El Maldonado sent him the last of the *quinina*."

Mr. Hanna said, "What's that?"

"Quinine powder," I said.

Mr. Hanna nodded and said, "Ah. For malaria."

"Among other things," Charlie said. "He also sent this to wash it down." He pulled forth a clay jug with a cork in the top. "*Tequila terapéutica*." Charlie grinned at me, saying, "Pure-D, grade-A *nectar de maguey*. For medicinal purposes only. It's the reason he's sound asleep now." He put the jug down with a thump. "Ah. Just remembered. Aunt Savannah is sending Rachel and Rebeccah with some food. Mary Pearl told us not to let you start fixing supper, even if we have to tie you down."

"Savannah used those words?" I asked.

"Well, not precisely," he said.

I shook my head. "Well, tuck that jug out of sight before they get here."

"The other thing is, El Maldonado asked us to come back. The boys watching the herd need someone to spell them. Everybody's good and tired. We figured to head back soon as we have supper. We'll be home at midnight, when the watch is through."

"Where's Willie?" I asked.

Gil said, "Stayed put. He's going to eat with the hands down there."

"You all didn't let Mary Pearl stay there, did you? It's getting dark."

Charlie shrugged and said, "Sure. Why not?"

"A girl alone with all those cowpunchers?"

Charlie said, "She's not just a girl. Mary Pearl can take care of herself. And when we left, she was in the house. I'll be back there before nightfall anyway."

"Fine, then," I said. "When you get home, wake me up, if I'm not already."

August 6, 1906

I'd always expected it to be the other way around—that eventually parents would get through to their children and they'd quit balking at every word. The older my children get the *less* inclined they are to mind me. I had told them to wake me when they got in at midnight. Said I'd take a turn changing the dressings on Aubrey Hanna. As it turned out, I slept the whole night away and they did the doctoring while I laid abed.

In the morning, I had to stop every other step and take accounts, as if my body was awake but my mind was back there on the pillow. Aubrey was up, not minding at all that Rachel and Rebeccah were ministering over his burned face. He managed to keep his moaning trimmed to a few hisses, no doubt for the sake of the girls nursing him. Rose was walking with all four feet around the corral, like her old self. Shiner was under the porch, exhausted. We hadn't found Nip.

For breakfast, I cooked everyone a stack of Indian-flour flapjacks, served up next to a side of bacon with a jug of sorghum syrup. It made my heart lighten up, watching everyone enjoy the food I laid on the table. While we ate, we talked. Mr. Hanna had been paying on a farm with planted pastures, fruit trees, barns, sheds, and a good-size house, not to mention the trainload of sheep and goats he'd had delivered the week before the fire. What he had to make payments on now were a few hundred acres of burnt scrabble without a living thing on them. Although he'd just told us how he'd lost everything, I saw how he kept eyeing his son, and how when Aubrey began eating, Mr. Hanna's spirits lifted. Even a wasted farm, in the light of day, tempered with a full stomach, didn't seem as bad now that his son was on the mend. I made two batches of flapjacks, then had to quit because I was out of eggs. We laughed at Aubrey, too, because before we were done, he'd eaten eleven flapjacks before he came up for air. When nothing was left but the smell hanging in the air, I pushed them all outside and said I wanted to clean up the dishes all by myself, since they'd done the doctoring through the night. I told the boys to get that fire going before they mounted up, and we'd rinse out the bedclothes at last. The smells of breakfast lingered and made the house smell good again, instead of like ashes and burnt feathers. The rain had cooled things, but the air was heavy and close. Mr. Hanna went to tend Aubrey's sores another time.

I was alone again, but not lonesome. No longer in a hollow house. In fact, I was glad to have them all busy working outside. It is especially good to have none but your own company when you plan to act a fool. I wept from the bottom of my soul.

While I washed and wiped and stacked, I cried. I reckon I cried first for the love of my family and the fact that they were all still alive. Then I cried for my dead chickens and missing dog. I wept over the thought of having to shoot my favorite horse, even though I hadn't done it in the end. I cried for things I didn't know, like who'd gotten hurt or maybe killed in the stampedes, people we hadn't found yet, and for animals that had suffered in ways Providence would never have intended. I cried for the Hannas and all their burned sheep in the field. I cried with thanks for the Maldonados, for Savannah and Albert and their children, and for any people I didn't know who might have lost their land, too. I let tears run right down into the basin. Then I dropped a big spoon, which splashed the wash water a little. I wiped my eyes with my arm, a coffee cup in my hand and soap running from my elbow. Someone took hold of the cup and pulled it gently out of my fingers. I turned with a start. Mr. Hanna.

I was still feeling skittish about having odd men slipping up on me, but he wasn't questioning or threatening me. He wasn't even looking at me. He plopped the cup into the rinse water and took the dish towel from the table and started wiping it dry. Then he took other things setting there clean and wiped and stacked them. All that, he did without one word or without ever looking toward me. Each dish I finished, he took from me without a sound and dipped and dried it. Finally, they were all done. By that time, too, my tears had dried, though my shirtwaist was dark and wet. I chanced a peek at him, and he looked up as if I'd startled him. I said, "Thank you Mr. Hanna, but, as I said, I didn't mind doing them myself."

He said, "Soon as I started, I figured out you wanted to be left alone. I'd already stuck my nose where it didn't belong, but I figured to help a little. I'll leave you be."

"Reckon you don't have to go. I'm done . . . being alone."

"Thank you for what you've done for Aubrey."

"Glad to do it. Glad it worked, too. My mama told me about the tea. Never tried it firsthand."

"I'm no doctor," he said, "but it's healed like a miracle. Mrs. Elliot, I can't repay—"

"Hush."

"Mrs. Elliot?"

"Hand me that towel." We dried our hands. Then I put the coffeepot under the pump. Before I could reach for it, he took the pump handle, started moving it up and down, and filled the coffeepot. "What did you do in the war?" I asked. Then I felt ashamed the minute the words cleared my mouth. I knew what men did in war. "What I meant was, were you in the army before the war?"

He handed me the heavy coffeepot, saying, "Oh, no. I was a shepherd before, too. Wyoming is good sheep country. There's nothing like a sheepskin-lined coat when the wind is howling and the ice is coming in sidelong. Figure I'm all done with that now. What I can't figure is why they just stood there and died. Didn't run."

My lip started to shake and my chin tightened. If there was one thing I wanted, it was not to start in weeping again. I clung to that heavy pot of water. I said, "Did your people always run sheep?"

"I never thought much about it, but I figure they did. Way back to the old country. Of course, they came here before the ink dried on the Declaration of Independence, so 'the old country' is just a saying. Still, they've always been shepherds. My pa used to say it was the first calling of King David, and that every time you put out your hands to shear a sheep, you are reaching back through the ages."

"That's pretty romantic talk for a sheep rancher."

He nodded. "He was a man of poetry. He wrote songs. Maybe that's why he always considered King David when he worked the lambs. And his name was David."

I said, "What about you? Do you write poetry?"

"Aw. Most of what I ever thought or meant to write . . . well, I figure it sort of got 'lost in the noise of war.'"

I smiled, and said, "I reckon Plutarch understood war, but he was talking about law, not poetry."

He smiled. "Mrs. Elliot, you are most certainly right," he said. "I reckon he was at that. Are you going to make that coffee now, or is it for later?"

"The reason I filled it was to heat some water and take a bath. It's the easiest thing to heat it and carry it hot, because of the handle. Unless you'd care for coffee?"

He said, "I'm full up, thank you kindly. Will you let me haul the tub for you?"

I felt a quiver in my chest. It was a boylike request, and it pulled a girl-like flutter from me, which immediately turned to anger. I have no use for female fluttering. I pulled the coffeepot closer to my chest and wrapped my arms about it. "I believe I will manage by myself," I said.

He said, "Well, there's plenty to do. Can't help my own, but I can help the rest. Thank you again for the meal." He left my kitchen.

I took the water to the stove and stoked and poked at the firebox. Then I dragged the bathtub down from where it hung on the back porch. I felt the strength in my arms as I did, and the rawness of my hands. I was certainly able to get my own bath. None of us on this ranch needed some stranger to help. None of us wanted some man in the kitchen wiping cups. I set another pan of water on to heat, too. Then I took a quick walk up to the cemetery while it did.

My heart was near in my ears and I could feel sweat running from my collar down to the middle of my back. "Jack Elliot," I said, "if you'd a been here where you belonged, none of this would have happened. And if I need someone to wipe my dishes, I'll lasso someone who belongs in that kitchen. Which I've got plenty of. Plenty! You hear me? There's no reason—" I stopped fussing, because I didn't know what I planned to say next. No reason for Mr. Hanna—the sheep man, for goodness sake!—to be wiping cups in my kitchen. No reason for my heart to flutter because he did. You'd think I was as dry for a helping hand as Chess said I was for a compliment.

"Jack," I said, "everything is near lost. If you were here, you'd probably choose *now* to go hunting some claim jumper in Cochise County or someplace. It'd still be all left up to me. Well, you'll just have to hear about it later. I didn't ask for all this work to do. Sure don't need someone else's problems on my hands. Some strange man and his son. I've got no time for the likes of you, any of you. You hear that?"

Another rain came in the early afternoon, rumbling and complaining like a spoiled child who then cries great sobs that disappear quickly when some new toy is chosen. At least it left a peaceful and cool dampness. It would have been nice to smell the greasewood and sage, too, but all we could smell was the odor of fire.

Aubrey Hanna was fairly camped on our sleeping porch with the rest of the boys, so there he stayed. His papa went back to their place to get started on it again. Gilbert warned Aubrey not to expose the open burns to the dirt of cattle work, but he said he'd be ready to do some work after another day. In the morning, I made him wrap a clean pillow slip over his head and neck, with two holes cut for eyes, which about scared poor Shiner to conniptions. Then he helped me shake the sheets and pillows out, plunge them in hot water, and hang them up. He went to fixing up the brush shade on my ramada, using some planks I showed him in the barn. I went with him, for I didn't want him to come across Mr. Sparks sitting in the back there and *really* be scared out of his life. The scarecrow was gone. I figured I'd have to ask the boys later what they'd done with him, as I was purely not in the mood for any heart-pounding surprises. Once the ramada was built, I got another fire going and started in on the mountain of washing I had to do.

Aubrey said he'd build us a chicken coop, too, but I told him he'd better rest awhile. Said I wasn't used to having young men go contrary to my orders. He believed that and perched himself on the front porch. Truth is, none of my menfolk seem to care a hoot what I say. Well, no sooner had I gotten him to sit down than along came Mary Pearl walking with Zack and Ezra. The little boys were lugging an enormous crate, which was balanced between them on their little toy wagon. Ezra carried a live colored rooster by the feet. Mary Pearl had a woven basket covered with gingham and bulging with something. Aubrey sat right up and said hello, and tried to smile. Mary Pearl sort of tossed her greeting over her shoulder as she came to the porch. Aubrey all but had to wrestle the basket from her to carry it in the house.

The children had been sent with the basket of jarred-apple pies for the men, and a dozen laying hens were in the crate for me. They left the crate of chickens outside, but Zack and Ezra followed Mary Pearl and Aubrey into the house. Ezra held up the fluttering rooster and said, "And here's the old fellow Mama says you'll need to wake the hens up to start their laying of a morning."

I laughed then. Aubrey made a funny face, trying not to hurt his sores, and Mary Pearl blushed a deep crimson. Neither one of those two would look up. Seems there was something mighty interesting happening on the porch floor that they both had to stare hard at.

Ezra said, "Mama said it'd be all right if we eat some of these here pies."

"She did not!" said Zack. "Did no such a thing."

Mary Pearl looked tired. "Mama told me that you can give 'em all to the men or let the renegades take one, as you please, Aunt Sarah."

"I think," I said, "with all those chickens needing a home, I'll have to rig up some kind of pen until we can really get the coop rebuilt. So I'll pay you fellows in pie—*after* the work is done." The two boys moaned and stuck out their lips.

Mary Pearl sat on a kitchen chair and bent down. She fiddled with her boot, tightening the spur. "Mr. Hanna?" she said over her shoulder. "I see you are feeling better. May I ask you to do me a favor?" As I watched, that young man's face lit up near to glowing, then fell just as quick when the favor was spoken. "I need you to keep an eye on my little brothers so I can ride out with Aunt Sarah and the men. They're a mighty nuisance, but if you're stern with them, they'll help you out. Maybe you-all can put up a chicken house together. Make sure you get to the pies before they do, though."

Aubrey looked helplessly toward me. "Make up your own mind," I said.

Aubrey smiled. "Long as the boys don't mind," he said, pulling the pillow slip back over his head, "taking orders from the Ghost of Cienega Creek!" The little boys squealed and hooted. They were plum tickled, what with him wearing a ready-made ghost getup, and planned some fun times. Zack and Ezra were always glad to have something to do that involved hammering and making noise. Aubrey stood and said, "Men? We have our orders. About-face and march, two, three, four."

I caught Mary Pearl's face as she watched them march away. She was grinning from ear to ear. When she saw me looking her way, though, she turned her head. I said, "You're not fooling me, Miss Mary Pearl."

"He's acting silly, that's all. Don't you see?"

"Reckon I do see right well," I said.

We left with Charlie and Gilbert. Mary Pearl said Willie had not come back. He had stayed down by Maldonado's with the other ranch hands. I wish I could get him to talk to me. Something's surely stuck in his craw. He'd come a long journey since he'd gotten here. He had been turning into a right fine boy, I believe, until Felicity's letter came.

Rudolfo's men had done a good job gathering what they could. The brands were mixed, but the hands had rebuilt the large pen, which was good as the old one. We'd have to run them through a chute, with fellows counting on each side, and see what was left. I spotted only a few dozen head carrying my Lazy Bar E. That added to the sick hollowness that came to me as we worked. There should have been a lot more with my brand on them. Scattered to the winds, I suspected.

Mary Pearl and I rode with Charlie in a wide sweep, starting at the west edge of my land and working northeast. She told me Esther had gotten more letters from her secret friend, and was getting Savannah all worked up about it. Mary Pearl said Esther was enjoying the attention. Every day now, there was a flower laid on their windowsill, with a note attached. It always began "To My Lovely," or "For My Heart's Prayer," or some such. Mary Pearl said she tried to stay awake all night long to catch him, but never could do it. At night, the two girls whispered about whether he could be a prince from a foreign land, or the handsome son of a wealthy *hacendado* from Mexico.

I said, "Likely he's some sawed-off runt of a cowboy with no more spine than a tumbleweed and wanted under a different name in Texas. Probably not got two cents to rub together," I said, "and only one good eye and a book of poems he can copy from." I was trying to make light of it, but I wondered if it was the only new young man around here: Aubrey.

Mary Pearl laughed. "Lands sakes," she said. "He could be any one of those sorry old rusty things. I'll pick out the poorest cur of the lot and tell her I've found him."

It was my turn to laugh. "You do that, she's likely to set her cap for him anyway, because of the romantic notions he's plying her with, and make some excuse like 'Him being so homely, he's lovable.' Before long, you'd have some sawed-off nephews and nieces to mind. It's better if we ignore it."

"Mama does not appreciate the ardor of the letters one bit," Mary Pearl said. "Every letter has to be read aloud to the entire family, and usually it falls to me. You should see Esther nearly swoon while I read them. Papa asked her to promise she would write and tell the man to stop. Today there were no letters or flowers. What do you reckon that means?"

"His ink went dry." I said. "Not many new folks around."

Her face went serious, and then after a bit, she said, "These letters are full of fancy talk. All the sentences are real complicated and flowery. Aubrey's talk is pretty simple. Not that he's stupid. I'm just saying he don't—doesn't use that language."

"Well, if a fellow wrote fancy words to me and then never told his name, I'd say he was a yellow coward. Besides his being short and splay-eyed."

We spotted a calf then, bawling, and alone. "Aubrey's not short and splay-eyed." She laughed and shook her head as she let out a loop. As Mary Pearl's rope landed over the little calf's neck, I dropped from my saddle and went to him to see if he was hurt.

I said, "I reckon he's not."

We found what looked to be the beginnings of the fire. Beyond that, as the desert will do with just a spoonful of rain, it was already greening and blooming. We stopped for a bit just to breathe the fresh smell, and then turned to circle back. Just when I thought Mary Pearl and I were going to come up empty, we found nearly twenty head pushed up a ravine and afraid to get loose because of some fallen mesquite at the mouth of it. She roped the biggest tree and had Duende haul it out, and then I worked my horse in behind. We pushed them real slow to the big pen.

The sky to the south filled with clouds stacked like white cliffs in the sky. A couple of hands spotted us and rode up to drag the line, so Mary Pearl and I took the flanks. We turned them to Rudolfo's place. After the first bunch, Charlie pointed a few of us to the south and I rode that way. I passed Flores and some of Rudolfo's hired men. They had a pile of carcasses they were setting fire to. One of those Spanish fellows said he and his brother would stay on without pay until they weren't needed anymore. I told him that was a fine thing to do, and he just smiled and rode on.

That afternoon, Willie ate with everyone else. He slouched, more than sat, at the table. I came up behind him, my plate stacked high with steak and roasted chili and tortillas. From the back, I again saw my brother Ernest in him. I pushed in beside him and said, "How do?" when I sat. He was chewing and just nodded. I wanted to put my arm around his shoulder like I'd do with my sons, but I suspected he would not take to that.

Finding that clean land this morning had made me realize that life was going to continue. It shook off that hollow feeling and filled me with a warmth, set me to thinking that maybe we'd survived to give Willie another chance, too. If a person was willing to take it—just like Udell Hanna—he could be handed a good deal, but he'd have to be willing to take hold of it. When everyone else was fixing to get back their chores, I asked Willie to stay for just a minute. Finally, it seemed folks were separated enough that we could talk without being overheard. I said to him, "Walk over here with me." I waited. Finally, with an exasperated jerking of his head, he followed. I said, "That cottonwood ridge, right there? That's the line where my ranch meets El Maldonado's."

"Yeah. They done already told me a couple hunnert times."

"Did you like your steak? Rudolfo sets a fine board."

"It 'as fine."

"Well, do you want a bath and some clean clothes, son? I'll go up to the house with you and draw up—"

"I ain't your son."

"I know that you aren't really. But you came here, wanting to stay. We took you right in. I meant it just being friendly."

"Well, these clothes're fine."

He was wearing someone else's duds, not the cheap, thready stuff he'd come here with. Still, he smelled fairly ripe. I said, "The boys told me you have worked hard."

"Reckon."

I put my hand on his shoulder. "I want to tell you something, Willie. You came to this place hoping to have a stake in it. Thinking your papa would meet you here and you'd have a home. And I know you've had a hard time, having to take up things you never learned before. You've done well, too. We haven't made it easy on you, but living here has never been easy. You've done a pretty good job, though, and stayed with it. Starting to earn your own place here. The way I see it, you're welcome to stay. I haven't treated you any different from the way I would my own boys, except maybe gentler."

He twisted out from under my touch with a jerk of his shoulder. "My pa owns this place. All that—that there farm with the trees and this'n with the cows and all."

I shook my head. "No, son. He didn't own any of this. My first husband homesteaded this land. When he died, I worked this place like a dog until I remarried, and then I kept working it, year in and out. My second husband gave me money enough to buy four times the land of the original place. Then with raising beef, I bought more land to double *that*. I own that place. All of it."

He put his arms out from his sides and stepped back. "Ma told me, all my life she told me, my pa was a soldier and a rancher with a spread out in the territories."

"Willie, did you *ever* see your father?"

A long time passed before he said, "No."

"All you've ever had are stories about him. Hard way for a boy to grow up."

"I'm growed all right."

"Mostly. The word is *grown*. I want you to start thinking about getting down to your studies after we get this herd on the road north."

"I figured to go with 'em."

"Well, you've got school to tend to. There'll be other cattle drives, if we have any luck at all. We have to think about your future."

"Why don't you think about leaving me alone?" He turned, his arms crooked outward.

It occurred to me that was a shape a man would take if he reckoned to be punched right in the middle. The boy had probably fought his whole life. I said, "If you're going to live here—"

"Who says I'm going to live here? I can live any durn *where* that pleases me."

I pointed to a turned-over tree. It made a natural fence. "Sit here and I'll tell you. Willie, your papa joined up with the army before we got that claim filed. He *never* worked that place. Never put another red cent into it from his pay. He did, however, send me ten dollars once. Just because your pa didn't own this ranch doesn't mean he had no place in this family. He had a fourth share in the first batch of pecan trees Uncle Albert planted twenty-some years ago. Planting those trees was to take care of Granny all her days. Albert and Savannah and their children have worked that land for twenty-five years. It's theirs."

"When do I get my share? That's a inheritance coming rightly to me."

"Can't you see that we may have lost half our stock? Even before that, there'd been three years of drought. Albert puts his money back into supplies, feed, and equipment. Just since the fire, he's spent over two hundred dollars hauling feed for all these loose cattle. I'm putting up the payroll for the cattle drive, which will about tap me out. The way I see it, for having put absolutely nothing into it, your share is to come here to live, become part of the family. Share in the blessings we have and the hard times, like you've been doing. Granny is going to move to my house. You can stay there, too. I'll add on a couple of rooms. You belong, all your days. The way I see it, you're family."

He used his toe to draw a circle in the dirt. Then he looked up. "How much my pa put in? I want it back. All of it. And interest."

"Well," I said, "it was sixteen dollars and thirty cents. Each of us was allowed to keep some of what we—"

"I want it back. That's all. It's coming to me. With interest over twenty years, I figure that oughta make—make about twenty dollars. That ten he sent. Makes thirty."

"You go work that farm and earn it, then. I'm sure the boys told you they get paid. You'll get paid a daily wage, too."

He sat again, then started picking at the bark of the tree. He mashed an ant with his finger. "Ain't no farmer."

"You can be more, don't you see? You stay here and keep on trying like you've been doing. Then we'll start your schooling in the fall. In a year or two, you can go to the university in town. I'll see your tuition is paid, and you can become a banker if you want, like April's husband, or some such. You're *not* stupid, Willie. I can tell that. Anything you want to be, you can be."

He stood and paced in a tight circle. "Banker? Nothing in that for me. Damn it, I want to be a high roller. No long face and dirty elbow cuffs. I want my own table on a riverboat. Have all kinds of racehorses and girls in spangly dresses and be able to tell people like these sodbuster squattin' relations to get the hell off my land." His voice had risen to a near squeal by the time he finished.

I felt all the warmth I'd held for him chill down so far that I shivered. "You'd better take back those words, young man."

"You said anything I want to be. That's what I want. You going to learn me it?"

"I'd never tolerate that kind of talk from my boys, and I'm not about to take it from you. You'd better straighten yourself up, and I mean before you go another step."

"You people owe me thirty dollars!" He slapped his hat against the tree trunk and walked away through the brush like before.

Willie looks like my brother, but he doesn't act like Ernest much. There was nothing mean in Ernest, and there's something awfully sinister lurking under Willie's skin. I thought I was offering him the one thing he'd never had: a home. Seemed like the things he wanted the most were the things he was most ready to throw away. How does a person undo all the tangles in a boy's thinking? I'd give anything to get past that part of him that seemed like leaky dynamite— just waiting for the spark to make it explode.

I got back to Maldonado's and found two punchers making cow eyes at Mary Pearl, and the very thought of all these young people shaking loose of their reins just set me on fire. I sent them packing, too. Mary Pearl looked peeved, but she didn't say anything, just rode off to find Charlie and get to work. I reckon I felt like getting my hands dirty. Luz told me that a couple of the men had gone down to the Hanna place to do some salvage, so I headed that way.

Mr. Hanna saw me coming and waved. "Aubrey all right?" he called.

I hollered back, "He's right as rain. Can't keep him pinned down."

He looked over toward where his house had been and said, "I keep think-ing it must be some kind of mirage, that I'll just open my eyes and wake up from this."

A square rock-built foundation showed where the house had stood. Part of it was completely turned to ash and blown away. Some of it still had pieces of the collapsed roof. An iron bedstead stuck up through two rafters. A chimney pointed skyward. A piece of broken glass caught sunshine and flashed like a mirror. He said, "I've started a pit fire to take care of what can't be cleaned up. Maldonado told me this morning that if I'd get the trash off the foundation, he'd buy me out."

I drew a breath and let it out with a whistle. Panic leapt in my heart. "Well," I said, "you don't have to decide today. You'll have an easier time put-ting a house back up with it cleared. Maybe last out the winter and see what comes. I'll stake you fifty head, providing we find fifty. Most all my heifers were carrying. Some will have lost calves, but the others will produce. Still, by next year they'll be ready to breed again, and by the following year, you sell off the first of them and pay me back. That'll start you. If you're willing to change to cows that is."

Mr. Hanna frowned. "Mrs. Elliot," he said, "I'll not be indebted more."

"Are you declining my offer?" I said. I looked toward the setting sun. It was behind a cloud rimmed in gold like a fancy plate.

He stuck out his jaw for a bit, then pulled his lips in, thinking hard. "I don't know about cattle," he said. "Nothing at all."

"You could learn."

"No experience. No fence. No. I'd better just write Baker and tell him I failed. Take the offer at hand. Twenty cents on the dollar is better than nothing."

I was getting my back up—toward Rudolfo and Udell Hanna both. "Twenty cents? That's robbery. Where would you go?" I said. "Hire out? There's not a sheep outfit in this part of the state that I know of. You'd have to go clear up to the Mogollon, or even back to Wyoming, and you said you didn't want that." My horse fidgeted and turned around, jerking its reins from my hand. "The of-fer stands."

"You'd do that for a stranger?"

"You planning to rebuild?"

"I figured to, before Maldonado came by."

"Then you're not a stranger. You're a neighbor. Now, show me where we're starting and where you want stuff piled."

I spent the last couple of hours of twilight helping him search for anything worth saving. We burrowed and sorted, now and then lifted burnt timbers, hoping for some miracle to be found whole underneath. There were a handful of those. We found a few dishes and cooking pans. The stove was still good. Most of their clothes were gone, and Mr. Hanna said he'd had some family pictures where we found metal frames. The paper under the glass had blackened, but the silver gleamed in the sunlight and showed the images if they were held just right. I told him I thought that if he was to write to the photographer who took them, the man could make a new one from the print he'd made initially. So he said he'd try first chance he got.

My hands turned black. I thought they looked bad before, but now they were the color of ink, and I knew from handling enough ashes that it will take two weeks to get the stain off. I'd like to have a long talk with Rudolfo Maldonado. I'd tell him a thing or two. Now that Udell had said he'd take my offer, I felt as if I'd thwarted Rudolfo again. Thwarted. How could I possibly consider living with a man I felt I had to battle?

By the time the supper triangle rang from up the road at Maldonado's we were working by lantern light. One of the hands worked the handle on an iron pump that looked like a black old crow sitting amidst the ashes in the yard. He got some water running, so at least the first layer of tarry black ran off our hands. My fingers looked foreign, all stained and wrinkled from the alkali in the ash. The other men found their horses and left.

"Mr. Hanna?" I said, "will you come and have some supper with the rest of us?"

He acted as if he hadn't heard. He reached for something. From a heap of burned cinders that had been a trunk, he pulled a piece of metal out of the pitch. It was a cross. He held it up and brushed at it with his gloves. "The silver has partly melted," he said.

"That looks like it belongs in a church," I said, raising the lantern higher.

"It was meant to. My wife, she did sewing and raised money. Sent off for it through the mail. I believe it came to the house before she was killed. After the funeral, Aubrey packed up the house, and this was still in its box. By the time I got home from the war and all, I tried to find the church, but the people had voted to transplant themselves to Oregon. Sold the building to be a warehouse, and all moved off. I kept it because I knew it meant a lot to her. A lot of handsome stitching bought this."

I nodded. After too long a silence, I said, "What was your wife's name?"

"Frances."

"My husband's name was Jack. Actually, it was John Edward, but he was called Jack."

Mr. Hanna fingered the cross in his hands. "I was going to bury this with her, since it meant so much. In the end, I couldn't let go of it."

I felt fingers squeezing my heart. I said, "It's something to hold in your hands."

Then he gave a sigh and smiled. He said, "Besides, it's a reminder of the bigger scheme, seeing it every day. I've come to believe that it is a good thing to stay on first-name terms with your Maker, in case you bump into Him unexpectedly some afternoon." He stared at the bent cross. "She told me once it took seventy-five yards of crinoline to make a single skirt. Her fingers would be nearly raw from making one."

Something familiar-looking caught my eye. I leaned down and tugged. A small box, covered with heavy black cloth, came loose in my hands. "This looks to be another keepsake," I said. It was a presentation box, from the army. The lid fell as I lifted it, and a medal on a sooty ribbon was inside.

He took the box. "Oh," he said. "It's mine."

I rubbed my hands on the only place on my skirt that wasn't already filthy, making its appearance complete. I said, "Mr. Hanna, we're going to miss supper."

He stepped over the trash in front of him, carrying the cross and the medal under his arm. I started pumping water so he could rinse them off. He said, "I can hardly believe I've already lost what little Aubrey and I had left."

"Well," I said, "you've got your land paper and a start on that. That's all any of us had here at first, a homestead we had to make good on to keep. And that bottomland where the hay grew isn't bad off. Albert hauls ash to his hayfield to make it grow better. This summer is a bust, but you start over, and by next year, it'll all look different. If you don't want the cattle I offered, sell 'em off now with the herd. Get more sheep."

He put the cross at the stack with the saved dishes, then laid the medal right beside it. He took our horses' reins with one hand and my arm with the other. I carried the lantern. We started up the road on foot. We were still around the bend from the hacienda when he said to me, "Mrs. Elliot, I've never known a strong woman before. Never cared to, I expect. Always thought that wasn't natural. My Frances was as timid as a mouse. I believe I'm getting where I look at that differently. I believe a woman couldn't survive here, not being strong. I just want to say—that is, without being forward, I'd like to say I admire you, Mrs. Elliot. To be strong *and* a lady. And I'm obliged for all your help."

"Well, you're welcome. For the help." We crossed a little ridge. From the top of it, we could see the Maldonado spread bustling with movement.

"Ma'am, I've never been eloquent. Never been anything but a sheep farmer. Never meant to be a soldier and don't plan to lift a gun or a sword ever again. I've lost my wife and most of my children. Lost the animals I invested in, and the house and supplies that came with this place, down to the ground. All I want in life is a farm. Some land to plant, animals to raise. My son to live, maybe someday bring me some grandchildren. I felt so like it had all slipped from my grip. You come along holding everything up in a different light for me, making it all look not as bad."

It sounded pretty eloquent to me. I said, "I guarantee, this fire like to took the life out of me, too, and I haven't lost half what you have. I know you don't feel like you've got roots yet. Me, I'm dug in deep and wouldn't know how to live anywhere else."

We came to the tables. Rudolfo's girls were running around, serving up dishes and hauling water in gourds. He said, "I'll be obliged if you'd allow me to fetch you a plate." I caught sight of Rudolfo watching our way. His eyes followed Mr. Hanna to the food tables, and the look on his face was bitter and dark. Rudolfo went in the house.

My boys had changed their day horses to some fresh ones, and they were set to ride out again in the moonlight. Charlie came to me while I was eating. "Mama? Old 'Boots' started up some trouble. Him and one of the boys got into the liquor and had themselves a snort. We sent him on home."

Willie was going to turn my hair gray. "What else have we got to do?" I asked.

"They're stringing a few up from the Cujillos'. Me and these boys are going up to Wainbridges and haul out the odd brands they've got. Nobody expects them to make trouble, as we're going to tell them we're sure it was account of the fire. Take your pick. And Mr. Hanna? Xavier Cujillo said he's hauling you up some lumber he had coming from Patagonia for a shed. You can put up a little line house at least, to live in until things get turned around. You want to ride with us, Mama?"

Mr. Hanna shook his head, then said, "Thank you, son. Thank you."

I said, "I'll take Baldy and go to Cujillos'. I'm fresh out of steam, and I'd rather follow a couple of dogies through some brush than look at a Wainbridge right now. I'll see you when you get done. That is, if you want to sleep under the mosquito screen on the porch instead of here. Up to you."

"G'night, Mama," he said, and walked away. Everything from the rope slung over his shoulder to the fan of his chaps looked as if he was grown. There is nothing to hold on to when a boy grows up. Gilbert was fast on his heels. I reckoned he'd be gone soon, too. Maybe that's why I wanted Willie to come along. Maybe I needed Willie to be here much as he needed it himself.

Udell Hanna said, "Mrs. Elliot, if a stranger in this country can hand me a roof and four walls, I believe I'd better go to his place and lend a hand. Mind I ride with you?"

"Not at all," I said. For me, that'd just make it that much easier.

Chapter Seventeen

The grating howl of a mountain lion woke me before dawn. The clock in the parlor struck the half hour, but I'd not heard what hour it was. Dark as it was, I decided to lie there and await either the lighting of the eastern sky or more sleep, whichever came first. The boys had both slept on the cool porch. Odd, how when I wanted them here, they cut and ran, but long as they knew they could do what they pleased, well, here they both were. Even if I had to tempt them with cooler breezes and cooking, it was good to have my sons and my father-in-law back around me, to know Shiner was under the porch and all my horses in their pens, and to sleep to the rhythms of their collective breathing.

I closed my eyes and heard the cat again, then Shiner growling. A puma wouldn't feast on the animal carcasses out on the range. Far off, coyotes gaggled with one another. Then I heard another sound, slow and rhythmic. First I thought it was a wandering steer. They stump along and don't care what they bang into. This sound was the soft and careful stepping of an unshod horse, then a horse's unmistakable snorting and tossing.

I reached toward the wall in the corner next to my bed, where my .410 stood. With it in my hands, I got up, went to Charlie's side, and knelt by him. "Charlie," I whispered. "Keep still."

His eyes opened and he was immediately alert, the way Jack always was. Without making a sound, he rolled from his bed, pulled a pistol from under the bunk, and knelt beside me. His eyes lowered when the hooves moved again. He motioned toward the door leading off the porch. Halfway up, the porch had been boarded in and the top half was stretched with screens. We could crawl low to the floor and stay hidden. We skirted the door and came up, one on each side of it. Though the moon was waning, it was bright. It shone on the screen, so that seeing in would be harder than for us to see out. Even so, I nearly jumped through my own skin when I saw the figure of a man out there. I pointed and we studied the fellow for a while. He stood stock-still, hands out, facing our house, his face shrouded in the same shadows that made it easy for us to hide behind the mosquito screen. First, I thought it was Willie, the way he stood sometimes, his arms and hands ready to fend off a blow. Then I wasn't so sure. This man wasn't shaped like Willie. His feet seemed to be wrapped up in blankets.

Charlie whispered, "Is that old Lazrus?" at the moment I thought it.

I nodded. "What's he doing?" I said. "Can you tell?"

"No. What did you hear?"

"The mule walking. Or something unshod—I knew that much."

Charlie peered at him again. Lazrus hadn't moved. Charlie said, "He's got his arms out like he's chanting a spell. Does he carry a gun? I don't see one on him."

I said, "I never saw one. Bowie knife, though."

Charlie put his head down and spoke into my ear. "I'll chase him out and shoot over his head. You back me in case he is toting iron."

"If he doesn't run fast enough to suit me, I'll let fly with the shotgun just to motivate him a little." We both stood at the same moment. Charlie flung wide the screen door. Lazrus was gone. Charlie hollered out, but no one answered. Chess and Gilbert came out of their beds, ready for a fight, but there was nothing to do.

When daylight broke, we searched more carefully than I'd ever tracked anything in my life. There were no footprints where Lazrus had been. Even a moccasin will leave a track in the silt. It was as if he had not been there. Surely, that was only the result of those wrapped leggings, instead of boots or moccasins. He'd probably wrapped the animal's feet, too. I remembered how in the old days the Apaches used to do that.

Gilbert went to feed the stock, and Charlie headed for the remuda to bring us mounts while I added wood to the stove and put some lard and buttermilk in the flour for biscuits. Chess leaned against the doorjamb for a while, his arms folded across his chest, pondering, I suppose, the morning's work before us.

While I rolled and cut the dough with a little tin cup that was really made for children, he poured me a cup of coffee. Before the biscuits were out of the oven, Gilbert came back, not running, but hurrying just the same.

"Mama?" he said, "did you turn Pillbox into the corral without Hunter?"

I was bent over, looking into the stove at those biscuits. "No," I said. I stood. I could feel my face turn white. "She's in the barn."

"No, ma'am. Little feller is hungry, and his mama's nowhere around. With him squealing, she'd come running if she could hear him."

I hurried toward the barn, the boys and Chess at my heels. My heart was pounding with fury at the thought of that Lazrus stealing my prize little mare. There were Pillbox's tracks, leading toward Granny's house. We opened the barn door and let the sunlight in. Next to Pillbox's prints were the heel prints of boots. In the corner where Chess builds the fancy saddles, one had been dragged down, but when the thief found that it wasn't complete and couldn't be used, it had been dropped. One of the work saddles was missing.

"Look here," Charlie said, hunched down next to the track. "A piece of hard-waxed thread. The kind that comes off fancy boots."

I breathed easier. Willie was just full of himself and ornery, showing he could ride any horse he wanted. I'd walk up to Albert's and he'd be there, eating his weight in pork chops and gravy. Or down at Maldonado's, filling up on eggs and chorizo in tortillas. I planned to scold the daylights out of him for taking Pillbox.

Chess shook his head, as if he was reading my thoughts. "That boy stole that horse." He walked to where Pillbox's little colt skittered around the big stall, trying to bump his mama out of the wooden walls. "Stole that prize mare like a damned rustler."

I said, "Likely he's just up at Albert's place. I'll see if Savannah's milk cow has some extra. We'll try giving Hunter that, with some sugar and eggs in it." Albert would remember what Papa used to give a foal if the mother wouldn't feed. This was the first time I'd ever come to this with a horse. "Chess, would you fix up some breakfast while I get dressed? And grab those biscuits out before they're ruined." He and the boys headed for the house ahead of me. The morning breeze was strong and smelled of rain.

As I got to the porch, here came a rider from the south, moving like a fury. There was just the sound of hooves at first, then the rattles of vaquero-style tack, more silver and buckles than work saddles have. I purely wanted to see who was coming this way on such a tear. The figure was hunched in the saddle, spurring his horse.

Rudolfo drew up close. "Sarah," he said, panting, "at least four hundred head, El Capitan and our bulls and finest cows, have been let out. Two of my men gone, too, along with your boy, the one they call 'Boots.'" I'd paid seven hundred dollars for my half of El Capitan, the champion bull I shared with Maldonado. And the younger bulls, bred from him, were worth the full price, too. They were how I was going to survive and keep the ranch going. One man with a good horse could move thirty head. It would take more than one to push four hundred, especially with a half dozen randy young bulls in the bunch.

"We'll be there soon as we get mounted," I called. Rudolfo turned his horse and left. I heard the men clanking coffee cups and talking behind the door. They looked up as I entered, and everyone dropped their forks and headed for the barn when I told them what Rudolfo had said. I called, "I'll see if Willie is up at Albert's. I'll just get my hat."

At my bedroom door, I stopped and turned. Putting my hand on the knob, a cold chill ran through me. That same haunted feeling ran up my neck as when I'd spotted Lazrus peeping at us through the leaves. Without breathing, I scanned the room. I went to the armoire and flung wide the doors. I dropped to my hands and knees and looked under the bed. Dust balls scuttered around in the breeze I'd created, nothing more. I went to the door and felt behind it for the string that hangs on the doorknob every night—the string that holds my scissors and key. It lay coiled on the floor, cut in two by the scissors that hung from it. The key was gone.

I threw back the door and ran to the smokehouse. The men followed me out of curiosity. Our smokehouse was an adobe shed with walls two feet thick and a heavy plank and pinioned door. The floor was always tarry with old charcoal and dripped grease. In the far corner was a metal sheet with a handle on it, and under there was my strongbox. I left the door ajar for light. Under the swinging hams and beef ribs, I stepped aside to let light into the corner. The strongbox lay upside down in the black grease. I turned it over. The key was still stuck in the lock. I let out a yell, my teeth gritted tightly together, my body shaking at the very memory of the gold coins stacked in that little box. I carried it out of the building and dropped it at the feet of my family. I couldn't speak, just shook my head, my hands clenched into fists that I couldn't undo.

Charlie knelt by the door to the smokehouse. "These tracks," he said, "come from bullfighting fandango boots. Seen enough of them lately. Only tracks on top of them come from your feet, Mama."

"Are you sure?" I asked, holding a fist against my forehead.

Charlie looked shaken and angry at the same time. "I'm sure."

The four of us rode to Albert and Savannah's house, and we barely slowed as we went in the door. Their family was seated at the table, about halfway done with breakfast. Before I could ask if they'd seen Willie, Chess called out, "That boy stole Sarah's best mare and run off. El Rudolfo says the prime stock is missing."

"And at least one man, maybe two," Charlie said.

Albert jumped up and looked toward the back porch, then came back and said, "I thought Willie was asleep on the porch. Ezra, run to Granny's and see if he's in there again."

Ezra came back and said no one was there, and no horse tracks went close to Granny's house. We backtracked toward my place and followed the trail. The tracks went north, then turned off the road, leading east, almost to the Wainbridges' fence. From there, the tracks joined up with those of another horse. Two miles farther, the horse hooves were nearly lost in the tracks of more cattle than any of us could speculate, headed due south—toward Mexico.

Chapter Eighteen

Rudolfo was coiling a rope. Before him on his desk lay two pistols and some cleaning rags. The room smelled of kerosene. His face was dark and his eyes glinted with a sinister fire I'd never seen in him. Anger made him seem much younger and far more dangerous than I'd ever known my long time *compañero*. "Sarah," he said, "I'm going with the men to find the cattle thieves for only one reason. To keep them from hanging *all* of the rustlers. I'll bring *el sobrino* home to you."

"I'm going along," I said.

Rudolfo lowered his voice. "No. You will not go with us."

"Why not? They're my cattle, too." And it's *my* lunatic nephew they're after.

"In case I fail."

In case he failed to find them or failed to stop a lynching? I knew without question that rustlers and murderers would stand side by side under the nearest live oak tree. Just knowing they'd made a running iron made them guilty. It's just a bent poker that can add a line or hook to a brand, and when it heals, a rustler can claim those cows as his. If I could get Willie back alive, I might have a chance to talk to a judge in town. Rudolfo said, "*Escuche.* Will you listen? Get one of the men to organize the drive with the remaining cattle, and start for the well at Picacho. We'll meet them with the stolen herd on the road. I'll cut out some of your brand and leave them. Wait here until I return." He was packing bullets into a double bandolier. He was mighty sure of himself. Still, that seemed the more practical thing at the moment.

I said, "Take them all—all that you find—to sell. But if you find fifty, I promised Udell Hanna a stake for a couple of years. Reckon he'll be going along, too, so tell him to cut fifty for himself and take the rest to Tempe. I'll sort out what to do when I see what money is left. Sell them all. I can't pay the hands. I'm flat busted."

The large clock on the mantel ticked loudly ten or more times before Rudolfo said, "Fifty for Señor Hanna." He began methodically stoking bullets in the chamber of one pistol, and when it was full, he sighted in on something near the fireplace. "If there are fifty, you will need them yourself. We'll make a hard bargain with both the *bandoleros* and the cattle buyers. I'll get your money and our cattle. Another thing. Hanna is not going."

"Why not?"

"Cujillo is helping him build a house. If he stays in this *valle*, he has no time to drive cattle." He came and stood before me. "When I return, we will talk."

I couldn't read Rudolfo's face. Seemed like he might be wishing I'd throw my arms around his neck and beg him to stay or to send the new neighbor in his place. For a moment, I searched in my heart for that tug I used to feel when Jack would ride off, bound to take on some band of warriors or outlaws that no one in their sure mind would face. All I felt was hollowed out again. I said, "Rudolfo?"

"¿Sí?"

"I know you'll do the right thing," I said. But I didn't feel sure of that at all.

He nodded, fit his hat squarely on his head, and left without a backward glance.

Well, the idea that I should "get one of the men" to put together a trail drive rankled me no end. It was my place as an owner. I'd put together seven drives of our last ten. But Rudolfo was taking most of his hands and Charlie, while Gilbert, Chess, Shorty, and Flores were headed north with the remaining cattle. They'd need hands, and we'd have to choose from the strangers Rudolfo had hired, and hope they'd take orders from me. Usually, I just said things plain out, and I expected to be listened to. Handling strangers could sometimes take a kind of sweet talk that was not abundant in my makeup. I'd have to count on my trail boss, and I'd have to choose him carefully.

Gilbert knew business, but I needed someone as boss the other riders would listen to because they respected him, not because he was my son. If he'd had even three more years on him, I'd have used him for the job. I decided finally on Flores. Aubrey wanted to go, so Gilbert could show him the way. Soon as Rudolfo caught up to them the next day, he could put Charlie as a ramrod. Gil and Chess planned to leave the following morning with a wagon headed for Tucson to outfit the chuck, then come back and meet the herd on its way. The herd would move slowly. Should be well out by the time they got together.

The food would have to be bought in town on credit. I gave Gilbert the last cash I had, the twenty-dollar gold piece from under the candle stand. I told him to keep it for an emergency on the trail, such as a doctor's care if someone got hurt bad. We'd pay the supply bill and the payroll when the cattle were sold. I asked him to put it to every one of the men that way, too, seeing if they'd work for a promise and then get paid at the end, for I hadn't any more real cash than six bits I could rub together.

While we ate at my kitchen table, just Gilbert and Chess and I, a little sprinkle of rain settled all the morning's dust. It came with just a whisper of a breeze and no lightning or thunder close by at all. Gilbert said the Wainbridges were both gone, too, along with the cattle they'd held behind the fence during the fire. It seemed to him, he said, that Willie had been in cahoots with Dustin and Cole Wainbridge, and they'd rustled cattle even before the fire. Before we'd finished our meal, the rain quit and the clouds scattered like they were a herd just come to graze a spell and move on.

With half the cattle gone, a third of them dead—we'd lost count—and the rest moved, I was looking at being retired from the cattle business by the next morning. And, by then, all these chairs would be empty but mine. Had I really lost all? My cattle, my savings money, and maybe even part of my land to pay the debts on the windmill and pay Granny for the well? Not in all my life had I felt so much as if I were rolling my wheels backward. None of this had been easy to build or hold on to, but in the past it was all going uphill, and anytime I turned around and looked to see where I'd come from, why, I was always better off than before.

While they went about packing up, I went to pull some water and look at my garden. It had been a hardscrabble square of land, about a quarter acre, when Jimmy first built the fence around it. He was only thinking of keeping out a jackrabbit or so and hadn't known about the javelina packs. Nor had he estimated the mess a coyote chasing a mouse through rows of lettuce could make. I had used string and wire and added a row of ocotillo branches around Jimmy's wire fence, then put cholla buds at the bottom to keep the critters from digging under it. About half those ocotillo had taken roots and sprouted. Over twenty years of hoeing and weeding, spading in wet leaves, paper, and manure, the ground had turned rich and black. Now it was scattered with cholla burrs and thorns, every inch. I started at one corner, raking.

An hour later, I checked on the sourdough rising on the sideboard for biscuits. The smell of that night's pot of beans and beef wafted through the open kitchen window. I did the evening feed. I tried to imagine that I'd sold my land and moved off this place for good and all. Taken Granny, Chess, and the boys to town. Left Savannah and Albert behind, along with the Maldonados and Hannas, everything familiar.

After supper, I rode a circuit from Cujillo's place to Hanna's, Maldonado's, and then home by way of Albert's. It would take months to repair and rebuild all that had been lost. But I had water at last. Rain coming. I got back to the last hill south of my house just as the sun was setting and the sky turned to deep azure in the east. From there, clouds painted yellow and red and copper stretched across a turquoise sky that reached westward from one end of the horizon to the other. The earth glowed, as if it had been overlaid with gold, and in the far distance, the hills turned shades of faded purple. It was a sight I had witnessed before, but unlike the rays of sunlight, I had never seen anything this fine in a picture painting. I wished I knew how something so beautiful could exist in this hard old land. It looked as if Providence had repented for making our lives so troublesome and had sent a bouquet of colored clouds perfumed with the smell of wet creosote and clay. My heart swelled at the beauty of it.

With whatever money Gilbert got for the stock he had, and however many Rudolfo could rescue, I'd start over, too. I'd take the advice I gave to Udell, and just dig in. I could never sell this land. I felt a hard band let loose around my ribs and I took in a long breath. This was my home. I turned my pony toward the candlelight shining in my parlor window.

Chess turned in early, and in less than ten minutes I heard snoring coming from the back porch. I sat awhile by the open window in my parlor with just a single lamp lit. I could see Harland's painting of a San Francisco that would now be forever changed hanging on the wall near the bookshelves. The clock ticked loudly. Somewhere east, coyotes played and tussled and yelped. On the far wall, nearly hidden by a chest where I kept linens and extra blankets, were some tiny faded blue handprints. My April had made those on the wall with a bottle of blueing the day I found Jack nearly dead out on the hillside. I reckon if I hadn't known the hands were there on the wall, I'd have believed it was just a shadow. So much of life is a shadow, fleeting as a moment.

The lamplight was drawing critters against the screen window so thick I couldn't see out. So I blew the flame out and just sat there rocking in the dark. The sun set around half past nine. By then, the one star I watched for every year came out. In a couple of months, another would come up with it, too. In the fall, they'd make a triangle with the moon, which was always something to see. The first and biggest one, I'd named for Jack long ago.

Rudolfo will find Willie and bring his ragged hide back here with my money. Charlie and the men will find my cattle and bring them back, too. I smiled at myself. I had been so mad when Rudolfo told me to get a man to arrange the cattle drive, but I really needed these men around me to do things. None of us could manage without the others. The trouble with me was that there was just one man I wanted, and he wasn't much for taking care of things, even when he had been here.

Just as real blackness seemed to close in, a yellow glow shone in the eastern sky. I feared more wildfire, but soon as I saw the round light appear, I calmed. I put my hands together on the windowsill and laid my chin atop them, then waited until the moon rose above the hill. At least the moon still came over the same notch in the mountains. The only thing I'd been able to count on lately was that things change. Reckon a person has to take comfort in the eternity of a few things. On the beam over the porch, two doves cuddled together next to the wall. They rubbed their necks this way and that against each other and then settled like two gray stones. This ranch would be here long after I was gone. For my boys and their children, April's too, if they wanted it. I savored the smell of land. Even the soft perfume of the old wooden sill under my hand was good. It was all good, and we'd made it through the worst. As Granny used to say, we'd lived over it, but we didn't look like much come this side. I had to smile.

Morning came misty and verdant, as if the very earth beat with a rhythm of life and lust and heat, with the cattle drive moving. As if it all might recover from the fire. As if someday there'd be a reason to go on, scourged and tried, but alive. Yesterday, I'd worked from the smallest hours to the greatest, and nothing but more work stared me in the face. Today, there was hardly a blessed thing to do but wait. How fast life can turn its course. On a nickel, as the boys say, and give you some change.

Shiner stayed with me. I had only a few chickens, Savannah's gift, to feed. There was no need to haul water to the remuda anymore, just a little for the ones left in the corral. Most of my riding stock was gone with the men, one direction or the other, and all I had left were my wagon team, the old horses, and Hunter.

I spent the morning coaxing Hunter to eat. The cow's milk wasn't sitting well. He tried to chew the hay, but what he liked was the leaf. I knew better than to give him nothing but leaf. In the barn, I carried a sheaf of hay to a worktable and took a knife to it, cracking and chopping that hay into baby-size pieces, almost like grain. Then I mixed it with some oats and a little molasses and a chopped apple. He snorted over it suspiciously, then took a little bit. Hunter dropped more than half of it as he tried to chew it, but it looked like he was pleased with the recipe, for he went after the stuff he'd dropped and ate plenty to make his little sides fill out. I gave Rose and the others a couple of apples each on my way to the house. Rose's leg was looking bad, what with the skin peeling away and flesh showing through, but she was getting around better.

Then I sat and wrote April and Morris and told them the whole of what had happened. I'd mail it tomorrow, after Rudolfo got back with Willie. I folded the letter and put it under the sugar bowl on the table. I fetched a rocking chair from the porch and turned it over my head, carried it up and put it under the dead jacaranda tree, where I could see the whole of the graveyard. Amidst the calls of quail and mourning doves, I listened to the sounds of peace. This place, this day—this quiet, quiet day—felt to me as safe from all the world's harms as resting in my papa's lap when I was little. In my papa's arms, all my problems were regularly salved by a few kisses and a story and a nap. I pulled my hair out of its ties and raised my skirt to let the air waft around my ankles, then leaned back and closed my eyes to think.

I woke up when a stray twig from the tree whisked across my arm. All was quiet. The commotion of my life had moved on. I saw myself on Mama's front porch, in her life, happy in her role as Granny and happy, too, to live alone in her little house. No longer did she seem addled to me. Just worn-out. Bone-aching tired, so that just putting on her shoes was an awesome effort. I stood up, careful of the snarled branches over my head. There on one of them was the tiniest green dot. A leaf bud. The tree was alive.

I touched the blistered bark gently, as if it had been Aubrey Hanna's burned face. If there are no cows to mind and no men to cook for, I reckon to build a little flower bed here by the graves. Maybe I'll begin tomorrow at sunup and have it done before they all get back. When Rudolfo brings Willie, that boy is going to spend the next month hauling rocks and manure to build a flower bed at this graveyard. I'll work that boy down to manageable size. He's been asking to be taken down a peg since he strutted in here.

Yonder over the southern hills, thunderheads rose above the filmy clouds hovered low. In the midst of them, lightning flashed, making the clouds look as if the insides were on fire. The air around me had taken on that leaden feeling of another impending storm, still and hot as an oven. I left off feeling at peace, but I didn't take on the worry and trouble that had been mine over the last days. After all, Rudolfo will bring my money, too, for surely they couldn't have spent it all by now. I don't think even four men living high and wild could burn through over a thousand dollars in a day or two.

I moved my feet, which made a little gecko slip from under the chair, headed for the grass. "You sassy thing!" I said, laughing. "Hiding under there, peeking at my ankles like a heathen." Lands, it was hot. I picked up the chair again and lugged it back to the porch and drew myself a drink of water from the olla. Sweet and cool. I finished the rest of my chores with a song. All this would turn out fine.

When I opened the door, I caught my breath. From where I stood, I could see the back door to the other porch. It was swaying gently, halfway open. I started toward it to close it. Then remembered I had shut it tightly when I took my bath. I left the house from the front door. Someone else had left it ajar.

I'd let down my guard and someone had come in the house. I reached behind the door for my shotgun. It was there. Without trying to be quiet, I racked it and made sure it was loaded. I went through my house room by room, but found nothing but my own footsteps answering me. On the back porch, the screen door was latched from the inside. Anyone going out that way would have had to leave it unlatched. That didn't mean someone couldn't have gone out the front. I had been asleep. I went through every bedroom before I set the shotgun back in its place in the kitchen. Another, closer peal of thunder rang just as I did. Lightning close by lit the room for a second like daylight and something flashed.

"Aunt Sarah! Are you home?"

I turned with a start, banging the table with my hip. I said, "Who is that?"

"It's me. Zack. Mama sent me to tell you supper is ready."

"Supper?" I looked out the window. Zachary sat astride Big Boy, who looked to be all but dozing in the cool breeze. "Zack? Were you in the kitchen, looking for me?"

"Yes'm. I just comed. Mama figured you'd be all alone, and she sent me to bring you to supper."

"Just came," I said, correcting him.

"Yes'm. Storm's a-coming, and Mama said better hurry."

"All right. I'll be there shortly. You go on ahead if you've a mind."

Zachary kicked his heels, but his legs were so short, their effect was lost on the big horse. He slid from the animal's back to the ground and led him around, pointing him toward the Prines' place. Then Zack climbed upon the rail of my porch and threw himself onto Big Boy's back. Before you could say Jack Robinson, he was turned around and seated upright. Then he gave the horse a little slap on the rump with his hand and they started a slow amble up the hill.

"Oh," Zack said, arched on the horse's back. "By the by, Papa said if you'd bring the money box, he'll see can he fix it."

"I'll get it," I said. "Go along. I'm right behind you." They'd hardly be to the gate before I could catch up. I'd fetch the box and start walking, and probably get there the same time Big Boy lumbered to his stall.

I put the shotgun over my arm, crossing the yard to the smokehouse. As I bent to retrieve my metal strongbox, I thought with a smirk that they should call it "a weak box," or warn folks not to hang the key on a string in the bedroom. I knew the box still lay on the floor, but I couldn't see it. I waited for my eyes to change to the darkness inside. A gust of wind swirled in the open door, and the heavy, salty smell of the place covered me like a blanket. I stretched for the thing, my weight on my toes, so I wouldn't have to step all the way in and get my shoes black before walking on Savannah's clean kitchen floor.

"Lose something?" a man's voice said from behind me.

I dropped the box, not straight down, but flipping it in the air first. My foot slipped at the same moment. I lost my balance and fell against the door, which swung back and nearly threw me to the ground before I caught myself. I banged my ankle hard against the doorjamb as I swung the scattergun toward the voice. I panted and waited. My throat was dry in one little place and I tried to swallow a dozen times to fix it.

The voice spoke again, coming from the blackened stand of ironwood and horsetail. "What you seek cannot be found. Only ask and it shall be given."

I knew that voice. I said, "Come out of there and show yourself, Lazrus, or I'll fire blind with this scattergun, and maybe hit something vital."

Lazrus stepped from under two ironwood trees grown closest by the smokehouse. "That wouldn't be advantageous, nor righteous, nor wise." He said the three words over again silently, just moving his mouth. Then he smiled.

"Anyone with any sense would think it might not be wise to sneak up behind someone carrying a loaded shotgun."

"You'd never harm me. I know it."

No jury full of men would believe how rattled and tortured he could make a person feel. How could I explain I'd rather take off his head with both barrels than forever be afraid of him slipping up on me? I said, "You promised you were going to leave me alone." I was shaking. "If you go making yourself commonplace around here, you'd best know that I'm not above relieving the earth of a dangerous madman."

He scratched his chin and said, "Dangerous?" He leveled his gaze at me, and it had the result he wanted, I suspect, for I froze in my tracks, listening to the beating of my heart, which was so loud, it seemed to be outside my chest. He said, "Why do you say *dangerous*? I come unarmed to you, a simple wanderer, a poor pilgrim in a strange land. We have *all* relieved the earth of its tormented. Its cracked pots."

I did feel dangerous, both frightened and frightening. I said, "Wander away, then, back where you come from. I've got enough troubles right now without you being here."

"I've come for the bath you ordered."

I swung the shotgun up to my hip and leveled it at him, as straight and potent, I hoped, as his eyes had seemed before. Buckshot from this distance would be fatal, but I could aim low and scatter up dirt and rocks that would sting and smart without killing him—barring blood poisoning from the filth on him. "You're not getting a bath here, today or any other day. Next time I see you, or if I even think you might be around, I'll start shooting with this thing before I know for certain. That goes for your mule, too. I don't want any more midnight visits from that animal, whether you wrap its feet or not."

His eyes widened and he grinned again. "Why's that box in the dirt here? It's a keepsake? A memoir? A lock of hair from a loved one? Did it belong to . . . him?"

I racked the shotgun.

Lazrus's hands flew into the air. He said, "Alas, I bid farewell but not good-bye. Out of your sights, as it were, but never far from your mind, dear." He tore through the brush, disappearing like a coyote into the thick. I aimed high, at the top of the paloverdes, and pulled the trigger. Usually a shotgun would fairly kick me back a step, but I was so rattled and so purely mad that all it did was make a jerk as I held fast.

Supper at Savannah's table had to begin with me explaining the reason for the shot they'd heard. Savannah was relieved it was only Lazrus. I was more terrified than before, hearing myself tell it again. Soon as the blessing was said, rain fell in sheets, waves of fiercely pounding drops, then thin places between them, which made us think it had stopped entirely. While the life-giving water fell from the sky, we ate chicken and pork cooked with potatoes, tomatoes, and chilies. We talked about Esther starting studies and Joshua returning to them at the university. Albert offered to pay my boy's tuition as a gift. I told him it would just be good money after bad until they wanted to go.

After awhile, I asked Mary Pearl where she'd been hiding, as rarely did a day go by I didn't see her. She seemed too quiet. She peeked up from her plate and said softly, "I've been—well, having a mindful day." Savannah gave her a stern look. Mary Pearl said, "I'm learning to bridle my spirit."

Too old to spank, that girl, I knew, could be a handful, much as I loved her. And while the older girls were made to toe a fine line, she got by with a fare-thee-well on a lot of things. Poor Savannah looked so worn and peaked, I felt sorry that she'd cooked this meal. After supper, I made her put her feet up and rest while the girls and I put the kitchen in order. This coming baby is taking its toll on Savannah. She fairly ordered me to stay with them until the boys get home, because of Lazrus sneak-thieving about.

"Stay here until Charlie gets back with Willie," Albert said. "We can all go together."

Savannah said, "Surely you can use the rest. Lazrus won't bother you here. He wouldn't dare. Please, honey. Come up to our house and just set a spell."

The rain stopped, and as the clouds parted, the last bit of sunlight brightened the outdoors. There'd still be light to get home by. Savannah called Ezra and Zachary and told them to get ready to say their prayers and dress for bed. At last I said, "There are animals to feed. The men'll be back tonight, I'm sure. I don't want to leave my place empty."

"Why don't you take someone with you, then?" Albert said. "So you're not alone."

"I'll go, I'll go!" shouted Ezra from upstairs.

Savannah called out, "Young man, get in bed."

"Savannah," I said, "if it'll set your mind at ease, I'll stay here. I'll just go do the feed and come back." Rachel and Rebeccah walked to my house, helped me with the horses and chickens, and then we hitched my wagon and Rebeccah drove us up the road to their home.

The morning dawned clear, but the air was heavy as I returned to my place. I looked to the south and listened hard all morning, hoping to hear the unmistakable commotion of a herd coming this way. The sound would mean Rudolfo had found Willie and my cattle was driving them all back to where they belonged. I pulled up rocks and broke soil with a pickax for the flowers in the graveyard. Before noon, I had finished every chore I'd set for myself. I had sharpened all my kitchen knives. Cleaned the shotgun and my old rifle. I took the hoe and went to the vegetable garden, spent a couple of hours raking thorns. Got one through my shoe that made my toe burn the whole time. The chili plants were trying to come back, and they had sprouted new shoots from the burned stalks. I was walking slowly up and down the length of the garden, drizzling water from the tip of the can, when I saw Mr. Hanna coming up the road.

I called, but he only looked around, so I had to wave my bonnet before he caught sight of me in the garden. I shouted, "Hello! Heard from the men?"

Mr. Hanna got off his horse. "Not a word, Mrs. Elliot. Are you busy?"

"Well," I said, "chores are a mite scarce lately."

"Would you mind riding with me down to my place? There's something I'd like to show you."

It took me a few seconds to run through my mind what I wanted to do. In the end, I figured if Rudolfo came back from the south, it'd be nearby the

Hanna place. It wouldn't hurt to ride down there for a bit. "All right," I said.

Mr. Hanna followed me to the barn. He pulled a saddle while I went out the side door and brought back a pony. I left my bonnet on the latch of the barn door and took my old straw hat from inside, where it was hanging over the ready oats for the horses. We headed south side by side. Mr. Hanna said, "Sure I'm not taking you from your work?"

"I was up early," I said. "Finished and fiddling around."

I straightened my hat. Neither of us said another word, but when he got to the flat pasture on his land, he gave his horse a knee and took off at a canter. I followed. We rode up to a line of stinking black bundles, the remains of his sheep ranch, rotting clumps of burned wool and flesh. He reined in his horse, which was jerking hard at the bit, not wanting to be close to the dead sheep. "I'm asking you to bear witness, I believe," he said. "Do you see something odd?"

I studied the scene before me: a whole herd of animals killed where they'd stood. "I don't, I reckon," I said.

He pointed down the pasture. "Ever in your life know a herd of any animal, even people, to line up in a straight line?"

"Lord a'mighty," I whispered. I wiped sweat from my face. I could feel it trickling down the center of my chest, too. I got off my horse and dropped the reins. Closer to the nearest animal, I pried at it just a little with the heel of my shoe. I held my breath and turned it over. Wrapped around the sheep's hind leg was a piece of wire, running from the poor thing to a stake in the ground. The other end led to the next dead sheep. I said, "Somebody went to a lot of trouble to put you out of business, Mr. Hanna."

"Who?"

I shook my head. Of course, the first name that came to mind was Lazrus. But cruelty like this, as furious as he'd gotten over the poisoned windmill? I said, "It's not unusual for cattlemen to resent sheep coming to the land. But not a soul has said a word to me against you or your sheep." Next names on my tongue would have been those of the Wainbridge brothers. Or, if I was looking for a mean streak, I wouldn't have to look much further than Willie. But tying up these animals had taken some planning. One thing I didn't think anyone would accuse Willie of was planning ahead.

We mounted up. Two miles southwest of his sheep pasture, we crossed a blackened hill that, from the rubble of stumps and ash, had been a thicket of brush and weeds. At the bottom of that hill, scorched land made a seam against fresh greasewood and brittlebush as neat as two quilt blocks. It made me sick down inside, thinking it had been intentional. Sicker still, because I kept feeling Willie had been a part of this. We led our horses awhile, then rode farther south. That little green patch had been simply that. The valleys and hills beyond were charred and gray. What looked like a thousand black arrows pointed through the ash toward the sky. We passed the carcass of a deer. The horses got skittish and wouldn't go through the ashen land.

He said, "Someone set that fire." Then he turned his horse and we rode back where we'd come. In front of his rebuilt house—no more than a tiny shed with room for the man and his son to sleep side by side on the floor—he turned to me and said, "First thing, I could have killed the man who did it. Now I'm mad, mad enough to dig me a trench and plan a strategy. I didn't live through that war for *no* reason. I fought for this country and buried most of my family in it. My great-grandparents fought for the right to live here and do as they well pleased, and no man's going to tell me what I can raise on my land."

I said, "I have a deep-down belief that there are folks in the world who are good through and through, and others who came in mean and will go out mean. It's like coffee. Once it's roasted, it all looks brown. Until you pour hot water on it and see what comes out. Folks get into hot water, you see what comes out. When Aubrey gets home from the cattle drive, it'll come out all right. You and he together."

Mr. Hanna shook his head and smiled. "Mrs. Elliot, you have said a truth worthy of Scripture." He swept his gaze across the sky. I couldn't tell if he was watching something or just taking it in, the way I sometimes did. He said, "Will you stay for supper? My stove is out here next to the woodpile. I've made some little benches. My cellar was saved whole, for the most part. Dirt on everything, but it didn't fall in. We didn't have the stampede you all contended with. Mrs. Baker left it packed with a king's feast. None of those jarred goods would travel, I believe. Will you take a meal with me? If you think it's proper, that is, I'd be kindly obliged. It won't be anything fancy."

"Fancy doesn't suit me."

He leaned over a row of jars resting on two boards and said, "Will you have a seat, there while I cobble something? Good thing about having the stove outside is that it doesn't heat up the house." I poked kindling and rustled up the fire. Udell made corn pone on one of the stove lids and heated up a tin plate full of Mrs. Baker's mixed beans on the other. We sopped the pone in pot liquor and ate the beans from coffee cups. Mrs. Baker had been a fair cook, and her canning was first-rate.

I showed him where a new leaf was budding on a burned-over greasewood bush. He leaned in close and studied it. "Starting over," he said. Then he held my horse while I got on, and we rode to my place.

All the rest of the evening and into the night, Mr. Hanna and I sat on my front porch and talked until the stars came out. He asked me to call him Udell, and I told him I would if he'd call me Sarah. Udell suggested that since I didn't have both watchdogs anymore, I should put something noisy by every door, so after he left, I strung metal coffee cups on every door handle, so there'd be a big noise if anyone opened one. I made myself a footbath with salt water and sat in my rocker. I'd string cups until my boys came home.

August 15, 1906

Charlie rode up this morning looking thinned out and old around the eyes. I called his name, and he heeled his horse and dropped from the saddle the way his papa used to do. It was so familiar a motion, I didn't notice until *he* did it that Jack had done the same thing all his days. Neither of the boys had ever seen their papa do it; it must have come naturally after Charlie grew up. From the look in his eyes, he'd done some growing while he was gone. He said he hadn't eaten for two days and would be glad to have anything, cold or not.

Charlie told me a tale while I fixed him a plate of food. They'd gotten down nearly to Douglas, when the rustlers laid an ambush for them and all-out battle broke out. The cattle stampeded every which way. Rudolfo Maldonado has been shot, but Charlie said he'd live. Rudolfo was at his house, getting well, he said. Charlie was bound to ride to Tucson to find a deputy or Ranger to give them a hand.

"Well," I said, "and what about Willie?"

Charlie took a drink of water to wash his food down. "He was in the bunch at first, right there with the rest of them shooting at us. Then they broke off in two groups, what was left of them. I found two running irons they'd left, where they were changing brands. We—we killed a couple. Buried two. There're eight left. Most of them I've never seen before. Five in one group and three in another."

"Which group is Willie with?"

"The three. A vaquero named Calderon from Maldonado's roundup and a renegade Yaqui they picked up who'd been waiting down in Agua Prieta." He made fists with both hands as they stretched on the table before him. "Mama? I had him in my sights. I—I couldn't shoot that kid. I don't miss him any more than I'd miss a toothache, but I couldn't kill him."

"No. Of course you couldn't."

"Don't know if I could have stopped him. But Mama, I believe he's the one shot El Maldonado."

I gripped my elbows in each hand, held tightly to my sides.

"That's about it," he said. "The other part is that I did— I did shoot one of the others. Ain't slept—haven't, I mean—since." He rubbed his chin with the back of his hand.

I laid my hand on his shoulder and he put his hand on top of mine. He sat there staring out the window, pressing my hand, holding tight. I knew every fiber of what he had gone through. That feeling wasn't going to go away, nor tame down, either, until it could be held up to the light of what had brought him to it. I said, "And the cattle?"

"A couple of Maldonado's men caught a bunch and are headed back this way. They're pretty hot right now, and anybody rides up to them is going to taste lead. Tell anybody you know not to approach them without calling out first who they are."

I patted his shoulder in the same spot I'd been holding. This was good news at least. A little good news. Since he didn't mention the money from the strongbox, I reckoned it wasn't worth asking about. I said, "I'll get my horse."

"No, better just pack me some food, Mama. And stay here and wait until I get back. Luz is tending her papa with one of the girls from the Cujillo place. I'm going to Tucson. Did Grampa go with Gil to drive the herd?"

"Yes. They'll be couple more weeks. But we were *all* going to Tucson."

"You go on, then. But not without Uncle Albert. April will be there when I get back." He stood and finished off the water. "I'm going to change my shirt. Sorry for the holes I got in this one." Long as the holes were not in his hide, it'd be easy enough to mend. And just like that, Charlie was gone again.

Rudolfo lay fretful in his bed. The bedroom in the hacienda was one room I'd never seen before. He was a good-size man, but he looked small in the large bed. Luz went ahead of me, "Papa," she whispered. "Doña Elliot is here."

Rudolfo opened his eyes. "Sarah! At last a woman with some sense. These girls have stolen my last shred of dignity. Luz! You two hiding there by the door. *Andelé.*"

"Luz," I said, "stay right here."

Rudolfo cocked his head at me. "Ah, yes. Business to discuss, but circumstance dictates honor, too. You've already heard, then, that we found them but didn't catch them. My men have some of your herd. I think about a hundred total. Did Carlos—"

He meant Charlie. "He told me. I'm sorry. Truly sorry."

"What happened here while I was gone? My daughters act as if nothing has passed. All they have to do is open their eyes. Only my Elsa was clever as you." He winced and drew a ragged breath, holding his ribs, before he continued. "Gone to a convent. What a good wife she would have made some man."

If, I thought, any man could have been found equal to Rudolfo's expectations. Perhaps Elsa had found the only "Man" who could. I told him about finding Mr. Hanna's sheep pinned in a line, where they died, and about our searching for the start of the fire. Rudolfo listened with his eyes half-closed, so I thought he might have fallen asleep.

Suddenly, he interrupted me and said, "Nothing else? *¿Furtivamente?*"

I told him of Lazrus, but again he stopped me, waving one hand and grimacing. "No, no. Did that boy of yours come back? I thought he was headed this way."

"No."

"Then it was a trick. He has learned fast, that little *testarudo*. Turned coyote overnight. He promised he would surrender and go home. Return your money, too, as long as we let him pass. I would not have let him, but, of course, Carlos was not there when El Coyote escaped. Never mind. I'm going to live to see him hang. Murdering thief."

I stepped back. "He didn't murder you."

"Tried." He coughed a spell. "Help me up, Sarah." He reached for me, pulling himself to the side of the bed, coughing all the while.

When he got quiet, I said, "Do you need me to bring a chair?"

"I need you to bring me my pistols. And get those girls to hurry up with my shirt. I'm going with the cattle. We'll ride to the stockyards at Hayden's Ferry. We'll find more strays along the way."

"You've got no business on a horse."

"What? This? It doesn't hurt. What pains me is the rib I broke. The bullet tore skin, nothing more."

"You cough like you've got the ague. Something in the lungs."

"Smoke, that's all. Luz! *¡Los pantalones!* Sarah, that shirt! There, on the chair."
I handed it to him. "If you find Willie, I want you to bring him here."

He studied my face a long time before he said, "You want him back?"

Everything about Willie had gotten so complicated, I didn't know what to
think. "Yes, I do." I watched him doing buttons, brazenly, as if we were already
married. "What about cattle? How many did you get?"

"Eh?"

"Most of them were mine."

"*Unos cuantos.*" He shucked the pistols into holsters and tied down the
straps.

My ribs pressed in painfully, as if I'd been shot, too. "*¿A donde?*"

"Polinar Bienvenides takes the few of them north. You wait here."

"I'm really tired of being told that. It doesn't look to me as if you're going
to spend time in bed healing up, riding off to Tempe. I could go with you if I
pleased. I could. Well, you do what you're a mind to. I won't leave my place un-
tended. I'm going home. There's work to do." I was both sorry and beholden to
him for chasing after Willie and getting shot. My riding by his side surely
wasn't going to get my chores done, nor fetch my herd. What it would do was
make him think I wanted to be with him.

He looked as angry as he'd seemed when he first left. He raised his head
and said, "Go, then."

Back at my place, I tended my horse and went to the barn to get some feed
for Hunter. The ready oats had come unstacked; the hopsack bags had slid
apart, as they did sometimes. I pulled the sacks apart slowly and carefully, for a
stack of feed is as good a place as you'll find for a snake to hide. Mice like the
oats, and snakes like the mice. I had it all cleaned out underneath and put some
boards at the sides to keep the stack leaned in on itself, and then started piling
them up again.

From a long ways off, a man called out. It appeared to be Udell, and the
closer he came, the more certain it appeared. He'd come with another remedy
to get Hunter to drink. He had rigged up a big bottle he'd borrowed from the
Cujillos, and he told me how to mix a good milk for the colt. Well, we took it
to Hunter, and he balked at first, but then he guzzled that milk as if it was good
as sweet cream.

We talked a spell and I told Udell about April and her family expecting me
after the gathering. "I haven't seen my daughter in so long," I said.

"Stay all you like," he replied. "You know, there's more in my life that I regret not doing than what I *have* done. A man can work for forty years for his family and still lose it all and the family to boot. Stay with her. You don't get second chances."

"I want to be here when Willie comes back. Rudolfo Maldonado has been shot. Willie did it."

Udell said, "Xavier Cujillo sent for a woman he called *la cantadora*. He said she's got Maldonado fixed up. That cough he's got is from dust he's been eating. Least that's what Cujillo told me. I'll tend your place."

I put out my hand to shake on his words, and he took it. So, we had a bargain, the two of us. "Udell, have you had supper?" I asked.

"Yes, ma'am."

"Something sweet, then? I'll put on coffee, if you'd care to stay. I took a pie out of the oven this morning. Charlie ate half of it, but there's plenty left."

"I wouldn't want to impose."

I waved that thought away as I went toward the door. "Least I can do," I said.

Udell said, "Mrs. Elliot—Sarah—I know you didn't ask me, but since I've got nothing living at my place, and you have someone looking to do you harm, I'd be willing to *stay* here and keep watch for you. I'd leave you your privacy, of course. But I'd sleep better if you weren't here alone."

I said, "Well, I hadn't asked because I hadn't thought that far ahead." I thought back to the times in my life that had put me in situations just like this. I felt as sure of Udell being a gentleman as I did of Lazrus being a maniac. "Reckon I'd be obliged."

I made the coffee I'd promised him. We talked in the darkness, sipping our coffee. Then we hung the blanket up on the summer porch and turned in. In the morning, I carried the gun to the smokehouse to cut some steaks while Udell washed up, and then we had a breakfast together. When he went to get his horse, I followed him to where it was tied. Then I said, "Is that your pack over there?"

He walked to it, motioning to me to go to the house. I got my shotgun and then went back to follow him toward the lump on the ground. Lazrus's shirt, smelling of bear grease and sweat, stained with streaks of brown, had been pinioned to the dirt with a sharpened shaft of wood. Udell jerked out the stave and kicked at the pile. A scorpion darted out, tail arched, ready to take on anyone who'd wake him at this hour. Under the shirt, my name was scratched deep into the dirt. The wood had pierced the *S*. Udell said, "Suppose I'll go unpack my army Springfield. Never thought to point that at a man again. I'll be back shortly. You keep that with you all the time."

"You're doing a lot for a stranger."

He smiled, the kind of smile when things aren't really happy, but he wanted me to know he was sincere. He said, "A neighbor, you mean."

Chapter Nineteen

At last, we were going to town. Rachel and Rebeccah were leaving home to teach school. Esther would begin her studies at the university. Joshua would go there soon as he got back from accompanying Granny to Chicago and back. My boys should have been with them, except for the trials we'd lived through this summer. I couldn't pay their tuition anyway. Lands, that nearly breaks my spirit. Not in years have I been so low on cash.

We were used to having our grown boys riding with us. Albert would be the only man there. He's not a bad shot, but he said it would be better if I carried his rifle, and he took the shotgun, for you don't have to be but half paying attention to make use of a shotgun. Now anyone in the Territory knows I can pretty much hit what I aim at, but there could be those on the road not knowing me, people who'd not tangle with folks guarded by a few armed men.

I picked up his rifle and said, "Albert, how long has it been since you blew the dust off this?"

"While, I reckon," he said.

I checked the breech to make sure it was loaded. At that second, I heard a crash come from the kitchen. Snapping it shut quickly, we both ran to see what had happened. Savannah was already sweeping. She said, "Stop there at the door. It's everywhere, and you'll track it through the house. I just dropped three plates and my best bowl—the only one that didn't have a chip in it. You'd think

I could have been more careful." She moved that broom in a flurry as bits of china and pottery came together in a heap. "Purely distracted. Can't keep my mind on one thing for more than a minute."

Albert said, "Well, honey, are you missing your girls already? Mary Pearl will be here. And, of course, Clover, Ezra, and Zack."

"This is a natural part of the girls' growing up. They *should* leave home," Savannah said. "I've had their whole lives to prepare for it."

I knew just how she felt. "Savannah," I said, "all you can do is start looking forward to the days they'll come to visit. As long as they're not in the ground, they'll come back to you." If I could have stepped over the mess, I'd have hugged her.

She gave me a look that in half a minute went from anger to worry to sadness to resignation. "I wish I could be as strong as you," she said.

"I'm not strong about it," I said. "But think what it would be like if you kept them here? Can you just picture it, the girls all old maids, still bickering over hair ribbons, and you eighty-five, still cooking for an army every day?"

She laughed, shaking her head, and said, "Lands! What a thought. Shoo those chickens out the door."

"It's the only way to do it," I said. In my heart, though, I knew I had no desire whatever to shoo my own chickens out the door. They were just leaving on their own, all big feet and pinfeathered.

Zachary would ride in the buggy with Savannah, the twins, and Esther. Ezra was to sit tall in his saddle on Big Boy and look grown. Last, Mary Pearl was to put on a pair of Clover's pants, tuck her hair in her hat, and try to look for all the world as if she was a man riding with us. Mary Pearl said it made her feel really strange, and she was embarrassed to come out of her room in the pants. A man with his head in a carpetbag couldn't mistake that girl for a fellow.

I said, "You need a big shirt. Get one of your papa's and let it hang loose. Keep a bandanna on your neck, honey. If anyone comes up, you pull it up over your nose." Nothing was going to hide those big brown eyes and their heavy fringe of lashes, though.

Savannah looked at her youngest daughter and said, "You'll wear a coat."

"Oh, Mama, the heat. I'll perish!" Mary Pearl said. "See if the shirt will be enough. I'll pull it way out. See? No waist at all."

Ezra came from his room with a toy rifle Clover had carved for him, saying, "Here, Imp. If you're going to look like a fellow, this can look like a rifle, too."

I tried to travel light, so I had only the two carpetbags. Rachel and Rebeccah both had traveling trunks and a bag, plus sewing kits and hatboxes, and Esther had a valise and two bags, and nearly the same number of little boxes. Everyone had to bring things. The surrey wouldn't hold the luggage and the family, too. So now Zack would ride with Ezra on Big Boy. The boys were plum tickled with the plan, since they have never gotten to take a horse to town. We tied another pony on back of the surrey. Albert had bought that horse cheap, and he'd gotten his money's worth. They called him Flojo, but that horse was anything but lazy. He was a little Spanish thing, with pin ears and a turned-under nose. All trouble and a mile wide, I'd say.

I looked behind us as we moved up the road. Albert's house was empty. Granny's house was so empty, it looked abandoned, dusty, even on the outside. Farther up the road, my place was abandoned, too, except for Udell Hanna coming to feed each day. I thought about how close I was to riding away from it for all time. Reckoned I might yet be happy to have a small share in the pecan farm. At least that was still solvent. I just didn't know how I'd go on if I had to take the charity of my brother's family. The most familiar ground, my little cemetery— long out of view—felt to me if it were tearing loose from its bindings.

Halfway to town, we edged our way down the *arroyo grande* on foot. A few of the planks had washed down the streambed at the bottom. Albert and the little boys fetched them, then set to bracing them into place with some rocks they'd hauled up at the edges. Savannah sat in the surrey, trying to stay out of the sun, but Esther got down, watching the boys work. She pulled a fine net around her face, for the mosquitoes in the arroyo were thick. Holding a canteen, she passed it to one, then another. I think Esther is plum worried about going to college, and afraid a mosquito bite on her face will brand her for the country girl she is.

I went to stand in the shade of the surrey. "Savannah," I said, "how are you?"

"Melted down like a candle," she said. "And worried, too."

"About the new baby?"

"That one, and all the others."

I said, "Look at Mary Pearl there. She won't even get off the horse for anyone to see her in those trousers. You've raised them just fine." Savannah got a satisfied look on her face.

Albert frowned and said, "Any man fooled by that getup would have to be stone-blind."

The trip to town took no longer than it usually took us, but my lack of patience sorely taxed me. I wanted to gallop down the road, not wait for their overburdened wagon. As we turned up Soldier Trail toward the last bend and saw buildings in the distance, I felt purely giddy.

The sun was high overhead when we pulled up to the entrance circle of April and Morris's grand house; a wide swath of packed gravel cut through the yard, all lined with pots of geraniums. Once everyone was out of the surrey, I knocked on the front door.

"Yes, madam?" a stranger said. The woman looked like a catalog picture in her gray dress, all starched and ironed in this heat. I knew April was planning to hire help, but the lady looked as if she should own this house.

Behind her, a lady in blue cried out, "Mama!" April came running, and I took that girl in my arms. Oh, she felt so good. Such pretty hair. So plump and real and warm. She kissed my cheeks and clung to me, and took away my breath. I breathed in the smell of her, the scent of lilac water in her hair. My three grandchildren waited in a row on the steps. After some hugs all around, we bustled into April's "drawing room." The room was set all about with gas lamps, fine rugs, and upholstered furniture. But first thing was not to sit and rest, for April wanted us to see changes they'd made to the house. It took nearly half an hour for April and Morris to give us a tour.

Then April said, "It's past noon, and the girls need their naps. It's hard enough to keep them on any kind of schedule in this heat. I've got tea and cookies ready, though. Oh, Mother, I've found a perfectly wonderful cook, Yselle. She makes the best chiffon cake. Morris, ring for Lizzie, won't you?"

Rachel and Rebeccah rushed to sit on either side of April, their arms around her waist. They had all changed into remarkable young women. The twins looked less alike now, since Rachel'd had rheumatic fever last year, but there was still an essence of the *tres amigas* who used to run endlessly between my house and Savannah's. The girls sounded like a little flock of quail fluttering here and there. Rachel and Rebeccah had only nine days until their teaching started, and they wanted to spend every minute possible with April. I almost looked forward to the twins' leaving, so I could have my girl all to myself.

It hurt, too, to see the babies. It was different from having my sons tease me that I was old, or for me to use my age as an excuse for some kind of laziness. Those times amounted to no more than squalling with no proof. This here was proof with no sound, proof that seeped into the small places in my heart, where I never allowed any nonsense. The place inside that I thought of as me had just been informed its owner was old. At home, when I was busy, there were days and weeks that flew by and I didn't give time so much as a nod. I remembered Udell's words about not letting a moment by, and suddenly my eyes filled with tears.

"Mother!" April said. She took the little girls from me and set them back on the floor, then leaned onto my lap and put her cheek against mine. It was such an odd thing for her to do. How could I explain to a beautiful lady in a silk dress that when I picked up her baby girl, I felt that lady's long-ago chubby shape in my arms, smelled her sunshine-touched hair? That years and years of tiny memories flitted past my heart like a flock of birds spinning on invisible air? It was the smell of the little girls, slightly wet, somewhat soapy, the smell of porridge supper, and the taste of kissed-away tears. Here in my arms were the best parts of life, going on, blooming like a strong tree.

"Grandmother?" said Vallary, looking into my face. "Don't be sad. Would you like to see my toy horsey?"

The stinger of my age had been removed by a single word from a little boy with tousled yellow hair. I smiled. "Surely I would," I said.

While Val showed me the carved horse and saddle, April looped her arms through Rachel and Rebeccah's arms. "Come with me, ladies. We'll put the girls down for their naps in the nursery. Then I've got things to show you." April, Rachel, and Rebeccah dashed upstairs with little Patricia and Lorelei in their arms and Esther on their heels. Mary Pearl stayed in the parlor with her folks and Morris. April stood at the top of their shiny wooden stairway, which was lined with an Oriental rug all the way, top to bottom. "Mama? Aunt and Uncle? Do come up, too," she called.

What caught my eye was Mary Pearl. Her eyes went wide at first, then narrowed. One of the twins leaned over the rail at the top of the stairs then and called, "Mary Pearl, come on up, honey. Wait till you see this fabric!" But Mary Pearl didn't move, and the one calling down didn't wait at the railing.

"You going?" I asked her.

Fingering the fringe on the heavy curtain near her chair, Mary Pearl shrugged. "I think I'll go for a ride instead," she said.

Savannah said, "Cousin April didn't mean not to include you, honey. But she and the twins were like sisters when they were small. You just don't remember her."

I stood up, some dishes in my hands, and Lizzie came in suddenly and took them from me, saying, "Oh, madam, please visit with your folks." Then she disappeared.

Morris said, "Lizzie'd be fretful if you carried dirty plates into the kitchen. Besides, Yselle is busy with supper. It's better not to go in during her work. I told her there'll be company."

Savannah went to Mary Pearl and said, "Let's go upstairs, honey, and see what the girls are looking at." Arm in arm, they started for the staircase.

Zachary came bounding in the back door, Ezra and Vallary on his heels. Ezra bounced an India-rubber ball off the floor and caught it. He went straight to Savannah, who was standing at the foot of the stairs, and in a loud whisper that all of us heard, he said, "There's no privy out back, Mama. Mind if I go in the hedge at the back of the yard there?" Morris laughed, and sent him upstairs to the privy room.

Ezra and the other two boys ran toward the staircase. As they stampeded past Savannah and Mary Pearl, we could hear them on the stairs, Zack saying, "Hey, Val' old pal, where'd you get them sawed-off pants?"

Vallary said, "These are knickerbocker trousers. All the boys in my school wear them. Call them knickers for short."

"Don't your legs get full of stickers?" Zack asked.

Ezra's voice rang down the stairs, "Knicker-stickers! Knicker-stickers!"

The three boys shrieked with laughter, then vanished, too.

The men went outside to look at some kind of water-pump system and the newest buggy that Morris and April had. For a moment, I was alone in the entry of this lovely house. Then I began to make my way up the wide, carpeted staircase. I lingered in the hallway at the top of the stairs, wondering which of the doors to go through. I felt torn. Longing to do something about the problems at home, thrilled to be here, and wishing to forget everything else, to see my daughter and her husband and my grandchildren—to be happy. Yet, I wasn't happy. I felt like a rank stranger in ways I could not describe. April and her family had been back in Tucson for over a year now, but it seemed the grandchildren were my only connection to her. I missed Lorelei and Patricia while they were asleep.

I heard voices behind one door that was partway open. When I entered, April explained that this was the "morning room." She had laid out bolts of fabrics on chairs and tables. April wanted each cousin to choose a color and cut a length—enough for a dress—as a gift. I tried to sort out whether she was telling us we dressed too shabbily for her, but the girls were happy with the prospect. Savannah was silent, merely watching the going-on, fanning herself. Reckon I wouldn't want anyone to speculate on the motive behind a gift I gave them, although I wasn't in the habit of bestowing things much.

Supper was just as elegant as it could be, but it was pure relief to head toward my place in town after supper. That night, the slew of us bedded down there, and for a little while, I laid awake, listening to the empty old house settling. I suppose a person would think their oldest child and only daughter would somehow seem more akin to them.

August 21, 1906

In the morning, as I reached to pull the plug on the bath, I peered out the window overlooking the back of the house. The sun was up just enough to see the dry and weedy square of "yard." Once, I'd had flowers and mint beds back there. It used to be beautiful. If I lived here, I'd put in some mint. Put primrose against the fence. If I lived here, it'd mean selling the ranch. Coming to town for good and all. Just like the ranch, which is homesteaded, this house is paid for. All I owe are taxes each year. If I sold the ranch and paid the taxes up for fifty years, there'd be no drought could take this house away. The boys are all but on their own. I'd be nearer these grandchildren. Chess probably wouldn't mind as long as he gets his three squares and some tools to fiddle with. Mama would live here with me and do her quilting, and I'd read to her every night. Savannah and Albert could visit. That thought made something clutch in the pit of my stomach.

I could sell this house instead of the ranch. It might bring enough to keep solvent until we got turned around. Trouble was, the house was full of memories of Jack, too. We had built it together. Had children here. I had so many decisions to make. At breakfast, I talked all this over with Savannah and Albert. I thought Savannah might tell me it would be too lonely for her. Instead, her advice was to wait and pray. Albert agreed, and saying nothing that big should be decided quickly.

Savannah was to see the doctor about her condition at ten o'clock. I told Albert to drive her in my buggy and that the rest of us could walk to April's place. As I watched Albert and Savannah drive away, I said over my shoulder to Mary Pearl, "What got into you to volunteer to haul around the boys, instead of visiting with the girls?"

Mary Pearl fixed her hat squarely on her head. "I don't mean nothing harsh by it. It's just that at Cousin April's house, it's us that's strange. I feel like an old shoe left on the porch a couple of years."

"Why do you say that?"

Mary Pearl shrugged. "Folks in town will quick pull up a package or some such, but they're staring like I was the ugliest thing ever born. Papa says, except for taking Mama to the doctor, he ain't letting me out of his sight. I reckon they just expect me to end up bad."

"Honey, they won't let you out of their sight because you are the prettiest dove of the bunch. Your mama is just trying to make sure you don't get led astray. Like with that fellow writing those secret letters."

She blushed deeply. "They're Esther's. She wrote and told him she was going to town."

"Mary Pearl! Are you *coming*?" a boy shouted, his voice cracking on the last word. Ezra. Loud boots clambered on the stairway.

"I'm coming," she said, going toward the door. "You don't think I'm ugly?"

"Like a sty in the summer!" Ezra said.

I said, "Get on out of here, you varmint," then turned back to Mary Pearl. "Why, Mary Pearl, do you think I taught you to carry that knife? It's a face too pretty to let pass. Just remember, sometimes a girl can get right up against something before she's got it figured out. Now chase those critters out of here before they run headlong into a fence post."

"Yes, ma'am." Mary Pearl smiled as she turned.

That girl had dimples in her chin and both cheeks, and I knew sure as I was standing that if she'd turned that little smile on any grown fellow, he'd have dropped to his knees in a full-out swoon on the spot.

Before I got to April's place, Mary Pearl had caught up to me. She said, "I decided maybe I'd like a dress, too. Mama said it'd be all right, long as it was modest. No sense being stubborn about taking a gift that's offered. I sent the rascals to try panning for gold up at the flour mill by Sentinel Peak."

"Pull a lot of color out of that wash?" I asked.

"I figured the idea of it would keep them company until they figure that pie tin has better uses."

We laughed. I shook my head. "Likely that'll cause a run on property there."

Well, April and the girls had patterns and pins and a flurry of sewing in that upper room. Amidst the commotion, we told April about the cousin we'd never known, and how Willie'd turned out to be some sorry stuff. While we talked of serious things, I played patty-cake with Patricia and Lorelei and cut them paper dolls. Next thing, the girls got the idea of fixing up Mary Pearl's hair like a Gibson girl, and they spent half an hour doing that.

I told April then, "So long. I mean to head back to the house and fix the little boys some dinner."

Suddenly, April dropped the hat book on the table. "I thought they'd gone with Uncle Albert and Aunt Savannah. You didn't bring them with you?"

I said, "They're out playing at the riverbed. Took some horses."

"Vallary is riding *horses* through town without any adults with him?"

"The boys know their way around."

"Whose horse? Is it wild?" April ran to the front window and looked out.

Mary Pearl said, "They put him on Flojo. Zachary's got Big Boy. Ezra's got Duende. I told him if he ends up riding dirt, it's his hide. Duende's not going to put up with him jumping off the way he does."

April gasped. "That gigantic horse? It'll crush them with one foot. Mother, how could you let them take my son like that?"

"Well, they're good boys. There's not much trouble they'll get into that a good switching and some castor oil won't fix." No sooner had those words left my mouth than we heard a commotion in the back of the house. Footsteps lumbered from room to room, then about halfway up the stairs.

Zack's voice whispered, "Aunt Sarah? Cousin April? I think you better come outside. In the back there. Outside." The back door closed very quietly. That alone was a sure sign something was not right with those three boys.

April opened the door to see what was keeping them, calling out, "Vallary Winegold? Come in this house this very minute." I followed April to the porch. Her cousins followed me.

Vallary, covered with filth and beaming with pride, slipped off Flojo's back just as the door opened. When he caught his balance, he reached up and grabbed something long, like a hank of rope, and slid it from the horse's back, too. Val had a huge grin on his face and said, "Look, Mother!"

Ezra slid off Duende and was just touching his foot to the ground when both Flojo and Duende saw the dead snake in Val's hands. At the same time, both animals bucked, arching their backs, rearing up and jumping, twisting sideways, throwing sunlight and shadows on their bellies as they expressed their horror at the snake's presence.

Zack had started for the horses, but he ran back toward the porch. Ezra held his arms over his head, trying to catch Duende's reins. Even old Big Boy ambled away from the commotion. Val, terrified, stood between the two wildly bucking animals, their hooves nearer and nearer. He held one end of his snake and froze, mouth open.

I let go of April's arm and ran toward my grandson, a noise like a raging mountain lion coming from my throat. "Don't move!" I screamed. "Whoa, whoa!" I waved my hands over my head and flapped my apron. I had Vallary in my arms as I dashed to the porch.

The rattlesnake's body dangled from Val's grasp like a tail, whipping around my legs as I ran. Finally, setting the boy on the porch, my breathing returned to normal, and he began to cry. "Oh, honey. Oh, little baby," I said, hugging him close. Val smelled like the horse he'd been riding, and worse. Something swampy and rancid coated his hair.

Vallary grunted, trying to stop his tears. He struggled out of my arms and stood on his own feet, saying, "Grandmother, I'm not a baby. I just caught a snake. All by myself. Zack said it was real brave." He wiped his runny nose on his dirty sleeve, giving himself a mustache of mud.

April screamed and ran to Vallary, picking him up. He still gripped his snake tightly in one hand. "Put that down!" she ordered. He held on firmly. With a gasp, she set him on his feet on the porch.

I knelt by him. "That horse," I said, and shook Vallary's shoulder with frustration. He stood transfixed, watching Flojo writhing in the yard. Flojo squealed and snorted; strings of mucus and foam flew from his nose. His hoof caught the blue glass "viewing ball" that stood on a stand at the beginning of the flower bed, and it exploded like a firecracker. April hollered.

I shouted, "That horse could have killed you with one hoof. You had that snake slung across— Oh, Vallary. The meanest little brute of a horse. Oh Lord."

April, hands on her hips, her face red and hair all fluttered out, said, "Drop that nasty thing this instant."

"But Mother, it was the bravest thing I ever done did. I want Ezra to clip off the rattles. Wait till you hear this, Mother," Val said to April, sniffing. He told a story of getting lost at the stream by the mill house, and of killing the snake with a rock because the horse wouldn't step over it. Then he told about his trip home, and a lady wearing a lacy dress—smoking a cigar just like a man—who'd hollered at him to show her his little snake. "But it's not little, is it, Mother? Look here. It's bigger than me. Zachary said I could wear it on my hat. How about that?"

The horses at last had settled down. April leaned against the rail on the porch and buried her face in her hands. "Oh dear God in Heaven," she said. "Castor oil, Mother? Fixed with castor oil?"

"Ezra James?" I said. "Zachary Taylor Prine? The two of you come here this minute." I glared at Ezra and Zack. These boys had led an innocent, frail little boy all the way to the river on the meanest horse they owned, and left him to risk killing himself many times over with a snake so large, it could have eaten the child after it struck him. There they stood, hooligans in the making, half-grinning, sassy, their freckles obscured by dirt. And Albert not there to take a strap to them. Under my care, they'd grow up to become rogues and drifters, and frighten old ladies, and rob banks. Rustle cattle. Just like Willie.

"You—you three boys," April said, breathing audibly two times, "take a bath!" Then she burst into tears, crying so heartily, she lost her footing and sank to the floor of the porch. She wadded her apron into a knot and rocked back and forth, totally besieged by misery.

The boys watched her, shocked. Never, ever, had Ezra and Zack seen someone's mother dissolve like this before their eyes. Val sobbed, too, sympathetically, still clenching his snake, its head gobby with mud and drying blood. Ezra's face turned red. Zachary said softly, "We're sorry, cousin," and tears dribbled from his eyes.

I said, "You two get those horses. Go on to my house, and take a bath, like she said. Val, put that thing out in the barn, where those horses can't see it. You've tormented your mama just about enough today. We'll talk about skinning it to-morrow." I was ready for my own company for a while. I surely wasn't accustomed to all this folderol, no matter that they were all blood relations. "I'll follow them home, and talk with Savannah and Albert about this," I said.

Rebeccah said, "We'll be there later. April wants us to stay here, sleep in their spare bedrooms. If Mama and Papa allow, that is."

Mary Pearl said, "Aunt Sarah, I'd be pleased to help you watch the little renegades. I believe I'll just let the big girls stay here." Mary Pearl and I walked back to the house. Well, we'd hardly gotten in the door than Savannah saw Mary Pearl's swept-up hair, which made her look older and modern and all. Savannah got cross, and she told Mary Pearl to get herself upstairs and take down her hair, then fetch her prayer book. Savannah's fussing had as much to do with the boys causing trouble as Mary Pearl's hair sweep, and I reckoned the girl would resent every word of it.

Mary Pearl said, "Yes, ma'am," but there was fire in her eyes. I watched sparks fly between them like a house cat in a thunderstorm. She was the same age my April was when she ran away with Morris. Girls around those years seem to get in a frame of mind that is prickly as a cholla patch.

Savannah was supposed to stay happy and peaceful, and she was more worried about Mary Pearl's hair fixing than she had a call to be. I got our supper and left Mary Pearl and her mother with the dishes. Then I read Ezra and Zack some history from a little book I'd found in a cupboard upstairs. They went to bed early. As I put out the lights and headed upstairs myself, I thought about being home, down on the ranch. Firestorms and dust and plagues of scorpions and cattle stampedes—all of that seemed peaceful compared to what was happening here.

The next morning, I awakened to the rhythmic scraping sound of metal hitting rock. My backyard was overgrown with weeds, some more than waist-high. Ezra had risen before the sun. He was hoeing and scraping, leaving a turned-up wake of freshened dirt. The soil was poor, mixed heavily with caliche and gravel. He stacked rocks in piles as he worked. When I called him to have breakfast, he cleaned up his face and hands, then sat without speaking. That boy was feeling mighty guilty for his part in yesterday's shenanigans.

The older girls had stayed at April's house. Mary Pearl rode herd on Ezra, Zack, and Val while I washed and hung out their duds. They ate like badgers, competing to see who could eat the most pancakes the fastest. Then the three went to the barn to finish doing their dirty work from the day before, skinning and mounting that snakeskin on a board to dry. April had been appalled when I'd said I was going to make them do it all by themselves.

Ezra, Zack, and Val clattered and banged on the back porch, laughing and hollering at each other. One of them said, "You were going to urp all over the barn!"

"No, I wasn't."

"You were slinging the snake's guts ever'where."

"I saw you. Just like a girl. Yurp, urp, slurp!"

"I did not!"

"Girlie-girlie!"

"Boys!" I shouted through the open window. "Everyone in town can hear you. Why don't you go play some baseball or something?"

"Aunt Sarah, does a snake have three livers?"

I couldn't tell the three apart by their voices. "No," I said. "That isn't natural."

"Told you! That warn't no liver," another young voice said.

Zack's head popped up in the window. "Aunt Sarah, Val says there's a swimming pool in town."

"Well," I said, "they won't take you as filthy as you are. You'd have to take a bath first, and it costs money to get in. Go down to the river and play in the water there. When you get home, we'll rinse the river mud off with a bucket."

They weren't gone half an hour before they came back. Apparently, some girls in the road had made fun of the way they looked and called them names, and the boys needed something to declare their scorn with. Naturally, the first things handy were road biscuits. They chased the girls and then came back to the house hot and tired, smelling awful. I pulled a metal tub from the barn and set it in the open doors there. Then I made a cover on a third side with a horse blanket hung on the clothesline. I told them to take off their overalls and play to their heart's content. That ought to keep them busy for at least an hour.

Chapter Twenty

On Saturday, it hadn't got warm yet when clouds started to boil up from the south. It had let up raining for some days but looked about to start again. As the morning went on, the sky got darker and the air smelled of wet creosote bush and clay. Rain in the distance dimmed the Rincons from view, and pretty soon the Catalina Mountains, too. I opened up the house, letting in the fresh air.

There was a tapping at the front door, and I was plenty surprised when April smiled prettily as I opened the door. She had a bundle in her hands. "Mother," she said. "I'm so glad you're up. I know it's early."

"Well, come on in," I said. "You know you don't have to knock. I'm fixing to work on this quilt of Granny's. Have you had some coffee yet?"

She looked about the front parlor. "I remember," she said, "when this used to be— I wish you'd put furniture back in this place. It feels abandoned."

"It's temporary," I said. Although I couldn't say myself right then if the temporariness applied to the abandonment or to my staying there. "Come on in."

April followed me to the kitchen. She chattered as she began opening her bundle, fussing with the strings that bound it. "I'm planning a tea party, to introduce the girls to some of my friends. Some important people in town. I was wondering if you'd like to have my dressmaker sew you a new dress. I've brought a pattern for you to look at. Where are Aunt Savannah and Uncle Albert? Upstairs?"

"Aunt Savannah is having a little baby sickness this morning. Albert went to buy horseshoes."

April's face went pale. "Baby sickness?" Her hand flew to her mouth, the way mine sometimes did when I was thinking hard. "I wanted to have a tea— I'm sure no one would— It wouldn't be fair to— I couldn't ask Aunt Savannah to— oh mercy."

I felt my neck grow stiff. "If you're wondering how to invite her out the door—"

"Oh no, Mother. I would never do that." For a few seconds, she stared at the tabletop. Then April turned to me with that beguiling, pretty smile I'd seen on her face recently and said, "I'd be devastated if she didn't come."

"Snake oil and hen's teeth. Why don't you talk to Savannah yourself? Maybe she'd surprise you." It made me simmer inside, this hoity-toity foolishness of hers. I'd just never had much truck with a person who didn't say what they meant and come right out with things. And to think a married woman couldn't sympathize with another's trouble. April kept up talking, trying to smooth things over. The only thing I could think of as we worked was that my daughter would throw a shindig and "receive" her aunt, all the while wishing that sweet lady had stayed home, and Savannah would smile and attend a gathering of silly women twittering about fashions and recipes, wishing all the while that she'd stayed home. Now I had to be betwixt the two, and not tell either one where her rope landed. April stayed just another minute and then took off for her shopping. I rolled up the pattern she'd brought and folded it back into the brown paper wrapping.

I was still staring at it when a voice said, "Mama wants some toast. If the fellows aren't here, I hoped to take a ride."

"Anyplace special?" I motioned toward the bread bin.

"Just getting Duende's legs under him again." Mary Pearl laid two cuts of bread on the griddle and slid it into the coals in the oven, watching it as she crouched by the door. "Mama said she wants it dry. Don't you think she'd like some peach preserve instead?"

"No. A woman having baby sickness only wants what she wants and nothing more." Mary Pearl took the toast upstairs, and awhile later I heard the back door open and close. I put my quilt on the table and laid it out flat. Purely homespun, that's what it looked. Scraps of clothes sewn in little bits. Nothing new but the backing. I reckoned April hadn't got a quilt in her whole house. At that moment, I felt like Mary Pearl's other old shoe.

I heard riders in the yard, horses drawn up, and the sound of hard-soled boots on the porch. Without knocking, someone opened the front door. Gilbert. And Chess right behind him. I made a whooping noise and ran to them, calling out, "Come in this house, you two." Shiner barked and skittered around when she saw them.

Gilbert said, "Mama? Didn't expect you to be here. I thought we'd just knock off some dust and eat something in town, then keep heading home." They told me how they'd had some trouble, and a two-day dust storm on the flats above Picacho. After that, they'd had rustlers try to cut out a few, but they'd chased them off, and then had to stand guard day and night. They'd sold the combined herd, got a good price for the 110 of ours. When Rudolfo Maldonado finally caught up to them, he brought 150 head. Only ten of them wore our Lazy Bar E.

"Here it is, Sarah," Chess said. "Four hundred and thirteen miserable dollars. Most of the cattle were the angle Slash—Maldonado's. He got two thousand and some for himself. That jasper bother to come by here? Likely halfway home." He slapped his hat against the floor as he dropped into a chair in the kitchen. I took the stack of bills. Four hundred and thirteen dollars. With no garden, no cattle, we'd be lucky to last to spring, put seed in the garden and hope to live on canned goods.

Gilbert said, "We've been talking to Cujillo and Flores. El Maldonado has cut into everyone's profit, trying to run too many. We've been doing some talking, Grandpa and me. We think there's only one way to make it fair. Fence." He opened the icebox and pulled out a jug, then yanked the cork and smelled it. "Milk!" he said. "You saving this for anything?"

I said, "A man comes around every other day selling fresh milk for the little boys. I'm taking it on credit, and I owe him two dollars. Have it if you like. More's coming tomorrow."

"What little boys? You got any biscuits?"

Then it was my turn to tell how we came to be here. "You two stay here, won't you? Stay until Sunday or Monday, and we'll head south together. April's going down to visit us a week or two later."

Chess said, "Any bed not laid on the ground will do me."

"All I can offer you is a pallet on the springs upstairs. I'll move my things out of there. There are two cots. Gilbert, you take one and sleep down here. Zack, Val, and Ezra can sleep on the floor."

Chess said, "I won't be putting you out of your bed."

"Don't argue with me, Chess. I've had all the aggravation I can take lately, and I'm feeling raw and mean. I'll pull a cot into Jack's and my old room. About time I slept there again."

Gilbert finished the milk, then said, "All right if I take a bath? I know it's the middle of the day. If you'll pull me some water, Mama, I'll wash these clothes. Grandpa and I need to scrape a little trail dust off us. Then we'll go say hello to Aprilcakes."

"You mean to tell me you're volunteering to wash your own clothes?"

He nodded. "Grampa Chess said you'd likely drop your teeth."

"Not likely. But I might want to hire a picture taker for the event. You go peel off. I'll start the kettle boiling."

Gilbert headed up the stairs. Chess sat on a kitchen chair, leaning back against the wall, snoring. I reckoned Gil had learned a thing or two about appreciation while he was on the trail drive. After he washed both their clothes with a scrub board and lye soap, I hung them out on the line for them, since the two had nothing but quilts to wear until they dried. I fixed them some food, and they ate dressed in quilts, now and then giving Shiner some bits of biscuit sopped in chicken gravy. I pushed a pan of gingerbread into the oven and suddenly straightened. "Where's Aubrey Hanna?" I asked.

Gilbert said, "He's staying in town. Got himself a job and a room at the Classical Boarding House up on Main Street. He wants us to tell his pa what he's up to. Says he's going to make a good life for him and a certain girl he's got an eye on. Says he's finished with schooling and thinks she'd be proud if he could earn a couple of dollars a week doing something useful—besides ranching, that is."

"That so?" I said. I looked from Gilbert to Chess. "Well, that's all right, if he wants to." I swan. Finished with school? Everyone wants to go to college except the two fellows I have been aiming toward education their whole lives. "There's nothing wrong with ranching to make a life, either, if that's what a man wants. Long as there's rain." I felt a little shamed I hadn't missed Aubrey at first. Udell would be completely alone down there, waiting on his son. I hurt for him, thinking how I'd waited on mine.

Gil and I left Chess resting while we bustled up the road, grown familiar now, toward April's house. She was tickled as a little bird to see her little brother. They hugged and squeezed each other, and April filled his hands with cookies and lemonade with ice and phosphate in it. Ezra and Zachary hung on him like little monkeys and pleaded with him to throw them a baseball. Val—nothing sissy about him anymore—sported a black-and-blue ring under his eye from a ball he'd caught with his face. The boys went outside in a flurry to show Gill the snakeskin, and the girls and I were left in the house.

April said, "How is your new dress coming, Mother?"

"Well, it's just cloth yet," I said. "Gil and Grandpa Chess came home, and that took some time. What are you sewing here?"

"It's Rachel's. Hasn't she got the smallest waist?" Rebeccah said, holding up a narrow strip of cloth. "Mary Pearl, that piece there has a wrinkle you've pinned in."

Well, we'd just got the rest of the pattern pinned down and marked when someone knocked at the door. Pretty soon, there was tapping at the pocket door, too. When April opened it barely an inch, the girls and I kept quiet. Lizzie whispered. April whispered. Then she pushed the door open with a whoosh, sending it into its pocket. "Charlie," she called. "Charlie!"

I rushed toward the sound of April's excited cries but had to stop short when I saw the man who stood before us. It had been only a couple of weeks since I'd seen him. He was the living image of Jack. A memory of Jack stood before me, mustache and all. Young. Handsome. Home. "Charlie," I said with a stutter, "let me look at you."

April called, "Lizzie, bring him something to eat." Then she said, "Come here, brother Charles. Sit, sit."

After we got gathered around him and I'd hugged him good, I stood back and just looked at him again. "Did you go to the house?" I asked.

"Grandpa Chess told me how to find you. Filled my hands with ginger-bread. My favorite kind. How'd you know I was coming?"

I said, "I wish I could say I made it specially for you. Chess looked a little peaked. I made it to perk him up."

Ezra, Zack, and Val burst into the room, and Charlie stood abruptly at the racket they made. While Zack and Ezra raced toward Charlie, Val stopped in his tracks, his mouth hanging open, as if he were seeing an elephant in the parlor. "Look!" he hollered. "A cowboy! Mother, there's a real cowboy in the house!"

Ezra and Zack attacked Charlie and climbed on him, much the same as they had on Gilbert. The difference, however, was that Charlie was taller—tall enough that his sleeves didn't touch his wrists anymore. And when the boys hung on his arms, Charlie lifted them off the ground, each of them poking and shouting for joy, wanting another turn to ride Charlie's arm-lifter. Val didn't want a turn. He just stared. I tapped Val's shoulder and said, "He's not a cowboy. That's your uncle Charlie."

Val just said, "Whoa! My uncle's a cowboy."

I'd have to explain it to him later that we didn't hold with cowboys. Seemed everyone from the other side of the Rio Grande thought any man wearing spurs should now be called a cowboy. That'd be like us calling every man in a bowler hat a grifter.

Lizzie put a plate of food in Charlie's hands, blushing hard as she did, as April peeled the boys off him for the fourth time. The skin around his eyes crinkled, his face now darkened to a bronze color from the sun. That mustache! Hair too long. Jack always let his get too long before he'd get it cut. Said he hated a haircut almost as much as having a tooth pulled. I had asked him when he'd had a tooth pulled, and he would just laugh and say, "Guess!" and kiss me. I felt so glad to see Charlie—and deep, aching sad to see Charlie, too, the very image of his papa. "Charlie," I said, "did you find Willie?"

He gazed from me to April and then to his cousins. "That skunk is holed up down in Cochise County, near the Chiricahua Mountains. There's been some other trouble. I had to get here first. I'm going to find him. I won't come back without him."

Charlie ate the sandwiches Lizzie had brought. I waited for him to say something, the way I'd always waited for Jack. He'd talk when he got his mind around the subject.

Then Mary Pearl said, "You know, he wants our farm. That's what he came for."

Rachel said, "Now, Mary Pearl. Willie *may* have come to be part of the family."

Charlie said, "Maybe at first. Any rate, I aim to settle his affairs once and for all. Mama, I've got a job to do. To get Willie." There was something in his expression I just couldn't read. He stared at his empty plate for a second, then looked me in the eye. "I'm saying you're looking at the newest member of the Arizona Rangers. Hired on through a man down to Bisbee. Came to town to get my papers and some ammunition. And to see somebody and ask her something. What's wrong?"

Suddenly, it was as if there was no one else in the room but my oldest son and me. I said, "You didn't have to do that to get Willie."

"Yes, I did. Two men with guns facing off, town doesn't know which one's right. Gives me jurisdiction in places where they weren't willing to take my word on it."

"But Charlie, what about school?"

He pulled something out of his pocket and held it out to me. A badge. He said, "I've been thinking about this a long time. Not just while I was gone, but way back, when I first went to school. I aim to bring Boots back with as many of our cattle as I can muster."

"Are you going alone?"

"Pretty much."

"When are you coming back?"

"There's a price on his head. I want to get him before some bounty hunter puts a slug through him for fifty dollars." The girls were talking. I felt as if the room were spinning around. Gilbert's voice added to the commotion. Charlie said, "Before I leave, I aim to ask Miss Esperanza to wait for me until I get back. Then I aim to court her serious. I'll have a salary. Be able to build a house of our own, just like you said I needed. I've been thinking about it, and you were right, Mama. I want my own house. And a family."

"I'll ride with you," Gilbert said.

"No," I said again. "You've both got school to get to. You're too young to be doing this." I could almost hear the rolling of their eyes, rattling as loudly as old Sparky's glass ones wobbling in their hollow holes. They exchanged glances with their cousins.

Gilbert said, "Old Charliehorse could use someone watching his back."

"It's all right with me," Charlie said, "only they aren't going to pay you."

Gilbert grinned. "Mama can tell Mr. Hanna about his wayward son. Shoot, Mama. If you wait around a while, old Aubrey'll probably pay you a social call."

April went to Charlie, patted his hand. "I think it's a noble thing for you to do."

My children have all plum left their senses. Loony as coots, the lot of them. Lost as their granny. Crazed beyond my control. I rubbed my face. There was nothing I could say. Everyone in the room talked, and the sound swirled around me like the clucking of a flock of chickens. I went to the window and pulled back the heavy drapes, stared into the hot afternoon outside. Voices wove a mesh of colors. Charlie spoke and someone said "Esperanza," and Ezra and Zack fluttered among the older cousins. Girls' voices said "Esperanza," and Charlie said yes about something. Whenever I got my fill of men and need an ear to bend, some woman who can see things straight, I need Savannah. I wanted to go home.

I heard Charlie say, "Well, I better git if I'm going."

April said, "I'll have our cook make you some food to take."

"You have a cook?" Charlie said. "I thought that girl was some friend of yours."

Mary Pearl said, "They have a cook and a maid to clean house, and they send out their laundry."

Charlie laughed, straightening his hat and pinning the badge on his shirt. "A cook and a maid? Only three children? What're *you* going to do all day?"

Gilbert said, "Guilds and societies and suffragette marches."

April sat dumbfounded for a moment as her younger brothers tossed the word *suffragettes* about, laughing. Finally, she said, "Someone has to feed the poor. Clothe the naked orphans of the world. Spread the Gospel to China."

"And vote the men out of office," Charlie added. He strapped his gunbelt on. Val said, "Whoa!" again. "Is that a real one?"

Ezra piped up with "Colt forty-five. It's a real buster! I shot one before."

Val circled around Charlie. I needed to have a talk with that little boy as soon as I could get a moment. I turned away from Val, away from Charlie. I faced April. Her face flushed a dark pink. I said loudly, "Anybody who's got to live by the law ought to have a voice in it. Women's votes wouldn't be swayed by a hand of cards or bought with a case of watered-down whiskey."

Charlie broke the silence. "Mayor Sarah A. Elliot, *del pueblo de Tucson*. It has a ring." Then everyone busted out laughing.

I waved my hand and said, "Politics. I don't have time for foolishness. I *work* for my living. If April has the money to have someone else do her laundry, why on earth should she run her hands to the bone doing it?" No one had a word to say to that.

Charlie said he'd come back and tell me Miss Esperanza's answer before he left, but he was headed down toward the Chiricahuas this very day. I watched Charlie through the curtains of the front window. The three little boys went after him into the yard, hollering farewells after him.

"I'm going back to the house," I said.

Mary Pearl caught my arm. "All right if I tag along?" she said. "Everybody here is planning a nap. I ain't had a nap, except for being sick, since I was four years old."

"Come ahead," I said.

She pulled Duende behind us, and we got all the way to my front door without talking. Then Mary Pearl said, "Cousin April said her tea party will have to wait for the spring season. Like them society balls and such."

All I said was, "That's likely a good idea."

Inside, Charlie sat on the bare floor, cleaning a Colt pistol I didn't recognize. Must have bought it new with his job money. Beside him, broken down in pieces, was a Remington rifle, one of those new ones that load from the stock. He was peering down the pistol barrel from the business end, but the cylinder was on the floor. Heaven knows I raised my children with enough sense not to stare down a loaded gun. He didn't look up, except for a glance. Charlie said, "Grandpa's gone to get my horse shod. Gilbert's around here somewhere. I'm leaving soon as I get this done."

I sat in the chair across the room. Put the basket at my feet. Watched his face. There was a wildness in his eyes, a fever. He took a bristle brush to the hammer and drew it back a couple of times. Charlie said, "My old pistol was getting a creep in the pull. Griego wouldn't give me a plug nickel for it, he said. He claimed it looked to be from the Mexican War. I told him better, and he just laughed. Had to lay out nine dollars for this one, but it's nice and tight." He sighted down the barrel, aimed at the floor.

I said, "You'll want the best."

He nodded. "Mr. Griego let me fire it out back into some old wadded blankets. She's got a mean kick. Take a look. Krags with the rim out." He scooted a box toward me, and I had to lean down to pick it up. I admired the ready-made bullets. Hefted one from the box. What a difference they might have made thirty years ago, every one a twin to the next one, loaded true and molded smooth. A lot different from pot lead poured into a mold by a campfire and then carefully beaten into a shell with a hammer.

"Well? Are you getting married?" I asked, scooting the box back toward him.

"She said she'd never rest being married to a lawman. Had no intention waiting at home for who knows when I'd be back."

All I said was, "She's made a sorry choice, then. You're a good man."

"I'm done talking about it, Mama." His neck grew flushed and dark.

Over my shoulder, I saw Ezra, Val, and Zack come into the room. They stayed quiet and listened. Mary Pearl watched over their heads. I said, "Who else's going, down south with you?"

"Only Gilbert, and only maybe. I told him any nuisance and I'd send him home with his tail between his legs. I'm boss on this ride, come high water or hellfire."

"No posse?"

"Rangers send one man at a time, maybe two. If you've got a badge and a gun, a warrant is enough. They issued me a rope and told me to use it. Will you load that thing for me while I put this together?" He nodded toward the pistol, which was set on a rag.

So I did load it. Pushed the shells into the chamber and lined up twenty-five of them in the belt loops. Wondering all the while if one of those bullets I was handling would be the end of Willie Prine.

Mary Pearl leaned against the door frame. She said, "Charlie, I'll go, too. I can ride and shoot. There'd be three of us."

Charlie stood up and took the pistol and belt from me. He went to Mary Pearl and put his arm around her shoulder. "Thanks, Little Biscuits. You stay here and go to April's tea party." He kissed the top of her head.

"I'd be more use riding with you boys," she said.

Charlie smiled. I swear to goodness, but his mustache wrinkled up just like Jack's always had. He said, "Probably more use than Gilbert in the long run. I've seen you peg a fence post from the back of a moving horse. But I'd feel responsible for you, like I had to protect you. It's going to be tough enough to bring in someone I don't *want* to peg if I can help it. I'm asking you to stay home. Besides, when Mama goes home with the little fellers, she'll need you riding shotgun, won't she?"

Mary Pearl looked at me, her brows raised, and I nodded. Chess announced that Charlie's horse was ready. Gilbert came down the stairs, raring to go, too. I made them wait while I wrote a note to Mr. Hanna. Told him I was sorry his boy had stayed up here but said that hard work was probably good for him if he wanted to try it. It would make him sure appreciate living at the ranch, and he'd be itching to get home before long. Told him to try not to feel too bad about it. Then I added that I'd be there soon.

Charlie went outside, and I heard him talking to his grandpa. Well, there was no one around but Gilbert and me, and he pulled up a chair. "Mama?" he said, "mind if I interrupt you for a minute?"

"No," I said. Would this be the boy getting hitched? "What's on your mind?"

"I want you to know why I'm going with Charlie. It's my fault Willie went bad." He laid his hands on the table between us. I waited. "See," he said, "old Boots was tormenting Ezra. Teasing Zachary until he cried, and that little kid doesn't cry all that easy. We—I mean *I*—I had this idea that Boots should have a talk with Mr. Sparky, to sort of straighten him out. We planted him next to Willie's bedroll. Just sitting there in the dark. When Willie woke up, he got crazy and kicked Sparks and beat him all to pieces. After that, well, he just got kind of crazy mad. He went off with those old Wainbridge boys. They'd brought their corn liquor, and he sat with them, acting stupid and laughing at the stars. I'm sorry, Mama."

Maybe that explained Willie turning sour just about overnight. He'd seemed to be getting hold of things, helping with the roundup. I'd been plenty mad myself, caught off my watch by that skull and scarecrow thing. Got hot under the collar and wanted to wring someone's neck. I said, "You boys had some tussles, didn't you?"

"Pure sideways, after a bit."

"Where's Sparks now?" I asked.

"Willie busted him up, sorta. What's left is in a feed sack in the barn."

I patted Gilbert's hand. His hands were larger than mine. Meaty and strong. Steady as a rock. I said, "Son, that might explain him getting mad and cussing. Or throwing a rock at the side of the barn, even. It doesn't give him leave to make threatening moves with a gun. It doesn't in any way give him leave to steal a thousand and some dollars. And it surely doesn't allow him the taking of what was left of my herd." I folded my letter and set the pen on its little holder. "Gilbert, did you threaten him? Offer to chase him off, or beat him senseless, or knock some holes in his grin?"

Gilbert kept shaking his head as I asked those questions. He said, "No, ma'am. Nothing like that. We just dropped old Sparks next to him while he was sleeping. Tapped him on the shoulder. He come up cussing, but it was all over with that."

"I don't think you made Willie go bad. I don't think any of us could have stopped him if we'd tried. Go on with your brother if you want to help him out."

My sons put their things in saddlebags, just like their papa used to do. Carried my heart in his saddlebag, he told me once. Charles Elliot put on his hat, cocked down against the sun in his eyes, and rode south with his kid brother to bring an outlaw in.

I stood on the front porch, watching Charlie's back, big and square, narrow at the waist. I made him that shirt he was wearing for Christmas last. I remember every stitch in that shirt. Behind him, Gilbert was not as rangy, but still young and slim and handsome, their steps as full of lightning as little Hunter's. Reckon I should be thankful he's not chasing Apaches, but many a white man I've known makes an Apache warrior seem like a parlor guest when it came to meanness. All I could hope was that Willie hadn't gone that bad yet. That he'd have some feelings for his own cousin when he sees Charlie. Not shoot him. All I could do was watch them go and pray God they'd come home and grow old.

Talking to Gil had made me realize that all the hoping and praying and talking in the world didn't matter a hill of beans to a boy who was bent on really being a "cowboy." Not the way little Val saw Charlie; to me, a cowboy was the same thing as an outlaw. Willie had said as much the first time I laid eyes on him, talking of changing his name to Frank or Jesse. I still felt as if I'd failed Willie somewhere along the line, although I wasn't as certain of it as before.

Mary Pearl and I fixed five plates of cold meat and fruit and some leftover biscuits with coffee for us and Chess and the little boys. The wind started to kick up. We had to close the windows or get blanketed with dust. The house was hot, though, so I told the boys we'd go to the very top—the third floor, where the cupola pulled a draft—to have some lessons and tell stories until it was time for bed. As I talked to the little boys, I thought of Charlie, figuring he had to have passed the arroyo by now. Suddenly, out of nowhere, Zack said, "Aunt Sarah, aren't you going to finish? What happened next?"

"I don't remember," I said.

Val said, "Grandma, is that cowboy fella really my cousin?"

"Yes," I said, thinking of Willie.

"Is he going to shoot somebody?" Val asked.

"Certainly not. You all get to bed." They grumbled, but they went. Leastways I left them to it. Whether they went right to bed, if I was asked later, I couldn't rightly say.

The house was dark except for my lanterns as Chess followed me into the kitchen. I started pumping water at the sink and filled the coffeepot. Chess saw what I was doing, and he pulled down the coffee grinder, went to putting some beans in the top. The crunching of the beans and their comfortable perfume filled the kitchen. After awhile, he said, "Got a lot of their papa in 'em yet. Can't change a leopard's spots."

I stared out the window. I wished Clove and Joshua had been here to go with my boys. If all the boys were riding together, at least that'd be safer. Charlie so resembled Jack.

"You say something?" Chess said.

"Charlie went and joined the Rangers."

"I know it. I declare. Just like that."

I said, " 'Just like that'? Just like Jack."

Chess said, "He'd be proud of that boy."

"He'd take a strap to his backside and send him to school."

"There's plenty to learn outside those walls you always put such a store in."

"Hmm." I opened a lid on the stove and took a towel in hand to make sure the flue was wide-open. "This'll need to cool. I don't much feel like cooking."

"Supper's over. I thought we were making coffee," he said.

"That's right. We were." I bent to push kindling into the stove. It caught quickly on the coals banked at the back. "I'm feeling scatterbrained," I said.

"Charlie's a full-growed man. 'Bout time he shirked off them apron strings you're trying to strangle him with."

"I'm doing no such a thing."

Chess spilled grinds on the table. He picked up a rag and went for them, but coffee grinds stick to everything, and if the rag is dry, you're likely to spread them instead of catching them. He worked at it awhile and then said, "Looks like it from here."

"You're polishing a hole in that table and leaving crumbs everywhere else."

"Reckon so, Mrs. Elliot? Sort of like sending a man to sit and learn postulatin' and polishin' words, when there's useful work that needs doin'?"

"I can't talk to you anymore."

" 'At's a fact, Sarah."

I let out my breath and went to the doorway. "Chess," I said. "He doesn't know what he's doing."

Chess took the dish towel from my hands and patted my arm. "He'll find out."

That night, I rose from my bed. Off in the distance, clouds arched across the sky, blue above them, indigo beneath. Instead of being in town, I was in strange house down on familiar land at the ranch. The clouds were yellows and oranges, pinks and shades of violet. Something moved, and I looked to the horizon. A so-familiar form. "Jack," I whispered. "Come here, across the arroyo." I saw him plain as day, waiting on the other side, reins in his hands, smile on his face, cavalry hat cocked a little to one side. I wasn't in town, but out in the desert in a great hacienda of vast empty rooms. From each window in every room, I saw the same view. I called to him. "I need you, Jack. Come on to the house."

He took one step toward me and was suddenly right outside the window. The openings in the walls were two feet thick, like a nice fat adobe, and the window glass was raised. I put my hand through the opening and reached toward his outstretched hand. Jack said, "Stay inside, Sarah." My heart fluttered at the sound of his voice. I reached farther. My fingertip touched his.

My eyes opened. Sweat glued me to the pallet and a chill ran through me. If I could have stayed asleep one more second, he'd have taken my hand. Never before had I heard his voice like that. I got up and went to the window, opened it, and breathed the sweet rain-clean air. I lit a lamp and lay down again, then stared a long time at the tin tiles over my head.

Chapter Twenty-One

Monday morning, we started packing to return to the ranch. We'd leave the twins to their jobs and Esther to her schooling. Until Josh, Charlie, and Gilbert returned, Esther would live at April's house. April promised to visit us, but of course it would have to be arranged during a break from school and not interfere with Val's piano lessons. Then she squeezed me and kissed my face again. "Mama," she said, "I do promise I'll come. We'll send you a note at the station down there. Just a few weeks from now."

As we packed, I thought about how I felt connected to April's family, despite the differences between us, and deep-down sorry to leave her behind. I felt torn, needing to be home and wanting to be in town. But it was good to be sad to leave, rather than being thankful to be alone.

What with having all the children in and out of both houses at a moment's notice, and those grandchildren of mine, who were so little, I had hidden the rifle I always carried. I'd taken the precaution to hide the shells in a brown crock labeled CASTOR OIL. I knew the children would stay away from that. It was so out of sight—up on a shelf in a little room we rarely used—that I nearly forgot it. The moment I had the box of shells in my hands, I heard a great crashing of glass from the floor below me. I tucked the rifle under my arm, along with the satchel I was carrying, and hurried downstairs.

In the kitchen, Mary Pearl stood with her hands on her hips, dripping water and suds down her sides. Esther was at the far side of room, standing near a pile of broken dishes. She was sobbing into her hands.

"Esther? What in heaven's name were you thinking?" Mary Pearl said. Esther ran from the room. Mary Pearl said Esther had picked up a stack of plates from the rinse water and for some odd reason had decided to dry them at the table, rather than on the board near the tub. She'd whirled around, and every last one had tumbled from her hands. Mary Pearl frowned and said, "She's having a conniption about something. Mama's going to be really upset, and now there aren't three plates left in this house."

Esther, the middle daughter, who never gave anyone a moment's trouble, never was a lick of nuisance in her life, was in the parlor, sobbing loudly. Savannah was fuming. "Are you afraid of going to school?" she asked. "You've worked so hard for this opportunity to be a teacher, just like your sisters. What has possessed you, Esther?"

Savannah asked me to be stern with her, thinking, I suspect, that my words might sound more severe than her own. However, I doubted even Savannah knew just how much her own children craved her approval and would brave anything to get it. Every last person gave her the best "Cheer up; you'll pass muster" speech we could come up with, and still Esther cried. Finally, we got her packed. Albert was fixing to drive her to April's place in my old buggy. She kissed everyone and hugged us, and seemed cheered some. As they drove off, Savannah watched from the front window, concern on her face.

"She'll settle in," I said. Savannah just nodded. Well, Albert returned after a bit, and he said Esther had finally quit crying at April's house. She bade him leave her bags on the porch, saying she'd just take them in later. Of course, by the time he came and told us that, Savannah had found the letter.

Dear Mama and Papa and All,

I know this will come as a surprise, but it is a happy one at that. One of the fellows who worked for Mr. Maldonado has been writing to me all this time. We love each other more than words can say. I know you will understand, Mama, as you have said so many times that love cannot be measured. How I long for the wedded bliss April and Morris have found, and know in my heart I am not meant for teaching, but motherhood. Polinar and I will be very happy, and though you will miss our wedding, we will visit you at the farm in a

few weeks. We will build a house nearby. Poli is from Spain and has
castles and horses there, which we will own when his wicked uncle
dies. I love you all. Yours ever and always, Esther.

Well, Savannah and Albert were fit to be tied. They drove right back to
April's house, but Esther and her bags were long gone. April said there'd been a
fellow waiting with a buckboard at the corner of the street all morning, and he
just drove right up and Esther hopped in with barely a by-your-leave. She only
told April that she took the notion since April and Morris eloped and all seemed
well with them, it should just naturally turn out that way for her and this Polinar fellow, too.

"Bienvenides," I told them. "Rudolfo had a man name of Polinar Bienvenides." After hearing that, Albert set off to see the sheriff.

We decided to wait one more day to leave, on the hope Esther might have a
change of heart and return. Toward dark, I helped Savannah up the stairs to the
nearly empty room she and Albert had shared. The night cooled, and with the
windows open, it was pleasant in the room upstairs. Still, Savannah had a film
of sweat on her brow. "Bring me my Esther," she said. "Then I'll sleep. What
could have possessed her? Bring me Zack. And Ezra. Rachel and Rebeccah.
Clover and Joshua, too. Bring my children. I don't want to sleep so far from
them all."

I was afraid she was becoming feverish, and I wished so hard for one of the
children to come into the room just then that I looked toward the door. Mary
Pearl stood there. She stared not at us but at the open window. Hers was the one
name Savannah had *not* said aloud. I know with all my bones that Savannah
treasured all her children. But she had left out a name, and the girl had been feeling mighty outside the fence lately, what with all the folderol at April's. "Mary
Pearl?" I said.

The doorway was dark and empty. Savannah sat up, shaking. "Mary Pearl?
Where is my daughter? Where is Mary Pearl?"

"Probably gone to get ready for bed," I said. "Don't you worry."

"Mary Pearl's so much like you, Sarah. I don't worry about her nearly as
much as the other girls. Sensible."

Though I nodded in agreement, I was *more* worried about Mary Pearl than
the other girls. I didn't think Mary Pearl knew at all what her mother thought.
Again, I was betwixt and between her and her mother. I wanted to run to the

girl, pull her to her mother's side, and make them say the things to each other they both needed to hear. I said, "I'll go get her for you."

"No, don't wake her. Sarah, there's a pulling in my back. Pray with me that I don't lose this baby."

"Stay strong, honey," I said. I looked toward the door, hoping to see Mary Pearl had returned. Before long, Albert would return, and then I'd fetch the wounded daughter. For now, I would stay with the burdened mother. I sat next to Savannah's pallet and unbraided her hair while Savannah told me things about Esther. How she'd been such a quiet child. Always the one to lose a shoe-button hook. Always the first to cry over a dead rabbit or a sparrow. I let her talk wander in whatever direction she wished, wondering now and again whether or not she would start labor during the night. After a while, Savannah closed her eyes, but her lips continued to move. Maybe in prayer—I don't know. Maybe just succumbed to sorrow.

My mind went to a thousand places. Charlie and Gilbert. Willie. Chess. Udell. Jack. Rudolfo. Too many men. If I lose the ranch, they will have lost, too. And . . . April. Strange having a daughter that doesn't seem as close as my sons. I will love her until I die, but she doesn't need me. Nor does my losing the ranch affect her family. She has her own life, very separate from mine. All these others may not need me, but they are not separate at all. And Esther, a girl I realized I hardly knew, why had I not reached out to her?

Albert came in after a while, but Savannah was asleep, so I held my finger to my lips. He motioned to me to follow him. We sat in the kitchen and poured some cold coffee. There'd be deputies sent in the morning, he said. But only two. And not until daybreak. My brother pulled at his hair.

I couldn't say what he was feeling. I knew what I was feeling, and that was as if the whole of Creation was working to crush me. Still, I didn't want to say that to Albert, as worried as he was. "I reckon it's our season of trials and tribulations," I said. "I don't remember a worse one. Not since Papa died."

"That's the honest truth," he said. Albert drained his cup, eyeing me over the top of it before he said, "Sarah? I'll ask you to take the children home with you in the morning. I'll stay here with Savannah until we hear one way or another. And Savannah, I believe, needs to be close to a doctor right now."

"I should stay with her. Don't you reckon she'll want the little ones close by?"

"Maybe. I'm thinking they'll be better off in your care and out of town. Get their lives back to normal, much as they can."

More people in the care of Sarah Elliot. And me not at all sure I've done well by the others. I nodded. "I'll do that. Are you going to sit with Savannah tonight?"

"I don't want to disturb her. Mary Pearl's in there with the two boys, sleeping in a chair, watching over them. I'm going to stay here in the parlor, just in case some message should come."

I waited a while, pondering the message that might come, and from where. Finally, I said, "I'll stay with Savannah, then. But I'll be ready to leave before dawn." Well, I was ready to ask him what else I could do, when there was a very soft knocking at the side door. Both of us rushed to it, disturbing Chess, who was sleeping there on the kitchen floor. He roused behind us as Albert opened the door.

Morris Winegold stood there, his bowler hat in hand. He had a coat and tie on, but the tie hung loosely at his throat and his collar was open. His face brightened. "You're here," he said. "Thank heavens. April urged me to see if by some chance you'd stayed one more day. May I come in?"

We drew him inside and pulled chairs up to the kitchen table. Morris set his hat on his knee. Albert brightened the lamp. By the time we got done explaining what had happened, Chess decided he wanted a pot of coffee and started in lighting up the stove. Finally, we got to hear what had brought Morris driving over late at night on the barest chance we'd not left.

Morris cleared his throat. "First, there is no word about Miss Esther. I'm sorry. Second, I have to tell you something that stretches the bounds of my ethics. Someone," he said, "has been checking your land records. Hand-copied every legal description, date, the deed of homestead, and every new parcel-purchase agreement." I was thinking it had to be railroaders. Maybe even Rudolfo. Morris squinted his eyes and leaned forward, whispering, "Felicity Prine's lawyer."

"Lawyer?" Chess all but shouted.

Morris went on. "The gal has gotten herself a lawyer who's agreed to work on a contingency basis to sue you for illegally occupying that land."

"I reckon I don't know what that means," I said.

"It's contingent on him taking the land from you. If he wins, he's got a whole lot of rangeland, free and clear in the settlement, and you could end up owing the court and him the cost of his fees."

"I never heard such nonsense," I said.

Morris said, "It means they'll be stopping at nothing to swindle you out of it. Make it look like a legitimate case. You haven't been served yet?"

"No," I said. I laid my hands on the table, staring at them, letting these words pummel me as if they were fists. "When will that happen?"

"Soon," he said. "I'd get out of town as soon as you possibly can, just to put them off. Do you have a lawyer?"

I thought of Mr. Baramon and wondered if he'd work for me, seeing as how I probably wouldn't be able to pay him for years to come, even if I kept the place. Albert turned and took my hands. "Sarah, you get the best lawyer you can find. Don't you even mention that you haven't got the cash. I'll pay the bill. I'll pay a retainer up front, too, if he asks it." Then Albert said to Morris, "Don't you have a legal man at the bank?"

Morris nodded. "I've already taken the initiative to ask a couple of hypothetical questions. We have a superb young man there; two years past the bar, with an appellate court win under his belt already. Asked him in confidence if he thought there'd be any real case. He said with a proper letter and a couple of affidavits, any judge in the country would throw that baggage—well, what he said isn't for polite company. At any rate, if you'll allow me to hire Mr. Hanna for you—"

"Hanna?" I said.

"Yes, ma'am. Aubrey David Hanna, Esquire."

"Aubrey Hanna is a lawyer? Why, he's just a boy."

Morris looked at me, sort of stunned. "Mother Elliot, he's older than I am."

"Lands sakes," I said. "Yes, yes. Hire him. Albert, that is, if—"

"Call it done," my brother said.

"I'll pay you back," I told him.

Albert allowed himself a small, exhausted smile. He said, "I'll arm-wrestle you for it."

Morris smiled, but his look was quickly replaced with one of concern. "There's one more thing. The county books were easy to find. Sitting right on top. When I watched that fellow copying the deeds, I acted as if I was interested in what he was doing. Asked him what he charged and all. They're supposed to be kept in dated order. All your deeds and agreements were right on top of thirty years of land records. Even had paper markers at the pages he needed. He figured someone had looked them up recently. I asked about that, too. He got fishy-acting, shooting his eyes around and talking low. He said the books were taken out a month ago and not put back. He said he was told to keep them on top for a while and now was glad, since they'd come to be such popular volumes."

I said, "A month?" Morris just nodded.

Chess said, "That'd be Maldonado or the train company."

"Couldn't say. Leastways, he wouldn't say," Morris said.

The coffee was finally ready, but Morris was fixing to leave. He sipped just a little to be polite; then Albert and Chess and I were left alone to ponder this news. We spent another hour locking the house up, even padlocked the front door, which I'd never done, even when no one lived here. Chess went back to his bed in the kitchen, and Albert took the shotgun, setting it on his lap as he sat in the rocking chair in the parlor.

Upstairs, Savannah slept. I sat on an old rush chair I'd pulled up against the far wall, turned the lamp down, then blew across its chimney to put out the flame. I wondered if somehow all the things that had come our way that summer were not real, but some terrible long nightmare that I'd soon waken from, feeling rattled, but all would be right again. Or was it instead all part and parcel of some plan by the Almighty to wear me to the bone, or see if I'd either give up or dig in? I've had ups and downs, tribulation of one sort or another, just like any woman. I've buried two children and two husbands. This time I've been given a stony cliff to climb. Nothing but destruction behind and a precipice ahead. I feel as if I'm being attacked on all sides, same as in the old days, fighting Indians on one hand and outlaws on the other, with the desert heat and cold to the north, black widow spiders and pestilence to the south.

If Willie isn't lynched by some posse he could just as easily be shot in the back by one of the renegades he's running with, providing Charlie and Gil don't catch up to him. Cowboy. That's what Willie wanted to be. Reckon he'd gotten his wish at that. I wanted a lot more for that boy than what was in store for him. Then there were Charlie and Gil, gone hunting him. And Granny clear up in Chicago, where she could misstep on the train stairs, teeter and fall, and be gone.

At last, I unfastened my shoe buttons and pulled off my shoes. There was a new crack in one of the toes, and my stocking was full of the same sand we'd dug out from the wheels of the surrey. The sand scattered to the floor. I'd sweep it in the morning. It made me think again of Willie. Telling him to sweep up his own mess.

Was there anything I could have done or said to make Willie settle down, and not go crazy and wild? How I would have loved to see him walking up the road to the house. He'd say how sorry he was for doing wrong. He'd let me hug him and fuss at him, and I'd make him build me a rock fence while I went to the kitchen to make all the boys a pie or something. If he hadn't really gotten so sideways, maybe he'd tell Felicity himself to make some tracks in any direction but here.

I rose and walked barefoot to the window and pushed it open. There was a faint glow in the sky, but here in town, it wasn't from the moon. It was the gas streetlight, which they didn't put out until eleven o'clock. I pretended it was the moon, though, and thought, Lord, beg your pardon, Sir, but we are in a fix. I'm about wrung out from all this, and it's getting so I can barely tell which way is up. I've got kin scattered from Chicago to Mexico, less than half a herd of near-dead cattle, a vagabond abusing my niece, destroying Albert's family, and barely two bits in my pocket. I'm fresh out of backbone, Lord. And near out of fight. Near out.

In the morning, I hugged Savannah to my shoulder, and she clung to me, just frightened as a kitten. Then I pushed her away. Daylight was upon us. "I need to go," I said. "You have to be strong, and trust Albert to take care of you the best he can."

September 4, 1906

Chess, the little fellows, Mary Pearl, and I, on horseback, made better time than we could have with the surrey, even counting Zack and Ezra doubled up on Big Boy. Only one time on the long ride did we lay eyes on another soul. A man in Mexican getup was heading north toward Morenci, and he didn't stop or even look in our direction. Hopefully, Mary Pearl's disguise made us look more like five men than an old man, two women, and two little boys.

Well, I never thought home could look so fine as it did that afternoon. We stopped at Albert's farm to let the three children sort their clothes and pack more to take to my place. When Chess and I crossed Cienega Creek, my happiness was dampened by the low trickle between the banks. I stopped in the yard, getting a sense of something being different.

"Mrs. Elliot? Is that you?" a man hollered. Coming from the barn, mopping his brow, his sleeves rolled up, was Udell Hanna. "I've been looking for you the past few days. It's a real pleasure to see you."

"Mr. Hanna!" I said. "Good to see you, too."

He began to tell me then, as he led my horse to the barn, about this and that, the many things he'd done. We went to see the horses, and marveled at little Hunter and how he'd grown. "Oh," he said, his eyes suddenly growing wider, "wait until you see who's showed up." He smiled in a way that made me feel his anticipation.

"Who?" I said. "Willie?"

"No. You'll be *happy* to see this fellow. Come here and take a look." He led the way to a new little shed standing in the shadow of the barn. He knelt on the ground and called very softly, "Here, fella. Here, boy. Come on out, boy."

I knelt beside Udell. Something dark and furry moved in the shed. I drew up a breath. Nip. Alive and home. Chess said, "Well, I'll be."

My throat caught up tight and I nearly choked. I said, "Oh, Nip. Good dog. Come on here, boy." I reached carefully toward the dog. Even a good dog can be edgy when it's hurt. Nip stood on wobbly legs and limped toward me. One leg was misshapen and bandaged. A huge wound, still open but not infected, ran across his head and down nearly to his nose. I could see by the way he walked that he'd likely never be any good again. I was so happy to see him alive, though, I didn't care if he spent the next ten years on the porch. "Where did you find him?" I asked. Nip sniffed my fingers and then licked my hand. I scruffled him very, very gently behind the ears. Nip whined. By that time, Mary Pearl, Zack, and Ezra had crowded around to see, too.

"All beat-up, near that rock outcrop north of the bend. Just about starved to death, too. I think he'll live, but I can't say he'll be a working dog anymore. I'll put him down for you if you want, but I didn't want to make that decision for you. He's gone through a lot to keep on living."

"No, no," I said. "Long as he's not just lingering, suffering. If he's on the mend, I want him to live." As I said that, the dog nuzzled my hands. "Good old Nip. Good old Nip," I cooed to him. "You boys stay away from this dog until he's good and well. I don't want you bothering him. If he's hurting, he could be snappy." I could see the wounds closer. Nip's hide had been sewn up in many places, doctored just like a person's would be. He smelled of Mercurochrome and his fur was clean. The bandage was new, not dirty, except for where he'd lain in the sand. Udell had taken care of this dog as if he'd been a person. I turned to the man and fought the urge to hug his neck. Instead, I squeezed his hand. "Thank you," I said. One small creature saved. If Nip could be saved, maybe others could be, too. Esther. This ranch. Willie. "Thank you so very much," I said again.

Udell looked at the ground and nodded. Then he glanced at the little boys and Mary Pearl. He said, "Sarah? Since you're home, it'll just take me a minute to clear my things out of the house. I've been spending most of my time out here in the barn, watching over the horses and old Nipper here."

My house was good and familiar, cooler by some than outside, and yet a little odd. Udell had moved my rocker close by the kitchen table, were where a lamp and a book lay waiting. He'd washed up the dishes, too, as there was nothing waiting on the sideboard but a clean plate turned upside down under a cloth.

Well, I found myself asking him to stay to supper, and to spend at least one more night. I said he could bunk down on the sleeping porch with Chess and the boys, while Mary Pearl and I took the other side of the privacy sheet. We spent the evening recounting what had happened in town, beginning with the story of Esther's eloping. Through all, Udell nodded and listened without saying much. Only when Zack and Ezra started telling about the fun they'd had showing their cousin Vallary through town did Udell liven up and ask the children questions.

Then Udell said Rudolfo had indeed turned off some of my herd to him. Not fifty, as I'd promised, but eleven. A hard start, but better than none. He said he would return them to me, of course. Truth was, I didn't see how I'd make it without them, but he had less to go on than I did, and I couldn't reckon with taking away something I'd promised to a man who had so little else.

When we finally bedded down, I listened in the darkness for a spell to the sounds of sleeping all around me. The little fellows' childish breathing was quiet and deep. Chess rattled and snuffled, as always. The fourth man, Udell, had added a new rhythm to the place. I could hear his breathing just as clearly as if he were beside me. I smiled. Lands! What a thought. A chill ran down my arms and legs, and I straightened the single layer of sheeting over myself.

After a long time, Mary Pearl whispered, "Aunt Sarah?"

"Yes?"

"Is Mama going to be all right?"

"I believe so. I think it's better she's near the hospital, in case she gets sick." I rolled to my side, facing her. "Try not to worry. She'd be telling you to say your prayers for Esther."

"I reckon Esther never thought she'd create such a stir."

"She thought about this awhile, didn't she?"

After another spell, she said, "I don't want folks mad at Esther. I didn't think she'd really do it. It seemed so stupid to up and leave with a fellow she hardly knew. He said he'd sweep her away like a knight rescuing a damsel, speeding away on his fiery steed or some such. There were lots more letters than the ones Mama knew of. And Esther wrote to him, too. Promising she'd be a good wife, things like that. I knew all of it."

"Glory," I said, and let my head sink into the thin pillow. "And why didn't you tell someone before now?"

I heard her sigh loudly. "I thought it was hog wallow. But Esther wanted a fairy prince to take her to his castle. She was scared to death to go to college in town. Last night, I was going in to tell Mama. I thought it would soothe her to know Esther had gotten it in her head that this fellow was going to be her true love. Then Mama was so upset, I just couldn't tell her. I was afraid she'd lose the baby. Or die."

"That's why you left? Even after I called you?" Mary Pearl hadn't heard the list that left off her name, merely a slip caused by her mother's worry? Thank heavens I hadn't gone after her to apologize! What pain that would have caused both the girl and her mother, to have aired all that had gone on in that moment. How blessed was the silence that had saved them both from needless suffering.

"I just couldn't tell her."

I reached across the dark place between our cots and patted Mary Pearl's arm. "It's probably the best decision for the time," I said. "When April ran off, I worried night and day. Cried a river over her. If I'd known she was happy and healthy and— Even so, it's better to let your mother know the truth. Do you still have all those letters?"

"I should have told Esther he really wrote to me. That would have hurt her feelings, but she wouldn't have run off with him."

I said, "She must have been more headstrong than anyone knew. Chances are, she wouldn't have believed you."

"I could have tried," Mary Pearl said. Her voice sounded pinched.

"We'll write your mama a letter. We'll start soon as we get the boys out doing chores in the morning."

"I'd give her my new bristle hairbrush and looking-glass set if she'd just come home."

"I know," I said.

The next morning, I read those letters, feeling guilty at first, then just angrily looking for something that would lead us to Esther. I'll say one thing. That boy could have turned the head of any girl in the county with the poetry and love telling in them. Time and again, he wrote, "To the image of my heart's desire. I have built for you a bower lined with wild roses." It was a hard thing to tell Savannah. It was equally hard to imagine Albert reading about what we'd found. Both Mary Pearl and I signed the paper. She insisted that she alone carry it to the mail station. "Ezra, you ride along, too," I said. Ez puffed up and said, "On Flojo?"

"Well, you'll never keep up on Big Boy. Get a move on." I stingily peeled off a dollar from the money I had left to give them for postage. I made sure that besides the knife she usually carried, Mary Pearl had a pistol at her side and my old rifle in a scabbard. I had told her in the past how to know when she might need to use it. I told her again now for good measure. Her hands trembled a little as she took the thing, and that was good. It isn't right for a person to be either too ready to use a bullet or too afraid. As she got into the saddle, I shook the toe of her stirrup just a little and said, "If anything happens, I know you'll know what to do." I stopped myself from adding "Be careful," or any of the hundred things I usually sent my boys off with. Mary Pearl nodded, pulled her Stetson hat low over her eyes, and gave Duende both heels. Ezra was fast on their dust.

Udell stayed most of the morning, and I was glad for the help. He said there was nothing living down at his place but that he would ride down and have a look-see, then check on us in a day or two. It wasn't until he was long gone that I found he'd left his wife's silver cross on my mantel. I hadn't noticed it the day before. Too tired, I reckon. It looked kind of pretty standing there, watching over my little box with the cut-in swan where Jack's watch and our wedding rings lay, resting.

Zack and I plum fiddled out the rest of the day, feeding hens and horses, coaxing Nip to eat. We tried to concentrate on some lessons, but neither he nor I had much heart for it. I told him he could just read aloud after supper, then go play some. Late in the afternoon, Mary Pearl and Ezra came home. The rains had caused the greasewood to bloom, and its perfume helped to cover up the lingering dank smell of ashes. Rose looked to have healed up just fine from her snakebite, and she whinnied to me when she saw me. Hunter had grown, and he was friendly when he wasn't busy frisking in the corral.

My heart felt softened by sitting in the evening on my own front porch, listening to Zack recite a four-line stanza of a poem. Then he wanted to read a book that Vallary had given to him—a story about a flying machine. So he read and I listened with one ear. In the other, I heard nighthawks trilling and a big owl in the distance. I heard, too, one of the little dove-size owls that make a trilling sound that's closer to a nighthawk's than a barn owl's.

Coyotes set up a yip in the hills. "Aunt Sarah, are we done?" asked Zack. The boy startled me. I said, "Yes. It'll be dark in half an hour."

Chess went to bed at dusk. Mary Pearl took a book to the parlor and sat by a lamp. I told Ezra and Zack that after they washed up and got changed, they could play checkers for a while. I stepped off the porch and looked at the stars. Jack's star came up with the moon now; and along with a second star, they made a triangle in the sky. The sign of September. This was the time of year I always felt him closer than at any other. The sky turned azure, which faded to turquoise on the western horizon. I took up my snake stick from by the door and ambled up the rise toward the graveyard. Surely, Jack's grave will have been overgrown with that old cholla. Likely, it would be done blooming now, so I wouldn't feel as bad knocking off the seed pods as I would the pretty flowers smiling down on Jack's face. "Jack?" I said softly, "I'm in a real fix here."

The moon was bright. The stars closed in, resting, it seemed, on my shoulders. I felt powerfully alone until I bothered a covey of quail, which resettled twenty feet away. I'd thought to find a mess in the graveyard, but the ground between the graves had been swept. The stones were all lined up, and new soil had been mounded over each grave. Even the cholla had been trimmed back, although not pulled out. As if Udell had thought I meant it to be there—not knowing those things just plant themselves wherever they can be the most nuisance.

I put my hand on Jack's headstone. "Udell Hanna's a nice man," I said to him, "to do all this." Listening, I waited for some movement in the brush, some sign of Lazrus jumping out at me. I knelt there in the dirt. A cottontail rabbit meandered through the graves, coming toward me. I held my breath. I looked in my direction, but since I didn't move, it ambled on its way, unhurried and unafraid. I waited until the little animal had moved far enough away that I wouldn't startle it, then went home to bed.

That night, Jack rode a horse I'd never seen before, coming right up to the porch rail. It was a full seventeen hands high as I'm standing. I smiled when I saw him but didn't call out. Always before, when I called, he'd only wave and ride away. I heard his boots clear as day on the floorboards. "Sarah?" he called. "Sarah? Don't wake the children."

I saw no children around, but I reached toward him. His hand brushed mine. I felt his sleeve. He stood just past my reach then, so very close that I could see that he needed a shave. Little whiskers glimmered in the half-light of the full moon, making his face edged in light. I said, "I've been waiting for you. Take me with you."

He smiled and then Jack said, "No. I'm leaving for good now. You're all right."

Tears streaked my nightgown as I said, "But I need you now more than ever. Take me, please. I'm so blessed tired. And I'm so alone. Tired of being alone."

"I've stayed too long. You don't need me now. Good-bye, Sarah. Good-bye."

"Jack?" Then, I felt something cool and warm at the same time wrap around me. Like a quilt in the winter, like a drink of deep well water in the summer, a breeze softer than the breath of a newborn baby passed over my skin and lingered in my hair, and then it was gone. "Jack?" I called.

"Sarah?" called Chess. "What in tarnation are you doing out there in the middle of the night?"

I was behind the house, off the sleeping porch, under the full moon. "Having a dream, is all," I said. I crept back into bed.

It was hot. I laid uncovered except for my nightgown. The threadbare gown, faded to gray, though once upon a time it had been white, glowed in reflected moonlight even there under the porch roof. Setting my hand lightly against the sheet, I remembered Jack's sleeve under my fingertips. Instead of longing and sorrow, however, what I felt was peace. Peace, from either deep inside my soul or from the far reaches of heaven. In a single strange breath, Jack's touch and his saying good-bye seemed to be the things I wanted most in the world to hear. I asked myself how that could be, since of course I wanted him to stay, needed him by my side. I had more to wrangle with now than ever before in my life. But he'd said good-bye, and that was enough. I touched my hair, remembering the lifting air that had gone through it. "Good-bye, Jack," I whispered to the night.

Chapter Twenty-Two

I slept well past sunup and woke to the smell of bacon and coffee. Mary Pearl had risen early. She said, "You must have been purely tuckered. It feels strange not having chores to do. I'll ride to our place and check on the chickens. See if Conciliada is feeding them well enough."

"First," I said, "run by the barn and get Shorty to go with you."

"Oh, Aunt Sarah. I went all the way to the station just yesterday."

"With Ezra. It's either that or don't go at all. And don't be rolling those eyes at me."

"Yes'm. My back was turned. How did you know?"

"Same way I know which way a calf is going to bolt."

When Mary Pearl had gotten on down the road, I sent Zack and Ezra to pull weeds and rake more cactus out of the garden. Chess had climbed up on the roof and was fixing more loose shingles he'd seen yesterday. I went to the pump and filled the metal trough that runs by way of a water pipe to the garden. Though the sounds of cattle were gone, the sounds of life at this ranch were coming back. A hummingbird buzzed through the air like some great hornet, paused to stare at me as I worked the pump handle, and then settled on the edge of the trough. It dipped its little bill into the water three or four times and watched me again. A glistening drop of water perched on the tip of its beak. I stopped moving to see what the tiny bird would do, but soon as I quit, it flew away.

Well, I washed up some beans to start a pot for supper, and about the time I got them over a bed of coals on the outside fire pit where I make soap, along came a rider from the south. The man on the horse was leading another horse and a pack mule. It was Rudolfo, dressed up pretty fine for a hot day like this one. I waved when I recognized him. "Amigo!" I hollered. *"¿Adónde?"* We had things to talk about. I knew some of them were troublesome; still, Rudolfo was a friend and I was glad to see him.

As Rudolfo drew closer, I saw he was grinning from ear to ear. He drew up the reins at my yard and dismounted. Before I knew it, Rudolfo had swept me up in his arms and hugged me tightly. He set me down and said, "I have heard you are home at last. All is well with *tu hija?*"

I said, "You look like you just ate your weight in liver pills. *¿Que?*"

He grinned broadly, striding toward the horse he'd had in tow. He pulled the filly, leading her toward me. She was a silvery gray, with a smoky mane and tail. I saw right away that the horse stepped lightly, as if her hooves hardly touched the dirt. Nice breadth. Good head and well-set eyes. My papa would have said she was "a pretty" all right. Rudolfo said, "For you, Sarah. A gift from me to you."

"A gift?" I said, patting the animal's side. He'd plum taken my breath away. I didn't want a gift from Rudolfo, and there was no occasion, but I couldn't take my eyes off that fine horse. The filly nuzzled at me, as if she were mine from that instant, and chortled in her throat—about the most soothing sound there is.

"The saddle, too. Brought from Mexico City."

Now I did look right into his face. "This is really fine, Rudolfo. But I can't accept these things. This horse and rig must have cost—well, way yonder too much for a gift. It's all very kind of you, but I can't take it."

"You must. You must. Please, amiga. Accept this from me. I've had good luck at the sale. Good rain here. Already there are letters mailed to everyone who can vote. Signs posted. Business attended to. All of that may be boring to you, but six weeks from now, I will be governor of the territory. While you were gone, I have ridden to Flagstaff and Holbrook, Prescott and Miami. All the miners from Globe are voting for me. I have a contingent in Douglas and even Agua Prieta. It's all good, you see?"

Contingent. That word made me remember the rest of what was stewing on my back burners. I had a few things I wanted to talk about with Mr. Rudolfo

Maldonado. First of which was why my cattle sale amounted to four hundred and some change and his was nearer to three thousand. I said, "Come on in the house, Rudolfo." As I stepped up on the porch, I felt him take my arm from behind and tug.

Rudolfo went down on his knee on the porch floor, clinging to my hand. "Sarah, make me happy. Make this a great day for us. I present you with this *contrato matrimonial.*" He pulled a box from his jacket pocket. Opening it, he said, "There will be more like it. As many as you wish."

What was in that little box took my breath away: a length of gold chain, all set with emeralds and diamonds, some as big as my little fingernail. I said, "I— we have some business to discuss. I cannot accept these things, Rudolfo."

He waited, watching my face. "See there on the mule? Fabrics from the Orient. *Sedas.* Perfumes and laces from Europe. All for you. More awaiting my bride, in your rooms at my hacienda."

"Oh, Rudolfo. Get up. I can't talk to you there."

He obeyed, pushing the necklace toward me. Then I remembered the dream. Jack on the strange horse, telling me to go on, that he was letting me go. The filly whinnied sweetly. The necklace gleamed in the sunlight, blinding me. Jack had said I didn't need him anymore. And I hadn't felt alone, or as needful. I sat in my rocker.

Rudolfo pulled another chair toward mine and sat, too, waiting. "Sarah," he began again, this time in a different, more serious tone of voice. "Are you my friend?"

"Yes, of course."

"Give me a thousand dollars, then."

I stiffened.

Rudolfo said, "Give me a hundred dollars, Sarah."

By the end of December, I'll need to pay nearly a hundred dollars in taxes up in Tucson if I'm going to keep the house in town. Another $110 to the county on all the acres I own here. With luck, I might stretch the rest until March. With a trainload of luck. We could live on deer and corn bread, the way we did when we first came here. I knew Rudolfo was testing me, though. Wanting something I couldn't figure. He didn't need money. Still, I said, "All right. If you need it, Rudolfo, I'll spare it. I'll fix up some beans and tortillas. Are you hungry?"

"Give me ten *centavos,* Sarah."

"What are you driving at?" I asked.

"That your nephew has destroyed you. You have almost nothing left. No way to live. Nothing to sell next year and nothing to live on until then. Marry me. As *mi esposa,* you will never need to think about money for the rest of your life. You will have servants and plenty, always. Am I so horrible that you cannot bear the thought of me?"

I've known Rudolfo more than twenty years. "No, not so horrible."

"And will you think of it?"

My heart was pounding. I looked into the face of my friend. "I will think of it," I said. "Consider, and think of it some."

His face lit up. "Take this, then. And when you start to doubt my intentions, you wear this, and know that I am very serious. We can be married after the election. Or—or before, if you wish."

"I only said I'd think of it. I'm not ready to plan a wedding."

He pushed the box holding the necklace into my hands and swept his hat back onto his head. "Farewell, dear friend," he said. He rode alone, leaving the mule and the gray filly behind.

As he got beyond the yard, Rudolfo let out a whoop and slapped his horse's rump with his hat, charging down the road toward his hacienda. I stared at the jewels in my hands and pictured myself wakening in the big bedroom in Rudolfo's house. Then I closed the box.

Chess wandered up from the barn. "What was all the commotion?" he asked.

"Rudolfo Maldonado wants me to marry him. He brought this to convince me."

"And did he?"

"I told him I'd consider his offer. That's all."

"Nice pony."

"Chess? What's your opinion?"

"You do what you think is right."

"I'm asking you. I don't want to make a choice and then hear two years later that you thought it was a bad idea from the start."

Chess leaned against the post that held up the porch roof. He pulled off his hat and mopped his forehead with his handkerchief before he spoke. "Reckon if I was you, I'd look at it as a square deal. But I ain't the one's got to live with him."

"You'd come live there, too. I'm not going without you."

"No. I'll stay here with the boys. We'll bunk here until they off and marry."

I held the box toward him. "You see this here?"

"Folderol." He turned away, refusing to look.

I held the box with its gilt chain and all those pretty stones in the sunlight so they flashed and sparked like a hundred dozen little fires. That many diamonds and emeralds would buy me a small herd. Enough to start over. That's all I'd really needed. Not sparkles to wear around my collar. Where would I wear such a thing? Feeding chickens? Rudolfo had plans for living up at the capital. Tea parties. That's where you'd wear it. Of all the knotheaded, insulting things. Did he think I was a woman whose head was turned by sparkles? I'd always despised women who would chase after such things.

I put the box of Rudolfo's wife bait on top of the pantry shelves. Then I went back out to Chess. "I didn't get a chance to ask him about the cattle," I said. Rudolfo had swept in here like a whirlwind, then left before I knew what had hit me. "I'll ride over there tomorrow. I'd better put up that filly and the mule."

September 16, 1906

Twice in the last ten days, I'd tried to talk to Rudolfo about my missing cattle. Each time, he swirled the conversation around every other subject, showing off things he'd put in his house, parading his daughters before me in new clothes.

The third time, I asked Mary Pearl to ride with me while Chess watched out for the little fellows. Nip was starting to come out of his little house now and then, so they planned to see if they could coax him to walk a little bit. I told them as long as they kept it really short and did what Grampa Chess said, they could feed him some corn bread, and gravy, too.

While we waited for Rudolfo to appear, Mary Pearl tried to talk to Luz. Mary Pearl had always been friends with Elsa, who'd gone to the convent of the Sisters of Saint Joseph of Carondelet in Tucson. But Luz had nothing to say. She was polite, but she offered no answers other than yes and no, and no conversation of her own. I got to thinking of April then, and I figured Luz probably *did* need to read a novel to have two words to rub together. Finally, Rudolfo sent word to us that he was going to be detained an hour. I told Luz to relay to her papa that I'd come back some other time.

Well, Mary Pearl and I rode south to Udell Hanna's place. We found him building a corral. The cattle he had penned were treading on soggy hay. We could see he needed some help knowing just how to get them going. Udell seemed stiff to me. He was polite, but nothing more. There was no light in his eyes at all when he said hello. He asked me if I wanted him to drive the cattle back to my place, as he couldn't rightly see taking them. I said, "Well, you need some better feed. I've got hay and leaf, and no cattle to feed. Haul your wagon up and get some."

"I'd be pretty much an all-around failure, I suppose," Udell said.

I pulled off my gloves, saying, "Did I do something to get sideways of you?"

"No."

I watched Mary Pearl from the corner of my eye. She was fidgeting nervously and trying not to pay attention. "Want the hay?" I asked.

"Yes."

"Well, come on up when you've a mind." I mounted my horse, and although I heard Mary Pearl say something to Udell, I was already headed for home. I'm about fed up with men right now. It's just trouble, always trying to figure what one's got caught in his craw that he isn't telling. Always trying to keep a step ahead just to keep from being run over. Lands. I passed right by Rudolfo's place without turning off toward the house. Let him come to me. For now, I wanted to go get some work done.

I heard hooves coming fast behind me. Mary Pearl flew by on Duende, as if I was barely moving on my old cow pony. She reined up to a halt and turned him, nearly flying up in the air, then coming back toward me after raising a bit of dust. As she settled into a walk beside me, I said, "That horse see a spook?"

"Mr. Hanna had a letter from Aubrey."

"Oh? What's he say? Is it about Felicity? Is she taking my land?"

"It wasn't about that. He's buying a property."

"What sort of a property?" I declare if I saw Felicity Prine *or* Aubrey Hanna's name on a deed to *my* land, there's going to be Arizona Rangers out looking for Sarah Elliot next. "Is that a buggy at my house, yonder?"

Mary Pearl said, "He says he's been given a salary."

"Look. It's your papa's surrey."

We loped toward the yard and climbed down, rushing into the house. My voice and Mary Pearl's mingled together. "Albert? Savannah? Mama? Papa?"

Albert and Chess sat at the kitchen table, and for a solid minute, my heart paused in its tracks. My mind became a great wooden block. Savannah was not with them. My heart ached and stopped beating, thinking my dearest friend and sister had left this earth. The color drained from the room and all was gray. Then I found my voice. "Savannah? How is Savannah?"

"I'm better, honey," I heard behind me from the parlor. I turned, to find Savannah sitting in a chair, her feet propped up on an overturned bucket. "It's going to be all right." Zack and Ezra burst in at that moment, presenting whittled animals they had carved, gifts for her. Mary Pearl sank at her mother's knee and put her head in her lap.

I took Savannah's hand over the cluster of children and mouthed the word *baby* with raised brows. Savannah shook her head. There would be no child to offset the loss of Esther, but also no labor, no fears for its life or hers. I sat by Savannah and the world turned back to color. I mouthed, "I'm sorry."

She said something to Ezra, admiring his handiwork, then said, "I've been feeling poorly for a while, and I'm mighty tired, children. Run along now. Let me talk to Aunt Sarah."

"Mama?" said Mary Pearl. "Did you get a letter? Mine and Aunt Sarah's?"

Savannah allowed her glance to meet mine for a second; then she turned to Mary Pearl. "I did."

"Are you terribly angry with me?"

"It wasn't *you* planned that. We'll pray for Esther night and day. The Lord watches over those that are His."

"Yes, Mama," Mary Pearl said. "I've cleaned the house and kept the chickens every day. We sleep here. Ezra is taller."

"Yup, I am," Ezra said, standing on his toes. "Look how them pants are short."

Savannah looked peaked and drawn, but there was some fire in her, too. "I'm proud of you, son. Now scoot and help Papa." She no longer had that resigned look of desperation she'd worn while we were in Tucson, even before Esther left. All she told me was that she had managed through the ordeal and the nurses had been very kind. Said she felt quite a bit better, too. Then along came the boys again, this time with an argument for her to settle over who'd had the baseball last. For now, it was enough that Savannah was home.

I spread out the fixings for our supper. Savannah rested while I stoked the stove. They'd brought mail. Sorting through it, I saw a letter on thick paper from Aubrey Hanna, Esquire, and another from April and Morris. I opened the lawyer's letter first. I put my feet flat on the floor before I began reading the first line. It was a lot of legal whys and wherefores, but the final word of it seemed to ring out right off the paper. "Judge Marks refuses to hear the case and has thrown it out of court. The aforementioned claims are found to be baseless." I pictured a fence rail with a string of rusty old cans set on it. With the word *baseless,* the first can flew off the fence, pinged square on with a good clean shot.

Felicity would not take this place. I might sell it to the railroad, or if I marry Rudolfo, it will go to him, but it will not go to her. Mary Pearl read the letter aloud as I started dishing out our supper. April's letter went on about some ladies in town and a few tidbits about Val, how he missed Ezra and Zack. Lorelei was talking more. Patricia asked for "Gramma" to come back.

After supper, the Prines all headed for their house, leaving just me and Chess on the sleeping porch. He went to sleep quickly. I heard something on the porch just after I'd come from my room in my nightgown. I pulled the shotgun from behind the door and opened it slowly, peering into the darkness. It was just old Nip. The dog had limped all the way from the barn to the porch and was sitting right by the door. The tip of his tail raised four times when he saw me. He turned his back to the door and his head to the yard and lay down. The Old Guard was back at his post. Another can fell off that fence.

Tomorrow I will go and sit with Savannah. Tonight, I will rest. I went to bed feeling more right and quiet on the inside than I have in many, many a night.

September 18, 1906

In the afternoon, I sent Ezra and Zack home from their schooling with their hands full of cookies I'd made before the stove cooled off from breakfast. The air is thick again, damp and miserable. All we want to do is sit and fan. I spent the afternoon writing letters to April, Harland, and Granny. I asked each of them what they thought of me marrying up with Rudolfo Maldonado. Of course, it would be my decision, but I still wondered what they'd think.

While I rode to Marsh Station to post the letters, spending four bits of my hard-won cash for those opinions, Chess had the gall to ride to Udell Hanna's place and have a talk with him. The very idea of that rankled me. I didn't know he was planning to go, and when he came back, he wouldn't tell me anything they'd said to each other, except that they'd talked about some cattle business. He did manage to remember to tell me that he'd also stopped by Rudolfo's hacienda and that it was busy with strangers. One of them, he said, looked very much like the railroad fellow we'd had here on the land. The railroad company is trying everyone around, I reckon, hoping to find someone else besides my poor addled mama to let them take part of their place for a noisy, smelly old track. What with Rudolfo running for governor, likely he'd be real pleased to have a train come right by his front door, so he could just step on it and ride to town anytime he pleases. When Chess finished telling me about what he'd done, I said to him, "Why didn't you ask Udell to come up for supper?" I still had his wife's cross on the mantel.

Chess fanned himself with his hat and said, "Why didn't you tell me you wanted me to fetch him?"

There was a hard tone in my voice when I said, "You never told me you were going there."

"If I had, you'd have said to stay put. I declare, Sarah. You think you know men, but you don't."

"I know far too many of 'em; that's my problem."

"Well, I've got work to do," he said, and stomped off, mad.

What do I care if Udell Hanna has supper? Or Rudolfo, either? Didn't I have enough to contend with, having a cantankerous father-in-law living with me, brushing against my grain every day of his life? I reckon there's a good that comes of being aggravated, for I got my washing out and done in no time. Worked myself tired before the day was gone, and then started supper for Chess and myself.

September 20, 1906

Who would have guessed I'd hear from April just two days after I'd sent my letter. She was, she said, quite happy that I should be making so prudent a marriage, and glad that all my worries would be ended. She assured me that she'd begin looking into arrangements as soon as possible, especially if I were to be marrying the territorial governor, and that it should be a grand affair. I read that letter twice over. Then I sat for a spell and put my head against the back of the rocking chair. Marrying Rudolfo. Territorial governor. Odd how April's measure of delight pushed me in the other direction. I wish I could take some joy in it. Wish I could feel even a little pleased.

A gleam of light struck my eyes as I sat there. Udell's silver cross flashed from the top of the mantel. Reckon if I'm to be marrying the governor, I had better take Mrs. Hanna's silver piece to Udell's house. I felt deep down sad, though, as I saddled Baldy. If I could pin a name on that sadness, I'd likely know what to do about it.

As I loaded the cross into the saddlebag, it was heavier than I would ever have expected it to be, and it made the satchel droop so low, I finally decided to carry it in my lap. I wrapped it up in flannel and put it in a hopsacking bag, then headed south. I rode the long way around, far from Rudolfo's house as I could get.

Udell was out in his corral again, this time putting up a shade at one end. His shirt was wet through and through with sweat, and he groaned as he lifted a piece of wood onto the rafters he'd built. It was a pretty fine shed roof. When he saw me coming, he said, "Mrs. Elliot? What brings you down this way?"

I thought we were using first names now, and I didn't miss that he'd gotten formal again. I said, "You forgot to take the silver cross. Thought I would bring it to you."

Udell climbed down from the rafters. He went to a bucket near where he'd been working, poured a dipper of water over his head, and used a rag to wipe his face. He nodded politely and held out his hands. I put the bag into them. "Thank you kindly," he said, not opening the sack. "I'd been missing it. Just thought I'd get some work done and wait for a good time to call. To fetch the cross, that is. Not a *call*, exactly."

I was still on the horse. "No," I said, "I wouldn't expect you to *call*, exactly."

"Will you rest a spell? Have a cup of water?"

This would be a good time to explain to Udell what Rudolfo had asked me. Maybe see what he thought of the idea. Tell him that nothing was decided yet. "Listen, Udell," I began.

"If you're busy, Mrs. Elliot—"

"Sarah."

He put his head down, then raised it again. "Sarah? Would you sit a spell?"

I got off the horse. "Nice shade you're making there."

"Modeled it after yours. Thought the animals would like it, come next summer."

"Shouldn't you set that in the house?" I pointed to the hopsack.

We went into his house, and Udell drew us each a tin cup of water. He took me out back. He said he'd decided to use the pasture where the sheep had died for a garden. The soil lay open in neat rows, ready for seed. Grim as it was, come spring that ground would be fertile with lamb's blood and ashes, like nothing hereabouts ever was.

We talked about seeds and weeds and such, then ambled around to where the half-built shade stood. I told him I had learned to save chicken droppings under a layer of sand for a year before using them, so they wouldn't burn up the soil. Then I told him I'd seen that he was having a hard time with that last beam he'd been trying to hoist. Said maybe he needed Aubrey home to help. He grinned.

Udell said, "Aubrey wasn't ever much use with a hammer, although he does know which end of a shovel works. He's a lot smarter than his papa ever was."

"I reckon he helped me keep my place. I wrote and told him thank you."

"I know."

"Well," I said, "you lift that end, and I'll take this."

"Oh, I couldn't ask you—"

"Well, you aren't asking me. You going to tote your load or not?" I had my hands on the log, and I pushed it up as high as my shoulder.

I reckoned Udell was not one to waste an offer like that, so he got his end of the beam over his head, and together we heaved it up on the low angle of the shade. He had some cross-ties nailed there, and he lashed it in place with rawhide. Then we set the last pole, a much smaller one. After that, we started loading up brush on top, which he nailed down with more ties as fast as I could get it up to him.

That brush roof was about half done when I picked up another armload of leafy branches and then suddenly dropped them. It felt as if I'd grabbed a mighty big thorn in the tender part of my wrist. Well, I looked down at my arm, and right there, mean as you please, with his head stuck into my glove and swinging his tail around, was a scorpion. Soon as I saw him, he whipped that tail, and I felt that thorny spike again. "Lord a mercy," I hollered. I shook that thing off and stomped it three times before it finally quit moving. "That blessed thing got me twice."

My arm hurt like a firebrand had been laid on the skin and left there. I pulled up my sleeve clear to the elbow. Udell rushed to fetch water, then bathed my arm again and again. He had a little bit of soap. He'd been working outdoors all morning, and the soap served to clean our hands a little, but it didn't make the burning stop.

The two places where the critter stung me didn't look like much at all, except for the red swelling around them. Before any time had passed at all, my hand got stiff and hot and sore. It looked like a big leather glove. Udell said he didn't know what to do. He ran to the house and came back with some vinegar, and poured that over my arm. I felt shaken and my heart was pounding fast and hard. He took my knife and cut my sleeve loose, because I couldn't push it up or down, the band had grown so tight from the swelling. "I think I need to sit down," I said after he cut the sleeve. Gray spots swirled in the sky and I sank to my knees.

I opened my eyes. My head pounded as if I'd hit a fence post. I felt cold and chilled. Overhead, the branches of a tree rustled. I tried to sit up, and felt arms behind my back. Udell said, "There you are. Lost you for a moment. Here, drink this." He handed me a cup of cool water.

I felt plumb foolish, fainting like that. "Reckon I got overheated," I said.

He ran into the house yet again, then came back in a moment with a hand-ful of cotton rags, which he soaked in water and held to my forehead. "I'd offer to help you to the house, but it's probably cooler here in the shade," he said.

I nodded. My eyes ached. "Was I out long?"

"Barely a blink. Sit still until you get a little color in your face."

My eyes met his for a long second. He had blue eyes. Not gray and hawk-like, as Jack's were, just blue. The eyebrows, like his hair, were salted with a lit-tle gray. I pulled the wet cotton from my head. A drip of water trailed down my face from my hair, running exactly to the tip of my nose. It tickled and felt silly. I smiled and wiped at it.

Udell's kiss was soft as fresh bread—unexpected, though not entirely—just as natural as the path of the water that had caused me to smile. His lips lin-gered just a moment longer on mine, as if he was waiting for me to protest. I simply couldn't. His arm still circled my back, and my good hand rested easily on that arm. He was muscled out from a lifetime of hard work. My hand felt small there, safe.

When he pulled away, he turned his head from me, but he didn't let go. I couldn't look him in the eye again, either. The moments passed as we held our breath. Then he turned back toward me, his lips caught in a shy grin, his brows raised. I smiled.

"Well, you're a fair doctor," I said. "I've purely forgotten about the pain in my hand."

He laughed. "Sarah, you'd make a man be anything he ever thought about being."

"I don't know what you mean."

He lifted me to my feet. "I've taken advantage of your condition."

My heart beat right up in my throat. I steadied myself on his arm, looking about for something else to hold to, so I could cling to that and not appear as brazen as I felt at that moment. My mouth opened and words came out that I'd had no intention of saying—truth, as bare as day. I said, "Reckon I don't mind."

Udell stepped one foot closer to me, and this time we kissed the way Jack and I used to do. All the while, my mind raced here and there, wondering what on earth I was doing. What this meant to him. What it meant to me. At the same time, my heart kicked like Hunter scampering around the corral. I wrapped my good hand around the back of his neck and just leaned into him. I pondered Jack for a moment, but rather than feeling guilty or longing for him, I felt only good, sweet memories. Sweet, tender kisses. Just like this one. All thought left me, and then a thousand feelings tore through my mind and heart. And they all came suddenly to rest on—Rudolfo Maldonado.

"I have to go home," I said, stepping away, turning toward my horse.

Udell rubbed his face and nodded. "I'll ride with you. That bite could get worse by the time you get home. What do you have to dress it with?"

I said firmly, "I'll be all right." I swung my leg over the saddle, teetering at the high point, as if I were going to go clean over the other side. At the last second, I caught my balance and planted myself hard in the seat.

He looked puzzled for a minute; then he set his jaw and shook his head. He said, "I haven't ever argued with you before now, either. I was real taken with the way we agreed on things. But no, this time, you're wrong, and you need someone to go along with you. Wait here while I get my horse."

"I'm perfectly able—"

"It has nothing to do with you being able. Wait here."

When we got to my front porch, I was feeling miserable, and my hand throbbed with shooting pain. I didn't know how I'd manage supper or washing up, much less changing for bed. Those things were on my mind. That's why I didn't notice the horse meandering around the yard. That's why I was startled by the presence of a man on the rocker. Rudolfo stood as we rode toward him. The look on his face was dark as the day he'd gone after Willie. Troubled as the day he'd returned without him. "Rudolfo? What brings you here?" I asked.

"A little business with the woman I'm going to marry," Rudolfo said. His eyes bored into Udell as he spoke.

I saw only a glimpse of Udell's face as he turned his horse. "Wait!" I called, knowing perfectly well that he would not wait. I could have throttled Rudolfo for saying that. I hadn't told him I'd marry him. I hadn't told Udell anything, either. Lands. I was betwixt and between, and this was a stew of my own making.

"I need to put a plaster on this bite. A little soda ash and water will do," I said. To the sounds of a galloping horse fading over the hill, I got down and told Rudolfo about the scorpion, and how I had fainted. My words felt foolish, as if I was telling a whopper, though every word was true.

Rudolfo followed me into the house and talked while I fiddled clumsily with the soda and the bandage, using my off hand, spilling things. I couldn't help but think that Udell would have been busy wrapping my arm with it by now, the way he'd done Aubrey's face. Rudolfo said he had a grand idea. Told me that what this county needed was a rail spur to get cattle to town. Too many were lost when driving a herd.

"Not across my land," I said.

His face softened. He spoke as if he were explaining something to one of his little girls. "It will be our land, Sarah. And our prosperity depends on wise thinking. You will be wise to let me make the decisions that will keep our business going. Remember? I told you that never again will you worry about money. You will be living down at the hacienda in grand suites. A few iron rails and some beams—what does that hurt? After they set *las espigas,* the workers will disappear. You will never hear the train from your rooms there."

"You know someone from the rail company has already swindled my mama out of part of her land?" I still owed her eighteen hundred dollars for that well, too. Glory.

"They paid in gold. You have a well for it. It's all improving the land."

My plaster slipped and I set it back again. "They were scouting my land. I know for a fact that someone looked up the plat and legal section maps awhile back."

I couldn't read his face. He stepped back, startled, and said, "How do you know this?"

"I just do."

"You can't know this." Something changed in him. There was a smoothness to his expression. Some kind of glaze in his eyes. My head ached with ferocious pain. My hand throbbed. My gut twisted.

I faced him square on and said, "Who looked up the plats for my spread?"

Rudolfo smiled, his eyes crinkling. He said, "As you said, the rail company is far-thinking. They must have been looking for a good location for tracks. That's why they came to you with the offer."

Chess came up on the porch and into the kitchen, sitting down right next to Rudolfo without saying a word.

Rudolfo nodded at him and said, "Señor? I have come to ask Sarah's hand in marriage. And to present her with this." He pulled another gift from his pocket, a folded leather wallet about two inches square. He opened it and took out a ring of gold with rubies across it. Rudolfo took hold of my left hand, which was still gritty from the soda I'd been trying to hold to my other wrist. He slid the ring on my finger. It was small and only went past the first knuckle. He pulled it off and slid it easily upon my littlest finger. "Now," he said. "No more of useless trains and men's business. Say you'll be mine, Sarah. I ask *el suegro* for your hand. Señor Elliot, will you give her to me?" he said, glancing toward Chess.

Chess grinned and made a face. He slapped his knee and said, "You must not know what you're getting into, Maldonado, if you think anyone could give her away. You'll likely wake up next to a mountain lion one morning, wondering where you went wrong. I ain't saying a word. Nosirree. Not a word."

Rudolfo looked to me. I looked down at the ring. And I heard Morris's voice saying, ". . . books were easy to find. . . . right on top . . . paper markers . . ." The county records of my land had been interesting to someone. The ring on my finger felt as strangling as the band of the sleeve had on my swollen wrist before Udell had cut it off. The parlor clock ticked. It chimed the quarter hour. I felt Udell Hanna's lips against mine, still flushed with the warmth of rediscovering that joy.

Rudolfo suddenly stood. "I have to go to Tucson in two weeks, Sarah. The election campaign starts in full then. We could marry before that day, or you will need to bring *El* Chess with you as *carabino*. I must know soon whether the wedding will be before the election or after. It changes the campaign. I'll send for a seamstress to begin work on your wardrobe." He took my left hand in his, kissed the fingers just above the ring he'd placed there, and, tipping his head toward Chess, whistled for his horse.

When he was gone, I said, "Chess, take this thing off my hand." I held the ring toward him.

Chess said, "*Sí*, Doña Maldonado." He set the ring on the table, placing it in the larger ring of spilled soda ash and drips of water.

I said, "Stop that."

"You'd better make up your mind," he said. "I won't say a word either way. But what I see crossing your mind is some kind of foolishness I can't even put a blanket on. I saw you riding back here with Hanna, like you'd been on a picnic. Maldonado here waiting for you. Well, I figured to come to the house and watch the fireworks."

"I was helping Udell build a brush arbor to shade his animals."

"Why in blazes are you ten miles from home, building a shed in the middle of the day?"

"Same as anyone would do. Lending a hand where I saw one was needed."

"Ah."

"Ah what?"

"Just sitting here, come in late, watching you fuss with that plaster. Let me wrap it on for you. What got you?"

"Scorpion."

"Two little sores here. Sure it wasn't a rattler?"

"I saw it."

"Too late, though, to do you much good." He tied the ends of the rag with a snap, hurting the worst part of my wrist. His eyes were stern. They held a glimmer of Jack's expression. "Think of it as a supernatural message."

I knew he figured I should be understanding something, but my mind was so full of dust right then, I could barely breathe. I said, "I'm going for a ride. Dip my feet in the creek and cool down."

Chess said, "That sounds like a right fine plan. You do that. Take all afternoon and do that."

"I will, then," I said, and closed the door behind me with a slam. Nip crawled out from under the porch and wagged his tail at me. "Stay home, boy," I said. This time, I got straight into the saddle without wobbling.

I headed north toward Savannah and Albert's place, stopping where Cienega Creek crossed the road. I looped the reins loosely over a low branch so the horse could crop. It was quiet and cooler there. First thing I did was test the water with my left hand. It was barely flowing, and not as cool as I wished; still, it was pleasant. I plunged the right hand, bandage and all, into the water and sighed deeply as the pain lessened. Then I sat myself in the shade and pulled up my knees, resting my elbows on them and my head on my good hand.

Other times, I'd have run to the graveyard to talk to Jack. Now he was gone as the rest of the people there. A vapor. Disappeared in the heat and sunlight. At least when I'd been able to tell him things, they'd begun to make sense to me.

Quail scurried by, first on foot, then fluttering into the air when they noticed me. As they did, another movement caught my eye. A horned toad flattened himself against the ground, invisible except for his eyes, which darted back and forth, sizing up his territory for enemies. I watched the horned toad dash away into some grass. Then I smelled an odor, halfway between a skunk spray and rotted meat. There was no time to lose. I was in the saddle just as the first javelina came ramming through the brush. Five more followed it, along with two babies, exact versions of their parents, but small.

The horse reared, and I held tight with my left hand, circling him around. We bolted away before the javelina herd came closer, but the horse was spooked and wanted to run. The wild pigs could cripple a horse, kill anything smaller. I pulled him back and made him trot to Savannah's house. She, of all people, would sort out my feelings for me. She would know exactly what I should do.

I found Savannah on her porch, fanning herself, a wet towel at her neck. Her expression was tired and gaunt. "We've heard from Esther this morning," she said soon as I dismounted.

What had I been thinking? That in the whole world, my problems were the only ones? I went to her side. "A letter, a note? What did she say?"

Savannah's voice was strained but flat, as if no emotion could express the anguish she felt. "That she was sorry to have eloped the way she did. Said she was happy, living in a tent in the bushes, for now. She could have *babies* out there."

All I could say was, "I'm so sorry, honey."

"I failed in everything I ever taught her. I was a no-account mother."

"Oh, Savannah, you didn't fail. You have eight. Seven have listened and learned. Surely Esther's not stupid, just—" I was about to say "young," but Savannah interrupted.

"Foolish," Savannah said. "The worst sin of all. Foolish."

Chapter Twenty-Three

I've told Shorty and Flores that I couldn't afford to pay them any longer. There wasn't much for them to do, anyway. We've been home for over three weeks and still no sign of Esther and Bienvenites. Albert says he wants to talk to the Sheriff again, so they are planning to head back to town. Chess and I will stay and mind their place with ours. While they are gone they'll pick up supplies, so I counted eight dollars into Albert's hand, over his protests, for a month's supply of coffee and flour and cornmeal. I'd do without anything else, and make do with what was already in my pantry. Chess asked Albert to take the fancy saddle he'd finished and see if he could sell it in town. Another hundred dollars or so would get us a little further.

Well, they're leaving this afternoon and Savannah said Mary Pearl had come down this morning with another note she'd found on her windowsill. This one was from Esther, by way of her man. Mary Pearl said Bienvenites promised Esther a castle in Spain.

Savannah stared hard into the distance and said, "You want to hear what she is proudest of? That he gave her a white mule to ride. Said it was a fine animal. She owns the clothes she left with, a Bible, and a mule. Castles in Spain, my hind foot."

I said, "Savannah, are you sure you're well enough to go? You could stay with me."

"I'm going," she said. Savannah hugged me, then searched my face, and the sadness in her eyes was as deep as a cave. If Esther had died instead of run off, it might have been easier for her mother to understand. I knew that feeling. And I knew there was no cure for it.

I said, "Maybe when your boys get home, they can go with Gil and Charlie to look for her." Misery made my own voice sound hollow. If I ever got to that girl I'd scold her for what she's done to this family until she was scared to lift a finger.

"Have you heard from Clove and Josh?" Savannah asked.

I shook my head. "But Granny should have gotten my letters. We'll hear soon."

"Will you check the mail for me? As often—not every day, I know—but some?"

Mary Pearl came out to the porch just then. She smiled, then saw her mother's expression, and made her own more serious. A gleam remained in her eyes, though, made more sparkling by the bright color of a new waistcoat. Mary Pearl seemed a far cry from the girl who had said a few weeks ago that a trip to town was just a long ride on a hard seat. Although Duende was tied to the back, she climbed into the surrey next to her mother.

When they pulled out, I rode alongside for a ways, and then I turned on the eastern trail and rode up to Marsh Station again. Might as well start today.

Weeks and months can go by without us getting so much as a Sears and Roebuck's Catalog, and now that we are spread to the winds, there's mail all the time. Henry, the stationmaster, said there was a little box for Savannah from the Singer Sewing Machine Company, a Seed and Feed catalog, and two letters from Aubrey Hanna. One was on thick paper, addressed in a fine hand to me. I opened it and read it quickly, before I left the station. It seems that a new judge had been appointed in town and Felicity's lawyer had somehow managed to get him to listen to her. I almost dropped the rest of the mail. Aubrey assured me that he would write another letter explaining everything again, but this new judge didn't know people in town the way his predecessor had. My heart sank.

I rode slowly, just thinking. Halfway to Albert's, I started to pull open the second letter from Aubrey, hoping that the two had been sent at different times and that in this one, he would tell me it had all been resolved. I stopped short because it felt so different from the first one. Not official at all. It was thin letter paper. I turned the envelope over. It was addressed to Mary Pearl.

I dropped Savannah's sewing machine parts and Mary Pearl's letter on their kitchen table. Fed their chickens and filled the water tubs in the chicken coops. The letter made me think of Aubrey, which led my mind to his papa. I hadn't seen Udell since that day I got the scorpion bite. I was just starting to get my hand back to use.

I stopped up on the ridge where I could see Granny's place, Albert's, and, yonder a ways, my own. At Granny's empty house, shingles hung loose and bird nests festooned the windowsills. I saw it differently now, not as our family home but just some ground with a tiny house on it, and for the first time, realized that when my mama passed into the next life, her section would rightly be split between us—Albert, Ernest, Harland, and me. Felicity would have an honest right to a fourth of Granny's place.

Then I imagined that my spread was no longer mine, either, but Rudolfo's. My fourth of Granny's place would also be his. And he'd stop at nothing. He wouldn't let that slattern take this land. Maybe he would be willing to pay cash and buy out her share. Surely, that would be more appealing to her. She doesn't want to work the land, just have the folderol. Rudolfo's so willing and eager to give me gifts; what I needed from him was a sack of gold to defend my land. But, if I *asked* him for something, especially that, it would firmly commit me to marrying him. All the other presents were just trifles I could put aside or give back. To do that sort of thing, well, that would be sealing my fate. It came to me then that if I had a sack of gold, I wouldn't be considering him at all. His life would be his and mine would be mine. When Charlie and Gilbert got back with the money and cattle Willie took, I'd find a way to make it on my own.

A breath of wind moved around me, hot air on a sultry day. A rider came this way. Udell. My throat went dry. My heart beat so loudly, I could hear it. What was he doing riding this way when I'd just been thinking of him? He tipped his hat, said, "Sarah?" as he rode up. "Been to the station?"

He'd not been looking for me after all. "If you're up to get mail, I'll save you the trip. There wasn't any for you or—" I started to say "Rudolfo," but I left it with "anyone."

"Thank you," he said. "Thank you. That saves me nearly half a day."

"I was hoping to hear from my mama by now," I said.

He merely turned his horse around. "Mind I ride back with you?"

"Not at all." We went a little way before I said, "I got a letter from your son. You can read it if you want, just to hear from him, although it's about a legal problem. We've got this family member trying to take my ranch."

"There's a lot of that going around."

I had to laugh, though it was a hard, bitter sound.

"How's the hand?" he asked.

"Better. Thanks. Someone else got a letter from Aubrey. Mary Pearl."

Udell smiled. "He wrote me that he's fond of her. Seems a likely girl."

We rode a long way without speaking, nearly to my front porch. Then he said, "Are you sure you don't mind if I read the letter? I don't want to pry." I handed it to him. Udell read it from the saddle, then handed it back. "He's got a fine hand."

I saw the pride in his face. "Yes," I said. "He does." His eyes were blue as the sky, and they held mine for just a moment.

He said, "I'm riding down to Benson today. Having a look around. I'll be back day after tomorrow. Here's a thing I've been thinking of. You offered me fifty head of cattle, and it's no blame of yours that there aren't fifty. It was a generous offer, well beyond what anyone would expect, unless they knew you. I'm inclined to return the eleven I've got, because we're both in straights. Only, if you marry Maldonado, and I give them back to you, they'll be his. That's your right, but you promised me fifty head, and he doesn't need them. If you don't marry him, I'll drive them all back, soon as I get back from Benson. Maybe you'd still let me keep just one to breed for a year or two. Ten may not be enough to keep you going. I don't know how much you need, and I'm eating antelope until it's like to make me grow antlers myself. I can't offer you a hacienda and a spread the size of his. I can't offer you two bits to save your land. Ten heifers. That's what I'm thinking."

He rode off then at a gallop, without another word. Didn't give me time to say as much as "Wait."

The sun was low in the sky when riders appeared on the horizon. Three men, who looked to be armed but, except for that, were traveling lightly and quickly. I watched them come down the track off the hill. They were nearly to the house when I saw who it was. I didn't know whether to drop to my knees in thanksgiving or run to them, so I didn't do either. Just stood there. Charlie and Gilbert. Between them, head down and hatless, rode Willie Prine. He wasn't on Pillbox, but some sorry nag that looked as forlorn as its rider. I hugged Charlie and Gilbert both, patting their broad backs. They looked sunbaked and wizened. Both sported mustaches, now, and Gilbert had a beard growing.

Willie stayed on his horse and didn't speak. He turned away, though I said hello to him. Charlie pulled the serape off Willie's saddle, and I saw the boy's hands were tied to the horn. He wore no boots or even stockings. Bare, beat-up and filthy, his long panhandle feet were tied at the ankles and rigged to the leather breast strap.

Gilbert unfastened Willie's feet. Charlie pulled a pistol from his belt and aimed it at the boy. "Get down."

Willie snarled, "Gimme back my book."

Charlie reached with one hand into the saddlebag on his own horse, pulled forth a thick wad of papers tied with strings into a roll, and pitched it on the ground in front of Willie's horse. "Get off," he said again.

"Get off your horse, Willie," I said.

After some minutes, Charlie said, "Answer her."

"Hey, Aint Sair."

Charlie said, "Gil, rig him up like last night. You try to take off from here, kid, I swear to the sky, I'll plug you. I'm worn thin of chasing you down. I'll let this Colt find you from here on in." Charlie turned to me and said, "Been real cooperative until I told him I aimed to turn off here and spend the night. Then I had to chase him to hell and back, and hog-tie him to that saddle to keep him."

The boys tied their cousin to the porch rail tighter than I'd ever seen man or beast tied. He could barely move his arms, but he stretched his long legs across the porch. I wasn't going to argue with the boys. Willie looked every bit the outlaw he was trying so hard to be—rangy, smelly, cut up, and mean. Charlie, too, had a different expression on his face. He looked like a lawman bent on doing his job. I had no intentions at all of stepping between him and that job, so I sidled closer to Gilbert.

"Can I have water?" Willie asked.

"I'll get you water, Willie," I said. "After I hear what's come of the herd you took. And the horse you rode off on. And the cash from the box. Is there a nickel left?"

He turned his head away from me and burst out crying. He wailed and gasped, and tears and spittle dribbled from his chin. I looked from him to my sons. Willie said between sobs, "I'm sorry, Aint Sair. I'm sorry!"

Gilbert started taking the saddle off his horse. "He's been bawling like that since last night. We tracked him north of Naco. That's where he split off with his gang."

"Wainbridges are both dead," Charlie ~~interrupted~~ interjected. "We didn't have any choice. Then Willie got into it with the Yaqui he was riding with, seems. Rest of them was scattered."

"I'm sorry!" Willie howled.

Gilbert walked to the olla and drank from the dipper. Then he handed a full one to Charlie. "Mama," Gil said, "the kid there says he's got religion. I don't much care, after what I've seen him do. We've come here to rest up a day. Then we're hauling his carcass to Tucson."

We talked on the porch while Willie sobbed, though his wailing had quieted and turned to childlike gulps of air. On the trip back, Charlie said, they'd rounded up thirteen head of cattle wearing my brand. They tried to keep them all, but three had to be put down. Ten remained and were north of the house, across the Cienega, where the grass hadn't burned. Just ten. Same offer I'd been given from Udell. One of them was the bull I owned with Rudolfo.

Charlie went to the horses again and picked up the roll of tied-up paper. He tossed it into Willie's lap, got down on his heels so his face was the same level as the boy's, and said, "There's your 'Good Book.' You hold that in your lap and tell my mother, who clothed you and fed you and treated you like a welcome member of this family, just what you done with her money. You tell her how it went into the nasty cribs of whores and opium parlors and was guzzled down in liquor. You tell her that her ranch is bankrupted because you are a high-timing gambler, betting a dollar a throw."

"I'm sorry, Aint Sair," was all Willie said.

Charlie pushed his hat back. "He's just sorry for getting caught." He pulled a short knife from his belt and appeared for a moment to be picking at his fingernails. "This your knife, boy?" Charlie said. "Got some stains on the handle, don't it?"

Willie blubbered and a new stream of tears rolled down his face.

I hated that boy. I said, "You're in a peck of trouble, Willie Prine." Myself, I was glad I was sitting, for my head felt as if it were feeling. "All the money is gone," I said, not as a question, but just to tell my own ears what I'd heard before. "The cattle are gone. Nothing left."

Gilbert pulled up a chair beside me. "Mama? I figure to go to town and get a job, too, like Charlie. We'll send you money. I'll live in the house there and won't have to pay rent, so I can save more. We'll get the taxes paid by the end of the year. Taxes for the house in town, too. I know how to work; someone will hire me. Shoot, maybe Maldonado needs a good hand. I won't even have to go to town."

"Maldonado?" I crossed my arms across my ribs and leaned back. "Rudolfo Maldonado has offered me another way to keep this land. He wants me to marry him." My sons looked at me as if I'd slapped their faces. Then they looked at each other.

Gilbert rose and stomped off the porch, but before he left, he took his hat and whopped Willie's head as he went past. "See what else you've done?"

"Gilbert," I called.

Gil stopped in the yard. He put his hands on his hips, staring into the round corral. "That what this horse is for?"

"Don't insult me, son," I said.

He turned. "You can't possibly love him. Can you?" Then he headed for the barn.

I tried to get Charlie's eyes. He wouldn't look at me, but I said to him, "There is sometimes more to marriage than love."

Charlie said, "He don't understand, Mama. That's all. He'll come around."

"Well, I haven't told Rudolfo I *would* marry him. Just that I would consider it."

"Can you put up with us a night? I'd surely like a bed and a meal before I go to town." I pulled up some fixings for a little supper. They retied Willie so he could eat supper. His hands were free, but his feet were nearly part of the chair he was on. He ate just as before, like a wolf half-starved. Now, though, instead of warming my heart, I'd as soon have thrown the food down the hole in the outhouse. All he was to me was a cowboy.

Chess stared at his plate, and after a while he set down a biscuit he'd been holding. "I can't eat. Not with that at this table. I'm going yonder to feed at Albert's place. While you boys got this outlaw here, I'm a-staying there."

"Grampa," Charlie said, "we'll have him out of here after breakfast tomorrow."

Chess looked right at me. "If I was you, I wouldn't be wasting a drop of rancid gravy on the likes of that." He left the kitchen without another word. After a while, the sounds of horse's hooves told me he'd left. Gilbert yanked Willie's hands behind his back, tied them to his feet, and pushed him to the floor. Charlie came in, rifle in hand, and sat in my rocker.

"What are you fixing to do," I asked Charlie, "stay there all night?"

"That's exactly right," Charlie said. My son looked five years older than he had when he left.

Willie said, "Can I have my book?"

Gilbert tossed it to Charlie, who laid it in front of Willie's face. Willie squirmed around until he could lay his head upon the tied-up roll of paper, then closed his eyes. I went out to the sleeping porch. Before long, Gilbert began to snore, exhausted to the bone.

I watched the stars. The moon triangle, with Jack's star and the other, shone too brightly, as if someone had set their wicks too high. "Jack?" I whispered. Nothing more. Waiting for sleep to come, I thought of Udell. Remembered the conversations we'd had so easily. Remembered the kiss we'd shared, too. Wondered if I could ever kiss Rudolfo that way. Wondered what lying with him would bring. Children? An early death? Embarrassment such as Savannah had felt, for my other children? *Embarrazada,* so close to a embarrassed—the Spanish word for carrying a child. And *esposa*—the word meant both wife and handcuff. Trussed and bound as Willie was on my floor. Rudolfo wanted an answer. So did Udell. One's offer was to give up everything for a life of ease. The other's was the chance to struggle back up from nearly nothing. Udell hadn't offered marriage. Or if he had, it wasn't clear. Yet lying with Udell seemed infinitely more welcome. As if he'd look at me while we did. Rudolfo's eyes would be on the land he was taking. I heard Willie crying. I got out of bed and put a wrap over my gown.

Charlie hadn't moved. He said, "Hush, you. Mama, did he wake you?"

"No," I said. "Can't sleep. Want some coffee?"

"Sure."

I chucked up the ashes in the stove and put in kindling. Pumped the coffeepot full of water. Then I sat by Charlie. He looked so thin. "Want a piece of that pie, too?"

"I already finished it off. Sorry."

I smiled. "Why don't you go get some sleep? I'll watch him for you."

He didn't want to leave his duty, he said. A Ranger couldn't turn the kid over to his *mother* to watch. I told Charlie it wouldn't be the first time I'd sat up beside a boy during the night. Then I said about five times that I understood Willie was not just a bad child brought home to face the music. He was a wanted man in the custody of an Arizona Ranger. Yes, yes, I said, until I was blue in the face. Still, he made me promise never to let Willie out of my sight, and if he needed the privy, not to let him near a door without a shotgun trained on him. "It's the law, Mama," Charlie said. "If I have to hunt him down again, I won't waste time bringing him to jail."

"I'll watch," I promised. "Get some rest." I took his chair and put the rifle across my lap. Charlie went to lie down out on the porch, still in his clothes.

Willie shuffled around in his ropes, shifting himself against the wall. "Are you hungry?" I asked him.

"No, ma'am. Thank you, Aint Sair."

"I'm getting myself some coffee. Don't you move."

"I'm staying, Aint Sair."

"There isn't much you've ever done gives me cause to believe you, boy."

"I know it. But I'm staying."

When I came back with coffee, Willie had not moved an inch from where I'd left him. He closed his eyes. I drank my coffee. After half an hour, Willie opened his eyes suddenly, startled by some dream. I said, "What's that book you've got your head on?"

"Half a Bible. It was give to me by a conjure."

"A what?"

"Maybe it was God. I was running and scared after what happened, before I met up with cousin Charlie. This feller came along out of the lightning, riding a snow-white mule, calling out to listen to the word of the Lord. He holds up a book and the storm comes right out of the pages, bolts of lightning. Them cows were split wide open. Hunnerds of 'em. Then he tore it right down the middle and handed this part to me. Said it would save my soul from hell's fire of eternal torment. When he tore that book, it screamed just like a woman."

I filled my coffee cup. "A man on a mule? Are you sure it was white?"

"Yes'm. It was God."

" 'It was God,' " I repeated, rocking the chair slightly. "And a woman screamed?"

"He let me live. After—after all. Said my soul was so blackened, I was looking into the eyes of the devil himself, heading for judgment, torment, and damnation. And if I'd read this book, it'd be all right. And I sat down and read all day. Somes I didn't understand."

The eyes of the devil? Lazrus should be on calling terms with the devil all right.

"Do you believe me, Aint Sair? That I'm sorry and all?"

"You took everything I had that wasn't nailed down. Being sorry doesn't fix what you did."

After a long while, he said, "No, it don't." More minutes passed.

My coffee got cold. I drank it anyway. I said, "What happened to Pillbox? Hunter's mama."

"With the rest of 'em. Lost somewheres."

I couldn't help myself. I said, "Wainbridges were in it with you?"

"It 'as their idea, mostly. They had this plan to take them cattle to a feller they knew in a place in Mexico. Rocko, Pocko, something."

"Naco?" I said.

"That's it. He'd give them a wad of cash and we'd set up a ranch down by the beach, where it's always cool and nice. The cows grow twicet the size down there." He was quiet while the clock chimed midnight. "Yep. Twicet." He rubbed his nose against his knee, saying, "This place ain't bankrupted fer real, is it?"

I couldn't answer him.

After a spell, he said, "What you going to do?"

I looked right at his eyes and said, "Keep going. All I can do. Living is getting knocked down time and again, then standing up time and again, and once more. It's easy to act honorable when things are coming along and all your pastures are green. Plenty difficult when the ground has dried and burned and people have connived to take even that from you. I'll sell this place, or I'll lose it. I'll go on. People who don't have hard times aren't living."

"You don't have to sell this ranch, do you?"

I thought of Rudolfo. That was exactly what I was doing: selling my ranch and myself. I decided to leave him out of the sums for now. "Willie, I'm out of money and in debt. We can't eat the dirt. There's only Chess and me left. I still have my boys and my daughter and her family, and my brother and his children. Charlie and Gil will marry someday and have children. That's all that matters."

"I done this to you."

"Savannah says it's a time to tear down. Ecclesiastes. A season for everything. Building up and tearing down."

He squirmed around and sat up. "I told cousin Charlie I come to own up. Take my licks. Go to the sheriff. Turn myself in. It's what I got to do. I seen the error of my ways. It's in this book here."

"Since you aren't hung yet, they'll maybe send you to prison."

"How long, you reckon?"

"Cattle rustling? Years. Maybe ten or twenty. Depends on what all the judge sees fit. I saw Charlie's papers. He could have hung you from the first tree he found."

"Twenty years is a long time. Charlie said likely up in Florence. Said I'd be an old man before I got out."

"You'd still not be an old man, even in twenty years. You might live another forty after that. A man can do some good in forty years, if he's a mind to."

Willie sniffed. In a broken voice he said, "I'll make it up to you. I'll come back and work here for nothing when my time is up. I'll work the rest of my life for no pay. You don't even have to feed me. Just let me make it up to you."

It wasn't in me to hate for very long. "That'd be fine, Willie. If you do that when you get out, you can stay here." I couldn't guarantee there'd be a "here" to stay at, though.

He laid his head back on his Bible and slept for a little while—nearly an hour. When the clock struck one, he awoke. "Is it morning?" Willie asked. "I'm so tired."

"It's a long ways until morning," I said.

We talked then about other things. About Esther running off. I asked him, "Do you remember whereabouts you were when you saw the fellow on the white mule?"

"Down from Bisbee, towards some little town. Just a place by a riverbed."

"Where were you when Charlie and Gilbert caught up with you?"

Willie said, "That storm there was where we lost the other steers. A feller—they called him Shank—he gets to saying he's going north, and I wanted us heading down to Mexico. I wanted to catch a few of them cattle. Not leave them all behind. We'd gone two—no, three days. Broke my tooth fighting him. That's it, three days up from Naco, after we got to Bisbee, but mostly reading all the time. Why?"

It didn't add up. Three days from Naco should have put them in Tucson, not just Bisbee. I said, "Do you want a drink of water?"

"That coffee smells all right. Cold water makes my tooth hurt."

"It's gone cold, too."

"Don't care."

I poured cold coffee in a tin cup and held it to his mouth. Willie drank. He closed his eyes and dozed. I decided to make more coffee. Walking around would help me stay awake. I stoked up the stove again. Drew more water.

When I dumped out the grounds, Willie awoke. He watched me while I measured in more coffee and set the pot down in the hole, close to the flames. He said, "I wisht I had a ma like you, Aint Sair."

I sighed. "Go ahead and sleep," I said.

"Cain't. Trussed up pretty tight."

"That, I'm not changing. Charlie may be my son, but he's a Ranger, too. I gave him my word you'd stay tied, and my word is good." I thought I'd try again to get him to tell me where he'd seen the "conjure." I said, "Do you remember the first town you came to after you met up with Charlie?"

"Sounded like a girl's name."

I fetched around in my memory. "St. Mary's? Elida? Galena?"

"That's it!"

"Well," I said, "so that was in a creek between Naco and Galena."

He said, "You know, I learnt to ride pretty good after awhile."

"Pillbox was a tough horse for anyone." I was right back to being angry, thinking of him taking my mare.

"Maldoraedo help you get the rest of your herd to town?"

"I had between eight and nine hundred head last year. Gilbert got paid for only a hundred and ten. There aren't a dozen left to start over with. Hunter nearly died not having a mother to nurse him."

"Here's something you should know, Aint Sair. That Maldoraedo feller paid Shank to pison your windmill and bung it all up."

I held my breath for what seemed like a minute, though I'm sure it was only a few seconds. I leaned forward to get a clear look at Willie's face in the dim lamplight. "How do you know that?"

"Shank told me himself."

Rudolfo would never—could not possibly—have poisoned my cattle. Nothing was worth that. I said, "Shank's a lying skunk." The coffeepot was boiling, and the smell started to perfume the room. I stretched and went to get a cup. My hands shook, and the cup clattered against the pot.

While I poured, Willie said, "Shank would do anything to anybody for half a dollar. I seen him. He told me where they hid the boxes. Said that stuff made him sick and all the skin peeled off 'n his hands. Leastways that was *one* thing I didn't never do."

When I turned toward Willie then, he hid his face. "Why would he make up something like that?" I said.

"I don't reckon he made it up. He told it to me just before he died." Willie chattered on. I nodded but didn't listen. I started counting back the days—before the fire, before the roundup. Around about the time someone ruined my windmill we were in Tucson last, was when Rudolfo said he was going all the way to Tempe to see how the price of beef was holding up. I remembered that day. He'd said it was down, dismal low prices. He'd said not to expect more than breaking even. It seemed only right to me that a drought would raise cattle prices due to scarcity, not lower them because of poor beef. Rudolfo was the one who'd suggested the herd be driven only as far as the McDowell feedlots east of Phoenix, instead of all the way to Kansas. Sure thing was, Rudolfo was throwing a lot of greenbacks around, nearly paving the way from my house to his with them.

Out of the clear blue—for I had no idea what he'd just been rambling on about—I said, "So was it Shank started the wildfire, too?"

Willie looked shocked. His mouth opened and closed several times. "Him. And some—some other fellows. Different ones. Dustin and Cole was there. They did most of it. They was only supposed to clear some brush, though. It got away from 'em just that quick." He sounded shaky.

"You had a hand in it, too," I said, certain of it, no matter what he said.

"Yes'm, I did. Only I didn't tie up them sheep. I hate sheep."

"It wasn't about clearing brush, then." Rudolfo Maldonado had it in his mind to own most of the county. If he couldn't buy Baker's land, he'd force off the new owner, especially if the new owner was strapped for cash. And if he couldn't buy mine or burn me off of it, he could marry me for it. It was a small price for him to pay, having a woman around the house. Someone to brush his children's hair. Make them say their prayers. "Go to sleep, Willie. I'm all done talking for now." I was too angry for talking. Too angry for thinking, too.

He started crying again. I told him to hush, and not wake Charlie and Gilbert.

I took down my cleaning kit from a shelf, and opened the action on my shotgun, then slowly and carefully eased the rag through each barrel a few times. As I worked some oil into the stock and polished the action with a little brush, I thought about this terrible summer. When I got the shotgun clean as glass inside and out, I loaded both barrels and left the works open. Willie watched my every move with frightened interest. Maybe he thought I'd use it on him. But I could barely think about Willie anymore; he was going to get his due.

Everything seemed a lot clearer by the time the sun started to green the sky in the east. I had in my mind exactly what I would say to Rudolfo, and what would happen next. When Charlie awoke, I left him watching his prisoner while I went to the smoke house and sliced steaks to feed my family. As I carried the plate back to the kitchen, I thought how we'd eaten some watery beans but never gone hungry. We'd had more and we'd had less. The combination of the bad weather, bad family, and bad neighbors was more trouble than I knew existed. I beat raw eggs into a bowl and stoked the fire tell it was hot. I forked lard into flour and stirred in buttermilk for biscuits. While I worked, I made a plan.

The bad weather, I had no control of. The bad family was being worked on by the law. The bad neighbor, I would set to rights myself.

Chapter Twenty-Four

Gilbert got up, groggy. I made a third pot of coffee. I kept one eye on their prisoner while my boys ate ham steaks and a dozen scrambled eggs, along with hot
biscuits dripping with sorghum. I finished off the pot of coffee with them.
Then we allowed Willie to eat. He got all the same food, but he just picked at a
single biscuit and pushed his eggs around the plate. Seemed he was looking
down the barrel of his fate.

I told the boys about what Willie had said about the well. Willie nodded
through it all, sunk into his chair, his head down, as if he was asleep on his plate,
hiding for shame or fear—I didn't know which. He shook all over. I hadn't slept,
but I wasn't tired. Not one bit. I picked up the shotgun, ran my hands down the
barrel, pushing every stray fleck of dust off it.

My sons eyed each other, then turned toward me. Charlie said, "Mama,
what are you fixing to do?"

Chess came up then, looking disgusted that Willie was still there. I told him
quickly what Willie had told me. Said I had something to say to El Maldonado
that wouldn't wait. I said, "Fixing to pay a call on a neighbor."

"Not without me," Chess said. "Boys?"

"Somebody's got to watch Willie," said Charlie. "Or we could lock him in
the smokehouse. I'd like to get a piece of that son of a gun."

I headed for the door. I didn't care what they did with Willie. I saddled

Baldy, put the rifle in the scabbard. One pocket in my split skirt hung heavy with shotgun shells. The other held the ruby ring and the emerald necklace. I pulled Rudolfo's little filly and the pack horse out of the corral and bridled them in the rigs he'd left for me. I slung the silver saddle on the filly's back loosely and tied one bolt of cloth to each side. Then I stuck a pistol in my waistband and laid the loaded shotgun across my lap.

Gilbert's rig carried a rifle, too, besides the crossed pistol belts around his middle. Chess had lost his aim, but he carried a good length of rope. Charlie filled his responsibility to the territorial government by way of a padlock on the smokehouse door. Willie seemed contrite enough when he was put there.

The four of us rode south by the pale green light of a morning sky, which was heavy as molasses with the night's dew. On our way, I asked about the white mule. Gil said that Willie had told them that story more than once, and it never changed. That the boy had been crazy sick with fear, and clung to that strung-up book when he gave himself up to Charlie. I didn't know what the rest were thinking, but myself, I would think of Esther and her lover and how that connected to Lazrus later. For the present, I rode toward Rudolfo Maldonado's house, planning to murder him before he got his morning shave. The hooves of our horses thundered like war drums.

Men worked in the yard in front of the house. Chickens scattered. A woman under a ramada stoked a fire beneath a *calderón*. I dropped the reins of the gift pony as I passed their yard gate and then approached the front door with my family close behind. With all the wind I owned, I shouted, "Rudolfo Maldonado! We have something to discuss."

Not waiting for an answer, I slung the shotgun from its resting place and fired one barrel at the roof tiles. The shot hit with a hissing crash, and shards of red tile flew like exploding feathers from a bird. Baldy circled and writhed beneath me. People in the yard scattered. Rudolfo appeared at the doorway. I lowered the barrel, keeping it level with his head. Rudolfo was dressed, even to his tie, for breakfast. He ducked behind the heavy door and then peered out with one eye.

"Come out here!" I called. "Come out, Maldonado. Tell these people. I want to know what you would do with a man who poisoned *your* well? What would you order, what kind of punishment?" I raised the shotgun just enough to miss him in the doorway, then took more tiles and a little drooping flag off the top of his house. Red tiles and dust rained down on him, and a man carrying a rifle came from around the corner of the house while I shucked out the shells and reloaded the shotgun. Gilbert trained his rifle on the man, and although the shooter didn't put down the rifle, he held very still. Charlie wheeled his horse in the opposite direction and held his rifle ready.

I shouted, "What does a man deserve who would drive a widow off her land? Starve her cattle? Poison her water? What would you do to a man who did those things, if you were *governor, El* Maldonado?"

Rudolfo pulled the napkin from his collar. He smiled as he waved that white napkin like a surrendering flag before he spoke. "Sarah? It is you? And you've brought your family. Come inside and let us talk." He smiled, all charm and smoothness; he had that flat look to his face, and the edgy, nervous eyes. He laughed and said to no one particularly, *"¿Cervesa anoche?"* Clucking, nervous laughs came from peons in the yard who gathered next to the well and fence posts. Rudolfo stepped off his porch and came about two feet closer. He repeated, "Come inside, Sarah. Don't make yourself look foolish. Please." He edged toward me, the handkerchief fluttering. I leveled the shotgun at him, and the expression in his eyes turned serious.

Chess rode his horse nose-to-nose with mine, but he kept silent. The boys were on the ground now, guarding our backs. I said, "I would be completely justified if I cut you in half with this. No jury in the Territory would convict me of other than killing vermin."

Rudolfo held up his hands and smiled. He said, "What insult have I made to deserve this from my future wife?"

I pulled the box with the necklace in it from my right pocket. I threw that box toward him. It opened in midair, the baubles crashing against the adobe wall behind him. A few sparkling stones came loose and scattered across the porch, mixing with the crumbs of red tile. I threw the ring in the dirt at his feet. "You'll not take my land that easily, even if I have to drop you where you stand. Come out here, where I can see you clear. Get out here, or the next one goes through the window."

Rudolfo seemed truly alarmed. "My daughters are in there."

"Then get your sorry hide out in the yard."

As he took one more step, a loop of rope dropped around him faster than a snake striking. Chess held fast to the other end, which was tied to his saddle horn. He backed his horse, pulling Rudolfo off balance. He tripped and scuffed up dust, trying to stand. Rudolfo gasped and said, "You cannot mean to harm me, Sarah. After we've been friends for years. Let's be reasonable. Señor Chess, speak to her. Reason with her."

Chess said, "If she don't shoot you, I plan to hang you. You can't poison a well and think you can get away with it. Not while I'm breathing."

I rode closer to Rudolfo. White-hot anger boiled under my ribs and I shook when I said, "Friends for years? Why, Señor Maldonado, I mean no more harm to you than you did to my stock. No more than you were willing to do to me." I leapt down from the horse, pulled the pistol from my waistband, and, walking toward him, aimed it at Rudolfo's chest. I pointed the shotgun in the general direction of the man still holding the rifle. That fellow hadn't moved, waiting, I reckon, on Gilbert to flinch.

A child's voice came from the house "Papa?" Magdalena stood in the doorway.

Rudolfo pleaded. "You would not make her watch her father murdered, would you? Sarah? I can make it up to you. All is not lost. We will be wealthy, you and I. What is one windmill when you can have five hundred sections to call your own?"

Magdalena cried, wailing, "Papa, Papa!"

"Gilbert? Charlie?" I called. "What's around us?"

Charlie said, "There're two by the house there, one on the roof. Another in the barn. Thinks we don't see him."

Chess hollered, "Boys, take your aim off *los guardias* and sight in on the *hacendado* there. No matter what happens, no matter what anyone does, he dies first."

"Yes sir, Grampa," voices said behind me. I seethed. Chess was an old soldier, all right. Hired hands gathered. Women, too.

Rudolfo's eyes grew wide, and a tear slid from one of them. He said, "Sarah, please, be reasonable." Chess's horse backed, causing Rudolfo to stumble toward me a few steps. He said, "I wanted it for us. Please, not in front of my daughters. At least let me send someone to get them away from the windows."

As I bit back tears, suddenly my chin hurt. No, I would not kill a father in front of his child. I'd seen my own papa shot, only to watch him die a few days later. I gritted my teeth and said, "Admit it. You paid someone to tear up my windmill and poison it."

He started to protest. I drew aim with the pistol and pulled back the hammer. He said, "You wouldn't listen to me. I had to convince you that you needed to marry to be safe. How long can you live there, once your sons leave and your old men die?"

"Say it!" I screamed.

"It was a bad—terrible—decision. I can't undo it. It didn't seem so bad then, but I—I—am—truly—sorry. I only want to marry you, Sarah. *Quierria*—"

"*¡Mentiras!*" It was true. I'd expected to pull the trigger. I'd had it in my mind that the minute he admitted it, he'd die. Pain clenched my shoulders, and I was filled with an unexpected sorrow that brought along with it a feeling of holding some kind of terrible power over this man—even more if I let him live. Rudolfo was a big fellow by anyone's measure, though now he seemed ought but pitiful and small. I lowered my voice and said softly, "Nothing you say will undo what you did. You had your men start that fire to burn out Hanna's place, too. They should be hung for doing it, and hung again for letting it get away from them—but to spoil water in this land, to ruin a well in a drought, it takes a certain kind of snake to do that. Marry you? I have no intention of sleeping with snakes." I looked down the barrel, once more squaring up the sight. Rudolfo's face was ruddy and his eyes glared as if he had a fever. I really wanted to pull that trigger. I held my breath. Sweat rolled from his head, more tears from his eyes. All at once, I lowered the pistol. I whistled the little two-note call we trained our stock to. Chess's horse stepped forward and the rope slackened. "And another thing. Cut around my property when you go to town from now on. Take the north fork from your place, and don't set foot on my land. If that makes your trip longer, use the time to pray your children don't take after you, for your old age will be a misery and a torment. Sow to the wind and reap the whirlwind, Rudolfo." Putting the weapon back in my waistband, I turned to mount Baldy. At that instant, I saw the man at the corner of the house raising the rifle to his shoulder. I didn't know which of us he was aiming for, but I whirled around and pointed the shotgun straight at Rudolfo again. I jerked my head in the direction of the man. Rudolfo pulled Chess's rope over his head, put up his hand, and the rifle went down. The man with the rifle whistled a signal to shooters hidden in the yard. I leapt into the saddle, Chess hauled in his line, and Gilbert held the rifle upon his thigh. Charlie kept his pistol drawn, aimed it back and forth. We rode away without looking back.

In a few minutes, the sun rose over the distant hills. Rays of light split through the distant peaks and scattered clouds like those painted fingers from heaven, spreading across the land. We stopped where the trail turned south toward Udell's place. The marker we used, even when it was Baker's land, was an ocotillo, fifteen or more feet tall, its branches twenty feet wide. It was prospering from the recent rain and was covered with leaves, hiding the treacherous thorns along its bark. We circled our horses under it.

Chess said, "We still should have hung him."

Gilbert had an angry glare in his eyes as he said, "There were at least three vaqueros in that yard. You were right, Grampa, about taking him down first. He'd never let that happen. I say we go back and hang him, now."

I said, "That won't change things. What we need to do is go after Esther, now that we know where they are."

"Mama?" Charlie said, "that place Willie's talking about is only about two or three hours away. Where we first caught up with him was Galena all right, but it was a running gun battle all the way up, and a storm spooked the cattle north of Bisbee. By the time the kid was alone, he was kneeling in the mud of the San Pedro between Fairbank and Charleston, barefoot and praying. We dragged him the long way around from Sierra Vista because he and his gang raised such a ruckus here, we'd never have gotten him this far without him stretching a rope. I've got to head to town."

Gil straighted and looked toward the south, saying, "Yeah, but it's only two hours from here. We can get to her and back by sundown."

Chess leaned toward Gilbert. "Spare me one of them pistols, boy."

Gilbert followed orders. "Here, Grampa," he said.

"You're not going without me," I said.

Charlie said, "Mama, I'm telling you. Don't come. We'll find Esther."

Chess's horse stirred, and he ended up facing me. He said, "Listen to your son there. Prines'll be home tomorrow. We'll see if she's all right. If she wants to come home, we'll bring her."

"Take my horse, then," I said. "You will need something for Esther to ride. Take my pistol, Gilbert."

Gilbert said, "Don't need it, Mama."

Chess said, "Your ma's right. Take it." To me, he said, "Think Hanna will get you home?"

I told him, "It doesn't matter. I've walked it before."

My sons and my father-in-law rode into a rocky draw that hid them from sight, though I could hear hooves for a little while. Below where I stood, Udell Hanna's tiny house lay in morning shadows. I started walking toward it. I didn't want a ride home so much as a man to talk to, someone I felt I could trust. I found him kneeling by a fire pit in the yard, watching something in an iron skillet.

Udell looked up curiously at me, coming on foot out of nowhere. He stood. He eyed the shotgun in my hand and said, "G'morning, Mrs. Elliot."

"Morning, Mr. Hanna."

"I heard some shooting. Were you hunting?"

"Rudolfo Maldonado poisoned my well," I said. "Burned your sheep to death."

He frowned, Rubbed at his lips with the back of one hand. Scratched the back of his neck. Finally, he said, "I suspected. I did at that. You teach him some respect for his neighbors' property?"

My face flushed hot and my lips tightened as I tried not to cry. "I shot his roof to pieces. I wanted to—meant to kill him."

Udell's arm circled my shoulders. He took the shotgun from my hands and cocked it open, then laid it carefully against a post. "Any man would have done the same thing. Shot *him*, I mean. Not his roof."

I laughed a little, and then all the pain and anger boiled over inside and I bowed and wept into my hands. Udell held me, and we rocked back and forth. He didn't say "Hush, now," or "Don't cry; it'll be all right," or any of the useless things people are inclined to say to someone sorrowing. He said, "Are you hungry? I caught a trout."

He bade me sit on a seat he'd drawn up—a box any other time. He had one plate and two forks. He split that little trout in half, raking meat from the bones. It was a tiny morsel for a hungry man, and he shared it with me, bite for bite. Every fragment of it tasted so good, I told him I'd never known a trout done better. Then he took the plate and forks and washed them himself.

He brought me a cup of coffee. He'd put sugar in it. Usually, I didn't waste the sugar in coffee, but it surely tasted fine. I reckoned he was trying to make it special. We sipped it slowly. The coffee was gone before he said softly, "Believe I'll be moving those cattle back up to your place, then."

"You are not like any man I have ever known," I said.

"I loved my wife," he said. "I don't think she ever knew how much. No. I'm sure of it. She never knew. I wasted a lot of time being proud. Made up my mind to do things different here on out."

I finished my coffee, then said, "I'd do a lot of things differently if I could, too."

"Your life's not over, Sarah."

I shook my head and said, "I feel as if I'm standing on the brink, slipping in sand." Lord a mercy. Had I really been counting on Rudolfo, somewhere in the back of my mind, to rescue me from the drought? Udell extended his hand across the space between us, palm up, and waited. He was so patient, so certain that

I would do it, I had to smile a little as I took his hand. His fingers closed around mine, gentle and strong together. Calloused, soft. I wanted to find strength there, safety, the way I'd let myself believe Jack kept me. But I knew that Udell could also slip away. Tire of my company, like Jimmy. Betray, like Rudolfo. Die, like Jack. I loosened my grip. I didn't need any more dying. I'd seen enough. Maybe that was why I couldn't really shoot Rudolfo, though heaven knows he deserved it. Just couldn't look upon another headstone.

Udell held on tighter. "Right now," he said. "Don't look down. Keep seeing the here and now. This is what you've got. It's all we've got. Any of us."

I put my other hand on top of his, and he clasped both mine in his. It was the second time in my life I'd felt as if I were being held to the earth by the strength of a man's hands. It got harder to draw a breath, and I felt tired down to the depths of my bones.

"I'm going home," I said, "and rest. I was up all night. Then I put in a busy morning, what with killing all that tile."

Udell smirked. He said, "He's lucky you are such a good shot."

"I planned to kill him."

"I know you did. It would have been the usual thing to do. I've heard from more than one person hereabouts that if you aim at something, it's as good as shot. I'll ride you home. Wait while I saddle up. My horse'll take two."

I unloaded the shotgun while he saddled the horse. The shotgun wouldn't fit in a scabbard, so I had to carry it in one hand, sitting—all but in his lap—on the saddle. We went slowly because of the extra weight, although the horse was nearly the size of Big Boy and probably could have kept up just fine.

Udell kept the reins in his left hand; his right hand, he laid gently against my side. As we rode the uneven path, as far wide of Rudolfo's house as possible, now and again my back touched his chest. As we neared the last rise before my house came into view, I said, "What was I thinking? I must have lost my mind."

"Making the man pay for poisoning your cattle? Sounds reasonable to me."

"It isn't like I never—I nearly shot someone I used to think of as a friend."

"You didn't. A woman ought to have a level of mercy."

"He did all those things so I'd be forced to marry him, because I'd have lost so many cattle."

"Mutual affection being a silly reason to marry these days."

I turned and tried to peer over my shoulder at him. "I suppose I was hoping there was a little affection and a measure of respect," I said.

Udell's legs pushed against mine as he spurred the horse up the knoll. "I was hoping there was *very* little affection, myself. Or am I equally mistaken?"

Baffling questions seemed to hang in the air whenever I was with Udell. I said, "There was a little, once. Not—not the kind I felt for Jack. Just a practical kind of friendship."

"Never heard of that kind of friendship." The horse stepped in a little dip and rocked us forward. Udell wrapped his arm right around my middle and squeezed me to him. Then he loosed his hold. After awhile he said, "Sarah? Is there any possibility—I mean, could—" He took a deep breath before continuing. "I had a hard time placing you with Maldonado. Not because I had aught against him before now, but I couldn't figure you as a matched team. What I'm asking is, did I only take advantage of your fainting the other day? Or is it possible you feel—What I mean is, now there's no promise between you and him, would you be inclined to let me call on you? *Call,* that is."

He sounded so formal. "There was never a promise," I said. "If he told you that, he lied." The horse's hooves clopped along. After awhile, I teased him a little, saying, "I believe I do feel inclined to that prospect, sir."

When we reached my yard, Udell got down and said, "I'm not sorry I kissed you, you know." He held up his hands for me, setting me lightly on the ground.

Standing so close to him, his hands still on my waist, I said, "I'm not sorry you kissed me, either." Then we strolled toward the house, not touching each other, although I could still feel the warm impression of his hands.

Udell said he'd drive up the eleven herd of cattle wearing my brand. Seven of them were heifers, the rest yearling steers.

I said, "You keep those. The boys brought back ten more. One's a champion bull. Next year, you send those girls home after they give you a little herd of your own."

After a minute's thought, Udell said, "You'd give away half of all you own, just to keep a promise?"

I hadn't been thinking of them as half of a whole twenty head. I'd been thinking of them as ten out of eight hundred. Odd how the same cows seemed more sacrifice the way he put it. I looked hard at Udell and said, "I don't promise things I won't stand to."

He said, "Promise you'll get a little rest now? You look exhausted."

"I will," I said. We drew into each other's arms at the same time, and his lips touched mine sweetly and gently. Then he also kissed the tip of my nose before he turned and settled his hat on his head. He mounted the horse and waved, whistling as he rode out of sight. Immediately, I ached for his company.

I walked up to the graveyard. There by Jack's grave, I knelt. I surveyed my house and the barn and all. That was when I saw it, nestled along the rock border. Tufts of green. The sweetgrass was returning. It would be a long time before the hills would sustain cattle, but if I had to feed only ten, why, I could make it. We could last until calving season. It was more than we'd come here with, and it would do.

I pulled weeds from graves, starting with that of my two-year-old girl, Suzanne. Paloverde sprouts were everywhere. A bit of stinkweed had taken hold by one of the unnamed soldiers' mounds. I never pulled that stuff without gloves, so I had to let it lie. As I worked, I thought of my sons and Chess going south. Reckon any mother could find reason enough to worry about that, but I saw them differently right then. They were men with their own minds and skills.

I'd done all right by them. Chess had nailed it right through the bull's-eye, telling me I was choking them with my apron strings. They were grown, and I'd have to let them go. I resolved to myself right then and there that they would catch up to Esther. And if they didn't, it couldn't be done. The world would be a bit better off, having my men in it. Then my eyes settled on the smokehouse. I'd clean forgotten Willie! Oh my heavens. I dropped the weeds and headed toward the place.

The smokehouse was a pretty miserable place to enter, much less sit for several hours. I had an idea to take Willie to the house and tie him to the porch rail. Then I remembered how easily he'd broken it. Even in his bare feet, the boy was big and strong. The barn had two posts made of tree trunks holding up its center beam. Those posts were at least thirty feet high, and they had been sunk six feet into the ground when this barn was built. There was no way a fellow could get over or around one, if he was caught to it good enough. I laid a circle with my mind, ten feet in all directions, and took away every tool, every lamp, even a dropped horseshoe nail, leaving nothing but the straw on the floor.

I pulled the hopsack bag that held Mr. Sparky's remains off the headstone waiting for me in the barn. As I did, I felt a hard twinge of guilt. Gilbert had been right. I'd wasted money on that stone, money I'm sorely longing for now, as I longed for what the stone meant when I did it. Foolishness. Savannah was right. The worst sin most decent people have is foolishness, and sometimes they don't even see it until they have to raise the claptrap and dust off their folly, looking for something they need far more. Tucked behind the stone, where I couldn't accidentally run across it and give myself torment, sat an unpainted wooden box of Jack's things.

There was an old army-issue bridle bit in there, wire twists, odd pieces I had never had use for on the ranch. I raised the lid carefully, checking for spiders and scorpions, and found what I wanted: two sets of army leg irons, the kind they used to use on prisoners in the stockade. In one corner, next to a broken whetstone and a leather awl, lay the key that opened them. I worked some axle grease into the irons and wiped them down. Then I called Nip to come with me while I carried the irons to the little window in the adobe smokehouse. I called out, "Willie, how are you doing in there?"

"All right, I reckon. It's sorta hard to breathe, Aint Sair."

"You want to sit in the barn instead?"

"All right."

I said, "Put these on your feet and tighten them up good." I pulled the bug netting off the slit of a window and pushed one set of leg irons through. I heard some fumbling and the rattle of chains. I said, "I'll be waiting for you with a shotgun. Don't think I won't wing you if I need to, boy."

"Yes, ma'am. I'm ready."

I unlocked the padlock and swung the door open, stepping back as I did, ready with the shotgun. I said, "Come on out." The boy came, his hands over his eyes. Nip, seeing Willie, raised his hackles and growled low. I said, "You got those tight? Hook your foot over that rock there and give it a tug. Now the other one." When I was satisfied he was caught, I marched him to the barn. Nip stayed close at my side, growling threats the entire time. There, the other set of irons lay on the floor, wrapped around one of the posts. "Link that one with the ones you're wearing," I said.

As Willie obeyed, he chuckled and said, "I smell like a ham dinner."

"Yes, you do," I said. That humor was his papa's for sure. There was that much of Ernest in him.

Willie said, "Aint Sair? Kin I ask you something?"

"Go ahead."

"How come you didn't just marry Maldoraedo? He'da give you the money and the cows."

"Because my self-respect is worth more than any amount of money."

"My ma would a married him. Shoot, she'd marry anybody with twenty dollars. Sometimes the barkeep did the wedding."

"I'm not your mother, Willie."

"Naw, you ain't."

"You going to be all right out here?"

"Yes'm."

I jerked on the leg irons. Those blessed big feet would not be able to slip through. "I'll be watching you from the house. I can see any move you make."

"I ain't leaving, Aint Sair."

A rattling noise out in the yard made me turn. A little Mexican two-wheeled buggy pulled up. Luz and Magdalena Maldonado were in the front seat. A white handkerchief flapped from the buggy whip Magdalena waved as if it were a flag in a parade. The pretty filly was tied to the back, her saddle and bridle still in place. I pushed the barn door halfway shut and anchored it with a chunk of wood we always kept there. No sense having to explain why I'd got this boy chained to the post.

Luz drove the cart closer to me. She looked around nervously. Her face paled and her lips quivered as she said, "Señora Elliot, Papa told us to bring back your horse. He wants to make it up to you, he said. He owes you much for the property you lost. Please accept this horse, he says. Please take it. He wants to be friends again."

"I don't want it."

Luz said, "The priest from the mission has been staying at our house, waiting to perform a marriage. Papa talked with him for an hour. The priest says he must make it all up to you, or he will never win the election. He will repay you tenfold, he said."

The election? Leave it to children to deliver a message too honestly. They hadn't yet learned to crawl on their bellies like their sidewinder of a father. I said, "Go on home, girls. There's nothing your papa has that I need. And quit bringing that animal here. You're teaching it the way to my house."

Luz looked disappointed, but relieved. She turned the little trap around. As it circled, Magdalena leaned out, smiled cheerfully, and waved. "Señora Elliot?" the girl called, "Leta Cujillo is going to be our *mamacita* now. Will you come to our wedding party?" Luz snapped that whip before I needed to answer, and the filly raised dust. Magdalena's voice faded, although she was still chirping. "I get to have two new dresses!"

Over the next hour, I sat with Willie, who slept stretched out on the dirt floor as if it were a feather bed. Clouds to the south rose and rose again. No matter. I thought of the grass in the graveyard. In the midst of the clouds, darkness began to grow, and in the darkness, lightning flashed like sparks behind a cloth. More rain coming meant more sweetgrass. I thought of the cattle Charlie had brought home. I had yet to see them. Once Willie was headed to town and no longer in my charge, I'd ride up and get a look. When the boy was sound asleep, I left him.

I fed the corral horses. Petted Rose and Hunter, who now came and nuzzled at my pockets, the source of apples and carrots. The clouds hovered closer, blocking out the mountains south of here. Looking at that sky, I thought if my fellows got caught up in some rain, I might not see them until tomorrow. Just for good measure, I led Rose and Hunter into the farthest stalls, safe and dark. Dan and Maize got the next ones over. I even made a place for Baldy, although he held his ears back nervously, for he'd only been in the barn for new shoes, not for any kind of weather.

All the commotion woke Willie. I told him I was going to the house, and he looked mighty worried. For half a second, I weighed whether or not to have him back in the house or simply close the barn door and save him from the rain. I'd promised Charlie to keep an eye on his prisoner. I didn't want to wait out the storm in the barn, nor did I want to march Willie to the house, where I wouldn't be able to keep him tied as tight. In the end, he decided a little shower wouldn't hurt the smell of him, and a little wind might just dry him off. "Besides," he said, "I won't be as scared if I can see you're watchin' me from in there."

Dark clouds gathered lower to the ground, and thunder tore across the sky without any lightning beforehand. Right up from the south it rumbled, though it wasn't dropping any rain yet. It came like a live animal, reaching far into the heavens. Then, like one I'd seen years back, the middle of it turned a likesome shade of blue. I knew that blue wasn't sky; it was water—a great pool of water carried up in the sky like a floating trough.

It was bearing straight toward my place. Nip and Shiner circled each other in the yard, barking. The air got heavy. So damp and hot and still, it pulled the lights out of a person. Unearthly quiet. Nip barked, dancing around me as I stared upward. Blackness covered half the sky, and the other half seemed clear and blue and perfectly at ease. I moved toward the porch, casting a glance over my shoulder at Willie. A drumming boomed from the midst of the stormy heavens. The noise rolled louder and louder. I watched overhead.

"Nip! Shiner!" I called, though I couldn't hear my own voice. Shiner headed for the barn. Nip tried to run past me, but I caught him by the scruff and pulled him into the house. I stood in the parlor with the dog in my arms. Nip whined from pure fear, as if he was in pain. The roaring came, sounding all at once like stampeding cattle, like tumbling water, or a freight train charging through town on a still night. The house shook when the first gust of wind hit. The dog yelped. Holding tightly to him, afraid of what the storm might be driving this way, I went to the kitchen. From the window, all was dark, then light. I heard a bang and peeked out the window, only to see another gust blow the barn door shut. I had to keep an eye on Willie! Nip struggled.

"Stay, boy," I said.

I heard a loud crack, just like when Willie'd broken the porch rail. I pictured him somehow mustering the strength to splinter the barn's post. At that second, hail slammed into the side of the house, clear up under the porch. The glass in the window cracked in two places but stayed in its frame.

Another, louder crack of thunder was followed by a grinding, screeching noise, like a train putting on its brakes too hot, and then a sound like the trampling sound of hooves sent shivers up my spine. I looked toward the barn, expecting to see Willie hightailing it out of there, but instead, I saw the cause of the drumming sound. Boards from my house were flying across the yard and beating against the barn door. If it had stayed open, Willie would surely have been beaten to death by them. Shiner, too. I turned around in the kitchen just as wind tore the glass from its frame. It hit my arm and cheek, cutting me before it fell to the floor. Then the whole kitchen ceiling raised up before my eyes, as if the house were giving a giant sigh, and fell in. Rain pummeled me. Nip squirmed.

I dragged him with me under the kitchen table. Holding the frantic dog, I couldn't get all the way under the table. Hail beat against my back, bruising me, as if the rocks of ice had been thrown deliberately at me. Rain poured around us. My arm flowed with blood. I buried my face in Nip's neck, murmuring reassurances to him. "Stay, boy. We're going to be all right, boy. No, no, don't run. Stay with me, boy." The water with the hail in it was freezing cold. The rain fell so hard that in less than a minute I was kneeling in an inch-deep pool, then a two-inch one. I gasped for air. There was another, cracking sound, even louder this time. The house shuddered. The floor moved as if it were on wheels. It gave way under me and dropped at an angle, flopping up mud and bits of branches and slop from under the foundation. The table came down upon us and was pinned by a heavy weight; it was held up from crushing the dog and me by a single leg caught at an angle.

The roaring sound and hail were replaced by the sizzling of rain, falling hard. I tried to budge the table by lifting straight up, using my back under the flat of it, my legs to shove upward. Nothing moved. We were caught at an angle. The smells of wet dog and old mouse nests filled the drenched air, made me choke. I let go of Nip. He scrambled through the cocked boards to freedom, and I followed him, wedging myself through the angle where the tabletop met those floorboards that had stayed in place. Once out from under the table, I could see right through the kitchen ceiling.

Overhead, gray sky was filled with starlike drops of rain that came straight downward. I followed Nip over the uneven floor to the bedroom. He hid under my bed. Thank heaven there was still a ceiling in there. Hail pelted the windows, hard as gravel. I sat on the bed, shaking all over. At least it isn't coming through the roof! I told myself. No sooner had I thought that than I noticed a bulging over my armoire, as if the ceiling were a blanket full of hay. I stood to run from the room. I'd just gotten to the door when the paper-mat ceiling came down in a gush. It splashed so hard, it knocked me on my backside into the parlor. I struggled to my feet. Water whirled around my ankles. "Nip?" I called.

The dog whined. I knew he was alive, but he wouldn't come out from under the bed. Lightning creased the sky outside, followed by deafening thunder. The rain softened. Then, as if the sky had taken a deep breath to let loose its full fury, rain dropped on the house, not like a shower or a storm, but as if a great river had suddenly been directed from on high to a waterfall right into my parlor.

I knelt on my bed just to stay off the floor, though the quilts held water like sponges. Rustling and thrashing came from beneath the bed and Nip struggled out of there. I caught him by the scruff again and hauled him up on the bed with me, where we both shivered in the rain for many minutes.

It quit the way it had started, without much warning, without tapering, just quit. A good four inches of water swirled around the floor in the bedroom and flowed toward the sunken floor in the kitchen. Over the fireplace, a small part of the roof held, and the box I kept Jack's watch in remained, too, wet but otherwise untouched on the mantel.

I trudged through the water, which flowed muddy and thick around my ankles, trying to see what I could save, where I could put things. Lightning snapped from every corner of heaven just then, and the thunder meeting in the middle, right over my head, drowned out my thoughts.

I pulled Granny's quilt from the frame in the parlor. It was wet through and through, but I folded it anyway and laid it on a chair. I took Harland's picture painting to keep safe it for him, placing it into the armoire, cramming it hard against my clothes in there.

I climbed over a slanted section of boards and under what had been the doorway to the sleeping porch. When my first husband, Jimmy, had built this place, he constructed a great square-framed roof over the floor, then just filled in the spaces with walls. The whole wall across the back was stove in, leaning at various angles.

Broken sunlight made the mess glow and steam. I had to see if Willie had lived through it. I walked around the side of the house and gasped when I saw the yard between the house and the barn. Boards of all sizes were scattered across the yard, tumbled and broken. Some were twisted up like straws, the dry old beams ripped in half. Squares of whole roof had been ripped from their places like discarded quilt squares that didn't match. One made a perfect lean-to against the corral fence, just large enough for a big dog to get inside. Most of the rest of it resembled a picture I'd seen once of a logjam in a river.

I found out soon enough that some of the boards still had nails in them, and though they were old, they were still sharp. Before I got across the yard, the sunlight closed up and rain fell again. A pile of lumber held the barn door closed. Dents and broken places scarred the big oak door, but it had held. I pried the lumber loose one piece at a time, moving sometimes just an inch before seeing I had to move something else to get to the one that was held. The rain started to pour down, though not as hard as before, and not cold rain, but warm. At last, I got two pieces free and managed to wedge the door open enough to force myself inside.

I hollered, "Willie? You all right?"

"Yes'm, Aint Sair. That lightning done yet? Heck of a storm, weren't it?"

I wanted to slap him. But I was relieved that he wasn't hurt, and equally relieved that he wasn't gone. I said, "Is Shiner in here?"

"Yes'm. I hate lightning. Always have. Feels like God is coming after me."

I stared at him for a minute. My house was torn asunder. Just like that house sitting off its foundation, my whole life was wrenched apart. If God was coming after Willie, His almighty aim was off. The horses whimpered and whinnied. They were nervous and scared, but they were safe, too. I could have used Willie's help, but I decided just to leave him be. I said, "I'm going to leave the door shut, to keep you out of the rain. You stay put, boy."

"Yes'm."

He was safe enough. Drier and cleaner than I might ever be again. I squeezed back through the slit of a door. I gritted my teeth, tripping back across the twisted pile of lumber toward the house. Nip was not to be found, but I was beyond fretting. All I could hope for was that he'd found a place to hide, as he had during the stampede.

Inside, I found Gilbert's room and changed my soggy shoes for a pair of my son's old boots. They hadn't fit Gil in awhile, and with a wad of paper, I could get them to stay on my feet. Gilbert's room didn't seem too bad off. The room that had been April's and was now Granny's had collapsed and ankle-deep water was everywhere, just like my bedroom. A single old housedress hanging from a nail was shredded and soaked. Granny's few possessions, she'd taken with her to Chicago.

Charlie's room was caved in just like the kitchen. The wall where he had tacked at least two dozen pictures of flying machines, horseless carriages, and bicycle machines was off-kilter and leaning over his bed. I couldn't move his highboy dresser, which was protecting its contents better than if I'd emptied it.

The table we'd hidden under in the kitchen was the fancy one Jack had bought us. Its top was cracked down the middle and part of the kitchen's south wall rested on it. The stove had keeled over onto the uneven floorboards, and I was instantly thankful that the fire had gone out long before this. Not that I thought anything could burn, I suppose, just because I'd always had a fear of leaving coals glowing in anything that could tip over. There had been jars of food in the pantry, foodstuffs we'd need to get us through the winter. Broken glass was everywhere. The contents of the broken jars mixed with mud, and filth covered it all. Mice scampered across the boards and up the walls. I had only two dozen jars of preserves left. Not a single pottery bowl was left whole. Three plates and the cast-iron skillets had survived. The coffeepot was hammered flat, pinned under the stove.

Thunder rumbled in the far distance. Rain, thick as a curtain, beat down, then stopped, as if some great hand had simply quit working the water pump. Outside, I took stock of the house. The rocks forming the foundation were in their places. One corner of the house had moved northward nearly six inches.

The south wall leaned in, stable on one side, where it crossed the kitchen and Charlie's bedroom, only teetering in place where it formed my bedroom wall.

As if Providence was satisfied that I'd seen the show and the curtain could be pulled again, rain began anew. The trough that sat by the side of the house to water visitors' horses had turned on its side. I sat there heaven knows how long, watching my house fall apart. April and Charlie had been born in that house, in that very room where my bed was now open to the rain. Jimmy had died right there, too. The grain of those walls held memories of sounds that screamed from the wood as parts buckled and bent, forced down by the weight of the beams that remained. They were the cries of newborn babes. Tears of heartbreak. Moans of ecstasy. Shouts of happiness. Arguments. Lullabies. The hiss of boiling-over beans on the stove. The crackle of a fire in winter, the setting with my feet curled up under me and Jack beside me. The gentle leafing of the pages of— Oh Lord! My books!

I stood before the bookcase, which held the singular possession I regarded with secret greed so powerful, I'd be ashamed for anyone to know of it. One hundred and seventy-one volumes of all shapes and sizes were arranged there. Some I hadn't read in years; some I'd read again and again. Every last one of them had been soaked to the core. Opening them would destroy them, and leaving them would doom them equally. Rain poured through the open roof. My heart crumbled. Books are made with glue and leather and paper, and none of those last in water. I sank to the floor and leaned against the bookshelf. I didn't weep. The destruction was too complete. I just sighed again and again, holding to the bookcase, watching water gushing off my books.

"Sarah!" I heard a man cry. I didn't answer—couldn't open my mouth. The voice cried out again. Udell Hanna came around the side of the house, running toward me. He stopped short, looked at me as if he were stunned, then stepped closer, slowly climbing over boards and overturned furniture.

"Sarah?" he said, kneeling in water. "Are you hurt?"

"No," I said, though I felt sore and pained, as if I'd been run over by a locomotive. "There's nothing left. It's gone."

He took my hands, looking hard at the blood on my arm. "But you're all right?"

"Willie's in the barn. He's fine."

"I came to see if the storm hit. I saw the tail of it but couldn't see if it touched down anywhere. It doesn't take much tornado to wreck a place."

"I've had some of these books since I was a girl."

"Let me see your neck there. What cut you? Do you remember?"

"I'm cold," I said. "My books are gone. Every last one."

He took both my hands as if I were some addled child. He said, "Sarah?"

"You don't understand. These are my books."

Udell pulled me to his chest and held me, rubbing my arms with his hands. I shivered against him, but his touch felt foreign, painful. I pushed him away. I couldn't stand anyone or anything touching me. I got up, pretending not to notice his outstretched hand and his confused expression. I reckon a woman ought want to fall into some fellow's arms and be comforted, but at that moment, I wanted nothing like it. Every fiber of me hurt in some way or other. I turned away, too, from the sight of those drenched books. "Will you help me see if my stove is racked? It's busted up. I want a fire. I'm cold." The shaking, which had been a tremble before, now overwhelmed me, and I shook so hard, my teeth rattled.

His eyes questioned, but he nodded and followed me. We pulled on the stove, tugged on the wall. He said he'd have to hitch his horse to the boards and pull them off, and he told me to stand back from it.

I watched that wall rise and crash down the other way as his big team moved it. When the weight holding it shifted, the stove rolled. A big crack in the iron side of it showed me it would never be of use again. Ashes poured out and lay atop the water like a slick of grease, curling around in eddies as the water flowed between the slanted boards.

I could see Udell working to unfasten the team from the wall. I looked at the tilted floor, the cracked glass, the broken table with its fancy carved legs, only one of which had remained whole. That one leg had saved Nip and me from being crushed by the stove and the wall. Jack had bought me that table. Had it shipped from Cincinnati. If there was, by gum, only one leg of it left, I wanted it.

I tugged at the wooden leg. Put my back into it. Strained and groaned, using every fiber I had, the same way I'd struggled to save Gilbert from the moving blades of the windmill. It tore loose, and I crashed against an overturned chair. Then I started to sob, not weep, exactly, for I was so wet, I couldn't tell if there were tears. I took that table leg in my arms and beat it against the stove. I pounded the flue pipe flat where it was still round. Stomped it with my foot. Banged the table leg at the edge of the counter where the water pump stood. The counter collapsed and only the pump handle, suspended on a pipe, stayed in place. The rain quit falling, but water dripped from every surface.

My hair fell around my shoulders. I said, "Udell? What's left of your place?"

"Didn't even get rain down there."

I felt stupid and insincere. "I'm glad. All I've got left is a barn."

"Your house can be rebuilt."

I felt as if I couldn't draw a whole breath. I held my ribs with my arms. Panting, I said, "I'm done. I've been wondering just how much I could take, and I just found my fence line. I don't ever want to look at this place again. When what's left of it dries out, I'm going to burn it to the ground. Move to town. Go to tea parties."

"I brought my wagon. We'll load your stuff up and carry it to the barn, where it will dry out and be safe until you get rebuilt."

I didn't have the strength to argue with him. I did what he said, moved where he pointed. Together, we carried things that felt as if they belonged to someone else, things I had no part of or ever wanted to. Heavy books made heavier by water left stains on my arms from the colored leather bindings. We hauled them to his wagon, and he piled up torn lumber so that the wagon could move the hundred feet or so to the barn.

Willie hid his head and stayed silent when he saw Udell open the door. We unloaded the highboy, a chest of drawers, things from the heavy armoire, and then the armoire itself. We moved beds out there, then hung the wet blankets and sheets over them to dry out. We stacked everything savable, and it all fit into two empty stalls. Udell cleared off the feed table where I'd mixed up Hunter's baby food, then placed books there one at a time. Then we strung forty lines of fine wire across from the table to the wall in rows of twos. He opened each of my books and then hung them one by one over two wires, dividing the pages by thirds, so air could get to them. I'd never have thought of that: a clothesline for books. Still, I doubted whether any could be saved. I couldn't stand to look at them, so I turned my head, even as I thanked him for the effort.

When that was done, we went toward the house, out of Willie's sight, and sat side by side to rest on the overturned trough. Udell held my hand. I shook all over. My body felt bruised from top to toe. After a bit, he put his arm around my waist. It didn't pain me as it had before. I leaned against his shoulder. I didn't cry. There weren't any tears bigger than the rain that had already fallen. I'd been so worried about hanging on to this place. All I could do was hold to his arm and sigh again and again.

"Sarah," he said. "You've been mucking through some awful filth."

"I smell pretty rough," I said.

"No, I'm talking about sepsis. You need a hot scrub on all those scratches and cuts. In the war, it was more often the mud than the bullet that killed a man."

"How am I going to light a fire?"

"Down at my place. Where it barely dropped a teaspoonful of rain."

Udell drove me to his one-room house. He started a big fire outside, where he'd cooked before, and laid over it his coffeepot, a washtub, and a copper kettle. Even the frying pan was used to boil as much water as it would hold. Udell ferried all the pans of steaming water to the doorway, showed me to a clean shirt and a pair of Aubrey's trousers, then left me alone in the house. All the while, I wondered what I'd do. Where I'd sleep. How I'd put a roof over my boys, my father-in-law, and my own mama. Up at Granny's, likely.

Across from the washtub, Udell had built a bed. I sat on the edge of it while I pulled dry stockings up over my scratched feet and ankles. They were fine stockings. Store-boughten, too. Looked expensive. Maybe he'd been accustomed to money, long ago. Left it behind with his dead wife and children. After all, somebody'd paid for Aubrey to go to lawyer college. I made a face, pulling Gilbert's muddy old boots over the stockings. When I opened the door, Udell looked at my face and smiled, then turned his head. Embarrassed seeing a woman in pants, I reckon. About as embarrassed as I felt wearing them. I remembered Mary Pearl saying as much. Although I surely could see now how a fellow could run and kick and hop on a horse so easy. Udell drove me back to the barn, where I looked in the armoire for a skirt of my own to wear. I put it over the pants so I'd feel more presentable. I couldn't find my hairbrush. Just let the hair hang down my back.

Chess, Charlie, and Gilbert rode up to find a mess they'd never expected. The sun was nearly down. They'd have thought supper would be waiting for them. It took me a few seconds to realize that neither Esther nor her paramour was with them. I watched them get off their horses and look around without speaking.

The three of them asked me so many times if I was hurt, I wanted to scold them. "The roof was torn off by a storm," I said. "Udell said it might have been a tornado. The house is lost. Did you find Esther?" Chess hung his head. Gilbert turned away, faced the barn. "Tell me," I said to Charlie.

Charlie's eyes watered up. He took my hand, then sat on his heels in front of me, squeezing my fingers. "Mama," he started softly. "Mama, we found her beneath an ironwood tree on the bank of the river. Two graves. Seemed to be her husband there, too. Their names were on two crosses."

"Oh Lord," I said. "Oh, poor Savannah." For a little while, we all fell silent. An ache that could have split me in two welled up inside me. That flowery-talking hired hand had wooed her to her grave. But two graves? I caught my breath. "Who'd have buried both of them?" I asked. "I thought you meant Esther had come to some calamity. But if they're buried side by side, somebody had to have . . . been there."

Chess spat on the ground. "There was a campground, well set up. Like it had been there for years." Gilbert wiped his eyes on his sleeve and sniffed.

"Indians?" I asked.

"White."

We rode up just before dark to check on Albert and Savannah's place. Birds twittered, splashing in puddles left from the rain. A couple of baskets had blown into the yard. Then the lot of us camped out in the barn overnight, next to Willie. No one told him about Esther. We kept our grief to ourselves. Chess told him we were sleeping in the barn because there was a leak in my roof. Willie said, "I meant to nail them shingles better than that," but nobody answered him.

Udell stayed. Off and on, I slept and woke, uncertain of my surroundings. Each time I awoke, I reached over and touched Udell's hand. Even sound asleep, he was quick to clasp my fingers in his.

Charlie said he meant to leave with Willie in tow before daylight. He'd be crossing paths with Savannah and Albert on their way home from town. I couldn't leave them to learn their daughter's fate that way. I decided to ride with Charlie until we came across the rest of the family headed home. I told Udell I'd follow Savannah, and then, whether she returned home or wanted to go back to town. I'd have to be with her.

Chess said he'd stay home. He asked Gilbert to stay put, too. Said they'd wait on me to come back. I packed some things I could wash in town. Took Granny's unfinished quilt and tied it to a pack horse. I looked at the remains of that house. No one could live there. Nothing would ever be the same. I said, "We may be in town awhile."

"That's all right, Sarah," Chess said. "We'll see you when you come down."

"Udell," I began, "thank you. For all your help last night. Thanks for staying."

"Sarah, be careful. We'll watch everything until you return." Well, he wrapped his arms around me in front of my sons and Chess and Willie, and he hugged me tight, then kissed my cheek.

I looked sheepishly at my men, worried they'd be upset at the boldness of the man and the foolishness of their mother, not slapping him silly for making advances. None of them looked the least bit worried. They just put their hats on their heads and pulled the horses out of the barn and into the daylight.

Chapter Twenty-Five

October 1, 1906

An hour outside of Tucson, Charlie, Willie, and I met up with Albert and Savannah, who were just starting their journey home. Mary Pearl rode alongside them. Ezra and Zack bounced along on Big Boy and Flojo. I hailed them and got off my horse, climbing into the seat beside Savannah. She started to weep the moment she saw my face, as if she already knew what I had rehearsed telling. Savannah sobbed deeply when I told her what had happened. Their whole family wept as one. Zack fell from Big Boy's back and threw himself into the dirt, skinning his nose. He wailed and gasped. Ezra cried, too, although more quietly. Mary Pearl buried her face in her father's shoulder. I held Savannah and rocked her as if she were a child.

Even Willie cried then, so complete was our sorrow.

I gave Albert my horse to ride and I drove the surrey back to town, not stopping until we were in the backyard of my house there. We unloaded everyone and pulled the shades. I left Savannah to her mourning then, for I needed to tell April before I stopped to rest. We would also need to find Rebeccah and get word to Rachel, call the family together.

Mary Pearl's eyes were swollen and her nose red. She called softly to me from the parlor doorway, "Aunt Sarah? Will you let me ride along with you?"

"Surely," I said.

Heading to April's house, Mary Pearl said after a few quiet moments, "Aubrey Hanna asked me to be his girl."

"That so?"

"I told him I expected to go to college. I'd planned at least a year, maybe two."

"And?"

"He said he'd wait a hundred. Said he'd bought some land for me. The Wainbridge place has been in foreclosure for nearly a year. That's what he bought."

"So you're really saying he asked you to marry him?"

"Yes."

"Thought you didn't want any truck with that?"

"Aubrey's not just any fellow."

I reached across the space between our horses and patted her arm. "I know, honey." I wanted to smile. Mary Pearl tried to smile, but she wept, instead, dabbing at her eyes with the back of her wrist. I clucked to my horse and she followed me. Her tears, for now, drowned her happiness. It would come back to her. She was young.

We delivered our sad news to April in the silence of her parlor. She cried on my shoulder. Then she raised herself stiffly. "I'll get a message to Morris. He'll come home and take me to Rebeccah and Rachel. Please let me do this, Mama. You go home and stay with Aunt Savannah. I'll handle it for you. It must come from family. Soon as we have the twins, we'll go to your house."

"You don't have to do this, April."

She pulled open the drawer of a mahogany secretary and dipped a pen quickly, tapping it against the blotter. Then she pulled the embroidered tassel that hung against the doorjamb. She whispered something to Lizzie, who disappeared. "It's done, Mama. Morris will be home in a few minutes. I'll be along with the girls as soon as I can."

I saw the determination in her eyes. "Thank you, honey," I said.

When Mary Pearl and I got our horses in the yard, Charlie stood and motioned to Willie. "Come on, Will," he said. "Time to go." Charlie still had his job to do.

"Aint Sair," Willie called. The boy was pale. His lean frame looked gaunt. "Kin I ask you something to do for me?"

"What is it, son?" Heavens to Betsy, I'd called him "son" again. Forgot what a curse he was to me, looking at him face-to-face. At that moment, I didn't care what he'd done. I was plum out of hardness.

"Go with us, there, would you?" Willie pleaded. "It's just a short walk. Would you carry my half a Bible? So's I can have it with me?"

Charlie had a hold on Willie's arm, and I walked behind him, stepping in the tracks of his bare feet, to the sheriff's office. Just outside the door, he hesitated. Willie turned to me and said, "Aint Sair, there's just one thing. I want to do this here by myself, but when I get to the judge, will you see me through it? Stay with me through it all, I mean? Clear to the end?"

"Well, it probably won't be a long trial. Don't worry. Sure I will. Of course."

"Promise? Just like you promised all them other things? No going back?"

I smiled at the childish insistence in words coming from an outlaw a good foot taller than I. "I promise."

"All right, then. I reckon I'm ready, Charlie. Mr. Ranger, sir." Charlie opened the door and took Willie inside.

Even though it was late in the day, Savannah begged Albert to take her home. We talked about it for a little while. No one wanted Savannah to suffer any more than she already was. I couldn't let go of her. Kept her hand in mine. In two hours, April, Morris, Rachel, and Rebeccah were there. All our shoulders were wet with tears.

"Savannah, I'm so sorry," I kept repeating, saying it enough times that it didn't mean much anymore. There was no cure for a mother grieving for a child. I knew that. When I used to long for my dead children—both Suzy and the two boys lost before they were ever born—I believed that if I could have had them for just a few more years, I would have managed better. If I could have seen them grown, I told myself, it would have been easier. But there is no easy way to mourn a child.

They finally decided to go on home. Albert declared he would ask Chess or Gilbert to show them where Esther was buried. They would build a marker for her in our family plot. I stiffened my backbone, planning to go along with them, hold Savannah up. See to the burying. Make supper for this family, even if I had to cook it out in the yard under my soap ramada.

As they were settling again into the surrey, another thought came to me. I'd promised Willie I would stay in town. A big part of me said I owed the boy no quarter whatever. But another part inside argued that he'd begged me to keep my word. That one thing, I couldn't turn away from.

I cast around in my mind and heart for all the reasons I had to go with them. Savannah was as dear as any sister, and her children nearly as close as my own. I ached for the loss of Esther. I needed to be with my family. To make sure they rested, and ate, and all the things a body forgets to do when they are mourning a child's passing. I was sick at heart, sick to my soul. Beat down and tired, too. I had two dozen reasons to go with them, and there was only one reason I had to stay with Willie. I'd given him my word.

I waved farewell to the sad family, my heart torn by the anguish on their faces and by my inconvenient promise to the hellion I'd let into my home and hearth.

Charlie and I stayed in the house. He talked with me about the times we'd come through. For the first time since he'd gotten so tall, I quit seeing Jack in his face and saw just Charlie Elliot. An Arizona Ranger. Quick with a gun. Handy with a rope and cattle. Smart. A good man to know. I was more proud of him than if he were graduating college.

The next day, we went down town to see the sheriff to find out when Willie's trial would be. The Sheriff said the new district judge would be there a week from next Tuesday morning, and he'd scheduled a trial the following week. Three weeks. I'd have to sit and wait, just biding my time. I should have gone with Albert and Savannah. I could be with them, but there was no use in it now. A clock only turns one direction.

We set out to fill our time. Charlie said he'd have to leave in two days, but for now, he helped me cut up the packed ground behind the house. All the while, I was thinking that this was where we'd call home from now one. We got a flower bed dug out and planted some flower seeds. Next morning, I went to the doctor, who put some liniment on my bruised back. I was sore through and through from the beating I'd gotten by the hail, and digging caliche all day hadn't improved it.

When I got home that afternoon, Charlie was painting the porch. That evening, he said he'd decided to ride down to the ranch, see what was happening. Told me he'd come back for the trial. He meant to ride all night. It was only after he'd packed up his gear and was saddling his horse that he asked my opinion of it. It would be midnight by the time he got there. I asked him, "Do you really want my opinion, or are you just telling me your plans?" He smiled. "Well," I said, "check on the cattle, and see the dogs are fed." I waved him farewell after supper, feeling a pulling in my soul.

Willie was locked behind bars in a horrible cage. The top and sides of the cell were steel plates; it was a giant vermin box. Hot, dank, smelling of outhouse and men's sweat. Each day when I got there, Willie was sitting on his bunk, reading quietly.

About a week passed. Something Willie'd said kept running through my mind. Instead of going back to the house one day, I went on to Aubrey Hanna's office.

Aubrey apologized, saying he was not a criminal lawyer. He was a money lawyer, he said, money and civil things, deeds and such. Still, I asked Aubrey to talk to Willie about one thing. I wanted Aubrey to get him to say again what he'd said to me in the barn: that his mother had often "married" anyone with twenty dollars. Aubrey's face lit up. He said that could change everything. I left his office with hope for at least one victory. Aubrey went to visit Willie the next day, then came to the house. Willie had confirmed the statement and even signed a paper with the words written in Aubrey's hand.

Well, not two more days had passed when Aubrey knocked on my door about four of the afternoon, breathless and red in the face. "Mrs. Elliot? I got the judge to listen to this move for dismissal. You've got to come with me right now. He said he'd hear it by four-thirty today, else it would have to wait a month. I'm thinking that since Willie could still be a legal heir and we don't know what his fate is yet, if he's sent to prison, the government could requisition the land that's his property. We shouldn't wait a month. It needs to be settled before Willie goes to trial, if that's possible. I brought a buggy."

The judge was an old, old man, who squinted through thick spectacles at the papers Aubrey Hanna placed before him. I sat on a wooden chair in a little room. When he finally turned to Aubrey, he said, "It is in my power to change people's lives. Much as I know I've made mistakes now and then, this one seems pretty clear. You, Mrs. Elliot, have lived on that land some years. This relative claims rightful ownership but ha'n't set foot on it in a month o' Sundays. Am I understanding this? Well, have you anything to say, Mrs. Elliot, on your side?"

There were a hundred things I could say to justify myself. I looked to Aubrey, wishing he'd told me the right words to use. After a minute, I said, "I'm not done fighting to keep my land, sir."

"Well, you are for a while. This is utter nonsense. Oh, oh, must be formal, eh? The court, as it were, myself, finds that Mrs. Elliot is the rightful owner of all claim to the property in question. Without prejudice."

"Thank you, sir," I said.

The judge made a face. "All right. Go along now. If I don't eat exactly at five o'clock, my insufferable bowel acts up. Good day."

As Aubrey drove me home, it was all I could do not to hug him right there in public. He'd done it. Felicity had legally abandoned my brother Ernest. There could be no lawsuit, no claim. The land was ours, fully and completely. Much as I felt like abandoning that ranch, that would happen when *I* decided it, not because someone came along with a story to take it away from me. At my house, Aubrey helped me from the buggy and I took his hand in both of mine and shook it. "Thank you," I said.

I told Aubrey to make me out a bill. I knew my brother Albert had said he'd pay Aubrey, but he'd done a lot of things for me. I wanted to make sure the money got put down in writing, so I could start working on it. He asked me two times if I was sure I wanted it right away, and I said, "I want the whole bill. Everything I owe you. I'll pay it back if I have to sell every inch of ground." He nodded and set his hat, then went on his way.

Well, the next day, by special delivery, I got a message from his office, written on that fine thick paper. I swallowed hard, wincing as I opened it. I had to read it several times over. "For services rendered, this receipt for the amount of one dollar, paid in full." I hugged it to my chest. Udell had raised a really fine boy. A man. Lord, I'll have to get used to the men around here, I told myself.

Now I had nothing to do but bide my time until Willie's trial. Then I could go home and start picking up the pieces. The house felt empty, a shell of a place. Never had I felt so shaken loose from everyone I loved. Almost all my family was tending to Savannah's mourning. As they should be. As I should be, too, not stuck here with Willie. I wandered through the place, top to bottom. The house had always been temporary. Not my home. Even when we built it, lived there, it had seemed only a way station, a place to sleep until I could get back to the land that was part of my blood and bones. That day, I swept it clean, from the attic down. Found a nickel on the back stairs. I'd come up a hundred percent in the world, financially speaking. Owned a beat-up ranch, ten and a half starving cattle, a house in town, and a nickel.

I reckoned, I could at least spend a little more time with April and her children. So that afternoon, I hitched up the wagon and set off for her place.

October 15, 1906

The days passed more quickly than I'd expected. April had said she'd be staying away from the trial and all the proceedings. Bad enough rumors flew through town. Still, bless her, April came to my place almost every afternoon, holding her head high, driving right to the front door proudly, not concerned if any of the hoity-toity ladies saw her.

I filled time. Wrote letters to Harland and Granny, to Savannah and Albert. Instead of feeding and hauling water, I rose every morning, made a little breakfast, and then lowered Granny's quilt on the frame Jack had built for me years ago. It hadn't been used in a decade. Each day, I'd work on the quilt for two or three hours, trying hard to make my stitches as tiny and perfect as my mama's had always been. The needle went up, down, four times. Pull, do four more—I heard Willie's voice with each one—when the thread grew short, tie a knot. Tried to read between his words to find what had sent him the way he went. Searched my own words to find where I'd gone wrong. Whether I could have said one thing or another, showed him a book, or explained better what I wanted from him. No answers came to me.

I stitched until my fingers hurt and grew blistered. I kept on until the blisters popped and I had to wrap my fingers to keep the quilt clean. I had done the best I knew how, and it hadn't been enough. Couldn't change the boy. And then along came some man riding hell-bent through a thunderstorm, ruining the only thing Esther took with her besides the clothes on her back, then handing it to Willie, to whom it was a biblical revelation. I reckoned some things would have turned out the way they had, no matter what. As if they'd been set in stone before we ever came to the dance.

Suddenly, I jammed the needle into the cloth and stood up, as if I'd seen a vision in the calico flowers marching in stair steps across the grain. Lazrus. A white man, living in the wilds, near a stream. Come across the foolish couple, her a moonstruck dreamer, him more useful at writing poetry than staying alive. They'd crossed paths with the crazy water witch. There may be no way to prove it, but I made up my mind then and there that I had to see that camp myself, see if it had a sign around that'd point a finger at its owner.

At ten o'clock each morning, I doctored my fingers with plasters, put on my nice gloves, and walked downtown to see Willie. I stopped on the way home and bought potatoes or lettuce, or got a chicken to roast for supper. April spent an hour in the afternoon, usually bringing the children so I could hold them in my lap and tell them a story or read to them. She always invited me over for supper, but I only went twice. In the evening, while there was light, I rolled down that quilt again and worked until I couldn't see it in front of me. After supper, when it was cooler, I dug weeds in the flower bed, hauled water, and tidied the yard, scraping up rocks where Ezra had started it.

As I sewed the front to the back of that quilt, I finally came one morning to the edge and had to repin it where it had slipped off at one corner. On the back, all the pattern of quilting was reversed. The knots I hadn't done well showed. Everything was in the right place, but not pretty like on top. I wondered if Willie had come to us like that. Every rule we made for him to follow turned upside down. Everything I wanted to help him with just looked backward and ugly to him. You couldn't know what was on a person's insides, just like this quilt here. Granny had pulled and stretched this layer of cotton batting between the two layers of cloth. She'd washed it and shrunk it, pieced it and shaped it just right, so that when the whole thing was finished, it could be washed. When it dried, it would be straight and neat, not shrunken or pulled off-kilter or with some old gray wool blanket—something I'd seen women use for stuffing a quilt—showing though. Maybe Willie had some dark place inside him that no pinning or shaping could reverse. When he hit the wash, all the worst came out of him. No telling what got into him to set him right. Fear, I reckon. Nothing like peering right down the barrel to change a person's point of view. It had changed mine more than once. That and a few words from the Good Book. Why, in all of Creation, any wisdom had to come connected to Lazrus, I'd never pretend to guess.

October 22, 1906

The day before the trial, I washed the best dress I had brought with me to town and my gloves in cool water. The clothes dried on the line in just a few minutes. Then I heated up the stove and opened all the windows so that I could have a bath and run the sadiron over them a few times. I hung those clothes over a chair right in the kitchen so they'd be ready for the following day.

When April came that afternoon, she brought with her a paper-wrapped package. It was a getup she'd had Mrs. Logan make for me, from the measurements she'd taken in preparation for the tea party. I suppose it will be quite a while until she has a party, now. It was a black skirt and jacket, with a lavender blouse. April carried a large hatbox, and in it was a wide Gibson of black straw with lavender tulle. I told her, "This is too fancy for me, honey. I washed my dress."

April picked at the tulle on the hat for a second before she said, "Mama, if you want to wear your old dress, that's fine. But you said yourself you don't know this judge. If you go there dressing proudly, as if we have some standing in this community, it will say a lot about our family."

"Why should I want to say anything about our family other than I'm sorry we have a no-account, horse-thieving nephew?" I asked.

"What we want to say is that we are good people. People of virtue and pride, merely subject to the vicissitudes of life."

I thought that over a minute. "Won't it seem, well, sassy?"

April smiled. "No, Mama. It'll seem proper."

I told her I'd think it over. So when she left, I laid that dress on another chair, the hatbox on the floor under it, and went and pulled down the quilt.

Good to his word, Charlie came back to the house that night. While he ate supper, he talked about how they had been trying to fix up the house. How he and Gilbert and Grampa Chess had worked the livelong day. How the heifers they'd found seemed to be happily getting a little fatter on the new grass, and how El Capitan was making good use of his time. He said Gilbert and Udell both wanted to run fence between our places and Rudolfo Maldonado's. He wanted to know my opinion. I told him I wanted an adobe wall twelve feet high between me and Rudolfo, and Charlie laughed. He said, "That stuff would take an army to move." Then he went to bed.

Next morning, on the twenty-third of October, I dressed carefully in the new clothes. My hands were swollen. While I struggled with the little buttons, I thought on things. I expected that I'd have to testify. It was my money, my cattle and horses that had been stolen. They'd ask me, I reckoned, what I thought of it, how I knew it was Willie who'd taken them. I rehearsed it over in my head, trying to come up with exact words to use. To tell the truth, but not send Willie to the gallows. I put gloves over my sore fingers, then placed the broad hat on my head, fixing it with a hairpin. This outfit would make them think I still had plenty left. Maybe hide the situation Willie had brought me to. But something told me April was right, so I went to help Charlie hitch the rig. He told me to wait at the front door and he'd drive around.

A light breeze rustled trees and bushes as Charlie drove me to the court-house. In just the few weeks living in town, the air had cooled, so it was no longer a misery to walk downtown. The hot weather was coming to a close. In the courtroom, I sat right behind the railing, close as I could be, so Willie would be able to see I was there.

There were about eighteen other people in the room besides the judge and myself. A deputy walked Willie in. Willie was wearing chains, like a trained bear. He seemed quiet and shrunken. He could hardly raise his head when the judge asked for his name. The judge asked him to step forward and be read his charges. Willie stood, his hands chained together but his arms held out as much as he could, in that old stance of his, as if he were expecting a punch in the stomach. The court clerk read, "Ernest William Prine, Jr., alias Willie, alias Boots the Kid, you are charged with loitering, disturbing the public peace, cattle rustling, and horse thieving. How do you plead, guilty or innocent?"

Willie said, "I plead guilty, Your Highness."

People around the room laughed. I hurt for him.

The boy tried again. "I done them things, sir," he said. "I'm ready to go to jail."

The judge leaned forward and glared at him. "Do you have a lawyer representing your case, boy?"

"No, sir. I come representing my case of guilty."

"Well, then—"

"And there's plenty more, sir. A whole plenty lot more."

The judge thundered at him, banging that gavel. All pompous and puffed up, it seemed to me. He hollered, "Do not interrupt a judge while he is talking."

"Yes, sir. But there's more I done. I come to confess it all. The honest truth is, I stole them horses and cattle, sure. I took my Aint Sair's cash box and busted it open and stole a thousand and one hunnert and four dollars. I got with some old boys and we run them cows near to Mexico. On the way there, though, oncet I shot a feller who was looking at me odd. He'd stuck a knife in a man for cheating him at dice, and I was scared of him, so I shot him dead. Then I killed another boy for some boots, 'cause mine were torn and he had some nice ones. Then it was raining and cold. We'd been driving them cows to kingdom come, and there was this little house. The man said to get away from there. He said I couldn't stay there 'counta he had a wife and children. So I shot them children. Shot the wife and shot the man and ate their supper and slept by their fire.

"Then I went on down south. Never even got across the border, 'cause the Ranger caught up with us. And some other banditos were there. There was

Rangers a-fighting us, and bandits trying to steal the cows, and it come a battle like a war, and then a storm started. The cattle spooked and lightning hit right in 'em. Killed a hunnert or more right like that. Another lightning bolt hit a man square in the saddle and tore him open like a gutted fish. Knocked me off my horse, and knocked all the sense out of the animal, too. Thought I was dead, but I rose up. And the sky opened like a hand, reached down, and got me. When the clouds busted up, a man come on a white burro and give me this here and told me to go home. I think it was Jesus. I really do. He ripped that Bible in half and it screamed just like a woman. That's when I come back. I done all that and more. Killed a outlaw name of Shank with my knife. Cut him until he bled to death, and even though I told him I was sorry, and he said that was all right, he still died. That's what I done. Stole and robbed 'n killed and murdered. I'm here to take my due."

I sat there with my mouth open. Numb. I'd never have imagined what he had done. I'd never be able to tell Albert and Savannah. I just held on to the seat of the chair until my hands ached, pinching the ends of my blistered fingers so I could feel the pain. It no longer mattered what I'd intended to say. Least of all, what I wore. Willie had just condemned himself.

The judge banged the gavel down to caution the crowd. My ears filled with cottony noise, and I rocked a little on my seat, as if I was quieting a baby. I heard words. They came through the noise in my ears, and still they didn't reach my understanding until the judge was long past them and saying something else. He left the room, and the crowd was standing all around me; people were moving toward the door. There would be no testimony. No need for my careful words. Willie'd said all the judge needed to hear.

I stared at the floor, hearing the strange words again. "Inasmuch as you have by your own admission . . . murder . . . by the neck until pronounced dead . . ."

Three days hence. How formal. Elizabethan. Like something from the Bible. I couldn't look at Willie, though I knew his shocked expression well. Mouth open, arms out, even in chains, his back hunched over. I could feel it from where I sat. All I'd considered was several years in jail. As long as he'd escaped a lynching somewhere along the line, I figured he'd just go to jail. In ten or twenty years, older and wiser, he'd come home and work and live on our place. Never in my life had I expected him to hang. I looked at him then, expecting him to be surprised, but there was no surprise on Willie's face. He'd known all along what he meant to do.

On the drive to the house, Charlie told me he again intended to ride south for the ranch. Couldn't bear it, he said. I told him that was all right, but I had made a promise, I said. I'd stay. Charlie rode away fast. Hardly said good-bye.

I went to see Willie again that afternoon. When I walked in, he looked up, and for the first time, he wasn't crying. Wasn't hunkered over on the cot. He stood up and came toward the bars. "Aint Sair? You got a new dress just for my trial?"

"Yes, Willie," I said. I wished it had been my idea.

"It 'as purty."

"Thank you. Why, Willie, did—"

"I don't want to talk about none of them things, Aint Sair. All right?"

"All right. Do you want to talk about anything else?"

"Naw. I reckon not. You're going to stand by me, aren't you? You promised. I don't mind if you don't, but you will, won't you?"

"I will, son."

He smiled and said, "I knew you would."

October 24, 1906

The next day passed, slow and fast at the same time. I quit working on the flower bed. Kept the curtains drawn. Sewed on that quilt until my fingers bled. I heard every tick of the clock in the parlor. The time between the sounds was eternal. At ten o'clock, I went to see the boy. I took him food, but he didn't eat. He sat on his bunk, holding his tied-up "half a Bible." He seemed thinner and more haggard.

The second day, I took him some doughnuts. I asked Willie if he remembered taking the sack of doughnut holes to the boys.

He grinned and said, "They sent me for postholes. Took me some time to laugh about that. I pulled it on a friend of mine, though. He got pretty mad, too, like I did. Rangers shot him, though." He put the doughnut to his mouth but couldn't eat. "Smells real nice."

"You doing all right? Anything I can get you?"

"You said how you'd see me through. You're going to be there, aren't you?"

I nodded. I said, "I didn't know about the other. I never thought you'd get more than prison."

"I knew I done murder. I was trying to be the meanest thing alive. Drinking all the time, just meaner than a one-eyed pirate. I couldn't admit it to you.

Had to tell the judge, 'cause he don't know me. I just need to know you'll come with me. I can't do this if you don't. You promise, Aint Sair, you'll see me through?"

"Promise."

"If my ma shows up, you don't have to explain nothing. If she wanted to know, she'da come here. If a lady like you could come here, she coulda."

I quilted all afternoon, and into the night. With every stitch, I watched my children grow up in my mind, saw them start their first days at school. Saw April give a recitation at the eighth-grade graduation. Saw Gilbert learning to strum his first guitar chords under Mason Sherrill's watchful eyes. Saw Charlie cut his hand on Jack's saber, practicing drawing it from a belt wrapped twice around his middle. Everything I had poured into my children, I stitched into that quilt.

Before the sun came up on the morning of the third day, I made myself some coffee. I repinned the quilt. Dressed. Tried to eat a cold biscuit from yesterday, but that took too much time. I was only inches from the last corner of the quilt. All morning, the street echoed with the *whack-bang* sound of the hangman testing the weights. I sewed faster and faster. At eleven o'clock, I tied the last knot. Searched every inch of it for a place I'd missed. I didn't stop to admire it, just folded it up in thirds, then set that quilt down in the chair I'd sat in—the empty chair for the extra woman, the one I had finally filled.

I dressed carefully in the new dress, donned the hat, pulled the veil over my face. I stepped out of the house at half past eleven and started for the courthouse on foot. I carried nothing but a handkerchief, which I held it tightly with both hands, as I stepped across the street.

It was the third day, noon. The time of banquets and siestas, wedding bells from San Augustine's, happy children let out from school, rolling hoops in the street, dogs snoozing in the sun. A crowd gathered around the scaffold behind the courthouse. My heart thundered. Two ropes hung from it. And it was noon.

There wasn't much ceremony involved. No drums rolled. No speeches were made. Willie was marched up the steps behind some other man they'd sentenced for horse thieving, too. Willie looked lost and scared, searching the faces before him. I waved. He caught sight of me, nodded. It even looked as if he tried to smile.

They put a black bandanna over the other man's eyes and lowered the rope around his neck. Then they came to Willie with a bandanna, and he jerked away. Although his hands were tied behind him, he wrenched and fought. "Don't put that on me," he hollered. The sheriff grabbed him roughly and another man held him. They tied the bandanna over his eyes while Willie cried out, weeping. "I can't see. I can't see. Take it off me. I can't see."

The men behind Willie whispered to each other, then one of them pulled off the bandanna. Willie sighed and gasped for air, as if it had choked him, then settled down and stood still as a fence post while they lowered the rope around his neck. "Thank you, sir," he said. People in the crowd murmured when they heard that. They got quieter.

The boy set his eyes on me.

I raised that veiling and pushed it to the back; I looked straight at him.

Willie's face got all set, like stone. His body moved back and forth, as if he were keeping time to some kind of musical tune.

I stared into his eyes. Heard the noise of wind but felt no breeze.

Somewhere, a man was reading forth something strange and distant.

Tears ran down my face, but I didn't look away.

The reading voice said something else.

I pulled hard on the handkerchief in my hands. Tore it in half. I felt every little thread pulled asunder, felt them let loose from where they belonged, joined.

The bell at St. Augustine's began to toll. His eyes boring straight into mine, Willie's face went white, but he didn't look away.

I held my breath.

The trap made a *whack-bang* sound.

I turned my face to the wall behind me and held to the doorjamb, shuddering. There were no cheers as in some executions. There was no sound at all.

Someone touched me. I opened my eyes, and Udell was there, firmly taking my arm. "Let's go," he said. "Let's go now, Sarah. Charlie came and got me. I brought my wagon. Thought the boy might have liked that, to ride where his papa rode. I'll carry him home for you. We'll put him next to his father."

I knew he'd have wanted that, too, but I couldn't have said it. I couldn't speak. Udell pulled my arm again. I found it hard to let go of the post. But Udell was there, and his arms seemed hard as iron, so I held to him and he walked me to where his wagon waited. When they set that pine coffin in the back, it sounded as if the trap was falling again, but this time softly—so gently—*whack-bang*. My heart ached as if it would tear apart.

It took only a few minutes to pack the few things I had brought with me. I rolled up my mama's quilt and held it tightly in my lap. Udell drove the wagon slowly. My back ached with each turn of the wheel. It was seven hours to home, on the front seat of Udell Hanna's big coffin-loading freight wagon.

Chapter Twenty-Six

We came around the bend, where the road cut off at Granny's house. "Stop here," I said. "This is where I'll be staying awhile. I want to leave off my things."

Udell didn't slow the horses at all. "Sarah, we've got to get this over and done. I'll carry you back here if you want, afterward. We've got to get down the road."

My heart stopped a beat. I thought I was going to be sick, right there in front of him. I put my hand on Udell's right arm, and he patted it with his gloved left hand.

We crossed in front of Albert's. It seemed deserted. Udell read my thoughts, for he said, "They've all gone down to your place. To see to the funeral arrangements."

The sun was lowering. It was already that late in the year. No more ten o'clock nightfalls. "Funeral," I said. "At least there's hay to sleep on."

"Yes, there's hay, if you want it." He tapped the horses and they picked up their steps a little. We crossed the Cienega. "Your brother and I put a few extra nails in the bridge here."

I looked down as we passed. Tried to pin my thoughts on the bridge. It did rattle differently, but I thought that was because this wagon wasn't my own. "Added some lumber, too?"

"Getup!" He snapped the reins. "Got to get there before the sun goes down." The horses clipped up a bit—not a trot, but a quick step. It was only a mile to my house, and only if you dawdled side to side the way my sons used to do, carrying some bread or cheese or other from one house to the cousins'. The sky turned red overhead. A few lingering clouds like streaks of amber paint blazed across the blue-green sky. I blinked. The house had completely fallen in. Someone had cleared all the broken and torn lumber from the yard.

"What," I said, "is that there? I thought it was the smokehouse. That's not my smokehouse. There's a house there. Somebody's gone and built a house on my land! Charlie and Gilbert were supposed to be watching the place. Where's Chess? Udell, I can't stand another battle. Did you know they were doing it? Couldn't you have written and told me? What am I going to do?" The closer we got, the bigger it grew. A Mexican-style hacienda, fancier than Rudolfo's, had sprouted from the land where my house had stood for twenty-five years. A veranda hanging with baskets of flowers spread across the front of the house. My old rosebush was tied up to one of the porch posts, and it looked as if it had been there forever. "Somebody's taken my land!" I said.

Udell patted my arm. "Right now, Sarah, we're going to bury Willie. We'll see the house afterward." He drove past the house and on up the rise to the graveyard. He helped me down from the wagon seat. My new black dress was dusty, but still fine. Albert and Savannah's family was there, waiting. Chess and my sons, too. I hugged everyone. Savannah held my hand. Rudolfo's family came. Dressed in black, somber, they stood at a respectful distance. Leta Cujillo, the new Doña Maldonado, nodded at me as I recognized her. I stared over their shoulders at that square box of a house.

Everything felt disjointed. Worse than other funerals where I couldn't concentrate, this one passed in a blur. I could barely take stock of what was happening around me. We put Willie next to his papa. Savannah held my hand. She had come through her trials without me by her side. She'd had her husband and children to comfort her and was never as alone as I felt. Aubrey was there, standing between Mary Pearl and Albert. Zachary held my other hand. Udell stood behind me. Chess said some words. I thought about Granny, and what she'd said to Willie—how he wanted to go on living so hard, he couldn't stand that his papa wasn't also. I wished so much that she could be here to say those words again. I wished to goodness I could tell her how right she was. I couldn't bear the thought of Willie being dead. Yet I wanted to go on living. Wanted to go on being at this place, loving these people. Oh Lord, I want my mother. Heaven help me if she is too old to live over the sad mission she is on with her two grandsons and my brother's family.

As the sod clumps fell on Willie's coffin, I thought of my children and grandchildren. Felt my mama's presence as clearly as if she'd been standing there. I straightened my back. I had to keep going. The battle of this existence wasn't done.

I looked toward Jack's grave marker. How foolish to look forward to lying there next to Jack. Not since he'd died had I felt so greatly the need to live. I loved him, but for the first time, it didn't hurt to think of him. Putting Willie in the ground suddenly made everything and everyone around me more precious, more urgent, more real. The moon rose before we finished, though the sky was still glowing in the west. The star that was Jack's twinkled at me, and instead of the twinge of longing to join him, I felt a glad satisfaction that I'd known and loved a fine man. Nothing more. Udell had said to think only of the here and now. To do that, I had to let go of everything I thought had been holding me up.

"Let's go home, Sarah," Chess said.

"I have no home. I expect to bed down at Granny's place."

"There's a house yonder," Chess said. "Waiting for you."

I looked from face to face, my family gathered around. I said, "Whose house?"

"Come see it now, Mama," Gilbert said. "We built this house for you. All your friends and family."

"What do you mean, 'my friends and family'?"

Charlie said, "The house there, Mama. You drove right past it."

"In three weeks, you built a house? Chess, what did you use for money? Who did this work?"

Charlie said, "Why, Mama, that isn't polite. Come on inside. We'll show you around. With the drought, everybody's out of work, got nothing to do. Flores and Conciliada came. Shorty and his whole clan. People from Willcox to Prescott and Douglas to Yuma pitched in."

I was ushered in and shown through a fine wide adobe house, with doors painted pale blue all around, a courtyard in the center. Lanterns flickered around the courtyard. Savannah and Albert's children presided over tables of food, keeping flies away. Willie's funeral supper was a banquet meant to welcome me to this strange house. High on the center walls were clerestory windows, which would pull up the heat of the summer and keep a breeze constantly blowing through the house. The ceiling was higher than at Rudolfo's hacienda, the rooms wide as a church, and then some. It reminded me of his place, yet it was different; the furnishings were spare, but mostly my own.

My armoire and my bedstead were set up in one room. Charlie and Gilbert's things were in others. Space had been made for Granny—a large room right next to mine. Harland's painting hung over a huge fireplace that was built right into the house, not added on and patched around later. All the rooms opened onto the courtyard, hacienda-style, with shade and screens stretched across one end of it for sleeping in the summer. I recognized the water pump, which had survived the destruction of my kitchen. It was now outside in the courtyard, ready for a cool drink or to water plants there, while a second one was in the room opposite my bedroom, a complete kitchen with a fine new stove.

I watched the people gathered around the tables, eating, talking, even laughing. Willie's passing had not meant so much to them except as a reason to have come tonight. They were here to celebrate this house, it seemed. At that moment, I felt exhausted and disgusted with them all. I told Chess I wanted to turn in, and then the party died down and everyone left for their homes, bearing lanterns in the darkness, the way some of them had come to watch my well being dug.

Udell made some coffee and we drank it, rocking slowly, watching the fire burn low. I kept seeing Willie's eyes staring back at mine. Hearing that echoing bang. I said, "I'm sorry for all the tears, Udell."

Udell said, "Take your time, Sarah."

"If he had told me . . ." I said. "If only he'd told me before we went to town."

Udell said, "Then you would have had a terrible decision to make. What would you have done? Broken the law? I doubt it. He spared you that choice. Made it himself."

"He did," I mumbled. "I could have forgiven him."

"Willie was a young man with a lot of chances to do right. Instead of living out here in the clean air, he spent his childhood in saloons and running the streets with criminals. I believe the only thing he ever did right in his life was what he did that day."

I turned on him, my jaws tight, and said, "Is that like the only good Indian is a dead one? Are you one of those men?"

Udell said, "I'm saying he went not like a coward, but like a young man standing up straight and true. Him not putting that on you, making that decision for himself—that was an act of honor. Maybe the first one in his life."

I sighed. Said, "Reckon so. Suppose I'm purely edgy."

"I collected his things from the sheriff. In his rolled-up book was a letter for you. I didn't open it. I believed it needed to wait until you had a moment of quiet."

Folded into the half a Bible was a slip of paper torn from blotter in the sheriff's office. My hands shook as I opened it at the crease. I stared at it blindly, unable to read the words. Udell took it from my hand and read aloud, though he stuttered over the poor handwriting, and his voice broke halfway through.

> *dear aunt Sarah—*
>
> *You been the best mother to me a boy could have and weren't no one to blame but me stoled them cattle and all your money. I done them other things too but I ain't writing them so's maybe you'll forget over time and remember this here. Tell the boys for me I hold no grudges and what we done to each other was all my fault. And say to them little fellers they should mind their ma and pa and you and grow up right and true—them things you told me about right and wrong and being a man is what makes me able to go to my Maker hoping I can make up for some of it I done. Thank you for sitting by me. Them were some hard days and long nights. Many a time I made up some story or other for the judge or thought to kill the deputy and get away. After I seen what misery I brung you and then the roof coming off, and still you stuck by me, why I just couldn't do less than I done. I reckon if saint Peter lets me in the gate it will be because of you, aunt Sarah, and he'll know you tried to put a halter on me much as I tried not to wear one, but for a while I rode for your brand and maybe that will be enough. Maybe he'll see I get another chance. Never would have guessed him to be a rancher myself, but the book give me says the Lord has cattle on a thousand hills. I reckon if I get in, the best part of heaven will be riding watch at sunup, don't you?*
>
> *Kind regards. Ever your son, Willie—Ernest, Junior—Prine."*

My son? My son—maybe *I* hadn't failed Willie. My brother Ernest had failed him, not knowing he was alive, and Felicity had failed him, raising him like she did. It was almost as if he'd found what he was hungry for, what was haunting him, and after that, his life was done.

A breeze came in the large deep-set windows of this fine adobe house I'd done nothing to deserve, or to earn, or to construct. All at once, I felt as if something came on that breeze that made things seem clearer. Here I'd been raising my boys the best I could, trying to balance good humor with straight talk and hard work, and they'd followed right along and then slipped down other paths without me noticing. But their paths weren't bad or wrong; they were just different from the ones I'd had my eyes on. Charlie will make a fine lawman, if that's what he wants to do. I raised him up to be a man who believes in right and decency, and he made a choice to stand up for it. And Gilbert, he's as clever as the day is long, and knows horses like my papa did, an instinct. He wants to breed horses and there's no wrong in that, even if he doesn't have any degrees written after his name on an envelope. My April, I'd always thought she ran away from me. Thought she was angry, or hated me. But no, she was angry with Jack, same as I was, for dying. Mad at the world for her papa leaving her, and she couldn't face life without him, maybe because I was bound and determined to do exactly that. Reckon my being a mother is finished, like putting down a good long book. All this time, they'd been making choices of their own because I taught them to be clearheaded and go after what they wanted. I thought I was leading them, but the truth was, I was just following them, holding up a lantern.

Udell said nothing more. Our talk was replaced with the soft trilling of nighthawks and, somewhere off, an owl. I looked at him after a spell, and he'd fallen asleep, his head bent forward. I'd found a friend in this man. So I thought about that some, too. Finally, I had to turn in, so I touched his hand and said good night. The men all went out into the central courtyard. I went to the strange bedroom, made for me, where my bed waited on a raised platform near a window, where it would be cooled by the night breeze.

I slept fitfully, though Jack did not return. The sound of a gallows trap woke me at dawn. I saw Willie's eyes. I listened for the sound again, trying to decide where I was, and in a little while I remembered. I put my head back on my pillow and slept. When I awoke, I smelled food cooking. Dressed in my wrapper, I closed the courtyard to see who was cooking in that kitchen.

Mary Pearl had spent the night in Granny's room. She was bent in front of the stove as I came in. "This stove surely draws nice," she said.

I sat at the table. It was hewn from large boards sturdy enough to butcher a cow on. Half of the chairs were new. A large pie safe stood next to my old, smaller one. Mary Pearl told me Gilbert and Charlie were out checking the stock. Chess was working in the garden. Udell had gone home. They'd left me orders to sit and rest.

"Well, that's a fine thing," I said to Mary Pearl. "I'm supposed to take orders?"

"Aubrey is coming for supper. Mama wants me to stay here and help you out until you get back on your feet. I'm going to cook the whole thing. By myself."

Back on my feet? Did I seem that out of sorts to my family? "Well," I said, "what are you fixing?"

"Chicken and green peppers. While you were gone, we got a letter from Clove and Granny. They're headed back. Josh, too, of course."

"And Melissa?"

"Uncle Harland said she was finally at perfect rest. The letter's up at our place, if you want to read it."

"No, I know what that means." I looked over her shoulder at the pan. "You know Aubrey isn't from around here, don't you? He may not care for green peppers."

She shrugged and then said, "Well, he's going to get used to them."

When Udell came for supper, my sons and Chess were still out at work. Udell showed me around. He pointed to where pipes had been run from the well, explained how to open and shut the tiny windows up near the ceiling, and told me everything my neighbors had done to build me a house. He said when the word went out around the county that I had lost my place in a tornado, things started appearing so fast, they didn't have room to store them.

Then Udell pulled two folded sheets of paper from his shirt pocket. On them was a list of every person who'd given something for my house and what they'd brought. Everyone had signed it. Even those who couldn't write had made an X, and someone else penned in a name next to it.

Rudolfo had quickly made good on his promise to pay me back tenfold. I said I didn't want Rudolfo's money, but Chess said I'd be wise to accept it. Rudolfo would feel better, and money had been needed for a roof, even though neighbors had donated their time to build it. The Cujillos had donated twenty-five huge beams and all the vigas between them. Flores's family had brought two rugs, each big enough to fill a room. Albert and Savannah had bought all the glass for the windows. People from Tucson, too, had brought offerings of furniture, and, more often than not, had stayed to lend a hand.

"And," Udell said, "I prefer not to be in debt. Long before you needed the house, I had determined to buy the cattle from you if I could, but I hadn't heard yet what I had. Remember when I went to Benson that day? Well, I thought that cross was tarnished silver decorated with gold. Turned out, it was solid gold all the way through. I bought your cattle free and clear, and put in some for the house, too. Now I'm counting on you to teach me how to keep them alive."

My throat tightened. "You sold your cross? For that?"

"Part of a gift, Sarah, is that you have to accept it when it's given. My wife worked so hard to earn the money to buy the cross. Assayer said it was probably made from melted-down coins. Came out at .85. What was I going to do with it? Watch it sparkle, when there are bills to pay? When there are good folks in need?"

"I can't accept all this."

"It'd be unkind to everyone if you didn't. Why don't you accept that other folks want to repay your generosity?"

Charlie said, "Udell's right, Mama."

Gilbert added, "You been taking care of folks across the territory for twenty years, Mama. Let them take care of you one time. No one went broke doing it. It was just a good turn for everyone."

I said, "And Rudolfo Maldonado had a hand in this?"

Chess said, "There's nothing wrong with the man trying to make amends. He's not going to ask anything in return. This is what he's giving to repay you for what he did."

I said, "Somebody tell me how you all got a house built in just three weeks?"

"Twenty-five days, Mama," said Gilbert. "Working day and night. Cujillo's family makes adobe in Sonora. They borrowed two mule teams from a friend of Flores who works down at the copper mine in Bisbee. Some of their boys came back with the load, just to be sure we put it up right. One fellow did all that plaster nearly by himself. Fast as we could mix it up, he was waiting for more. You should have seen him work. You'd have wanted to adopt him." Everyone chuckled at that.

Charlie said, "Some days, we had upward of thirty people working here."

My sons pulled me into a room I realized I had not seen the night before. It was wide and had its own fireplace, surrounded by chairs and a large table. Two walls were lined with shelves. I whispered, "My books," and hurried to see them. I ran my fingertips over the bindings. Most of them were wrinkled, but all of them were there. "You saved my books," I said. "Thank you, boys. Thank you."

"Tell Mr. Hanna. He did all the books," said Charlie.

Albert and Savannah had made plans to see Esther's grave. Charlie was to lead the way. I said I'd ride along, but Savannah said, "No. It will be all right. Sarah, you stay here and rest. Ezra and Zachary will stay and do anything you need done. They are not to complain or shirk. You have had so much to bear. It will be all right." Albert said he would mark the place, then go back in a year and move her bones home. Their remaining daughters sat in the surrey. It would be nightfall before they got back.

I spent the day lost, wandering. The walls were a good eighteen or more inches thick, plastered white and smooth, inside and out. All the floors were new wood. The kitchen was fine and the stove was new and sleek. The oven box was big enough to put three cakes into at one time. Chili *ristras* hung like chandeliers from the beams overhead, showing off wealth I didn't have. But I couldn't find anything, couldn't lay my hands on a bowl or spoon that I recognized. I missed my old house. Missed feeling at home. I went out to the barn just to be someplace familiar. Hunter ate from my hand. Rose chortled at him, and he answered her back. Then she nosed me, wanting her apple, too.

Chess and Gilbert went down to help Udell put up the first of his corrals and some fence posts. Zack, Ezra, and I were to stay in the great house, which still seemed to belong to someone else. I asked them to feed the horses, and they went right to it. Then I said, "How about the hens?" and they went to that, too. When I said, "How about hoeing up some rows in the garden?" they eyed each other just like they used to in the old days. I smiled. I'd had just about enough cooperation, and it was good to see some spunk in them, like before all this sorrow came to us. I said, "Buck up, fellas. We won't do the *whole* garden." So we worked side by side, pulling out thorns and cholla and at least a hundred paloverde sprouts. We passed around a canteen of cool water, which tasted sweet as honey after all that work. Then I said, "Boys? Go on and see if there's enough water in the creek to cool off with, and I'll go fix us up some picnic lunches."

They headed toward the creek faster than they'd moved all morning. I pushed open the wide blue door. It was cool in the house, pleasant as only an adobe house can be. I meandered through the long room to the right of the main door. It led to the indoor kitchen, which had a door leading to the courtyard and its cooking area. The door across from that led to the side yard, close to the chicken coop and the garden. The big worktable was right in the center. First time I'd noticed that. Someone who knew cooking had helped make this kitchen. I uncovered a crockery bowl, where we had stored some extra tortillas the night before. Then I pulled three layers of cheesecloth off a salted ham and took up a knife from its hook to slice some. Just before I touched the meat, I saw there was a streak of something on the blade, so I reached for clean one, inspecting this one more closely. The edge had a tiny line from the shank to the tip. Blood. Dried on. One by one, I took all seven knives down, and each and every one had blood on it. I worked the pump handle and leaned over the windowsill for a pat of lye soap. The water splashed into the basin.

A man's voice said, "I've paid the price, you see."

I whirled around. "Lazrus!" He wore no shirt, and the lattice of scars on his chest was laid over with fresh wounds, some having only just dried. In his hand, balanced as if he were casually toying with it, was my kitchen pistol. I glanced at the knives lying in the shallow water. Had he used them on himself? I said, "Paid a price?"

"I couldn't let that go on. I have been sent to watch over you. That girl—"

"Did you murder Esther?"

"Murder? I offered hospitality. 'Twas her foolish husband wouldn't let well enough alone. See how I've paid for my transgression? There have been many over the years. See?" He looked down at his scarred body. "For all of them, I've offered a blood sacrifice." I watched him move the pistol from one hand to the other, hefting it for weight. He said, "That's over now. Done. Redeemed. I've tried to make you see. You belong to me. I've come for you."

The pistol glimmered in a shaft of light, and I could see the head of a bullet in the chamber. He bounced it to the other hand. I tried to remember where I'd seen my rifle. The shotgun. I'd always known which door they were behind in my old house. I hadn't spotted them since I'd come here. "What do you mean, 'all'? You've killed others?"

"Killed, no. There have been accidents. Things befall people, events of their own making. Those who had no civility. No shred of decency or sympathy. Not like you. I have loved you always, since before time began."

I sidled toward the door to the courtyard, the quickest way to my bedroom. "Let's talk about that," I said. "Let's see. Do you have a plan of some sort, something for us?"

He grinned and straightened. "I always have a plan. In case things are not as they seem. I have brooded long and suffered for this plan. Sacrificed. For you."

"Tell me about your plan, Lazrus." I glanced around the room, hoping to glimpse the doorway and see whether it was open. He looked toward the door, too, and for the second his head was turned, I reached into the basin and took a knife, holding it behind my back.

Lazrus stepped toward me. "Where are they?" he asked.

"Who? My sons? Working, that's all. Working. But they'll be back for dinner. That's why I came in—to fix them something to eat. They'll be here any moment. Here comes Chess now. Chess! Come on in. We've got company."

The lunatic cocked his head at me as if he were a dog, peering into my eyes. "They're too far to hear you. I hate it when you lie to me." He came another pace closer. I moved toward the door. "You won't go out there. That would be a mistake."

I knew my only chance was going to be to put more space between us. Run if I had to. He had a new rawness about him, something animal and wild, which told me I'd never fight him off with just the knife. I said, "It would? Well, then. Where could I go?"

"Take off your clothes."

I showed the knife. "You promised to go away. Get out of here. Go on. You promised."

"There's always a sacrifice to be made." He held the pistol to his lips, kissed the barrel, pointed it at my head, pointed it back at his own, and laughed, screeching. "Hand me the blade. You're not strong enough to do it. In my weakness am I made strong." He reached for my knife, and I swiped it at him. He laughed again, a wicked, low sound. Then he lunged at me, and before I could think, I struck him with it, aiming for his neck but only pulling it across his chest and shoulder. He took my blade hand in his and squeezed hard, holding the pistol to my middle with his other hand. He squeezed so hard, my fingers opened, useless. The knife fell to the floor. "Evil is purged," he said, looking down at the fresh red flow on his arm, "by blood."

I waited for the bullet to punch through me, made myself arch forward, the way Willie'd always stood, then felt nothing but surprise that he hadn't pulled the trigger. He kissed the fingers of my aching right hand. When he crushed his blackened hands into my flesh, I could still feel the tang of the scorpion's sting. "You're hurting me," I said softly.

Again he turned his head like a dog, listening to something strange. "Come!" He jerked me around the table, toward the outer door. "We must be under the heavens, not under some miserable excuse of mortal dwelling. We must have God as a witness." Lazrus knocked the door wide with his foot, whirling me through it, and I tried to turn still more in order to spin out of his grasp. He held my hand so tightly, I thought it would pull right off the bone. I landed on the porch on my knees. "No!" he shouted. "Not here! Out under the sky. On the rock cleft for you." He pointed the pistol toward the new windmill, which was standing on its platform of solid rock. "There, where the water of life flows. Where the fountain everlasting runs, there our blood will mingle through the ages. Think of it, Sarah. We will be linked throughout eternity, and our lives will fill all who drink of this water and taste of this cup!" He dragged me off the porch. I struggled to my feet, stumbling as he pulled me toward the windmill. As I tripped down the steps and landed in the dirt, I saw my old shotgun tucked behind the kitchen door.

Five paces and three stair steps lay between me and the gun. I fell again, purposely this time. He loosened his hold, and I yanked my hand from his grasp. He tugged at my hair, choking me with the bonnet strings hanging down my back. I yanked the ties loose and slipped from his grasp, rolling in the dirt like a little boy, just beyond his reach. I grunted and scrabbled toward the steps, getting to the top one on my hands and knees as he grabbed a chunk of my skirt and hauled me back into the dirt. He flipped me over, so that I was facing upward. Looming above me, he was a great black shadow that filled half the blue sky, so dark against the light that I couldn't make out his features. He pointed the pistol at my head, then said, "Not here? Of course. It has to be on the altar. I won't let him have you, you see. I know what evil lies in women's souls. They destroy men. Their hearts are wickedness itself, demon-possessed. You have tricked me and lied. And now you plan to toss me aside. I came to you honestly, and yet you seek to cast me away in order to ply your wiles upon another man. Adulterous heart, vile witch. That must be purged, and then we will be one. Don't you see? One." Lazrus reached down and lifted me by my arm, more gently this time, setting me on my feet. He didn't let go as he led me forward. I went two steps, then tore my arm away, racing for the porch. I laid my hands on the shotgun barrel.

"Aunt Sarah? Aren't you coming?" Ezra hollered. "We're getting mighty hungry."

Lazrus looked toward the sound. I turned. Lazrus was standing by the windmill. He raised the pistol and drew a bead on Ezra.

"Drop it," I said, "or I'll shoot."

"Aunt Sarah!"

"Stay where you are!" I called.

Lazrus yelled, "It's him!"

"He's a little boy!" I said.

As Lazrus raised the pistol again, I leveled my aim at him. Pulled the trigger. Nothing happened. I pulled the trigger again, then racked open the chamber. Empty as a cave. Not to have looked! I had to get the rifle that was in the house. Lazrus started walking slowly toward Ezra, who stood in his tracks, just clear of a copse of trees this side of the creek. I dropped the shotgun and tore through the house to the bedroom. The rifle was not to be seen. And though I'd never kept one under the bed, it was the only place I couldn't see at a glance, so I dropped to my knees heavily. There it was. I opened the chamber: loaded. I ran to the front of the house, which cut off some yards and put me between Lazrus and Ezra. The crazed man advanced on the boy, who at first just stood there, petrified, then turned when he saw me and headed back for the creek. I rushed into the line between the two and faced Lazrus. "Stop, Lazrus," I called. "It's me you want."

Lazrus pointed the pistol toward me and fired. The shot rang loud in the still air of noon, hit a rock, and pinged. I raised the rifle. "Lazrus!"

He held out his hands, making his form into a crucifix, and shook his head sadly. "Pierce well," he said.

I couldn't flat-out murder him. I stared down the barrel. "Get off my land."

"I cannot." He raised the pistol to aim again.

"Aunt Sarah?" a little voice wailed.

"Stay where you are," I called. I sighted in on Lazrus; I could see from the angle of his weapon that he'd more likely hit the chicken coop than either Ezra or me. He fired, then pulled the trigger a third time. Nothing happened. That would be the empty chamber I kept under the hammer in case it got bumped accidentally. He must have spun the cartridge. There were three more shots in that pistol.

"Come to me. Be forever immortal, as I am." Lazrus aimed closer this time, straight down my rifle barrel, as he hollered, "Today, thou shalt be with me in paradise!" I pulled the trigger. He fired. I felt a whap like the swatting of an insect slap against my leg. Lazrus fell in the dirt, groaning. My first thought was how that old pistol never had much range and that I had him by a hundred yards. I kept a bead on him and moved closer.

Lazrus bent both his knees, then raised himself to his elbows, the pistol still gripped in his hand. He glowered at me. On his left breast, blood ran from a small dot no bigger than my thimble. "As God is my witness," he said, and pointed that pistol toward me. I fired again, and he sagged to the ground, moaning pitifully.

It had been a long time since the days of Comanche attacks. Since the

Apaches were all rounded up. I hadn't pulled a trigger on a man in all those years. "Ezra?" I hollered. "Go get your brother. Stay there until I call you." Not for the life of me had I ever thought to kill that man. But what makes a person cross the border from lunacy to terror? Where is the line? Instead of rambling around in memories like Granny, what makes a person kill a young couple wandering by and then torture his own flesh to atone for it? I wasn't sure he was dead. Couldn't think whether to doctor him or put him down like a rabid skunk. I scrunched down on my knees to wait, the rifle ready in case he stirred again. My left leg was sore—too much gardening. Then I saw a flower of red blooming on my skirt, and I knew. I'd seen people get shot and then go on doing near-miraculous things. Sometimes the doctor hunting the lead caused more pain than the bullet itself. I reckoned I'd have to endure.

After a bit, he came to. Lazrus fidgeted and howled, writhing. He mumbled something as he arched his back, thrashing in the dirt. Red foam bubbled on his lips and his breathing was loud and haggard. I knew he was finished.

"Aunt Sarah, can we come out now?" a boy's voice called from behind me.

Lying on the ground, the man turned the pistol and, without looking or aiming, fired off a final shot. This time, his aim was truer than it had been with any of the other bullets fired. I'd felt the brush of death more than once before. I full-out expected that bullet to land right in my chest. When the sound of it whistled by and I kept on kneeling, I was purely amazed. I looked down at myself, then stared at Lazrus lying motionless now, twisted the way a snake will writhe around, already dead but snarled on itself. I wanted to feel some meanness in me toward him, but all I felt was that same empty feeling of loss. A man who'd been just plum crazy, loco as a bat, was finally done with his torment.

I stood up. My leg hurt plenty. I touched Lazrus's foot with the rifle barrel. The man was dead. Ezra came running. "Come get Zack. Get Mama and Papa!" said Ezra. His hat was gone. Sweat made his hair cling to his head. He gasped and coughed, arms swinging wildly as he propelled himself toward me. "Aunt Sarah! Come get Zack."

I said, "Tell him to come along with you."

"He says he's been shot. But he cain't say where, and there ain't any blood, but he ain't moving, he says. He won't let me near him. Bit me when I tussled him. You'll have to come get him."

I ran, following Ezra through the brush to where Zack stood. I said,

"Where's it hurt? Tell me. Open your mouth." Zack screwed his lips together, staring off at clouds or something in the sky. "If you're fooling me for some reason, I'm going to whale the tar out of you, boy. This is not the time for it. Now, have you been shot?"

"Yes, ma'am."

"Show me."

"Right here, and here." He pulled the front of his overalls out and poked a finger from each hand through two new holes. The skirtlike size of the heavy pants formed a tent away from his body. Zack said, "Went through m' pants, and out the other door like a whistle. If I'da been standing closer to the front of 'em, I'da got my skeezix shot clean *off*."

"You mean," I said, leaning over, examining the overalls, "you mean it went through and didn't hit anything? Oh Zack." I swept him up and crushed him to me.

"Don't, Aunt Sarah," hollered Zack.

I said, "Come on back to the house now."

Zack mumbled something, then said, "Wet my pants. Piddled right down my own leg like a baby."

"It doesn't matter," I said. "Of course it doesn't matter. It's no shame at all. I've seen men in soldiers' uniforms do the same thing, and they didn't get half that close to a bullet. Come on. Your folks will be back soon enough."

"Well, I don't want Mama to see me like this. The big girls will scold me."

"Oh honey," I said. "They'll be so glad to see you, it won't matter one little bit. Come on to the house."

Zack made a face of fear and worry. "Can't. I want to, but I can't." He scratched his head. "Just can't seem to move my feet. They're kind of stuck." He fidgeted a bit, leaned one way and then the other. "I told Ezra."

I knelt before him, too, and said, "The bullet didn't hit you? You're sure?"

Zack said, "I don't feel bad or nothing. Just sorta can't walk anymore. Like I forgot how. Like that time Clover nailed Josh's shoes to the floor. I stood in 'em while they were all laughing. Feels just like that."

Then I said, "We'll let Baldy do the walking for you until your feet remember how." I went back to the barn and got my horse. Then I lifted Zack, soggy britches and all, onto his back. The boy's legs hung limp. "Now, hold on to the mane with your hands, real tight. Chances are, your legs also forgot how to hold on."

"Am I going to be put in bed for the rest of my life?" Zack asked. "I *want* to remember how. I *do*."

"No, not for the rest of your life," I said. "You know sometimes when you run, you get to where you can't go any farther? This is the kind of thing where you just got tired out, and you can't go any farther. Once your legs get some rest, they'll be fine." It was getting mighty easy to peel off the whoppers I'd been telling this summer. What mattered, I suppose, was that Zachary believed it. We walked the horse back to the house, Ezra on the other side, holding his brother in place when he'd slip now and then.

We got some clean clothes for Zack, and although he could stand up just fine, he still seemed unable to take a step. I put him in my bed, and in minutes he was deep in asleep, snoring like a grizzly bear.

While he slept in my room, I pulled up a chair in the room set aside for Granny, and had a look at my own bullet hole. Clear through, just like Zack's. Well, there'd be no doctor gouging around with a poker in there. That was something to be thankful for. I hollered to Ezra to bring me a basin of water and soap, and I bandaged it right up.

Ezra fixed us both a little food. Brought me a drink of water. Then we just sat and waited for his folks to return. I left Lazrus in the yard. Figured I couldn't move him myself anyway, and likely shouldn't be digging a grave with this hole in my leg. Then, too, I didn't want him in the graveyard next to folks I loved, tormenting me the rest of my days, and afterward, too.

Well, the folks returned before dusk, and Ezra had no problem telling and retelling what he'd seen from the bushes. I just let him say it. The men hauled away what was left of the lunatic and buried him above a wash in that land Granny'd sold to the railroad.

I put together a supper for them, and no matter what, Savannah couldn't make me sit down, or convince Zachary to stand up. Zack sat, stonelike and sullen, where he'd been placed. He couldn't be cajoled by anything we knew to put his feet under him and walk. He acted as if he didn't have any control of his legs at all, though he could feel the touch of our hands or the brush of a feather. His sisters carried him out to the privy and waited outside the door for him. His father carried him to the dining table for supper, then to a chair in the parlor.

Savannah said, "Come to me, Zachary, and sit in my lap," but he only fell from the chair and lay on the floor, sniffing back tears, refusing to move. Ezra accused him of being ornery. I picked him up, all fifty-five pounds of him, and lugged him to Savannah. On her lap, he listened without a sound to her talking and singing nursery rhymes and hymns and Bre'r Rabbit stories.

Finally, Savannah said, "Would you like to sleep here with Aunt Sarah tonight?"

"Yes'm," he said.

She said, "Well, I believe *my* legs are going to sleep. Do you think you can go to bed now? Give me a little kiss."

Zack said, "When legs go to sleep, do they ever wake up?"

Savannah said, "Yes, they do. We'll call the doctor to make sure. It might take some castor oil."

He shuddered, wiggling his entire frame. "What if they still don't wake up?"

Savannah hugged him, and he leaned against her neck. She said, "Legs that have run and played as much as these have probably need a rest now and then. No matter how long they have to rest, they'll wake up eventually. If they don't, that'll mean you've been chosen by Providence for a special life. You're a mighty young fellow to have the hand of God placed so squarely on your shoulders. No matter what, I'll always care for you."

In less time than it took her to slide off his battered shoes, Zack fell asleep, nuzzled against his mother's neck. Gilbert fixed him a pallet next to his bed on the porch. Albert carried him to his pallet, and the little boy lay there as if he were unconscious.

Then Savannah ordered me to the kitchen where she doctored my leg with carbolic acid and a clean bandage. Afterward, we sat in the shade of the porch, but didn't talk. We had no words left. Now and then, she'd sigh heavily. I patted her arm. "You don't mind if he sleeps here?" she asked.

"Of course not. Ezra can stay, too, if you want. You and your girls have a little peace and quiet." Albert came up then. My brother took off his hat. His hair had gone white at the sides, more than I'd ever noticed before. He just held out a hand and Savannah took it, and then he nodded to me and took her and the girls home.

I went to my room and got into bed.

I planned to think on all this, but sleep came quickly.

"Look, Aunt Sarah. You was right. My legs was just tired out from being shot at." I opened my eyes. Zack stood over my bed, balancing himself on first one leg, then the other. I wrapped my arms about myself and held my breath for a long moment, collecting my thoughts. Zack's legs had remembered how to walk. Hallelujah for one small miracle. Had I prayed for that? I couldn't remember. The sky was hazy and green; sunup was minutes away. "Are you still sleeping? Aunt Sarah, I'm awful hungry."

November 1, 1906

I heard a racket and hurried up to the garden, where I could see the road from the south. It was a buggy, coming up from Maldonado's place. Five men on horses followed it. Another flatbed wagon was piled up with luggage and chairs. I waved.

The buggy in front stopped. It stood a minute, then turned slowly and came in the direction of my house. Rudolfo was driving. Leta sat next to him. They stopped again, now just twenty yards away. Leta was dressed in coffee-colored silk, her hair curled and piled on her head, under a stylish bonnet covered in lace. The diamond necklace was lost in more lace at her throat. She was barely twenty-two. She was a plain woman, with a large sloping nose and a down-turned mouth that looked to be forever scowling. At least she no longer needed to be fearful of being left an old maid. She cast her eyes from me to her husband, and I wondered what she was thinking, whether she worried for his loyalty. I reckoned she should fear for it, for I knew what its value was. However, she had no reason to think I'd want to take that seat she was sitting on. *"¡Buenos días!"* Rudolfo called. He smiled, but his eyes were cold.

"Heading to town for the elections?" I asked.

"Sí," he said. "We will be staying for a while." He smiled again—too broadly.

It was in my nature to want to thank someone who'd done me a good turn. Putting up money for my house was certainly that, though I couldn't reconcile it with what I felt he'd taken from me. The words *thank you* stuck in my craw. Right next to *curse you.* So I said, "We should come to an understanding, you and I."

Rudolfo's eyes darted furtively toward his child bride. "What more may I do for you, Señora Elliot?"

"Drive your people across my land—on the old road, the one you used before. No sense taking two extra hours to get to town."

Rudolfo was silent for a while. He began to nod just a little. "That, I can do."

Next to him, Leta fidgeted, and slipped her hand over his arm. I smiled at her. Silly girl. Probably already carrying a baby. I said, "I'm using El Capitan for a little while. Trying to build my herd again. December, you come lead him to your place for a bit, if you're still in the cattle business, and not in the governor's office."

"Ah. ¿*El toro?* I expected he was dead. Bought another *toro grande* from Mexico City. El Capitan is yours." Leta glanced sidelong at him.

I nodded, and then I said, "I'm thinking about putting up some fence."

Rudolfo said, "If you wish. Two *vecinos* should share the cost."

I knew right then I probably wouldn't put up a fence. He was being far yonder too accommodating. I said, "*Vaya con Dios,* El Maldonado *y* Señora Leta."

Rudolfo smiled then. He said, "*Y tu,*" and snapped the reins. The little parade turned and went across my land toward Mama's house, where they would catch the main road. I stayed put until they were out of sight.

Well, Savannah and Albert's family brought food that evening. We passed around Savannah's daughters' good cooking. We talked about Clove, Josh, and Granny coming home. About April and Morris coming to visit. While we talked, I reckoned I could accept this house for my own. It meant a place to have those people gathered together. All our living family, here at one time, in the care of Mrs. Sarah Elliot. What a wonder and a blessing.

November 6, 1906

Chess and I spent the morning moving some things around in the barn. In the corner where that headstone lay, I stacked sacks of feed and grain nearly as high as my shoulders. My folly could wait under the needs of the present and be forgotten.

In the afternoon, two conveyances stopped at my gate. One was a beautiful black trap pulled by a double team of horses. The other was a painted surrey, its four corners adorned with tassels, which danced in the breeze. It was pulled by a matched team of four. They disturbed a covey of quail, which scattered toward the yard with a flutter and murmur of surprise. The sight of them filled me with childish glee. April and Morris had come to the house. There were my grandchildren. Behind them, Harland stepped down and helped Granny alight. His children stood sheepishly in the shadow of the trap.

My mama stood there in the yard, puzzling, I'm sure, over the strange house that sat where my faded white wooden house had been. Everything around was lush and growing, shortened by the fire, but green. Fall was always a pretty time of year hereabouts. Must have been a real sight to her. Granny pushed her bonnet back on her head and turned this way and that, until I could stand waiting no longer.

I rushed to them, hollering for joy. I squeezed all those children until they squawked like little chickens. I said, "Well, come along in the house, then, everyone. We'll have some lemonade, and I'll tell you what's gone on. We had a tornado."

"It drop this house on your old one?" Granny asked. Everyone laughed.

Arm in arm with my mama and my daughter, we toured my hacienda. We sent the children out to play. Granny went to the porch and found her familiar old rocking chair. She turned to me and said, "It's chilly out here. Do you have an old blanket or other?"

To me, the day felt as warm as September, but I brought her Granny's Garden quilt to her and covered her knees. She looked at the stitches and ran her hands this way and that. Then she said, "Well, I'll be. That looks like one I made one time. I left it in town."

"No, Mama. You left it in my parlor. I finished up the quilting. I had the time, after all." She patted it, looking puzzled by it, and then nodded. And soon she was napping, snug as a cat.

Well, Clover and Joshua were glad to be home, too, so the horde of us had a big picnic supper both inside the house and outdoors. Clove had bought himself a photographic machine, and he lined us all up and counted noses. Twenty of us had come through this season. After supper, Savannah and Albert's bunch headed home. Harland's little girl, Blessing, fell asleep in my lap. Harland carried her off and then he and April and Morris went about tucking their children into beds and pallets and turned in.

I don't know when my sons slipped out of the room. I just turned around and found that we were alone. Udell stoked up the big fireplace and pushed the kindling around a little before he struck a match. He used the iron rod to poke the wood up where it had begun to roll down. When the blaze was going fairly well, he set the grate in front of it and then pulled a chair next to mine. It was pleasant to have weather cool enough that the fire was a comfort.

Udell put a coffee cup in my hand. It smelled good. He makes it strong. I sipped that coffee and peered at the man. Udell had been right: I had to hold on to what was in front of me, not spend my life looking for what had been lost or what might never come. I believed I loved Udell Hanna. It was different from any love I'd ever felt before. His eyes were not keen and wary, as Jack's had been, nor was he young and bounding with energy. Udell's manner was slow, befitting a man who was used to animals and knew not to frighten them. His words were few, but they always held something good as a drink of cool water in them. I loved the quietness of him, the scars on his heart. There'd be no saying whether the future held marriage for us. For now, it was enough to have him beside me. To know I loved him without feeling tied to the past. To let Jack rest, as Jimmy did, with my people, biding his time until we met again.

I watched Udell, wondering if he was feeling empty, with Aubrey gone, the way I sometimes did. A thread from my pocket caught my eye in the flicker of light from the stove. I twisted it to make a knot, wrapping the tip around my finger. Niddy-noddy, knitting needles, busybody, butter beetles. When will I meet my fair, true love? I smiled. Udell looked up then, surprise on his face, as if I'd caught him at something. He brushed his hands against his pants and held his right hand out to me. I put my hand in his, and Udell and I held hands and watched that fire burn down, listening to the wood crackling and sputtering.

Reading
Group
Gold

SARAH'S QUILT
by Nancy E. Turner

Get to Know the Author
· Seeing the World as a Witness:
  How I Became a Writer
· The Process:
  Writing Fiction from History

Get to Know the Story
· Behind *Sarah's Quilt*

Keep on Reading
· Suggestions from the Author
· Reading Group Questions

For more reading group suggestions
visit www.readinggroupgold.com

 ST. MARTIN'S GRIFFIN

A
Reading
Group Gold
Selection

I spent my formative years growing up almost literally in the shadow of Disneyland's Matterhorn in Anaheim, California. My three sisters and I were rabid readers. Days, I went to an innovative school program for gifted children; evenings were spent at libraries, doing homework. Saturdays were for piano lessons. Our family was old fashioned and tightly knit, and to this day we girls all have a literary bent.

"I'd always loved hearing stories about my great-grandparents... and imagining... their day-to-day lives."

I didn't start out to be a writer when I began my college education at the age of forty. I thought I was headed toward teaching high school English classes. However, as one of the most terrified freshmen ever to step onto a campus, I put off the major state university in favor of a couple of years at our local community college, intending to take it slow and easy. After all, I'd waited twenty-plus years to get back to college, and I still had a family at home, so I wasn't planning to set the corporate world on its ear. I enrolled in a Creative Nonfiction Writing class, hoping it would spark my abilities for upcoming term paper requirements in my coursework. After two years at Pima Community College, I was highly dismayed when I came to registration for the fall and there were no "real" classes in writing left other than a fiction class. Besides, I loved science. I loved to write, too, but I wanted to write about science. Full of doubts, I signed up for Advanced Fiction Writing thinking at least it wouldn't hurt anything. I'd skate through and collect an easy three semester hours. How hard could it be?

A day or two later, the instructor, Meg Files, called and told me the registration computer had mistakenly allowed me into the class, that it was by invitation only, and that in order to receive said invitation, I was required to submit a portfolio of thirty pages of my best short stories and poetry. I'd never written a short story. My last poetry consisted of two stanzas of haiku for a class in high school and a solitary tome of teen angst in 1969. Determined that the only thing I could do was hope she'd appreciate my best term paper, ("real" writing, I smugly mused) I submitted a forty-page thesis on plate tectonics and specific zones of subduction created by movement of the North American and Juan De Fuca plates. She let me in the fiction class. I didn't know if that meant my scientific theory was hokey, or that wiser heads prevailed at prodding an erstwhile but misguided sophomore away from some abyss, but I was in.

That year had also been the year of my dad's retirement, and with time on his hands, he began researching our genealogy. I'd grown up with no knowledge of our ancestry, no sense of belonging to any place or people. I'd always loved hearing stories about my great-grandparents from my grandparents, and imagining, with a healthy dose of Laura Ingalls Wilder's Little House novels, their day-to-day lives. When the first assignment in my fiction class was to write a short story about someone with whom each student would like to spend time, the one person I could think of was my great grandmother, Sarah Agnes Prine. My imagination had been fueled throughout childhood by breaking away from the high-tech world of California and spending weeks every summer on my grandparents' farm in West Texas, where I learned to set irrigation pipes, shoot a .22 rifle, pull weeds, collect eggs, spoil horses with apples, and annoy sheep. Along with general kid stuff, my sisters and I heard many a tale of pioneer life. My grandmother told about her mother Sarah as if she were a character in a book. When Dad came up with a little hand-written memoir we thought was by Sarah's brother, outlining places they lived and how they worked in Arizona and New Mexico Territories, the new information threw kindling on the embers of my inspiration. That short story ended up being the first chapter of my first novel, *These Is My Words.*

"While [Sarah's Quilt] *travels further from the family history, it is very close to my heart."*

I did finally graduate in 1999 from the University of Arizona with a BFA and three majors: Music, Studio Art, and Creative Writing. I have taught a couple of classes back at my first stop, Pima Community College, but I never got certified to teach high school, and I don't think I'm going to pursue that. I have too many more stories to write!

Sarah's Quilt is the sequel to that very first short story, still focusing on the imagined life of my great-grandmother, a woman whose reputation was bigger than she was. Some of the family details are there, but for the most part, I have transmuted oral history and research into a fictional set of characters set against a very real background. As my third novel, I think it is a stronger, deeper story, and while it travels further from the family history, it is very close to my heart.

While I started out intending to write a story about Sarah and her sons, one day Willie came sauntering up, swaggering and ridiculous, one part scared and two parts mean, wanting to cut himself out a place in the story. I tried writing it without the rascal, but he wouldn't go away. I had to give him his voice. I also tried my best to save the kid, but he was headstrong and dangerous, a threat to himself as much as to anyone else. A coming, hidden danger lurks beyond the knowledge of the characters in *Sarah's Quilt,* which I have decided to use as the springboard for the follow-up novel. Sabers are already rattling, heralding the coming Mexican Revolution, which will greatly impact Sarah's family and neighbors. I originally intended to carry *Sarah's Quilt* along to a much later date, but the story took on a life of its own and the weight of a volume that size simply didn't allow it.

I think a writer is an ordinary person who just happens to live on the outside of things, seeing the world as a witness, an evaluator, in a second, secret life, populated by diverse characters and places and times, a world that can be as real but less threatening than the one in which we're forced to move. It is both a refuge and a vast domain where anything is possible, even realizing almost-forgotten dreams.

I use meticulous research to fill in details around my characters. I rely on books, microfilm, travel, and interviews to make a story come to life in as real a setting as possible. Just as in the previous novel, where every Indian battle and most of the peripheral characters lived in the Tucson area, I spent a great effort getting the facts right, from the build of a work saddle to the cut of flannel underwear. Five days of poring through *The Rifle in America* and *Guns of the Old West,* note taking and cross-referencing, all amounted to a single line of dialogue—"See those? Krags with the rim out." But the line felt like the thing Charlie would have said. His mother is anxious about his being dumped by his fiancée, his cousin has run off with the herd and their livelihood, land grabbers and lunatics glare from every side, and yet, the young man answers Sarah with a notice that he's bought some new technology.

I am compelled to get it right. I sometimes draw upon my own life to broaden events as well as the scope of emotion experienced by the characters, though, of course, any novel exists as just the gloss on the tip of the iceberg of a writer's foundation of study material. It took me nearly two years of hunting and pecking for information to find out how to stop a pre-1940 Aeromotor windmill!

"I believe there's nothing like being there—smelling the soil, feeling the rain, the gnawing desperation and the joy, to add breath and soul to your writing."

But, the incident with the twenty-foot wide dust devil bearing animal rabbit droppings was a reality I experienced firsthand. I believe there's nothing like being there—smelling the soil, feeling the rain, the gnawing desperation and the joy, to add breadth and soul to your writing.

The best writing advice I ever got? You have permission to write a book. It's just that simple. Now go do it. The second best advice is, be prepared to throw away your first million words, and I would add, to change every last one of the next million. Only then you are ready for someone to read it. Lastly, only listen to critics when you hear the same comment three times.

Sarah's Quilt opens in April of 1906, a time following three years of devastating drought in the Southwestern United States. Years of overgrazing and poor land management combined with the drought finally culminated in the destruction of natural grasslands of Southern Arizona. To this day, the range is covered with chaparral and cactus and supports only a small percentage of the livestock that roamed there a hundred years ago. The soil in the Basin and Range is mottled with heavy clays and caliches, steeped with alkali, and generally hard to farm. Underground caverns pit the landscape, and it is upon one of these natural wells that Sarah's main water supply depends. When that supply is exhausted, the family is desperate. I remember one hot, dismal summer day at my grandparent's farm when my uncle came into the house with a bucket of mud to announce that he had just pulled it from the well. I remember the looks of fear on the faces of the adults. Even as a child, I knew an empty well meant disaster.

In contrast, April of 1906 marked the great San Francisco earthquake and fire chronicled firsthand by Jack London in *Collier's Magazine.* The irony of bone-dry, baked caliche and animal-starving drought superimposed on California's quaking ground and torrential rains set the stage for the main element of the story, a human fight against the elements complicated by the dynamism of other characters.

The turn of the last century in Arizona Territory was an era of great changes juxtaposed against centuries-old lifestyles. Ranchers' horses were often stampeded by horseless carriages, gas lighting and sewer systems replaced candles and outhouses in town, where an ice factory provided children with

respite from the summer sun. Medical care was bar-
baric, and more children died than lived to ten years
old. Multiple marriages were common as adults
were felled by disease and childbirth. Social mores
of Eastern cities had reached the West, and brought
the Temperance Movement and Women's Suffrage
along with the banning of any "artificial" means of
birth control. The first speed limit was imposed on a
Tucson thoroughfare, Speedway Boulevard, and a
hefty fine could be imposed on anyone barreling
down the lane faster than nine miles an hour. A
paved road was a near miracle. The average age of
the students at the University of Arizona was fourteen, and for over twenty years the school never finished all four quarters of a football game because by
the third quarter there weren't enough players left
without broken bones to field a team. There was
flowing water in the Santa Cruz and Rillito
riverbeds—now dry washes unless we get a frog-
choking rainstorm during the wet season—and, at
the base of Sentinel Peak, a working wheat mill
ground flour by means of a water powered wheel.
The Presidio and Spanish Mission feel separate
from Tucson until you poke further.

Much of downtown Tucson is changed and paved
over, but unlike some cities, there is still much that
remains of the territorial days. Adobe railroad work-
er's 1880 row houses have become trendy and
upscale, high-rent real estate. Convent Street and
Meyers Road still serve their purposes, although the
sisters of the convent have moved away as have the
ladies of the evening on Meyers.

The most powerful book I can turn back to that made me first think how wonderful it would be to own the skill of storytelling was Truman Capote's *In Cold Blood.* It's not a novel, but told in such a looking-over-the-shoulder narrative style that it chilled me to the bone as no thriller ever has. But, common sense (or blind ignorance) had long convinced me that writers were all journalists with PhD's and years of reporting expertise, and housewives from Arizona weren't likely to get their names on the cover of a novel. I didn't think about it again until I began to write for that fiction class.

"The best book is one that ends with an almost audible gasp... 'oh no, it's really over'."

Probably the second writerly inspirational book was a tiny novel called *The Ladies of Missalonghi* by Colleen McCullough. It's a sweet, romantic story full of delicious details, about as far removed from Capote's true-crime drama as possible. What made me reread it more than once was the fantastic skill McCullough used in painting memorable characters with so few deft strokes. Again, it honed my longing but not my bravado. It was to be twenty years later, before I began to study the craft of writing, and only in secret did I start to put words to paper. I still didn't think of my work in progress as a novel, but just as a short story that got out of hand. Thinking no one would read it anyway left me free to do as I pleased!

Reading suggestions? I think in terms of authors, rather than a particular work. Every reader brings her own baggage into play, too, so it's all so very subjective. It's the between-the-lines style that gets to me. Mark Twain and Stephen King, Zane Grey and John Grisham, Mary Stewart and Alice Walker, Tony Hillerman and Alfred Lord Tennyson, Margaret Mitchell and Thomas Cahill have all brightened my world. The best book is one that ends with an almost audible gasp, an immediate twinge, that "oh, no, it's really *over*," combined with the hollowness of letting go, and a slightly bitter, envious voice from somewhere that murmurs, "I wish *I'd* written *that!*"

I read reams of nonfiction, particularly military history, which often gives great tidbits about terrain and other natural elements, plus has insightful maps. I find it helpful, too, to read anything I can find that was written in the era about which I want to write. Diaries, newspapers, and personal journals are the most enlightening. I study photographs, maps, and love to walk through an old building and soak in the ambiance.

📖 Reading Group Questions

1. Why the title *Sarah's Quilt*? And, how does the quilting metaphor apply to Sarah's story?

2. The story takes place over a mere seven months' time. Discuss the book's narrative structure, and why the author might have chosen to map the action this way. Does the pace seem appropriate for a novel this size?

3. Do you feel the depictions of Territorial life in 1906 were historically accurate? How much did you know about this era before reading *Sarah's Quilt*? What do you know now?

4. Discuss secondary plot elements such as letting go of the past, the concept of "home," pride vs. courage, and family as fortress.

5. The book focuses on Sarah Agnes Prine's relationship with her sons and nephews. How does that compare with her relationship to her only daughter, April?

6. How does Granny's mental detachment affect the other characters?

7. How important is Esther's eloping to the plot, and overall theme of the book? Do you think Mary Pearl could have stopped Esther from eloping? In what ways could things have turned out differently for each character?

8. Arriving at the ranch, Willie was given a second chance at his life. Was it too unlike anything he knew to work? Was there anything Sarah might have done differently to reach his heart?

9. Why did Willie confess only to the judge? What in his background led him to make that association?

10. Did Charlie and Gilbert go too far in their teasing Willie? What were the consequences of their actions? Do you feel any sympathy for them? Why or why not?

11. How does Sarah's want of education color her every decision? Discuss some examples of her stigmatic behavior.

12. What in Sarah's personality is the trigger point for how she reacts to Udell Hanna? What role does he serve in the story? What would Sarah's story be without him?

13. What are the different roles that Lazarus and Rudolfo play in Sarah's life? Discuss the ways in which they alternately influence her character.

14. Does Sarah really know Rudolfo? What if she had married him? Would you be left with an altogether different impression of Sarah? And/or *Sarah's Quilt*?